The Doves of Primrose Book 2

Emmylou

By
Krista Kedrick

The Doves of Primrose, Book 2: Emmylou
Copyright © 2014, Cowboy Capital Productions; Krista Kedrick, all rights reserved

This is a work of fiction. All of the characters, organizations, and events portrayed in this novel are either products of the authors imagination or used fictitiously.

Cover: © Krista Kedrick, 2014
Pictures: ©Jensen Geisert, Fotolio, ©Krista Kedrick, ©Prairie Preservations

Other Books by Krista Kedrick

Under a Prairie Moon
Family Ties

Other Books in this series

Lacy

Special Recognition

To my cover models, Shelby and Colby, what a fun day we had together creating these amazing images. I thank you for all of your help and your friendship. You are so very dear to my heart.

To Prairie Preservations and Val its owner and creative genius; thank you for the use of your farm and your buildings. They were the perfect backdrop for the models. Your hospitality and artistic flair are rare gems in the Nebraska prairie.

Dedication

In every book I write, I weave in names and character traits of the members of my family and friends. As it turns out, this book has extra special meaning with the sudden loss of a man who helped to shape me into the person I am. He was my phone call whenever anything exciting happened. I will miss that.

Emmylou's namesake is my darling Emma. While she may be a quiet, beautiful girl, I know of the sardonic humor that colors her every thought and most of her comments.

She gets her grace from her mother, Evelyn, who has demonstrated more strength than any woman should have to. I will always be thankful that Troy brought you into our family.

And to Colby. It has been my extreme joy to watch you grow into such a wonderful man. I marvel – and snicker – at how much we have in common.

Chapter 1

The tinkling of bells was a homecoming to Shane Newbury when he pushed open the door to *Bake My Day*. It had been recommended to him by his landlady. Apparently, the owner was some kind of culinary genius. Shane would be happy with a cup of coffee and a bagel. Actually, he would kill for a western omelet, bacon and toast, but the moving truck carrying all his worldly possessions wasn't set to arrive until tomorrow, and he had been told that the woman who ran the café was on a doctor-ordered bed rest for the next two weeks.

Well, he would find out about that as soon as he got to the clinic and started his rounds. He stepped inside the delightfully scented bakery and found a longer line than he had expected. He glanced around, wondering where all the people had come from. This was a tiny town. He had gotten used to the hustle and bustle of the city while obtaining his medical degree, working as a resident for four years and then a fellowship for two more. He had been grateful when his assignment had finally come through, and he was sent to Primrose, Nebraska.

Shane leaned to the side counting seven people in front of him, then pulled his sleeve up to check his watch. Damn it, he was going to be late on his first day. Had he had his alarm, he wouldn't be running behind schedule. He tapped his foot, debating between leaving and trying to get through the day without the much needed caffeine or drinking whatever was available at work. His experience with hospital coffee was an unpleasant memory of black tar in a paper cup. He shuddered and turned his attention to the chalkboard behind the glass display case.

The line moved, and he stepped with it, a smile twitching at his lips. He had never seen anything like this before. The person who ran this place must be interesting. He wasn't sure what to make of a menu that categorized things into columns with names like *Little Miss Muffins*, *Kneadful Things* and *Batter-up*.

The next board was titled *Percolicious*. He assumed that was the coffee. He squinted, remembering his glasses were on the dash of his pick-up. Where in the hell was the plain coffee? He scrolled through *Amber Haven*, *Minty Fresh* and *One-night Stand*. The writing was loopy and girlish. It was impossible to read what the descriptions were. He was growing impatient and irritated with his landlady for suggesting this place. This was the last time he'd trust a woman with aluminum foil curlers in her hair.

Shane felt the seconds ticking by, moving closer and closer to seven-thirty. He decided to try his luck with whatever brew was available at the clinic. He turned to step out of line and slammed into a tray-carrying waitress, dousing himself in hot liquid as everything clattered to the ground. He quickly pulled his shirt away from his scorched skin, gaping at the spreading stain. His feet crunched on the shards of ceramic as he shifted to keep the fabric from making contact.

"Damn it!"

"Are you okay?" A woman's voice asked, and Shane felt a slender hand on his shoulder.

"Yeah. I'm just great," he answered, unsuccessfully attempting to stay out of the mess. "You only ruined my entire day."

The hand recoiled. "Oh, well if *that's* the only damage that was done, then I'll consider this little accident a success."

Shane raised his head and narrowed his eyes on the sassy worker preparing to lecture her on etiquette, only her startling bright-blue eyes distracted his thoughts. He found himself staring and blinking, trying to grasp the anomaly of this beauty and her ill-mannered mouth. It just didn't add up.

"Here." She whisked the dish towel from her shoulder and waved it at him.

He snatched it from her hand. "Gee, thanks. This will fix everything." He swiped at the stain.

"Hey, you were the one piling out of line like your hair was on fire. Maybe you could've signaled first, and this whole thing would have been avoided." The woman dropped to the floor and began to pick up the broken cup.

"Excuse me?" he snapped.

"Yes, that would've worked better." She continued to clink pieces onto the tray.

"Can I help you, Emmylou?"

Shane closed his mouth and looked at the old man who had sweetly offered his assistance to the rude barista.

He watched in bewilderment as her face transformed into a grateful smile. She pushed her long hair away from her face. "No, thank you, Don. I'm sorry about your coffee. Lindy will make you another one right away."

"Don't you worry about that, darlin'. I can wait."

Shane had had enough of this. "Well, that's nice of you since there's a whole line of people waiting for service."

"What's the matter with you?" she asked with a scowl.

"With me?" he scoffed. "What's the matter with *me*?" He shook his head. "Unbelievable! I stand in line for fifteen minutes unable to translate one word on that ridiculous menu, risking being late simply to get a cup of coffee, which is blatantly apparent you don't even make here, only to be scalded from head to toe and insulted by some airhead waitress who obviously got this job because of her ability to turn old codger's heads. I'm the victim here, and you have the gall to insinuate that I'm the problem? Trust me, lady, *I* am not the problem."

There was absolute silence. He felt like an ass after he said it. Her eyes glistened with tears, but she fought them back. He had to respect her for that. His eyes darted around the shop, unable to settle on anyone, while she rose from the floor.

"I'm sorry that you find this place – and me – absurd," she spoke firmly, but quietly.

He sighed, but before he could apologize, she walked to the counter with her tray. He could feel a dozen eyes boring holes through him. His skin was ablaze, and not from the coffee burns. His only option was to slink out the door before they all started throwing coffee at him. What a great first impression he had made on the town where he was supposed to be putting down roots. He set the towel on the back of a chair and grabbed the door handle.

"Here ya go."

Shane turned to see the woman holding out a white paper sack and a to-go coffee cup. He stared at them, then looked to her expectant face. He reached to his back pocket to get his wallet.

"It's on the house." She held them out further.

"Oh, I can't let you do that." He shook his head.

"Just take them." She scrunched up her nose, and it had the strangest effect on him. He wasn't sure if that was a good thing or a bad thing. He hadn't had that feeling in more years than he would care to admit.

Slowly he took them, grazing her soft hands in the exchange. "Thank you."

"You're welcome." She brushed her hands on her white apron. "And I'm sorry about ruining your day."

His face crumpled while his conscience dug into him. *Had he really said that?* "Oh." He swallowed. "You didn't."

With a customary smile, she nodded and turned. Shirt still soaking, he pulled the door open making the bells jingle and stepped into the frigid morning. Good thing the heat of mortification was roaring through his body.

*****

Emmylou pinched her thumb and forefinger at the bridge of her nose. This could very well be the worst day of her life, and that included the time she had blanked on her state final informative speech, thrown up on stage and then slipped in it as she rushed behind the curtain, thoroughly embarrassing her parents. Not that that was anything new. She had been disappointing them her entire life.

She walked behind the counter and told her employee Lindy that she was going to get more sour cream-raisin muffins for the display. In the sanctity of her kitchen, she leaned against the cool stainless steel counter and bowed her head, playing back the scene with that extremely rude man. In all honesty, she hadn't been watching where she was going and had run into him. On the other hand, she had apologized and asked if he was hurt. He was the one who had jumped down her throat.

No, Emmy was never rude to customers. Her business meant everything to her. She had fought so hard to get it going, and she valued every moment she got to do the thing she loved most of all. She lifted the edge of her specially designed black and white apron with her custom logo of the horizon and curved wording to wipe at the tears brimming over her eyes.

Emmylou thought of the poor man who had been on the receiving end of her bad day. She had never seen him before and would probably never see him again. Most likely he was one of the many new guests at The Dove House, her best friend's bed and breakfast. In the past five months, there had been an explosion of visitors to the town. Ever since the news of the trouble-ridden movie set and the tragic death of one of the assistants had lit up the media stream, people had been flocking to Primrose, clogging up the pristine prairie town. They even had their own Twitter hashtag and Facebook fan page. It was all really insane and disruptive, so she wasn't too worried about her lack of customer service for one guy. Although, there was always the possibility the man had been burned from the coffee and would sue her for everything she had. Tears welled in her eyes again, and she hunched further in self-pity.

If only she hadn't been so distracted this morning. If only she wasn't a complete failure, a worthless airhead, a hopeless mess. She closed her eyes and sighed deeply. Finally swallowing the sorrow, she tossed her head back, mentally restoring her self-esteem. It had taken a real battering last night when her boyfriend - no, that's right, ex-boyfriend – had called to tell her he had found someone else. But this time was different. This time she had thought this was it for her. After years of playing in the minors with every Tom, Rick and Steve in town, she thought she had finally caught her all-star. Marcus had been so attentive and passionate. He was handsome and accomplished. He was larger than life to her, and she had wanted him as much as she wanted her bakery. They had handled the long distance relationship well.

Marcus was a film director, jet set and completely out of her league. They had met when his movie production came to town and filmed at her best friend's bed and breakfast, The Dove House. It had taken some time to get him to notice her, but once he did, it was like Christmas and the Fourth of July all rolled into one. When the movie had wrapped after some disturbing setbacks, they fostered a relationship flying back and forth, having Skype dates and mini-vacations. But then he had gone on location to Canada, and it was hard to contact him in such wild tundra.

And that's where he'd met *her*. The so-called love of his life. Emmy rolled her eyes a moment before burying her face in her hand. She could still hear the phone conversation echoing in her ears. She shouldn't be surprised. It was the same old conversation dozens of men had had with her before. They didn't need her anymore, it wasn't her, it was them, she would find someone else; blah, blah, blah. Of course, that revelation only came after she had poured her heart and soul into the relationship.

What was wrong with her?

At first, she had convinced herself that it really *was* them. They had the problem, and she just hadn't met "the one" yet. But she was pushing thirty now, had been on more dates and had more boyfriends than she could remember, and here she was. Still single. Still alone. All she had was Bake my Day.

She pulled the stool up to the counter and sat down, even though she knew Lindy was manning the morning rush all by herself. Emmylou was in no condition to handle people. She wouldn't be able to smile at them. She didn't feel very friendly this morning, and she feared the questions her patrons would press on her. They all knew the wreckage that was her love life, and she just couldn't bear the pity one more time. Sometimes, living in a small town really sucked.

Emmylou's thoughts turned to her best friend Lacy and her new husband Kyle. Their love had survived betrayal, hurt and separation and come out strong on the other side. They were sickeningly devoted to each other and so deeply in love that Emmylou found it hard to be around sometimes. She was so jealous of what they had she wanted to scream.

A wavering smile tugged at her lips. She was also very happy for them. They made it seem like everlasting love was possible and that Emmylou could have the same thing. And damn it, she thought she'd had it. How many times can a heart get broken before it dies? Emmylou was pretty sure hers was close to termination.

Her career was eminently successful; why on earth couldn't she get love right? She ran a bakery in town, did online consulting with hundreds of people and just last year had launched a production line called Prairie Goodness that shipped baked goods all over the country. She could teach an online webinar on the proper techniques of creating realistic molding chocolate sculptures to seventy-five people at once while actually performing the craft. She should be able to manage a relationship with one measly man.

The continual ringing of the front door bells roused her from her pity-party. She pushed out of her seat and slumped to the rolling tray of goodies. She retrieved her one-of-a-kind muffins, already sick of herself pouting over another break-up. She was sick of the whole thing; men, dating, the perpetual ups and downs, but especially of her always ending up on the bottom. She transferred the fresh muffins to a white tray with her tongs and backed out of the kitchen door.

The moment she spun with the tray, her eyes settled on Scarlett and Lacy, her two best friends, standing at the counter. They wore twin expressions of disappointment and tenderness.

"Don't," Emmylou warned calmly.

"We were just here ordering coffee," Lacy tried to assure her.

Emmy wasn't buying it. She looked to a guilty-faced Scarlett trying valiantly to hang on to her innocence. Emmy had to give her credit; Scarlett held her gaze, only tucking her lip between her teeth once.

"You aren't even supposed to be drinking coffee, Lace."

Emmylou transferred her suspicions to her other friend.

Lacy straightened her shoulders. "My new doctor told me it was fine to have a little coffee every day."

Emmylou raised her eyebrows and curled her lip up.

"At least that's what he's going to tell me when I see him tomorrow." Lacy's voice rose and fell, and it was suddenly difficult for her to look at Emmylou.

"Uh-huh." Emmy turned to Lindy. "Do not give her coffee under any circumstances. I don't care if she tells you that it's for Kyle or Scarlett or a homeless man with one leg. Don't believe her." She placed a hand on her worker's shoulder and shook her head. "She'll tell you anything for caffeine."

Lindy nodded in earnest. "You've got it boss lady." She picked up the dish cloth and took off for the seating area.

Lacy grunted her protest. "I've been drinking coffee since I was ten-years-old. My system is used to it. I don't think it's possible that one little cup is going to affect the baby." She crossed her arms over her chest, drawing Emmy's gaze to her belly with a tiny stab to her heart. It was still flat. Lacy was only four months along, but simply knowing that a little person was growing in there brought every maternal reflex to the surface for Emmylou.

"Well, we don't want to find out, do we?"

"For Pete's sake! Between you, Scarlett and Kyle, I may very well run away from home. I feel like a rat in a science lab the way you all watch me." Lacy tossed her heavy hair over her shoulder and stuck her chin out.

"We have to. Kyle swore us to servitude in his absence," Scarlett divulged.

Lacy rolled her eyes, but the glow in her cheeks spoke of her secret pleasure in her husband's devotion. "I'm not a baby. I'm *having* one."

"You're a disaster. That's what you are." Emmylou hadn't meant for it to come out like that.

"Oh, thank you," Lacy drawled. "I think I could say the same about you."

Emmylou bobbed her head in acknowledgment. "You know I

8

love you, Lace." Emmy kissed the air toward her friend. "I was just trying to say that it's smart of Kyle to employ backups since you have a tendency to get into trouble."

Lacy composed a surrendering face. Even she couldn't argue with that. Not with her littered path of a disastrous marriage to a pathetic man, a rocky reunion with the love of her life and the fact that she had almost been murdered by Kyle's deranged assistant last fall. Lacy was a beacon for tricky situations.

"Besides, I don't have anything better to do." Emmylou sniffed and concentrated on putting the muffins into the display case.

She didn't mean to make her friends feel sorry for her; she already felt sorry enough for herself. But she had to admit that this last break-up was harder than the dozens before it. Scarlett reached across the counter to get Emmy's attention. Emmylou attempted a smile. It fell flat when her face crumpled, and the tears clogged in her throat.

"I don't know what happened," the words rushed out on a sob. Then, just as suddenly, she swallowed them and shook her head, getting control. She clutched Scarlett's hand and looked deep into her eyes for strength. "I'm okay." She sucked in a shaky breath and transferred her gaze to Lacy. "I promise. I'm okay."

Emmylou took Lacy's outstretched hand, feeling her friends' love and support like an electrical current flashing through her.

"Oh, honey." Lacy tilted her head and grimaced. "You don't always have to be so tough you know."

A hiccup escaped Emmylou's lips. "Look who's talking."

"Yeah, but you're so much smarter than me. I would've thought you could learn from all my mistakes." Lacy grinned, a glint shining behind the tears in her eyes.

"It's that stubborn Irish streak in me, I guess," Emmylou quipped.

The door bells jingled, and the friends jarred apart. Lacy and Scarlett shifted so Emmylou could wait on her customer, but their gazes never left her. Emmylou was very blessed in the friend department. They were the first ones in line, charging with guns blazing – Lacy literally – to her defense.

After ringing up the coffee and croissant and bidding the woman goodbye, Scarlett and Lacy were pushing back up to the counter.

"Okay, so Kyle's gone. I know." Lacy brushed off her friends' identical looks of annoyance. "But it's the last trip to Garberville. He has to close on his house there and then spend a few days with…" Lacy clamped her mouth shut, her eyes like saucers, staring at Emmylou.

Emmylou's chest tightened. She knew why Lacy had suddenly locked up like a virgin on prom night. Kyle was with Marcus, and Lacy was such a sweetheart she wouldn't even mention the man's name.

"It's fine, Lacy. Kyle is still allowed to be friends with him. You don't have to protect me." Emmy shrugged and sighed. "I think I'm immune to the pain this time. I've finally had my heart broken enough times that it's just numb."

"I'm going to take that as a good sign." Scarlett's eyes were sad, but her tone didn't let on. "That means he wasn't the one for you."

Emmylou's gaze moved fondly between her amazing friends. "I don't want to talk about it anymore." With a breath of strength, she turned to Lacy. "How are you feeling?"

Taking the cue, Lacy straightened and bravely smiled. "I'm pretty good, I guess. I mean, I don't know what pregnancy is supposed to feel like, but so far not much is different."

"Other than those huge knockers." Emmylou tried to pick up the mood even more, and her friends' laughs meant success.

Lacy put a hand on each side of her breasts and looked down. "Aren't they the weirdest thing? Kyle isn't complaining." She shrugged. "He probably hopes they're permanent."

Emmylou grinned and shook her head. "What about you, Scar? How's Louie doing?" Emmylou knew that the subject of her latest heartbreak would be completely forgotten if she asked about one of Scarlett's many rescued pets. They ruled the woman's life.

"Oh my goodness! Well, you know how he likes to wander the neighborhood?"

10

Emmylou nodded at the understatement. That cat was a cross between Houdini and Church from Stephen King's *Pet Cemetery* after he came back from the dead.

Chapter 2

Shane barreled into the parking lot of the clinic, praying he wouldn't run anyone over. His shirt was heavy and sticky beneath his coat; he was cold and more than a little annoyed at the way his first day on the job was going. He should have just come here without stopping at that ridiculous coffee shop. Then he would have been on time and had a clean shirt to wear. He grabbed the cup and paper sack from the seat of his pick-up, kicked the door shut and jogged across the freshly plowed concrete.

He tried the front door and found it locked. Before he could even think about looking for another door, a woman dressed in heart-patterned scrubs was smiling through the glass at him. She turned the lock, and a nervous thump landed in his gut.

"You must be Dr. Newberry," the woman said and gestured for him to enter. "We've been expecting you." He walked with her to the reception desk. "You can put that down right here." She patted the counter, and he placed his coffee and sack down.

"Sorry about that." Shane didn't believe in excuses. He met her gaze and caught an amused twinkle in her light colored eyes. He didn't know what else to say.

"Oh, we are too. It's such a shame."

He tilted his head, confused and off-balance. "Excuse me?"

"It's a shame you weren't able to get to town sooner. I'm sure you had a rough morning trying to find your way around." Her cocked grin and casual stance ignited his dormant sense of humor.

"How could you tell?" He returned her smile, beginning to relax.

"For starters, you slid your truck in here like you were making a pit stop at the Indy/500, then sprinted across the parking lot with your pants on fire. I'm guessing you were just about to break the glass and crawl through the door before I opened it."

He couldn't help but chuckle at her accuracy.

"Don't worry about it Doctor. Even though this place runs with the precision of an atomic clock, we leave room for humanity, and the clinic doesn't open for another fifteen minutes."

Shane let out a sigh, relaxing his muscles. "I can't tell you how happy I am to hear that. I've been running on a hectic schedule the past few years, I forgot what it was like in a small town."

"Well, we're sure glad that you decided to come here."

He started to take his coat off, then remembered the coffee stain. He grimaced in indecision.

"I see it really was quite the morning for you."

Shane wagged his eyebrows and looked at the massive stain with a shake of his head. "I'm not sure what gave it away. Could it be this coffee all over my shirt?"

The nurse laughed and patted his arm. "I think I have just the thing for you." She walked behind the desk and toward the filing cabinets. "It just so happens," she reached behind the wall and presented a blue striped shirt covered in a dry cleaner's sack, "that Dr. Miller always kept a spare shirt around here. I'm sure he wouldn't mind if you used it." She walked back to him and held it out. "You never know whether you'll be assisting a birth or reattaching a thumb."

"Thank you." Shane laughed and accepted the shirt. He dropped his shoulders and cocked his head. "Here I am talking up a storm, and I haven't even asked your name. I'm sorry."

She waved a hand and smiled. "I'm the one chewing your ear off. I'm Shelby, Shelby Stevens."

"It's nice to meet you, Shelby." He held his hand out. He almost reached for his hat out of habit but remembered he hadn't worn one in several years. It must be the friendly, small town bringing him back to his roots.

"And you, Dr. Newberry. I can see we're going to get along just fine."

Their hands released, and she walked around him. "You'd better eat that thing before Abigail gets here." Shelby pulled the pen from behind her ear and pointed at the paper sack on the counter.

"Oh, I was going to save it for later."

She gave him a funny look. "It's from Bake My Day isn't it?"

"Yeah. Emmylou gave it to me."

Shelby's eyebrows bounced up. "Emmylou is it? You're a fast worker, Doc."

Shane sputtered, unable to respond to Shelby's mistaken implication.

"Believe me, you won't want to wait." She clicked her tongue and winked a moment before walking down the hall.

Shane felt like he had been sucked into a whirlwind and twisted around. He stood for several moments looking around at the reception room. It had been nine years since he had worked at a job where he didn't have orders barked at him every second of the day. In this place, he was in charge, at least of the day-to-day operation. Next week he would meet with the board so they could go over all the policies.

Shane had submitted his resume with the understanding that Dr. Miller would be here to show him the ropes should he get the position. But three days ago, his phone had rung, and the man on the line had begged him to come as soon as he could. Shane had been thrown into this position when Dr. Miller had suffered a massive stroke not two weeks after announcing his desire to retire.

Shane was at the end of his fellowship and just picking up shifts at the hospital, so he jumped at the chance to be back in rural Nebraska. The years he would spend serving this community would fulfill his scholarship obligation of serving a rural community. He had been awarded an RHOP scholarship from the State of Nebraska. He got to go to college for free as long as he returned to a rural community to practice. It was a good fit all around.

But now he was feeling a bit like he had been tossed to the wolves. He didn't know anyone here, he had only just met his nurse, and he had no idea where the examination rooms were or how a typical day in this clinic went. To say he was in over his head would be an understatement.

Shane opened the sack, and the heavenly aroma slipped into his nostrils, instantly making his mouth water. The huge muffin he pulled out was spongy and delectable. He took his first bite and grunted with satisfaction as the soft, delicious, raisin-filled creation danced on his taste buds. It was the best thing he had tasted in his life, hands-down. He had just filled his mouth with another bite when Shelby reappeared.

"I heard moans and grunts out here. Thought I'd better come and check it out, make sure there wasn't somebody having *too* good a time." She gave him the "if-you-know-what-I-mean?" look. "You can finish that while I show you around, although I can see you won't need that much time." He tried to chuckle through a mouthful of muffin. "We'll have just enough time for you to change your shirt before this place turns into Grand Central Station." She waved for him to follow her.

To emphasize her point, the phone rang. A dark haired woman came out of nowhere, picked it up, and sat in her chair while pulling out the computer keyboard. This place really was efficient.

*****

Emmylou adjusted the belt on her pink, oversized sweater for the third time, anxiously glancing around the clinic waiting room. She wasn't big on clinics or hospitals. She had spent too much time in them as a kid being poked, prodded, x-rayed and interviewed. Her parents had dragged her to every doctor and specialist in the Western Hemisphere to make sure she was as perfect as they wanted her to be.

The Bennett's weren't supposed to be able to have children. When her mother had been surprised by pregnancy, they went to extremes to get their baby to term, then went overboard on Emmylou's care after she was born and on into puberty. Her mother didn't cope well with surprises. She fared even worse with imperfection.

Emmylou chafed her arms, staving off a chill, but not from the cold day this time. Had she not been so distracted during their conversation at the bakery yesterday, she wouldn't have gotten herself roped into going to the doctor with Lacy. She had hoped to be able to spend the afternoon working on that stupid birthday cake she was supposed to get done by Friday night.

Emmy closed her eyes and clenched her fists. This break-up was affecting her outlook on everything. If she wasn't careful, she was going to turn into a bitter old maid just like Bonnie Pike, the woman who lived at the end of her block and threw sunflower seeds at the children who rode their bikes or walked to closely too her immaculate yard. Heck, the woman did that to the adults, too.

"Thanks for coming with me." Lacy flicked a glance at Emmylou over her magazine. "I know it wasn't at the top of your list of things you wanted to do today, but I really appreciate it. I would've asked Scarlett, but she would have ended up asking the doctor all about how to treat some injured raccoon or how he felt about de-clawing cats."

"Lace, it's no problem. Really. I'm happy that you asked me. Since this baby is going to be my niece or nephew, I'm thrilled that I get to be one of the first to meet it."

Emmylou was an only child and thought of Scarlett and Lacy as her sisters. It was nice to feel that she wasn't alone in the world.

"Have you met the new doctor?" Lacy asked, then held her copy of *Inns and Cottages Magazine* for Emmylou to look at the pages.

"Oh, that's pretty. You should get Kyle to make that for the entrance." Lacy was constantly updating and restoring The Dove House, and now that she had an unlimited supply of cash, she was able to do whatever she wanted. "No, I haven't met him yet. I was doing a webinar the afternoon he arrived in town."

Emmylou was on the board that ran the town's clinic. She had even helped with obtaining the funds to build the new six-room addition that they were sitting in. She didn't really enjoy it, but her mother had retired from it the year before, and it was understood that Emmy would fill her place. *The Bennett's were public servants.* How many times had she heard her mother's speech? At least one thousand.

"He's thirty-two and from a small farming town in the eastern part of Nebraska," Emmylou informed her friend to help her relax. She didn't want to tell her that he had virtually no experience in obstetrics or that Emmy thought he was the worst of all the available candidates.

"Oh." Lacy perked up and nodded.

Emmylou knew she had put Lacy at ease even if her insides were twisting with guilt. Nebraska people automatically accept other Nebraskans no matter what part of the state they are from. It's a kinship they all share.

"Lacy McClintock," Shelby, the nurse, called out.

"I'm still not used to that," Lacy divulged under her breath as she rose from her chair and stuffed her magazine under her arm. "Ready?"

As I'll ever be, Emmylou answered silently while nodding.

They followed Shelby to an examining room while chatting about their families and such. Emmylou took the blue vinyl chair along the wall, while Lacy hopped up on the exam table. All of the things on her list buzzing through her mind drowned out the chatter between Lacy and Shelby.

"Earth to Emmylou."

"Hmm?" Emmy blinked and turned toward Lacy. She hadn't even been aware the nurse had left the room.

"What's on your mind?"

Lacy's smile tried to hide the underlying question. Emmylou knew Lacy was asking if she was thinking about Marcus.

"Oh, just thinking about the cake I need to get done for a Conner Stapleton's birthday this weekend."

Lacy tilted her head, surveying her for a moment with a thoughtful expression before straightening. "Yeah, that's going to be a blast. Kyle can't wait for the practice. It was his idea to start offering Dove House as an event venue. I saw Conner yesterday with his mom. I don't think he knows we're doing it. Or he's a really great actor. I'm not a great judge of those things you know."

"Oh, Lace. When are you going to let go of that? The woman was crazy. She even had Kyle fooled. And that's saying something."

Lacy's face crumpled in a mixture of sorrow and anger. Emmylou knew she had had a hard time dealing with the accidental death of Lauren Michaels, Kyle's assistant who had tried to murder Lacy and set The Dove House on fire. But Emmylou figured it would always be hard once a person had seen a woman plummet out of a window. And Lacy felt responsible for it even though it had been self-defense.

"I think I need to apologize to one of your guests," Emmylou changed the subject hoping Lacy would come around.

"Really? For what?" Lacy tapped her heels against the side of the exam table.

"Yesterday, before you and Scarlett came in, I ran into a guy, dousing him in hot coffee. I didn't know who he was. I assumed he was a tourist. I wasn't very nice about it." She pulled a face, waiting for Lacy to either laugh or scold her, but her friend was thinking.

"I don't think any of the guests were out of the house before nine this morning. Most of them were opting for the fire and hot breakfast that Mrs. Walters was cooking up."

"Oh." Now Emmylou was baffled. She knew everyone in town and most of the surrounding area. She was sure he had to be one of the guests.

"What did he look like?" The paper on the table crunched as Lacy readjusted her seat.

"Well," Emmylou thought back to yesterday. "I didn't really look at him. But he had darkish brown hair, a little taller than me." She rolled her bottom lip, digging into her memory. "His eyes. They were this yummy, chocolate brown. Warm," Emmylou stuffed a giggle thinking about how angry he had been at first but had softened when she gave him the coffee and muffin for free. "Late twenties, maybe early thirties."

Lacy wrinkled her forehead and shook her head. "We don't have anyone that young at the B and B." She flipped her hair and turned her eyes up. "Kyle probably wouldn't have left for California if we had. He seems to be a touch on the–", Lacy wrinkled her nose, searching for the right term, "protective side."

Emmylou had to laugh. She knew if Kyle could lock Lacy up in a glass box, he would do it. After the incident with the movie set last year, he rarely let anyone he didn't know or trust around Lacy. An entirely stressful situation when the woman he loved and wanted to protect ran a bed and breakfast.

"I guess he must've been passing through town, or maybe he'd just arrived and wanted some coffee." Lacy lifted one shoulder, but Emmylou couldn't stop wondering who the guy was that she nearly scalded to death.

"I wonder what this new doctor is going to be like. I've never been to anyone except Dr. Miller." Lacy sighed, and Emmylou patted her leg. "Doctor Miller gave birth to me. This could be weird."

"He interviews well over the phone, and the three doctors we talked to gave him glowing reports. It's going to be fine. I'm sure that…" a knock at the door interrupted Emmylou, and she looked to the opening door. "He's – oh my God!"

If Emmylou could have crawled under the examination table and hidden for the next three months, she would have. Standing there in a white coat with his mouth open, utterly frozen, and his hand on the door handle was the man she had dumped coffee on and insulted this morning. Her stomach – well she couldn't even feel that anymore – and her heart slammed into her chest like a jackhammer. He wasn't just a tourist!

He cleared his throat, and a wave of composure washed over him while he continued into the room. "Good afternoon, ladies."

"Good afternoon," Lacy answered. "Emmy, honey, you're hurting my leg."

Emmylou was drawn from her paralysis and looked at Lacy. She was wearing her intrigued-concerned look that always made Emmy want to spill her guts. Instead, she clamped her tense jaw shut, glanced down to see that her hand was digging into Lacy's thigh and whisked it away. "Sorry."

Her heart was still as jumpy as a June bride at a shotgun wedding, but she managed to make it to the vinyl chair and lower herself into it. Her mind was racing in tandem with her heartbeat. The doctor moved to the desk next to Emmylou's chair and sat on the stool. His eyes flickered to her, and she swallowed hard. The manners driven into her by her parents popped back into her mind. She twisted in her chair and raised her hands to the desk to plead his forgiveness knocking his file folder to the floor and scattering the papers everywhere.

"I see accidents are a part of your protocol," he quipped and bent to pick up the mess.

An embarrassed whimper escaped her throat, and she slid off the chair to help him, but her pride rallied in a matter of seconds. "And you are the master of impertinence." He paused in his collecting to raise a brow and tip his head. She met his gaze, unwavering, then moved to gather several more sheets. She reached to get one that had skittered the furthest, and when she turned back to hand it to him, her head slammed into something hard making stars pop in front of her eyes. She both heard and stifled a grunt and a low "oww". Oh, why couldn't she just die this very moment?

"Sorry." That was all she could get out before his smart-assed reply came.

"An apology this time. Wow. I can see that I'm going to have to wear a helmet and a rain coat whenever I'm around you."

Emmylou's nostrils flared in annoyance. He had slid back onto his stool. She pushed against the floor to get up and whipped her head to look at Dr. High-and-Mighty. She raked her eyes over him noticing his nice, clean shirt. "You don't look the worse for wear after our little incident this morning. Besides, I said I was sorry," she finished, softer.

He tucked his pen into his white lab coat and leveled dark brown eyes on her. For once, she towered over him. She wished she felt the power that leverage normally brought, but with those intelligent eyes studying her, she couldn't harness it. He leaned back and crossed his arms. "I heard you."

She glared at him with her mouth dropped open. "Of all the rude, egotistical, self-absorbed, chauvinistic men I have encountered in my life, and believe me there have been many, you, sir, are the worst! I have half a mind to–"

"Emmylou!"

The no-nonsense interruption made Emmy turn and stare at her friend, but Lacy cut her off by widening her eyes, reminding her that she was a lady. Emmylou clamped her mouth shut and dragged in a heavy breath. She knew that she should apologize for her outburst, but she couldn't bring herself any lower. Besides, her mother always said that if you couldn't say anything nice, then don't say anything at all.

She dropped into the chair, crossed her arms and legs, and stared off to the side. She was sorry she had ever agreed to come along on this doctor's appointment. She could feel him looking at her, probably waiting for another outburst or gloating over her being effectively silenced.

"Now, Mrs. McClintock, how are you feeling today?"

Emmylou had to refrain from mimicking him with her nose turned up by thinking about how she was going to design the cake Lindy had just ordered for her wedding reception. Confections were the only thing that calmed her. She half- listened as Lacy and Dr. High-and-Mighty talked about Lacy's condition. She loved her friend and was excited beyond words about the baby, but if she had to tolerate this doctor for the entire pregnancy, she might have to bring cotton balls along to stuff in her ears – or down his throat.

Emmylou had never really hated anyone before, with the exception of Mrs. Hagstrom, her tenth grade French teacher – really, her name said it all, but Doctor Newbury was on the fast track to Revulsion City.

Emmylou's attention was drawn to the conversation when Doctor Newbury asked if Lacy wanted to hear the heartbeat.

"Can I?" Lacy asked in awe, and Emmylou smiled for her friend. "Emmy." Lacy shifted to look at Emmylou and wiggled her fingers at her. "Come stand with me so you can hear too."

With a sheen of tears in her eyes for both Lacy and herself, Emmylou went to the examining table. Lacy grasped her hand, and Emmylou returned the squeeze. Doctor Newbury squirted some clear jelly on Lacy's abdomen and took out a weird looking silver object with a black wire. Emmylou couldn't stop smiling while she watched his long fingers work the device back and forth. And then the room was filled with a rapid *whoosh-thump* of a heartbeat, and Emmy's smile grew to take up her entire face.

"It's so beautiful," Emmylou crooned and held Lacy's hand tighter.

"Can you even believe it? It's so fast." Lacy's dreamy tone made Emmylou's eyes overflow with absolute joy. Two tears slid down her cheeks, and she didn't bother to wipe them away before looking to the doctor when he spoke.

"Everything sounds normal." He leaned over and clicked a few buttons on the computer keyboard. "I'm making a recording of this for you and your husband. I will email it to you later this afternoon."

The grin that split his face surprised Emmylou, and she was struck by how handsome he was. His concern for Lacy and the baby was written in every crease of his smile. If she didn't hate him so much, she would think it was the sweetest thing she had ever seen.

Chapter 3

Emmylou reclined on the couch with her sketch pad resting against her knees, working up some rough ideas for Lindy's cake. She set her pencil down and reached for the half-empty wine glass. Her assistant was five years younger than Emmy and already getting married. Lindy had been dating her fiancé for six years. They had started dating their junior year of high school. Emmylou had had more dates and more boyfriends than the female population of Primrose combined and nothing to show for it other than a calloused heart and a pile of regrets.

She downed the lukewarm wine and picked up the bottle to refill it only to find it empty. "Damn." Her heart sunk with guilt. She couldn't remember if this was a fresh bottle that she had polished off or one that was leftover. She had a nagging suspicion she had just had an entire bottle of wine in a matter of two hours.

Emmylou set her pad on the coffee table and gathered the bottle and glass. She started for the kitchen with the memory of Lacy's doctor's appointment fresh in her mind and the picture of Lindy's beautiful three-tiered cake dancing before her eyes. Everyone's life was moving on while hers was stagnant, and there was a very good possibility that it was actually going backwards. She would be adopting cats and knitting doll clothes to dress them up very soon.

The doorbell chimed, and she closed her eyes on a curse. She wanted to wallow in solitude. She stood still in the dining room praying for the person to take the hint and go away. If she were really quiet, whoever it was would think she wasn't home. Another chime was followed by knocking. She hung her head. There was no way she was getting out of answering the door. She placed the glass and bottle on her table and dragged herself to the door.

The knock was harder this time. "Emmylou!"

Emmy groaned, and her shoulders drooped. She could sit down and cry at this very moment. As if her self-esteem wasn't low enough, her mother was now at her front door. It took all her effort, but Emmylou raised her hand to the knob while her mother kept rapping.

"Emmylou Marie Bennett, I know you're in there!"

Emmy swung the door open just as her mother had started to peek through the peephole. She took impish pleasure in making her stumble inside. She hid the smile by closing the door while her mother adjusted her wool coat.

"Well, it's about time. I thought you were going to leave me out there to freeze to death." Susan Bennett tugged her smooth leather gloves off.

"That thought never crossed my mind," Emmylou assured her mother, less than sure herself. "Come in, mother." Emmy scanned the room to see how messy her house was. She was relieved to find it in pretty good condition. These days she didn't have much enthusiasm for running a tight ship.

"Thank you, sweetheart."

A siren flared to life in Emmylou's head. Her mother was only nice when she wanted something. "Have a seat."

"That would be –" Emmy watched as her mother swept her gaze over the sofa, then the chair, "I think I'll just stand. I can see you haven't had time to tidy up."

The odds of Emmylou being compliant dropped several notches, but she didn't take the bait. Emmy folded her hands and waited with a forced smile. She loved her mother, but sometimes she was really hard to like.

Several seconds ticked by while the tension grew. "So, what brings you by tonight?" Emmy knew it had to be something pretty big to bring her mother out after dark. Usually she would be tucked away in her room planning her next church event, reading or talking with Emmy's father.

"I wondered if you'd had a chance to welcome the new doctor

to town today."

Emmylou choked a little and had to clear her throat. She stepped closer to lean against the antique buffet behind her couch. "I had the pleasure of meeting him today." She couldn't make eye contact with her mother.

"Oh, good." Susan sighed in relief. "Shelby mentioned to me that he had had a rough morning and I was worried that had set the tone for his acclimation into Primrose."

The fact that her mother had the utmost confidence in Emmylou's manners and hospitality burned her conscience.

"I'm happy that you were able to take my place on the board, Emmylou. I know things will be taken care of. I couldn't leave it up to the others." Susan slapped her gloves into the opposite hand. "That ridiculous Mrs. Walters couldn't find her way around a dead-end street with two guides and a map."

Emmylou had to bite back a smile. "Mother, why do you hate her so much? She's such a wonderful woman and a great help to Lacy."

Susan's lips flattened and nearly disappeared. "That's not saying much, dear."

Emmy knew better than to defend her friends further. She had been doing it since the beginning of time and nothing she had ever said made any difference in her mother's eyes. None of them were good enough for her darling daughter.

"Can I get you something to drink, mother?"

"No, thank you." Susan smiled and adjusted her stance. "I can't stay, and it looks like you have depleted your stock anyhow." Emmylou followed her mother's quick glance to the dining room table where the empty wine bottle sat. Her mother really had a way of making her feel like a failure whether she meant to or not.

"Well, I just wanted to make sure that you had taken care of Dr. Newbury, and you have. Thank you, dear." Susan gave her a warm smile, making Emmylou feel crazy for thinking that her mother disapproved of her.

"You're welcome, Mom."

Susan moved from her place near the sofa, then stopped. "Oh, I see you're still working on your art." She stepped to the sketch pad and picked it up, a frown taking over her previous smile. "It's another cake."

She said it like Emmylou had drawn a gorilla or a tree. "It's for Lindy's wedding in March. I want it to be the best cake I've ever made. She's been such a wonderful assistant, and she will be quitting after the wedding. I want to show her my appreciation."

Her mother was still inspecting the sketch. "Mmm." She wrinkled her forehead, but this time she kept her usual sermon about Emmy's wasted talent to herself. "That's nice of you, honey. You're always thinking of others."

That's what you taught me, Mother, Emmylou thought. *Suddenly that was not the thing to do?* Susan Bennett had spent her life volunteering and had taught Emmylou that she should always give back. Emmy guessed that attitude only applied to the community so she could look good and increase the family's good name, not to help individual people just to be kind.

She stood still as her mother approached and ran a loving hand over her hair. A smile met her eyes. "How about dinner tomorrow night? Your father will be out of town, and we can catch up." She rested her hand on Emmylou's shoulder with an expectant expression.

Emmylou looked away. "As lovely as that sounds," she hoped she sounded sincere, "that's Thursday and–"

"Of course, of course," her mother fluffed her hair and narrowed her brows. She backed away, averting her gaze. "That's your dinner night with your friends. I forgot."

"I can cancel. I'm sure that Lacy and Scarlett can do it without me."

"No, no, dear." Susan shook her head and made a job out of putting her gloves back on. "You go and have fun with your friends. We can do it another night."

Her mother had never acted like this before. She was usually so busy that spending time with Emmylou outside of a formal meeting or customary visit to criticize was unheard of.

"Maybe we can invite Dr. Newbury as well. We can help him

26

feel at home here."

Emmylou swallowed, "Sure, mom. That would be nice." Keeping her poker face was harder than normal. She could only imagine how awkward that would be.

"I'll see you soon, honey." Her mother's gaze settled on Emmylou a little longer, making her wonder what was going on.

"Are you all right, Mom?"

Susan gathered her familiar composure and answered with a steady voice, "Of course. Everything's fine."

Emmylou let her pass by in her walk to the door with a strange pressure behind her heart and a twist in her stomach.

"I'll call you about dinner." Susan pulled the door open.

"Sure, that sounds great."

Her mother looked like she wanted to say something else and Emmylou wished she would. Emmy opened her mouth to speak, but her mother gave her a quick smile and slipped out the door into the cold night.

Emmylou stood staring at the door trying to piece together the hidden meaning in their conversation. What it was her mother *hadn't* said. Her mother was such a sergeantmajor all of the time that the vulnerability she had shown just now was more than odd; it was disturbing.

*****

"Maybe she'd heard about your behavior and she was upset by it," Lacy said as she took a sip of her sparkling grape juice and grimaced.

"If that were the case, she would have jumped down my throat." Emmylou placed the paring knife next to the sink and scraped the bell peppers into the salad bowl. She loved Thursday night dinners at The Dove House. Even though it brought back memories of Marcus and the film he had made here, it was still closer to home than her parent's house.

"And maybe she just wanted to spend time with her only daughter," Scarlett added quietly before gathering the hot pad and opening the oven to check on the casserole.

Emmylou had a flippant answer for Scarlett, but she knew just how much Scarlett wished that her own mother wanted a relationship, so she kept it to herself. Scarlett hadn't heard from her mom since Christmas, and that was to ask for money. No one spoke of Scarlett's mother's addiction to gambling and her subsequent alcoholism. It had become the norm, as awful as it was.

"I suppose it's possible." Emmylou shrugged and picked up the bamboo bowl. "But why would she want one now? I've always been more of a project than an actual daughter to her." The three friends pushed through the kitchen door into the dining room, all carrying food. It was eight o'clock and the diners had gone home. They went to their favorite table next to the big window.

"Well, at least be happy she's interested in you at all." Scarlett slid into the chair closest to the window, averting her gaze.

"I know I should be, but it was just weird."

Lacy and Emmylou joined Scarlett at the table and passed the dishes around. It was Scarlett's turn to do the main dish, so Emmy knew it was going to be something they had never had before and mouth-wateringly delicious. Emmylou may be the baker and have the certificates to prove it, but Scarlett could put any professional chef to shame.

"When is Kyle getting home?" Emmylou asked Lacy.

Lacy was already working on a mouthful of food. She gave Emmy an embarrassed look and placed her hand over her mouth while she finished chewing. "Sorry." She swallowed and picked up her wine glass full of juice to wash it down. "Scar, this is awesome." She pointed to the plate with her finger, then directed her attention back to Emmy. "He should be home tomorrow sometime."

Emmylou nodded and took a forkful of casserole, "Are you going to let him listen to the heartbeat?" She took her bite with the ever-thankful taste buds rejoicing in her mouth.

"You got to hear it?" Scarlett perked up, a smile splitting her face.

"Mm-hum." Lacy leaned forward, her entire being glowing

28

with joy. "I wish you could have been there, Scar. It was the most amazing thing, and Dr. Newbury took a recording of it so Kyle can hear it too. Just think, a little person is in there right now, growing arms and legs, and fingers and toes." Lacy had to pause to catch her breath and stifle back some tears. "Nobody told me that the raging hormones are the worst part." She wiped her cheeks with a sheepish smile.

"I'm sure that's not the *worst* part," Emmylou smirked and the three of them burst into laughter.

They enjoyed more baby talk while devouring nearly every scrap of food on the table. Emmylou and Scarlett had finished the bottle of wine while Lacy scowled. She wouldn't be partaking in that particular tradition for quite a while. Soon they were cozied up on the floor next to a crackling fire, holding cups of melting marshmallows swimming in hot cocoa. They were enjoying the quiet company a lifetime of friendship ensured when Emmylou suddenly felt an atmospheric shift. She glanced over to see Lacy suddenly begin tugging at a loose thread in the antique quilt she was wrapped in and Scarlett become fascinated with her cup.

Emmy cocked her jaw and raised her brows. "Okay. What's up?"

If Lacy's face kept scrunching at that rate she would soon resemble a Shar-Pei, but Scarlett took a breath and spoke to the ceiling. "We wondered if you were up for a talk about Marcus."

"Is that a question?" Emmylou snapped, then sunk against the chair behind her, closing her eyes against the sting. "I'm sorry," she spoke on a sigh. "It's just that I thought maybe he was the one." She twirled a braid from the blanket around her finger. "I should've known better. I mean, he spent more time looking in the mirror than he ever did looking at me." She pinched her thumb and forefinger over the bridge of her nose.

"Oh, honey." Scarlett scooted closer and wrapped her in a hug while Lacy reached out and rubbed a comforting hand over her knee. "We didn't mean to upset you." Scarlett pulled her closer, and Emmylou tucked her head against her friend's neck.

"We heard you cussing at your muffins," Lacy added and

squeezed Emmylou's hand.

Emmylou looked at Lacy with a crooked smile. "It was that bad?" Both Lacy and Scarlett bobbed their heads, their gazes trained on her. Emmy pulled away a little. "Really? I'm so sorry." Emmy sat up and tossed her hair back. "I didn't mean to shut you guys out. I was just so… disappointed. And angry. Deeply angry."

"We understand." Lacy leaned forward, and Emmy caught the small gasp she let out.

"I guess I was a bit embarrassed, too. This is another relationship down the tubes. I'm twenty-nine years old, have had more relationships than pairs of shoes and now I have to start over. Again." She tucked her heavy hair behind her ear and saw Lacy slowly move her hand to her abdomen.

"Don't feel bad, Em. You and I can be spinsters together," Scarlett patted Emmy's leg. "Lord knows I'm not marrying anyone."

Emmylou hated that her friend only said that out of habit. Scarlett had convinced herself, after years of help from her grandfather, that she wasn't worthy of a respectable man or a family. So she had resigned herself to that idea and, consequently, spent her years tucked inside herself and away from anyone who might be interested in her.

"That's not true sweetie." Emmylou captured her friend's gaze hoping that what she was going to say would wake Scarlett up to life even though it never had before. "You have opportunities right in front of you. You simply choose to believe the crap your grandpa pumped into you instead of the truth that your best friends *know*."

"Now that we're talking about it, Scarlett, you really should listen to Emmy." Lacy winced on the last words and pressed her hand against her middle.

"Are you okay?" Emmylou didn't like the face Lacy was making.

"Yeah." Lacy let out a heavy breath. "It was only a little cramp." She sat up straighter and moved her hand away. "I'm okay."

Emmylou and Scarlett both watched Lacy until they were satisfied she was telling the truth.

"Okay." Emmylou adjusted her seating and blanket. "Well, I for one am sick of all this depressing talk. What's done is done. Marcus is gone." Emmylou waved her hand, then picked up the cool cup of cocoa. "Now, Lacy, tell us," Emmy puckered her lips, feeling more like herself, "what's the sex like now that you're pregnant?"

Lacy and Scarlett let out identical screams of shock. Scarlett covered her mouth ,and Lacy reached over and smacked her shoulder, her mouth gaping open and a red flare in her cheeks. Emmylou laughed. "What? We're not getting any." She glanced to Scarlett. "So we have to live vicariously through our married friend with the super-hot, movie star husband!"

They all laughed now, and Lacy shook her head. Her blush turned beet red and spanned from forehead to collarbone.

"I hear it's pretty hot," Emmylou managed to sputter through laughs, causing more hilarity among her friends. "Not that the two of you need any help with that! Seeing you two together makes me want to get the nearest hose and spray ya down!"

The three of them collapsed in a fit of giggles while Emmy was pummeled with couch pillows. Every joke she made and laugh that bubbled up made her feel better and better. She was almost back to normal. Almost. The moment lingered and drifted.

Emmylou rearranged her mass of messy hair. Scarlett and Lacy followed suit. Of the three of them, Emmy's was the longest and thickest and caused the most problems. Although Lacy and her waves would like to argue. And Scarlett was beautiful no matter what she did. Emmylou moved the tangled blanket off her legs, welcoming the cool air over her heated body. She fanned her shirt open to help the process.

"When did it get so hot in here?" she asked.

"About the time you said 'sex' and started talking about Kyle being super-hot," Lacy chuckled.

"Well, that always gets you going, honey." Emmy lifted the hair from her neck.

"It's true." Lacy grinned and wrinkled her nose.

Emmylou opened her mouth to joke more, but launched forward the second Lacy's face crumpled and she let out a groan.

"Lacy?" The panic rocketed to Emmy's throat, tightening it. "What's wrong?"

Lacy moaned and clutched her stomach, tucking into a ball.

"Oh my God! Lacy! Please tell me what's wrong?" Emmylou ran her hands helplessly over Lacy's body, desperate to make the pain go away. "Is it the baby?" *Please God, no!* She didn't want to ask it, but she had to.

"I think so," Lacy gasped the words as her fingers dug into the bunched shirt at her abdomen. "It hurts. Worse than cramps."

"Don't joke about it." Scarlett's voice was strained and quiet.

"Who's joking?" Lacy closed her eyes.

"Sorry." Scarlett blanched and her hand trembled as she went to place it on Lacy's shoulder. Emmylou reached out and got her attention, then nodded firmly when Scarlett straightened her shoulders and clamped her jaw shut.

"What can we do? Do you want an ambulance?" Emmylou asked.

Lacy turned her head and rolled her eyes. "Yeah. Please call Carl and have him dispatch the ambulance. It may get here about the time pinch-rolled jeans come back in style."

"Well, I don't know what to do, damn it! You're scaring the hell out of me!"

"Both of you stop yelling at each other!" Scarlett barked, making them stare at her. She returned it with an annoyed glare of her own. "Lacy, can you get to the couch or do you think we need to keep you where you are?"

"I think it would be okay to move to the couch, but I can do it." Lacy attempted to lift herself.

"Like hell you can." Scarlett could be bossy when she wanted to be. "We'll lift you to the couch. It's not like you weigh anything."

Lacy allowed Emmylou and Scarlett to lift her from the floor. Emmylou knew it was painful for her, but damn if Lacy didn't tough it out. They helped her lay down and Emmy brushed the hair out of her face. Scarlett placed a hand over the top of Lacy's that was wrapped protectively over the baby.

"See? No problem." Emmylou hoped her voice was confident, only she was sure it quivered with the panic raging inside of her.

"That's because you are both as tall as cranes, and I'm a short little duck." Lacy took a deep breath. Some of the tension left her face.

Emmylou and Scarlett let out airy, nervous laughs, trying to comfort Lacy. Until Lacy's brown gaze bored into Emmylou's with another wave of pain. "Dr. Newbury's number is in my purse. Can you call him?"

Emmylou nodded her head. "Of course." She glanced to Scarlett. Their silent exchange evoking the fear and uncertainty they both felt.

Emmylou scrambled to the office where Lacy kept her purse, knocking it to the floor with her trembling hands. "Damn it!" Rather than bother with the search, she dumped the contents on the wood floor and pushed the items around until she spotted the white rectangle. Hurrying to the phone on the front desk, she realized she wasn't going to be able to dial if she didn't calm down. She clenched her hands and tossed her head back, taking in a deep steadying breath.

Finally, she held the card up and scanned it. Finding his name first created a strange flutter around her heart. Her stomach fell to her ankles, and she wished to high heaven that Dr. Miller were still around. At least she could talk to him. Every time she had the misfortune of meeting Dr. Newbury, a hatred like no other banged around inside her until finally kicking her foot directly into her mouth.

She found his cell number and punched it into the phone. It rang. And rang. Emmy hitched her hip to the side and tapped her foot. On the fourth ring, she smashed her lips together feeling the rage flare to life in her chest; the fifth brought teeth clenching and eye rolling. By the sixth ring, she was cussing like a cowboy on branding day. *If this man is so incompetent that he can't even carry his damn cell phone with him , then how in the hell is he going to take care of Lacy and her baby?*

"Son of a bitch! If you can't –"

"Hello?"

Emmylou cut off her rant and pulled the phone away to stare at it while the idiot doctor kept saying hello and asking if someone was there.

"Yeah. Dr. Newbury?" Emmylou wanted to reach through and choke the man.

"Yes. Hello. Who is this?" he asked in a distracted, almost out of breath voice.

Emmy gaped at his tactlessness. "Tinkerbell," she snapped and shook her head, thinking she had probably interrupted his nap. "One of your patients you moron!" She couldn't help herself.

"Oh. I'm sorry. How can I help you?"

Emmylou could picture him on the other end of the line combing his hair with his hand, trying to gather his wits, if he had any. "This is Emmylou Bennett, and I'm calling for Lacy McClintock. She's in pain, clutching her abdomen. I think there may be something wrong with the…" Emmy felt her eyes sting and she had to swallow, "with the baby."

"Okay. I'm on my way. Just make sure she's lying down and as comfortable as possible."

Emmylou was about to tell him he could piss off and they would meet him at the hospital, but the click on the end of the line stopped her. "The bastard hung up on me."

She heard Scarlett holler from the other room. She tossed the phone down and ran for Lacy. If anything happened to that baby or her best friend, she would see to it that Dr. Newbury would go from a rooster to a hen in ten seconds.

Chapter 4

Shane pulled on some jeans and a t-shirt, slid his feet into his boots without any socks, grabbed his truck keys and dashed out the door. He had been in the shower when his phone rang and had nearly dropped it three times while talking to Emmylou. He could only imagine what he'd sounded like. Probably a jackass.

His phone had rung like that during his rotation in emergency, but he really hadn't expected to get called out the first day he was in practice in Primrose. It was a tiny country town just like the one he grew up in; nothing much happened. At least that was what he had thought when he was a kid. Maybe the doctor in his hometown was as busy as a cat covering ten mouse holes.

He skidded his truck to a stop in front of The Dove House five minutes later and launched himself up the stairs. His shirt was stuck to him in the places he hadn't dried off, chafing his skin as he moved. He knocked on the screen door with the hand not holding his doctor's bag. About the time he realized this was an emergency and he should just hurry inside, the inner door flew open.

"What the hell do you think you're doing?" Emmylou's eyes were flashing and her face was pale.

"I'm responding to your call about Lacy."

"Don't you think you should just come in instead of politely passing the time on her front porch? This isn't a date, Dr. Newbury."

God, that woman never knew when to quit!

Rather than debate the fine points, he jerked open the screen door and stepped inside. "Take me to her."

With a final glare, Emmylou spun on her heel, and Shane followed. Her long blonde hair was pulled into a low pony tail, the ends reaching almost to her waistline. The curls bounced and shimmered in the light with every rushed step. If only he could see this side of her all the time. At least, then he wouldn't have to deal with her sharp tongue and could enjoy the view.

As soon as they reached the next room, he saw another woman with very dark hair leaning over the sofa. She looked up with the most striking color of eyes he had ever seen. She was trying to stay strong, but inside, her control was rioting. It was a look he had been introduced to at a young age and was becoming more familiar with the longer he was in medicine. For a second he was transported to another time, a hospital room in a small town, a man who wore that expression, only his was mixed with accusation and disappointment.

Sickness rushed through him like it had that day, and he had to swallow it back. Shane shook his head, forcing himself to the present. He came around the sofa and got his first glimpse of Lacy.

"Hi, Lacy." His preliminary observation gave him little to go on. The only thing he noticed was her obvious discomfort. She wasn't pale or perspiring, and he didn't see any sign of convulsions.

"Glad you could make it to the party, Doctor."

"We should be at the hospital," Emmylou spoke under her breath.

Lacy scowled at her, and Shane observed her out of the corner of his eye. "I live three miles away. It would have taken more time for me to meet you at the clinic and longer yet to go to the hospital in Glenwood. You actually would've had to drive past my driveway in the process."

Emmylou opened her mouth most likely intending to tell him exactly what she thought of his stupid decision, but promptly clamped it and crossed her arms with his challenging look. She transferred her gaze to Lacy and it softened with concern. Satisfied, he began his examination of Lacy, pressing her abdomen, checking her blood pressure, and listening with his fetal Doppler. When he removed the blanket further, he spotted the blood stain.

"Lacy?" He looked up at her with his practiced look of calm and confidence. "How long have you been bleeding?"

Her eyes bulged, and she attempted to sit up. "I didn't know I was!" Her voice trembled and her face crumpled.

"It's not a lot. And this is totally normal." Shane was proud of Lacy for keeping her emotions in check. He had delivered this news before to a squalling woman who had shouted about hemorrhaging and dying. Lacy's way was more helpful.

"This is ridiculous!" Emmylou shouted behind him. "She's *bleeding!*"

Shane gaped at her and then glared to try to get her to shut up. He felt Lacy's hand contract in his.

"We're taking her to the hospital. To a *real* doctor."

Shane turned back to Lacy and smiled warmly. "It's going to be just fine, Lacy. There is no need to be scared."

"You're not going to *listen* to him are you, Lacy?"

Shane's shoulders tensed and his head came up, "Give me a minute, Lacy. I will be right back." He patted Lacy's hands and stood up. Emmylou jumped when he grasped her bicep. "Can I see you in the hallway for a minute?"

She swallowed at the harsh tone and sharp look he fixed her with. Before she could answer, he had excused them from her friends and was forcing her to walk beside him. They turned into the hallway, and he dropped her arm. "Are you a doctor? Do you have some secret medical training that I am unaware of? Or perhaps you possess some kind of X-ray vision." He took a step closer, but she held her ground. Damn she was stubborn! "Maybe… could it be that you're a healer? You can invoke the power of God to bring about a miracle healing." His voice had risen, and he flung his arms to make his point.

Emmylou's blue eyes were blazing daggers at him, but he didn't care. She had jeopardized his relationship with his patient. "Now if you will listen, you will find out I *am* a real doctor."

"Says who? One supervising doctor and three professors?" She crossed her arms and pursed her lips.

"What?" He was confused. How could she know who he used for his references?

"That is my friend in there bleeding on the couch. I'm pretty sure she doesn't need you out here arguing with me."

"No. She doesn't." His quiet reply seemed to chasten her. He held eye contact with Emmylou until he was satisfied she wouldn't interfere again. He hated having to reprimand her, but Lacy's confidence in him as a doctor was vital.

Shane returned to Lacy with Emmylou several feet behind him. He saw Lacy grimace thoughtfully at Emmylou with a glow in her eyes. Their friendship must run deep. The dark haired woman moved behind him to put her arm around Emmylou, leaning her head closer.

"Lacy, I need to inspect the blood and see what we're dealing with. Would you like to do that in private?" He waited for the round of protests from her friends, ready to roll with whatever decision Lacy made.

They didn't come. Shane excused himself to a corner of the room so Lacy could remove the clothing he had requested. The other two did the same but to the opposite corner. He surreptitiously watched the two of them, wondering what was coming next with all the whispering they were doing. Emmylou was pulling on her bottom lip and fidgeting. She was really quite beautiful, and he liked her spunk. If only she wouldn't announce every thought that crossed her mind. They could probably get along then. She was quite tall, almost able to look him in the eye. That would put her around the five foot eleven range.

The dark-haired lady said something that made Emmylou shake her head. A funny feeling prickled its way down his spine, settling in his gut. Something about the way the brunette stood shot him back to that long ago hospital. He heard the sobbing, felt the glossy mass beneath his hand. He started to tremble with the memory. Shane ran his hand over his chest, expecting to feel the crusted blood on his shirt. Her blood. His breath was coming in strangled bursts. He hadn't experienced this reaction in years. He thought he had moved on.

"I'm ready, Dr. Newbury."

He cleared his throat and ran a hand through his hair. Just to make sure or perhaps out of habit, he smoothed his shirt, assuring himself there was no blood there.

*****

Emmylou hated Dr. Newbury. His resume had looked good when the board was searching. He was a small town boy looking to fulfill his RHOP responsibilities. But she would have thought that when the state of Nebraska was awarding bright, young individuals from rural communities looking to obtain a degree in the medical field with full scholarships, they would at least screen those candidates. Apparently not.

"Shhh. I can't hear what he's saying to her." Emmy swatted her hand at Scarlet,t moving to see over her friend's shoulder. She and Scarlett were still standing next to the built in bookcases waiting for whatever idiocy the quack was going to spew. She was going to have to call an emergency meeting of the Willow County Clinic Board to discuss getting one of the other applicants to come and take Dr. Newbury's position.

"I'm sure that's what Lacy wants right now." Scarlett turned to watch the doctor and Lacy. "This is a private matter. We don't always need to know everything. Especially before Kyle knows." Scarlett whipped back with a guilty arch in her brows. "Do you think we should call him?"

Emmylou was too intent on garnering more information to use against the doctor to think about Kyle. "You just said that we don't need to interfere in Lacy's business all the time. That would classify as interfering."

"Oh, yeah. You're probably right."

The heartlessness of what she had just said rang in the hollow of her chest. Emmy closed her eyes and bent her head, rubbing her forehead. "That sounds awful. I'm such a pig." She raised her head to look into Scarlett's sea green eyes. "What's wrong with me? The moment that man stepped into town, I became some kind of mercenary sharpening my blade."

Scarlett reached out and rubbed Emmy's shoulder. "You got your heart broken. It's understandable that you would take it out on someone. Honey, we know you're hurting. It's okay."

Emmylou sighed and smiled sorrowfully. "I don't deserve you. My disastrous love life is no excuse for me to act like a gorilla smashing through the brush." Emmy's face fell and she clutched Scarlett's arms. "Am I always like this? I mean, I've had *a lot* of broken hearts and if I always behave like this then…"

"No." Scarlett's famous smile lit her face. "You've always bounced back like a champ. I think this time you put more into it. You really gave your heart to Marcus with the intensions of making it forever, and when he let you down, it crushed you." Scarlett took Emmylou's hands into her warm grasp. "Anger is normal." She shrugged her shoulders. "Heck, if I were you, there would be a bonfire in the middle of my yard turning all of his mementos into charred remains."

Emmylou grinned. "Remind me to never make you mad."

Scarlett flashed her gorgeous smile and tossed her head back. "I make you no promises."

They both chuckled and hugged before turning their attention back to Lacy. Emmylou still felt like a shrew. She would have to apologize to Lacy for causing a scene. She closed her eyes on the memory of the visit to the clinic. Twice. She really had been awful.

She focused her attention on Dr. Newbury, still feeling a keen dislike for him. Emmy caught the look on his face while he listened to what Lacy was saying, and it sent a ripple to her stomach. All of his attention was focused on her; he nodded, his brows were knitted in concern, and his lips were drawn tight until he spoke. His voice was soft; she couldn't make out what he had said, but whatever it was, it seemed to be helping Lacy. Emmylou watched her shoulders relax a bit. He held his hand out to clasp Lacy's and smiled.

Emmylou lifted a hand to her chest. Wow! That man had an amazing smile. It was genuine and made his eyes sparkle.

She knew that she could never like Dr. Newbury very much,

but it appeared that his skills weren't completely reprehensible. She couldn't hear what he and Lacy were talking about, but her friend was obviously at ease with him, and Lacy was never comfortable with anyone. She didn't hand her trust out lightly. For now, that would do for Emmylou. Although, she would reserve her final judgment for later.

"Okay you guys," Lacy spoke over her shoulder. "Dr. Newbury doesn't think there is anything to worry about. This sort of thing is common. There wasn't enough blood to warrant a trip to the hospital."

Emmylou took a breath and crossed her arms as she and Scarlett walked to the sofa. She kept her mouth shut, made her best attempt at a smile and bobbed her head in approval. "Mmm." She didn't believe she radiated a lot of confidence.

"But she has to take it easy, and I'm counting on both of you to help me with that. No lifting, no walking distances and stay sitting or lying down as much as possible," Shane addressed both Emmylou and Scarlett while pulling the blanket over Lacy.

"And I'm going to need to go to the clinic tomorrow for an ultrasound. He said I could wait for Kyle to get here so he can go with me."

"Oh that's wonderful, sweetie. But if you need me to go with you I will, and I'm staying the night with you tonight." Scarlett rubbed Lacy's shoulder and glanced to Dr. Newbury with a warm smile. He didn't quite return it. Emmylou looked closer at him and noticed he wouldn't make eye contact with Scarlett. He made a show out of repacking his doctor's bag before straightening and providing Lacy a few final orders to stay still and call if anything changed. Men always acted strangely around Scarlett, but usually they were in awe of her soft beauty and gentle mannerisms. Shane Newbury appeared to be the opposite.

He bid goodnight to the three of them and excused himself. Emmylou was still wondering about his strange attitude. Once he left the room, she followed him on the pretense of seeing him to the door.

"Do you think she's really fine?" Her question startled him. He jerked around still very distracted.

"Oh." He scratched his face. "Yes, Lacy is going to be fine. It's very normal to bleed some during pregnancy. You can talk to her about it. She will probably tell you what I explained to her. Or look it up on the Internet if you don't believe me. There's plenty of information out there." He tilted his head and lifted the corners of his mouth in a mock polite smile.

His forlorn expression made worms wiggle in her stomach. For a hair of one second, she wanted to reach out and stroke his smooth cheek, but she forcibly squashed the moment. "I may just do that."

He nodded with his coffee brown eyes probing hers. The seconds stretched as he held her gaze captive. Then he turned and went out the door, and Emmy had a strange hollowness bloom in her chest. She didn't know how long she stood in the large foyer with her hand pressed to her mouth staring out the front door. Long enough for Dr. Newbury to drive away and the dust to settle.

Slowly she turned and went back to clean up the dinner dishes. The evening of shared secrets and heart-to-heart conversation had evaporated. Emmylou was left with uncertainty and a headache. The out-of-control mess her life had transformed into disturbed her right down to her core. It seemed as if everything she knew, or thought she knew had been whisked out from under her, and she was flying with her feet in the air. She wondered when she was going to crash down.

*****

Shane set his bag on the small table next to his front door and wandered over to his leather chair, one of the only pieces of furniture in the place and where he planned to sleep until the moving truck arrived. The short drive hadn't been enough to sort through the feelings and images screaming through his mind.

Seeing that woman with the dark hair had awakened the memory of his darkest days. He had thought it was in the past, that he had pushed beyond and gotten on with his life, but he should have known better. Emotional scars were never gone. They were simply something you coped with for the rest of your life.

He kicked the footrest out and pulled a blanket over himself. It did nothing to warm the chill in his bones. A cold like that wasn't cured by a flimsy blanket or even one hundred blankets. It went deeper than that.

And why in the world did he allow that crazy Emmylou to get under his skin and in the way of his patients? She was pushy, opinionated and completely gorgeous.

His eyes popped open. *Gorgeous?* Where had that come from? In the past ten years, he hadn't had a thought like that enter his head so spontaneously. He had recognized beautiful women, but mostly in passing or while he was out to dinner or maybe – once – he had noticed a colleague. Never had it happened like this.

Now that she was in his head he could think of little else. There she was front and center, taking up every available space. Her shining, bright-blue eyes, creamy skin and glossy blonde hair. That damn hair. He had seen it both up and down, and every time it was full and bouncy; an all-consuming part of her. The women he had been around for the past years at college and working in hospitals had either cut it short or kept it up in varying styles of buns and pony tails. Emmylou's wavy locks were long, and Shane had an itching need to run his hands through them.

He threw the blanket off and shot out of the chair. If his television were here, he would turn on sports and forget all thoughts of women –Emmylou in particular– and be able to drift off into a refreshing sleep. Basketball cured all troubles, but here he was in a new town, a strange house with absolutely nothing to do but focus on the events of the past and the annoying blonde woman he couldn't shake.

He paced the floor several times, willing his mind to divert to something else. But it was useless. Now that his head was full of visions of the accident merging with his strange and unsettling thoughts of Emmylou, that would be all he could focus on until dawn. There was nothing his mind liked better than to obsess over some damn puzzle.

Shane grabbed his keys and left the house.

The five mile drive to town was quick. It hadn't become a habit yet, and the snowy roads required his concentration. He didn't want to slide into the ditch and get stuck or hit a meandering deer. For starters, he wouldn't know who to call to get him out. He had only been in town for two days. So he would be stuck walking, and February in Nebraska was vicious. The lights on the dash informed him that it was two degrees without the wind chill.

He drove down the main street. All the businesses were closed and dark except for the gas station. As he passed the bakery - their first encounter - a smile appeared. He usually went for the demure, graceful type, but there was something about that tall, hot-tempered baker that beckoned to him. He couldn't shake the feeling of life that had sparked in him the moment they locked eyes. He was soaring with excitement, wondering when they would bump into each other again. Only this time, without the scalding coffee. Maybe he could grab a muffin tomorrow.

No. That would be too obvious. He wondered when she grocery shopped, or maybe she would get sick and he would take care of her.

He pulled into the parking lot at the clinic and sat in the truck staring at the parking sign with Dr. Miller's name. What was he thinking? He hadn't been on a date in... he couldn't remember. He rubbed his eyes and sighed. Katie was the last person he had gone on a date with. This wasn't happening. Emmy was nothing like Katie. It wasn't possible for him to be attracted to her.

He told himself it would go away. It was a phase. He was being nostalgic about small town life. He felt at home in Primrose, and it was clouding his good judgment. Yes, that was exactly it. He let out a relieved scoff before leaving his truck. His heart still belonged to Katie. That familiar stab to his chest came with the memory of his beloved Katie. His face and nose burned, and his eyes filled as he made his way across the frozen parking lot.

Shane used the key Shelby had given him to get in. He planned to bury himself in files and paperwork until his mind was so full of conditions and medical records he couldn't think of anything else. That had always worked for him.

Sitting at his desk, Shane saw that the clock read 11:04. He let out a deep sigh and flipped open the first file folder he could find.

Riiiiinnnnngggggg!

Shane jumped with the shrill of the telephone on his desk. He stared at it through the second ring wondering if he should answer it, then questioned who would be calling here when everyone in town obviously knew when the clinic closed. A sharp sting of panic sliced through him when his mind turned to Lacy and the baby.

It was that thought that made him snatch up the receiver. "Hello." His voice was rushed and his hand clamped around the skinny black handle.

"I'm in the ambulance. I need you to follow me to the hospital right now!"

Everything went blank. He stared at the opposite wall, but it was taking that damn hamster in his brain a long time to wake up and start running in its ball.

"Do you think you can handle the roads by yourself, or do we need to come and get you?"

He heard the command to begin CPR, and finally, the ball spun into high speed. "Shelby?"

"Well it isn't Santa Clause." More counting came. He could hear the exertion in her voice and knew she was performing compressions.

"I'll be right there." He shot out of his seat and slammed down the phone. He grabbed his coat on the way out the door and slipped his arms into it while running to his truck.

Chapter 5

Emmylou yawned as she took the pan of fresh bagels from the oven. She baked a new batch every other day. They were one of her more popular items; she figured it was mostly due to the honey butter that she bought from the Andersons. They had nineteen hives and sold honey all over the state but made the butter special for Bake My Day. It cost her a premium, but customer satisfaction was vital to her business.

Most people around here could bake their own morning pastries and brew their own coffee. They came to Emmylou's bakery for the specialties and the fellowship. It was a great place to check in with all the locals in the morning and an excuse for moms to get out of the house.

She had had to come in forty-five minutes earlier than usual this morning to get the bagels and special orders done. And earlier yet due to the fact that she had to drive in from The Dove House instead of six blocks from her own house. She and Scarlett had insisted on staying the night with Lacy after the incident.

No one had slept well. Emmy couldn't stop worrying that something bad was going to happen, and she suspected that her friends felt the same way. Even though none of them mentioned it, the rustles and flip-flopping were loud and clear. Standing in the warm kitchen with the smells of sugar and cinnamon wasn't helping her stay awake.

Two more hours of mixing, rolling, glazing and frosting, and Emmylou was finally ready for the day. The back door opened, bringing a blast of cold air. Four o'clock had come sooner than she thought.

"Hey, boss lady." Lindy's rosy cheeks spoke of the cold or perhaps it was the fact that she had a loving fiancé she would soon be married to. Emmy wished for that kind of blissful innocence. To be marrying your high school sweetheart must be a sweet feeling. But Emmy's high school boyfriend wouldn't have been suitable for marriage. Unless you asked her parents who had already designed the invitations and compiled the guest list by senior prom.

"Hi, Lindy." Emmy turned to roll the cart she had loaded with trays out of the way.

"It's bagel day. Why didn't you call me? I would have come in and helped you get everything baked." Lindy pulled her scarf and coat off and hung it behind the door, replacing them with her apron.

"No, I knew you had your counseling session with Pastor Douglas last night, and I didn't want to bother you with it. But I do have a webinar today at eleven if you could cover me then."

"No problem. Do we need to bake any of that special gluten free bread for Nannette today?" Lindy dove right into the day's routine, spreading flour on the stainless steel surface and grabbing some dough to roll out and cut into doughnuts. Emmylou hated them, but the customers demanded she serve them.

They continued for the next hour in companionable silence until it was time to open. Emmy unlocked the door and checked to make sure the coffee had brewed. Lindy pulled out a couple of new syrups for the cappuccinos, replacing the empty bottles. The two of them worked so well together Emmylou didn't know what she would ever do without Lindy. They were always in sync.

The bells jingled, and Emmy turned to start her busy day. Her eyebrows raised as an unexpected face approached the counter. "Shelby Stevens. What brings you in here at this early hour?"

"Coffee. The strongest you have." Her limp figure all but collapsed on the counter. She laid her head on her hands and shook it back and forth. Her normally sleek red hair had been replaced with frayed pieces sticking out of her bun now slipping over her right ear.

"Rough night with the baby?" Emmylou asked as she poured coffee into the largest to-go cup she had.

Shelby raised her head enough to look at Emmy. The creases in her forehead were deep and the smudges beneath her eyes were dark. "I wouldn't know. She was all Daryl's responsibility last night. I haven't been home since ten-thirty last night."

"Oh, I'm so sorry. Were you out on a call?" Emmy handed her the steaming cup along with the pitcher of cream and bowl of sugar packets.

Shelby rubbed her face and lifted the pitcher over her coffee. "Yeah, and it was a tough one. I 'spose you'll be hearing about it all morning. You know how secrets are kept in this town." She ripped open three packets of sugar and dumped them in. "Like a fart in church."

Emmy grinned and handed her a stir stick. "Pretty much."

"Well," Shelby wrapped her hands around the cup, "Mr. Perkins had another heart attack last night."

"Oh no." Emmy put her hand over her chest. "His daughter must be so upset."

"She's the one who called it in. She had gone over to check on him for the night, and she found him in the kitchen." Shelby nodded with Emmylou's gasp of grief.

Mr. Perkins had suffered three heart attacks already. Emmylou was scared to ask if he had survived this one. He was a fixture in this town. Everyone knew and liked him. He had been a real crusader for the farmers back in the fifties and had earned the respect of the whole town. He was ornery as all get out and a bit of a drinker. He was also the man who had gotten Lacy out of trouble more times than her counterfeit mother. Emmy knew Lacy would be devastated by this news.

After Shelby's third or fourth sip, Emmylou asked, "Is he doing okay?"

Shelby shifted and darted her eyebrows up. "It was a struggle to keep him here, but yeah, he's doing okay. He's supposed to have surgery later this morning to replace a valve and put in two stints. We'll have to see after that."

Emmylou's heart was in her shoes. She made a mental note to take over some rolls and loaves of bread to his daughter Carol's house. She would be plagued with visitors soon and in need of anything she could find to serve them. Emmylou retrieved a cranberry-apple muffin from the case, put it on a plate and set it in front of Shelby.

"Thank you, Emmy." Shelby opened her wallet to pay.

"It's on the house. I'd say you earned some coffee and a muffin." Shelby's tired smile was payment enough. "You don't have to go in to work today do you?"

"Of course." She took a bite of the muffin and looked a smidgen better afterwards. "But Dr. Newbury is the one you should worry about. He worked on old Cletus trying to get his heart stabilized until I thought he might drop from exhaustion or worry."

Emmylou tilted her head in surprise. "Really?"

Shelby agreed through a bite of muffin. She took another sip, and Emmylou saw a touch of color return. "He was amazing. I've never seen a doctor quite like that. He was calm and in command during the whole thing." She shook her head with a faraway look glazing her light green eyes. "He wouldn't give up on Cletus… just kept working away."

Emmylou walked around the counter and gestured toward the closest table. Shelby gathered her plate and cup and sat.

"He had to be exhausted, but you'd have never known it. As many compressions as he had to perform and orders he had to give, I'm sure he'll be a hurting unit today. I'm hoping we have a light schedule, but I'm sure we won't with it being cold and flu season. And tonight's the basketball game at the high school. One of us will have to be around in case of an injury."

The longer the story went, the smaller Emmylou felt. She had called Dr. Newbury a moron. To his face! Well, over the phone, but it was the same thing. He had saved the life of one of the town's cherished citizens, and he'd rushed over to help Lacy when she had called. Maybe he wasn't so bad.

"I suppose I'd better get home and check on the kids. I'm sure Daryl served them chocolate cake for breakfast and dressed them in summer shorts and snow boots." Shelby shook her head and started for the door. "I love him, but sometimes." She backed into the glass door, her hands full.

"Wait." Emmylou popped up from her seat. "Will you take Dr. Newbury some coffee and a roll? Sounds like he's going to need it." She tucked her hands into the pockets of her apron to keep from fidgeting.

"I'd love to, but I'm afraid it'll get cold before I go into the clinic."

Emmylou looked away. "Oh, yeah. I suppose you're right."

"I can swing back by and pick it up."

"No." Emmylou brushed her hand through the air. "You don't need to add to your schedule by doing that."

"Well, just call me if you change your mind." Shelby pushed the door open with her behind. "Thanks for the coffee and muffin, Emmy." She lifted them in a toast. "And the company."

"Glad you came in, Shelby." Emmylou smiled and nodded.

"Oh, and I can trust you to keep this between us? I don't normally chat about our ambulance calls. Could be a real problem, me blabbing all over town about Cletus' medical emergency." Shelby shook her head and looked at the floor.

"Sure, honey. I know you're just concerned. It'll stay between us."

Emmylou wandered behind the counter and absently wiped the clean counter with a dry rag. Now that her conscience was killing her, and the idea of a peace offering had embedded itself in her mind, she couldn't focus on anything else.

"Why don't you take it over later?"

Emmylou jerked and looked at Lindy. "Huh?"

"I mean it. You should take it over to him. You talked about introducing yourself to him when he got into town anyway. Seems like as good a time as any other. I can handle the shop."

Emmylou scratched her head and scrunched up her mouth. "Well—"

"Don't worry. I'll be fine." Lindy nudged her shoulder.

Emmylou let out a self-deprecating laugh. "That's not it. I have every faith in your capabilities. It's…" Emmylou began wiping the counter again until Lindy placed her hand over the top of hers. Emmy let the rag go and crossed her arms, knowing she was going to have to spill her guts. "Okay. You know the guy I slammed into and spilled coffee all over?"

"Yeah." Lindy's attention was fully focused on Emmy.

"Well," Emmy pressed her lips together for a moment not wanting to continue the embarrassing story. "That was Dr. Newbury."

Lindy did a fantastic job of attempting to merge her eyebrows with her hairline and a less brilliant attempt at keeping her laughter inside.

"Oh, just wait. It gets better." The outburst from Lindy made it hard for Emmy to keep a straight face.

"I can't wait to hear it," Lindy managed to get out between fits of giggles.

Emmylou cleared her throat. "On our second encounter, I scattered all of the papers in his file folder and then head butted him when we gathered them up. I doubt I did any real damage." Emmy shook her head and closed her eyes with the memory. "I then proceeded to call him self-absorbed, egotistical and rude a moment before he let us listen to the baby's heart beat."

"You didn't?"

"Oh, yes I did." Emmy rubbed her hand over her face to block Lindy's display of enjoyment over her mortification.

Lindy clamped her side and bent over slightly. "I'm sure you can apologize and he'll get over it." She was recovering from the outburst of laughter and beginning to sober.

"I'm sure that I could." Emmy puckered her lips and rocked back on her heels. "If that was all I had done."

"Oh my goodness, Emmylou, don't tell me there's more to this story. The man's only been in town for three days. How many times can you insult him?"

"Apparently there is no limit." The look of pity and disbelief written all over Lindy's face made Emmy feel like a pissant. "My crowning glory was last night. I called him a moron, ridiculed his medical license, or lack of, and interfered with his treatment of a patient."

Lindy stood staring at her in shock. "Wow, boss-lady, you're three for three. And you're right. That last one probably put you over the top for a simple apology to work."

Emmylou bobbed her head in agreement. "Believe me, he got in a few good insults last night." She still had sunburn from Dr. Newbury's blazing anger while he put her in her place.

Emmylou was wondering if her usual kindness had been sucked away by Marcus. Or maybe it was all of the thoughtless men over the years that had slowly sapped her empathy and consideration for others. Either way, courtesy and good old country manners dictated that she make amends with the good doctor.

Damn it!

Chapter 6

Shane didn't even bother going home after his thirty minute drive from the Glenwood Hospital. Thank goodness the clinic Board of Directors had already established privileges for him or he wouldn't have been able to work on Mr. Perkins. He wasn't certain what he was going to encounter when he got to the hospital a few minutes after the ambulance arrived. Shelby had hung up so she could continue the compressions, and he found her talking with the hospital nurse about Mr. Perkins' vitals when he walked through the door.

Mr. Perkins had been a tough case. Shane had had the same trouble with a couple of patients in the past, and he knew that there was still hope for the man to survive and recover, so he continued to fight for him. Sure enough, after about four hours in the emergency room, he had stabilized Mr. Perkins' heart, and they moved him into the ICU. Which wasn't much better than the regular hospital, but he would have his very own nurse by his side twenty-four hours a day.

They would be transferring him to Lincoln to have heart surgery later today or tomorrow depending on the progress he made. Shane was grateful he didn't have to supervise that flight.

Shane collapsed into his desk chair and picked up the file he had been looking at before the emergency call. He rubbed his eyes and tried to concentrate, but it was no use. Even if he could see the pages through his blurry vision, he wouldn't remember a word of it. He moved over to the sofa in the corner to lie down. He was used to sleeping in hospitals and clinics. It wasn't sixty seconds before he was out.

"Dr. Newbury!"

Shane flung himself upright banging his feet into the little table by the couch. He shifted his head back and forth with half-open eyes trying to collect his senses into one focused consciousness. He heard his name again and was finally able to pry open his eyes. He scrubbed his hands over his face, his bleary gaze fixed on the shape in the doorway of his office.

"Yeah," his voice rushed a moment before he had to stifle a yawn.

"I just wanted to tell you that you did a great job with Mr. Perkins. The whole town will be thankful you were able to bring him back around. He's kind of a local hero."

Shane nodded, curving his mouth into a sleepy smile. "That's my job."

Shelby leaned further into the room; he didn't know why she didn't simply come in. "Well, you're really good at it."

He slanted his head. "Right back at 'cha. If you hadn't performed compressions for the thirty minute ambulance ride, he probably wouldn't have made it. So thank you for making my job easier."

Shelby's fair skin gave away her discomfort as red flamed from the top of her head to the tips of her fingers. She nodded stiffly and ducked into the hallway.

"Hey, Shelby," he called her back. "I've been wondering; why did you call the clinic instead of my cell phone?"

She grinned and chuckled with a shake of her head. "I saw your truck here when I went to pick up the ambulance."

"You drive the ambulance, too?" He leaned his elbows on his knees.

"Not this time. Tony Markum drove us to Glenwood while I worked on Mr. Perkins. He doesn't have his certification yet, so I take all the major cases."

"Oh, well, I'll have to thank him when I meet him."

A twinkle sparkled in Shelby's eyes as she studied him for a moment. "I'm sure he would rather you buy lumber or paint from him the next time you need them. He owns Markum's Home Improvement on the south side of town." She indicated the direction with her thumb.

"Oh." He stood up and tried to press out the wrinkles in his shirt with his hand. "I'll have to do that." He made it to the doorway and stopped short. Shelby slapped a hand on his chest.

"You're not in the big city anymore, Doc. Around here we're all volunteer." She pushed on his chest and spun around. He watched her walk down the hallway wondering how long it was going to take to get the city out of his system. He had gotten used to the fast pace and throngs of people in his years at college and in his residency.

It hadn't been easy to shed the country boy when he was getting his doctorate, and now it was going to be difficult to shed the city that had infiltrated. Strange that he always considered himself small-town.

Shane took the files back to the cabinet and was about to check the schedule on the computer when a knock at the door interrupted him. He tried to get a look by leaning over the counter, but he only succeeded in making Abigail, the receptionist, uncomfortable.

"I'll see who it is, Abigail."

The older woman scowled at him over the top of her glasses, and he realized exactly how this office ran like clockwork. No one dared to cross a woman who had mastered the don't-mess-with-me look.

The feeling that he hadn't turned in his homework and was about to be scolded beyond embarrassment came over him, and he shuffled away from the desk with an apology. The shocking similarity of Abigail and his high school history teacher was uncanny. Even down to the straight lined clothing and precise grey-brown bob.

He got to the glass door, and his hand stopped in mid-motion of pushing against it. He couldn't believe his eyes. It wasn't possible that this woman would voluntarily come to the clinic to see him unless she was toting a shotgun, and he was pretty certain she didn't have one of those on her.

Shane was still staring as she raised a white bag and steaming Styrofoam cup. His mind was still revving the engine before shifting into gear. He was confused. And shocked. And truthfully, a little scared. The last time they had spoken seemed like ages ago even though it was just last night. He had insulted her, and she was standing there, her beautiful hair spilling out of a cute stocking cap, the reflection of the sun off the snow providing a glowing silhouette and her cheeks pinked from the cold air. She was the epitome of a snow angel.

Finally, he realized he was staring and letting her stand in the cold. Two more ungentlemanly offenses; his mother would have slapped the back of his head. He pushed the first door open and took the two steps to the outer glass door. Her smile was a forced polite lifting of the corners of her lips, but it made his heart stutter and his fingers fumble with the metal deadbolt. He hated that feeling.

Emmylou stepped back when he opened the door. He looked down at the snowdrift it had made as it swung open.

"It snowed." He wanted to bang the door shut on his head. Could he be more of an idiot?

"I think it just blew off of the roof."

Her blue eyes were stunning. And her face… a peculiar warm sensation slithered through him. Her eyebrows raised and understanding slammed into him.

"Come in." He flung his arm out and pressed against the door.

"Thanks." She nodded and shifted past him.

Shane inhaled as she passed. She was a delightful fragrance of cold air and cinnamon. A walking dessert with golden, wavy locks. Emmylou tried to grip both the sack and the cup in one gloved hand, intent on opening the next door.

"Let me get that." He didn't coordinate the move, and the outer door rammed into his back. He clenched his jaw and staggered forward. He glanced at her out of the corner of his eye a second before opening the next door. The pinched amusement in her face told him she had witnessed his mishap.

"Thank you, Dr. Newbury." She really was enjoying his discomfort. He wanted to crawl under the desk and hide.

They stood in the waiting area, neither one making eye contact. Shane rubbed his hands together finally chancing a glance. She

56

was casually inspecting the room, looking at everything except him.

"So, what brings you here? I hope you're feeling well."

"Yep. I'm good." She rocked back on her heels. "Um, I talked to Shelby this morning and she told me you had a late night or early morning. Whatever you want to call it."

A puff of air escaped his throat, and he pressed his hands against his legs for lack of anything else to do with them. "Oh, yeah. We had an emergency we had to take care of." He nodded, and so did she as she continued to look around. "After your little emergency. Not that any emergency is little. It was a big emergency. Well, maybe not a *big* one, but a relatively good one. Or, no. No emergency is good." *Shut up, Shane.*

"Of course not. But I'm sure in comparison…" Her blue eyes finally found his and he forgot what he was going to say. Not that he was doing a good job of speaking.

He couldn't seem to control his hands. He ran one over his hair, then tucked them both in his pockets. The silence was becoming uncomfortable. Or maybe it was just him and his idiocy.

"So like I was saying, I talked to Shelby, and I thought you might like to have these this morning." Emmylou held out the cup and the sack.

"Thank you." He took them. "That was very thoughtful." *Apologize*, his brain said. "Is this some of that Percoliscious stuff from your menu?" He tried to smile to pass it off as a joke rather than an insult.

"I'm afraid so. I brewed up a batch of organic Sumatra Black Satin with amaretto and vanilla this morning. It's a local favorite."

"Mmm." Shane forced the corners of his mouth up. "That sounds great." He turned the cup in his hand wondering how he was going to suck the stuff down and look like he enjoyed it.

She licked her lips, and his attention was immediately drawn to their fullness. The top was thinner than the bottom, and the peaks pointed outward. They looked delicious… and kissable. He took in a sharp breath, shaking the heart-wrenching feeling. "Well, I can't wait to enjoy it." A grunt-like chortle stuck in his throat.

"That's nice to hear." Her artful brows raised, and her hypnotic gaze was trained on him.

He held it, swiftly losing ground in the stand-off. His hand stalled several times in his attempt to raise the cup to his mouth. As it got to the top of the arc, he tipped it in a toast and prepared himself for what was to come. Awareness shot through him as the smooth, familiar brew shocked his taste buds. He pulled the cup away, savoring the comfort and staring at it.

"What did you think of it?" Emmylou grasped her hands behind her and moved closer to him.

"It was fantastic."

"You sound surprised." Her voice was as warm as her coffee. He turned his head and finally realized how close she had moved to him. His breath thinned, and his heart ached with his alertness. He couldn't stand it. These feelings had died long ago. Katie had taken them with her.

"Just that it had stayed hot with the frigid temperature outside." The straight jacket that had effectively wrapped itself around him strangling every bit of air in his lungs became unbearable. He moved to the front desk and set the cup and sack down, picking up whatever file was within reach.

"That's just how we do things at Bake My Day."

The need to touch her cheek, to explore its velvety softness, throbbed in his hands. "Well, it's better than I expected designer coffee to be." He could feel the beads of sweat pop at his hair line. Any moment now they would be streaking down his temples, forever branding his unease.

"That's because it's not."

"It's not what."

Emmylou rolled her eyes and stepped closer. Shane's back hit the edge of the desk; he had nowhere to go. "Organic Sumatra Black Satin with amaretto and vanilla, dummy."

He could lose himself in the depths of her sea blue eyes. In fact, he was pretty sure he already had, and he didn't like it.

"It's plain old black coffee with a small shot of creamer in it."

No wonder it tasted so good. He looked at her, waiting for her to come back with one of her glib remarks, then realized he hadn't spoken his thought. His eyes fluttered, and his hand curled the file. "That's the way I always take it."

Emmylou tilted her chin and looked at him beneath her lashes.

"How did you know that?" His intrigue overpowered his discomfort.

She coyly lifted one shoulder. "I've been slinging coffee for five years. I can tell within thirty seconds of meeting someone how they take their coffee."

"I'm impressed." He answered through threaded breath.

"You should be."

It took a moment of confusion before he realized she was teasing him again. When he saw the sparkle in her eyes, he began to chuckle. A warm sensation poured over him releasing his tension. He had the distinct feeling it wasn't just the exhaustion and stress of his night, but the residential tension occupying his every bone, joint and muscle. It didn't set well with him. "Okay, well…" he stepped back and looked at the floor. His stomach was twisted with unwelcome emotion and his hands shook. His soul had awakened and it was like poison. "Thanks for dropping by. What do I owe you?"

He felt her shock and confusion and heard it in her next words. "Nothing. I was trying to be nice after the long night you put in. And for saving a man's life. A man we all love and respect."

Shane propped his elbow on the counter, swallowing against the need rising in his chest. "Mm-hmm." He lifted his leg, hitching his boot against what little counter he could get. "I appreciate it. But you didn't have to." He pressed his lips together, knowing he may as well have slapped her in the face.

She crossed her arms, finally destroying what was left of their peaceable moment. Her tongue clicked when she answered. "I know."

He wasn't certain, but it sounded like a whole conversation in those two little words.

"Have a great day, Dr. Newbury."

The inner door was almost closed before he answered

Emmylou. "You too."

She didn't glance back. Shane didn't blame her.

Chapter 7

How could she be so stupid? Emmylou took ground devouring strides on her way back to her vehicle. She hadn't bothered to re-button her coat after leaving. The fumes emanating from her would put a tropical island under a heat advisory. She had brought Shane coffee to make his day better after spending all night saving a man's life. And how had he thanked her? By insulting her. Again!

Why she had thought she had misjudged his character was beyond her. She was rarely if ever wrong about people. She was highly intuitive, or maybe after years of practice, she was an expert at reading through people's bullshit. Either way she wouldn't be making that mistake again. Shane Newbury might be a good doctor, or really lucky, but his people skills were severely lacking. She might just bring him before the board yet.

Emmylou punched the unlock button on the car remote and jerked open the door, dropping into her seat. She let out a scream of frustration and jammed the key into the ignition. The engine fired to life. She drove to her production house, Prairie Goodness, to check on the day's progress. She was so angry that she couldn't concentrate when she was talking about orders and shipments with Lorie, her manager, so she decided to take the paperwork with her instead of making the poor woman repeat herself four times. It was almost one o'clock, and Bake My Day would be closed. Friday afternoons were spent on special orders, custom baking and experimentation of new recipes.

Driving back to the bakery she couldn't get the thought out of her head that Shane had been nice, almost flirtatious, when she had first arrived. He had made eye contact, smiled and fumbled with his words. It was sort of sweet. And then - BAM! Right between the eyes like Bambi's mother. She never saw it coming.

He must have recovered his senses and realized he was being too nice to her. Or was he suffering from delirium? Perhaps he couldn't handle all those night shifts. Or was plagued with multiple personalities. She could vouch for that if it ever came up in his evaluations. She was convinced now more than ever that Lacy couldn't have him as her doctor. She wouldn't trust her best friend to anyone, especially a doctor with mercurial moods.

"How did it go?"

Emmylou kicked the back door of the bakery shut and stared at Lindy, not sure how to answer that. She took a couple of unsteady steps forward, still lost in thought. She reached for her coat to find it hanging haphazardly off one shoulder where the weight of her purse had tugged it down. She pulled them both off and rolled them into a ball, then chucked them into her office.

"Not well," Lindy answered her own question, scooting closer to the steel counter to spread flour over the surface. "What happened?"

"Don't ask because I don't know." Emmy tied on her apron and joined Lindy to roll out the special order cinnamon rolls for the Methodist church's chili feed.

The bells on the front door jingled, startling Emmylou out of her trance. She flashed a look at the clock and then at Lindy who looked just as surprised. "Didn't you lock the door?"

"I thought I did." Lindy brushed the flour from her hands onto her apron and slid from her stool, a worry wrinkle etched into her forehead.

"I'll go check. It's probably Scarlett." Emmy waved Lindy off and proceeded to the swinging door. Even though Scarlett had a key to the bakery, Emmylou had never known her to use it. She stepped into the store area behind the counter. "Hello?" She spoke to the man standing in her store.

He turned and removed the ungloved hands he had clasped in front of his mouth. His heavy wool coat had seen better days. The plaid was faded, and it was two sizes too large. He smiled warmly and stepped closer. It was a nice enough smile, but Emmy was glad for the glass display case between them.

"You must be Emmylou Bennett." His arms swung at his sides, and his last steps forward were more of a swagger than a walk.

Emmy hesitated to confirm his statement. "I don't believe I know you."

"Oh sure you do." His eyes lit with another smile, and Emmylou felt like she was missing some secret joke.

"No, I think I would remember if we had met before." Her gaze flicked to the handgun that she kept in the drawer below the cash register.

"Oh!" he exclaimed with mock disappointment and clutched his chest like she had stabbed him. "I'd hoped you would recognize me from my profile picture."

Emmylou clenched her jaw, as an angry fire rushed through her veins. If her friends had created a profile on one of those ridiculous dating websites, she was going to kill them. "I'm afraid not," she answered, tight-lipped.

He obviously felt the ice that edged her words because he quickly lost his previous humor. He straightened and licked his lips.

"Look, I don't know who you are or where you came from, but I'm not interested in dating right now. It's not you; I simply don't have the time for a relationship."

"How about a dirty little fling?" He laid his hand on the counter, leaning forward. He promptly cleared his throat and backed away, tugging his oversized coat down. "Sorry. Too soon?"

"What!?" Never in her life had a stranger talked to her like this. "Okay, it's time for you to go." She pointed to the front door.

The man held his hands up. "No, I'm sorry. I was trying to lighten the mood. I do actually know you. We've never met in person though. I swear!" His hands flew higher in protection from the impending right hook he correctly deduced was coming. "Edibites!"

Emmylou unclenched her fist and dropped her chin. "Excuse me?"

"Edibites." His words came out calmer. "I'm Edibites four-oh-two." He exhaled. "From Bakeology."

Her eyes narrowed while her mind whirred and shifted with this information.

"I absolutely love your webinars."

"You take my classes?" Her rage had calmed, but she hadn't relaxed. "What are you doing here?" What she really wanted to ask was *"How did you find where I lived?"* She tried to keep her online presence as separate from her personal life as humanly possible.

"I'm visiting some family in the area. As it happens, I have some relatives not too far from here. The Langenburgs. Imagine my excitement when Aunt Charlotte told me about this bakery in town and I find out that you are the owner." His voice rose with every word. "I mean I have watched every webinar and taken every class you offer. Your recipe for clafouti is by far the best thing I have ever made, and that includes the Marie Antoinette I learned at Escoffier from Chef Lafontaine."

"Wow, that's impressive. Thank you for the high praise." Emmylou was happy that this guy was just another chef. A very unprofessional, uncouth chef, but a chef nonetheless, and that, she could relate to. "I can't believe you trained with Lafontaine. I hear she's brutal, but I guess all geniuses would be."

He tucked his hands in his pockets and smiled. "She was. Unfortunately, I didn't get to stay as long as I would have liked." He twisted his mouth and shrugged his shoulders. "Lack of funds. I had to return to home."

"I'm sorry to hear that. But at least you got to go. I only attended the Midwest School of Arts." Emmy pursed her lips. "It was a dream of mine to go to Paris and study."

"Nah. It's overrated, and you don't need it. With your gift, you could teach them a thing or two."

She nearly blushed under his glowing praise and approving gaze. "So Charlotte and Steve are your aunt and uncle?"

"In a manner of speaking. They practically raised me. I didn't have much of a home life and they were always there for me. So I always think of them as the adoring aunt and uncle I never had."

That bit of news seemed strange to Emmylou. From what she knew, the Langenburgs weren't the type to show affection to anyone or anything. They were old school parents and even older school ranchers. Children were to be seen and not heard and animals were tools to get the job done, not pets.

The kitchen door swung open, presenting Lindy. She surveyed the two of them with nonchalance, but Emmy knew she was checking to see if everything was okay.

"Lindy." Emmylou drew her closer. "This is Mr. ... um." She couldn't very well introduce him as Edibites-four-oh-two. She looked to the man for help.

"Matthews. Evan Matthews." He stuck his hand out, and Lindy shook it with a sideways, questioning glance to Emmylou.

"He takes my online courses and even studied at Escoffier," she informed Lindy. "Isn't that fantastic?"

Lindy was still looking at Emmylou. Apparently the information didn't impress her as much as Emmy. "That's truly amazing, Mr. Matthews." She answered flatly, looking at the man with a deadpan stare. "I'm just going to take the rolls with me when they're finished, if that's all right."

"That sounds great. Thank you."

A pause followed with Emmylou expecting Lindy to go back into the kitchen, but she didn't budge.

"Well, I won't keep you from your work. I can only imagine how busy you are." His shoulders rose when he fisted his hands in his pockets.

"It was nice of you to stop in," Emmylou said.

"Crazy how things work out like that."

"It is." She smiled and looked to Lindy.

"Yeah, crazy." Emmy wasn't sure if Lindy was talking about the situation or Evan Matthews. The two women remained side by side as they watched him leave.

"Wasn't that nice?" Emmylou asked and followed Lindy to the kitchen door.

Lindy answered with a grunt and a grimace. "If he were so

nice, he would have checked the store hours and come back when we were open."

Emmylou laughed and pushed the metal door open.

"You may want to lock the front door before more adoring fans make an unannounced visit."

"Good point." Emmylou grabbed the keys from her coat pocket.

*****

Shane sat at his desk staring at the open files in front of him. He had expected to drop into his bed and sleep the moment he got back home last night. He had been awake and busy for more than thirty-six hours. He should have been exhausted. Under normal circumstances he would have been. But he had had trouble sleeping. The motor oil that passed for coffee in the clinic had been his only saving grace.

Thank goodness it had been a slow day, only the usual colds, flus and ear infections typical of the season and one eccentric older lady who he suspected was going to become a regular visitor claiming unusual and unlikely symptoms.

His encounter with Emmylou yesterday had been dogging his every minute. He had had a peculiar feeling in his chest every time she appeared in his mind. It was an uncomfortable, fluttering weight that threatened to cut off his air passage. He didn't like it. If he were a hypochondriac like so many of his fellow doctors, he would run some blood work, schedule a stress test and have a chest x-ray. But he knew it wasn't any medical condition causing his heart to act like an outboard motor every ten minutes.

It was that woman. Actually it was what she brought out in him. There had only been one other woman on the planet to cause him so much tension, and she was no longer on the planet. His stupidity had seen to that. The pen he was rolling in his hand turned to sticky, chestnut locks. He ran his thumb down the shaft, and his mind flooded with horrific images of his beautiful Katie's face caked in hot, red blood. He squeezed his eyes shut, snapping the pen in half with the searing pain slicing through him.

He sucked in a sharp breath, desperately trying to tackle the awful memories before they overtook him. He had been able to manage them for quite some time now. Shane had spent years compressing them into a tiny box he could bury beneath his heart. He had learned to rationalize it, to compartmentalize. His medical training helped with working through it.

And now...

"Dr. Newbury."

Shane jerked his head toward the doorway before he could compose himself. "What is it, Shelby?"

She had obviously intended to simply pop in, but she straightened and slid into his office. "Are you okay?"

Shane reclined in his chair, quickly gathering his wits. "Yes, I'm fine. Just a long week."

Shelby kept her gaze narrowed on him as she approached, "It has been that." She grasped the back of the chair in front of his desk. "Are you taking the weekend to get unpacked? I saw the U-Haul arrived yesterday."

He groaned and grinned, remembering that Shelby lived several miles past his house and had to drive by it on her way into town. "Yeah, I suppose I should do that. I've been sleeping in my recliner all week."

"Mmm." She nodded her head, making him wonder if she knew that, too. "Well, I'm heading home."

"Big plans for the weekend?" Shane dropped the bottom half of his pen into the holder on his desk.

"Oh yeah, Daryl and I are repairing the chicken coop tomorrow. It's a regular frat house around our place."

"Sounds like more fun than what I'll be having. If you want a break, you can come on over and unpack some boxes or move some furniture."

Shelby pulled at the stethoscope around her neck. "Don't temp me. You don't have four kids, a herd of cattle and a pile of laundry at your house."

"Four? I thought you told me you have three kids."

"Oh believe me, my husband is more of a kid than all the others combined, and I can't threaten him with a spanking; he might take me up on it."

Shane laughed and shook his head. He had never worked with a nurse quite like Shelby before. It was refreshing. "My door is always open if you need a break."

"If I wanted a real break, I'd go to the theater over in Glenwood and see the new Mark Wahlberg movie." Shelby sighed heavily and shrugged.

"You like action movies?"

She propped her hand on her hip and tilted her head. "I like any movie where Mark takes his shirt off." With that she spun on her heel and strutted out the door with Shane chuckling behind her.

Chapter 8

Shane allowed an hour for his travel time to Glenwood, thirty miles away. The last time he made this journey he had been trying to catch a speeding ambulance and hadn't exactly been gazing at the landscape out the windows. He had no idea where the theater was located and didn't feel like stopping and asking directions. Shelby probably could have told him, but he didn't want her to know that she had planted the idea of a night out in his mind.

Once she mentioned relaxing and watching a movie, he knew he had to come to Glenwood. He had skipped dinner and was still in his work clothes. He couldn't care less, though. No one knew him here. He had only been to the hospital and hadn't been in the area long enough to make any acquaintances.

Surprisingly, the theater was easy to find. Of course, it may have been that huge billboard on the edge of town telling him to turn left on 4th Street. He looked at the marquis for the times, then at the clock on his dash. Thirty minutes until show time. The lights were on, but there didn't seem to be anyone else around. Snow was beginning to gently cover his truck in a thin veil. He pulled the collar of his coat up and hunched inside of it.

When he got out of his truck, he jammed his hands into his pockets and jogged across the street. The door was open, and the theater was plenty warm. He turned toward the ticket counter, fully prepared to be asked to wait or to have to stand there until the worker was allowed to sell tickets. But a freckle-faced girl of about fifteen appeared behind the cash register with an open smile.

"What are you seeing this evening?"

Shane hadn't expected such professionalism from someone so young, but it had been several years since he'd been to watch a movie in the theater and then it was in Omaha with some fellow pre-meds. He actually had to look at the posters displayed behind the cute girls whose nametag read Kristen. He was surprised to find that this place had two screens and two movies. Smiling when he saw the photoshopped picture of Mark Wahlberg supposedly tearing his way out of the poster in a halo of flames, he spoke the title to her.

He paid, took his ticket and walked the ten feet to the concession stand. Popcorn was bubbling out of the popper, and his stomach growled. He tried to remember what he had eaten the past few days and came up with a vague memory of beef jerky, ramen noodle soup and some rice concoction Shelby had forced down him in the back break room of the clinic.

Somehow he ended up with his weight in junk food, tucked back in the corner of the theater happily positioning his various boxes in order of planned consumption in the seat next to him.

The theater was completely empty, and that wasn't an exaggeration. Shane wondered where everyone was or if he was just that early. It was a small town, after all. Maybe they didn't need to rush to the theater early in order to secure seating. He had been away from small towns for far too long. Funny enough, he was settling right back in. It must be something that a body never forgets. Like some kind of muscle memory.

He washed the salty popcorn down with an indulgence of soda and nearly sighed with pleasure. This was just what he needed after the week he had had. He glanced at his watch, then once more at the empty chairs. Watching a movie on the gigantic screen all by himself would put this in the top three best nights ever. He spun his head to the entrance when he detected movement. His chances of being alone evaporated when a familiar blonde appeared in the doorway.

*****

The theater was empty when Emmylou stopped in the entrance to scout out seating. Guess she had her pick of seats. She wandered down the red carpeted aisle with her extra-large soda in her hand. She was wishing she had brought a fifth of rum with her to dump in the cup. It had been a hell of a week. She and Scarlett had planned to come to the movie together, but as luck would have it, Scarlett was busy with her sick cat.

That girl had a regular zoo at her house; everything from cats to raccoons and even a salamander or two. Emmylou couldn't dislike her for it, though; Scarlett had a soft spot for living creatures, especially the abandoned and injured type. Every animal in her home had been rescued and lovingly nursed back to health by Scarlett. Emmylou could only imagine what her vet bills were. On occasion, Scarlett did like to find good homes for her critters, but overall, it was filled to the brim with fur balls.

Emmylou couldn't stand the thought of hanging out all alone, or worse, going out by herself. The movies were neither one of those things. Here she didn't have to socialize or make small talk; she didn't have to dress up and appear carefree. She didn't have any demands in this place, just two hours of viewing pleasure. It was exactly what the doctor ordered.

She made it halfway down the aisle and took a seat in the middle of the row. She wasn't sure why it was empty. The movie had been held over from the previous week, but it was enough of a blockbuster that the theater should be at least half full. She sucked down a gulp of refreshing nectar and closed her eyes as the bubbles tickled her insides. She rarely drank the stuff, but she couldn't resist tonight.

Emmy heard muffled footsteps coming up the aisle, but she focused on the screen that was now playing an advertisement for the local 4th of July Fireworks show. The footsteps stopped next to her, forcing her to look sideways. She groaned and turned her head back, rolling her eyes and praying he would just keep moving.

"Emmylou." The leering way he said it brought a bit of bile to her throat.

Emmylou glanced sideways and forced her lips into a painful smile of disgust. "Tim." She turned her attention back to the screen hoping he would get the hint.

"What are you up to?"

She tilted her head and slanted her eyes, "I'm building gluten networks and transforming them into sturdy webbing." She heard a low chuckle in the back of the theater. Probably some of Tim's posse. With any luck he would slither back to them.

"What?"

His black boots clicked on the floor as he sidestepped into her row. Emmylou pulled her jacket tighter around her. The only thing that accomplished was drawing Tim's gaze to her breasts. She knew she was now trapped. She couldn't get past by the wall, and he was blocking the aisle.

She shook her head. What could she have possibly seen in a man this dense? "Nothing. I'm just here to watch the movie," she answered.

"Yeah, me too."

Emmylou tried to avoid looking at him, but he was towering over her, making her skin vibrate with nerves. Their relationship hadn't ended on the best note, and Emmy suspected he was still pissed off about it. In retrospect, sending him a bouquet of burnt cookies spelling out the words "Go to Hell" in frosting maybe wasn't the best way to go about breaking up. But, then again, Tim shouldn't have cheated on her with Carmen from *The Curly Gates* salon either.

"One drink. You here by yourself?"

"Are those new boots?" she evaded.

Tim dropped into the empty seat next to her and propped his left foot on top of his right leg. She straightened and crowded to the far edge of her seat.

He grinned and leaned closer. "Cost me a pretty penny, but I think they're worth it." The gap between his teeth she had once thought endearing now seemed pompous, and the pouch of tobacco tucked in his bottom lip turned her stomach. He had quit that when they were together. His gaze lowered to her lips, and his hand slowly moved toward her. She stiffened and sucked in air, bracing for his touch.

"Got some new ink, too."

Emmylou opened her eyes and shifted her gaze to the place on his bicep he was staring at. The skin was red and scabbed and etched with a black band of barbed wire. "Wow." She drew it out trying to sound impressed. "So are you here with someone?"

Emmy must have sounded a little too hopeful because his eyes darkened. "Maybe. You jealous?"

"Not at all. I'm happy for you." More like sorry for whatever lady was idiot enough to go out on a date with Tim Potter.

He ran a finger from her shoulder to her wrist. When he stopped his path, she clamped down on his hand as hard as she could. She desperately wished she didn't keep her nails so short. With a clenched jaw and dagger gaze, she leaned in. "Oh, Tim. I would hate for your date to question your fidelity." Irony painted every word. With one last squeeze, she dropped his hand in his lap and moved to stand.

"There you are, honey."

Emmylou and Tim both turned at the voice. There stood Shane Newbury with a deadly smile on his face. Emmy simply stared at him, unsure what feelings were rushing through her. But Tim pulled his boots from the seat and squirmed under the piercing brown eyes like the snake he was.

"I think you're in my seat, Mr. ...."

Even Emmylou felt the leashed hostility pulsing beneath Shane's surface, masked with that broad, white smile.

"Tim," he stuttered.

"Mr. Tim." Shane didn't extend his hand; instead, he looped his thumb in his belt loop.

"Uh, yeah. No. It's Potter."

Shane twitched his head and looked at Tim like the simpleton he was.

"Tim Potter." Tim stood and brushed his hands on his jeans and fixed his shirt sleeve.

"Oh, I see." Shane gave Tim another half-smile. "Well, enjoy the movie."

"You, too."

Tim looked back at Emmylou. She wiggled her fingers at him, and he jerked his head in a nod, then slid out of the row under Shane's scalding gaze. Shane watched Tim all the way up the aisle. When he turned his gaze to Emmylou, he hitched one eyebrow high, and Emmylou couldn't hold back her smile.

"Thank you, but I was handling it."

"Yeah, I could see that. I particularly liked the line about you baking bread."

"Baking bread - you got that?"

He crossed his arms and shifted his jaw, tucking his tongue in his cheek. "I'm a doctor; by nature we tend to like science, and the reference to building gluten networks wasn't hard to figure out." He moved and sat down in the seat vacated by Tim.

A tingle surged up her arm when his forearm nudged hers. "What are you doing?" Emmy pulled her arm away, narrowing a sharp look at him.

"I just told what's-his-face that this was my place. You don't want him to think I lied, do you?"

Calling the seat his "place" was abnormally soothing. She didn't like it. "He left. I'll be fine. You can go back to your seat, now."

"From what I can see, your taste in men would keep any decent guy busy protecting you for decades."

Her jaw dropped, and she shot straight up in her seat. "You don't know anything about me or my taste in men."

"Don't get your knickers in a twist just because the truth hit a nerve."

Emmy's eyes flared and narrowed. "Just because you think you're John Wayne riding in to save the little lady from the savages doesn't make you movie-star appealing. In fact, it makes you look like a conceited ass!"

His grin and the stupid twinkle lighting his eyes stoked the angry fire inside of her. She twisted in her seat and rested her arm on the row of chairs in front of them.

"Hold that thought." Shane popped out of his seat and walked to the back of the theater.

Emmylou shook her head the entire time she watched him. She had been subjected to some pretty awful language and behavior, but never before had she experienced a man who didn't rise to her verbal sparring. This man seemed to enjoy it, which just made *her* feel like the ass. There was something wrong with him. Some sort of social malfunction or disorder to make him behave like this because every time they were near each other, he was a jerk. And he brought out her very worst behavior. She turned back into her seat to contemplate what had just happened.

She was chewing on her straw when footsteps and the sloshing of an iced beverage disrupted her thoughts. Shane settled back into the seat beside her. Her face contorted with the dumbfounded brain-stall in her head.

"Popcorn?" He leaned the bag toward her.

She shook her head. "Didn't I just tell you to go back to your seat?"

He settled against the plush cushion and stretched his long legs out. "I figure sitting next to you will deter anyone else from making a scene and disturbing my movie enjoyment. What can I say? I'm selfish like that. Raisinette?"

She glanced over at the assortment of treats lined up in the seat on the other side of Shane. "Aren't you supposed to be the example of health?"

He emptied a few of the candies into his hand and shrugged. "Why? Do you think they would follow it? Trust me, people are gonna do what they're gonna do whether I eat candy or not. My being the picture of healthy living does as much good as dressing in a three piece suit to train dogs." He tilted his head toward her and looked up from beneath his lashes. It was the cutest thing she had ever seen him do. "Do you always follow the doctor's advice?"

Her face answered for her.

"That's what I thought." He turned toward the screen again just as the lights dimmed. "Besides, the raisins offset the chocolate." He dumped the brown ovals into his open mouth. "This *is* a healthy snack."

Emmylou snatched the box from his hands. "In that case, I'd love some." She helped herself to a handful and leaned against the cushion. She glanced over at Shane and found a smirk on his face.

"You know that's not the truth?" he asked without looking at her.

The screen flickered with light, and the volume thundered as the movie began.

"I'm a baker. By nature we know what's in a Raisinette."

He chuckled and sipped from his straw. He glanced over, and she met his look of appreciation. Their eyes held for a charged moment before he broke it.

"The previews are starting," he whispered.

Emmylou looked harder at him. "You might be the only person I know that actually *likes* the previews."

Shane glanced back at her with a smile. He lowered his gaze to her mouth sending a shiver through her. "Shhhhh," his lips formed a perfect "O".

With one last look, they both turned to the movie screen and settled into their seats. Emmylou caught herself with a start before she snuggled closer to Shane. She was only this comfortable with Lacy and Scarlett. Wordlessly, Shane tilted the popcorn in her direction. Her hand shook as she reached inside and took a handful.

The booms, yells and crashes only stimulated her already overloaded nerves. Emmy had her hands shoved between her legs to keep them from reaching over. Shane offered her a piece of candy. She shook her head in a tight motion. She was scared to touch his hand. The last time they had brushed against each other in the popcorn sack, she thought she had been electrocuted. Now her body was on high alert.

His enjoyment of the show and completely relaxed positioning kept her teetering on the edge. Her mind wasn't helping any either. Mark Wahlberg was replaced with visions of Shane. He took his shirt off; she imagined Shane without his.

"Are you cold?"

His voice brought her attention back. She realized she was sitting on the front of the seat, leaning forward with her hands gripping the seat and her shoulders hunched. "Oh." She instantly reclined against the seat, but she wasn't relaxed. "No."

What was going on? She was feeling like a high school girl sitting next to her crush.

A better question would be why was he being so nice to her?

Halfway through the movie, Emmylou didn't even know what the storyline was. She had spent every moment analyzing her feelings and the puzzling lack of discomfort on Shane's part. It was as though he was watching a movie with his best friend. He kept nudging her arm or leg, pointing to the screen, laughing and stuffing his face with snacks.

She was having a meltdown and he was oblivious to it all. This had never happened to her before. Usually she was too busy trying to make sure her date had everything he needed and was having a nice time. She looked over at Shane and studied him. She caught herself smile when he smiled at the screen, and she shook her head.

She was still shaking it when she turned her attention back to the movie.

"Seriously, you're making me feel like a pig. I need you to eat some of this. Otherwise I'm going to be that single guy who walks out of the theater with a week's worth of TV snacks." Shane held out a box of Junior Mints and shook them. "Come on. Don't let people pity me." His playful pout was too much.

"Oh, for heaven's sake." She snatched the box and settled back into her seat opening it.

"Yes." He made a triumphant fist. She scowled at him and he shrugged.

Having something to keep her occupied helped her relax, somewhat, and his comfort was rubbing off on her. She was finally able to pay attention to the movie even though now it was pretty pointless since she had spent the entire thing watching him.

The credits were rolling, but both she and Shane took a few moments to stir to life. He leaned forward to pick up his mess. Emmy took in a wakeful breath when the lights brightened. The darkness had provided a cocoon, and it was difficult for Emmylou to regain her senses. She was already feeling the emptiness of separation, and Shane was still beside her.

"That was awesome. Thanks for letting me sit with you." He had blocked the path with his arms resting on both rows. "What did you think of it?"

His chocolate eyes warmed with his easy smile, striking a sensitive place in her abdomen. "It was good." Emmy pushed her hair away from her face with her finger. His gaze followed her hand's trail.

Shane scooted forward, his focus on her hair. He reached out, and Emmylou instinctively leaned forward. Her heart thudded, and her mouth softened. His hand tugged at her hair, and she started, pulling back.

"There ya go."

She looked to his outstretched hand and found a semi-smashed Junior Mint in his palm. Heat rushed to her face and an unwelcome disappointment bloomed in her chest. She moistened her lips. "Thank you."

He smiled and tossed the candy into his empty popcorn sack. Her jaw clenched with mortification. What was she thinking? He wasn't going to kiss her. He didn't even like her. She jammed a hand through her hair wondering why in the hell she had wanted him to kiss her. She didn't like him either. This wasn't a date.

"Well, are you ready to go?"

More politeness. She ran her tongue along the back of her teeth before nodding her head and standing up. They walked through the theater to the door in awkward silence. He pushed it open for her and waited for her to exit. Who was this guy?

"Have a good night," she said over her shoulder, her breath creating steam in the frigid air. She walked a few steps while digging in her purse for her keys. She stopped and spun around, slamming right into him. "Oh, shit! Sorry!"

She lifted her gaze from his chin to his eyes. His firm grip on her arms was reassuring and unsettling all at once. *Oh God, he smelled delicious.*

"That's okay." His words were delivered with a fatherly tone that deflated her hopes. "Did you forget something?"

"What?" She shook her head and tried to step back, but Shane didn't loosen his grip. Or maybe she hadn't moved at all; it could have been the earth that moved since it had spent all night tipped on its axis for her. "No. I forgot to thank you for…" she had to swallow before finishing, "helping me."

The heat radiating from him - or was it her - made her forget it was bitter cold outside. Their mingling breath was the only reminder.

"It was no big deal. Like I said, it was selfish on my part."

A group of teens passed by them laughing and chattering in excited voices.

"So that's where everybody was."

"Excuse me?" Emmylou asked.

He turned his attention back to her and she thought she might just melt into those chocolate pools. "I wondered why the theater was empty on a Friday night. Guess they were all at the basketball game."

"How do you know that?"

"Those kids just said so."

How on earth he could hear their conversation Emmy didn't know. Her ears were filled with her thundering heartbeat. She swiped the hair from her face and stepped back. This time he allowed it.

"I suppose. I'd better get going." She adjusted her purse strap and curled her hands into her sleeves. "Thanks, again."

"You're welcome. And thank you."

"For what?"

"For the great time I had."

She smiled and he returned it.

"Who would've thought?" Shane shoved his hands in his pockets, pushing his shoulders up to guard against the wind.

"What?" Emmylou stuttered and blinked several times.

"Well, that I would have fun with you."

Emmy was sure her face resembled a deer staring at an oncoming pick-up truck. "Definitely not me. Good night." She tipped her head, turned and started across the street.

"Emmylou," he drawled, but she kept walking. She threw her

hand up in dismissal.

When she reached her car, he caught her by the arm and turned her. "Hey." He understood her look and released her but didn't leave. "Am I wrong?"

Damn it if he didn't look like a little puppy who had just spilled his food dish. She chewed her bottom lip and averted her gaze before answering grudgingly, "No. You're not wrong." She leaned against her car door. "It's just –" she stopped before she blurted the rest out.

"What?"

No one has ever been honest with me. No one has ever treated me like a lady or an equal. I haven't been this comfortable with a man before. "Nothing. You're right. Based on our history, we should have been trading insults and throwing food at each other all night. But we didn't. It was nice."

She didn't like the way he was assessing her. She was sure he had just read all of her private thoughts.

"Okay." He chaffed his hands against the cold.

"Okay? That's all you have to say?"

"Yep. That's all."

His grin was infuriating. "Okay." Emmylou slapped her hands against her jeans and turned to open her door. Shane beat her to it. She stood staring at him, not sure what to do. "Uh, thank you."

She wiggled into her seat and fired up the engine. He was still standing outside her window. She waved and he backed away, slightly. She carefully pulled away from the curb. When she looked in her rearview mirror, Shane was still there watching her drive away. He didn't move until she turned onto the main street.

A strange sensation tingled in her heart.

Chapter 9

"It was weird." Emmylou set the steaming vanilla latte in front of Scarlett and slid into the chair across from her.

"Sounds to me like you enjoyed yourself, and you don't know how to feel about that." Scarlett took a sip of the frothy brew. Emmy was amazed that her friend never got any of the foam on her lip while she was usually covered in it.

"Nah, I don't think that's it. I can't stand him. He's abrasive and egotistical and constantly saying rude things to me. And just look at what he did with Lacy. I mean, she could've lost the baby, and he would have been standing there with his finger in his nose."

Scarlett shot her a look that made Emmylou bristle. "Well, it's true!"

"No, it's not. I think he did a great job with her. A lot of doctors overreact in my opinion, and besides Lacy loves him."

Emmy pursed her lips. "Lacy doesn't have the best judgment in men."

"Said the human doormat."

"You know, Scar, sometimes you're bluntness gets under my skin."

Scarlett set her cup down after her sip and delicately licked her lips. "That's only when I'm directing it at you." She tossed her dark brown hair over her shoulders and settled her green eyes on Emmylou. Emmylou always found comfort in their soulful depths.

"True." Emmy rested her chin in her palm. "You know, I think he may have followed me home. I'm not sure, but on the highway, a truck stayed about half a mile behind me all the way, and when I pulled into my driveway, it passed in front of my house and turned on the very next block to head *back* in the direction of the highway."

Scarlett arched her slim brow. "Or perhaps you have a stalker."

Emmylou grinned with a scoff. "Yeah. That's always a possibility. Primrose is such a dangerous town. Although, I didn't recognize the truck."

"See."

The door bells jingled and they both turned.

"Hello, Mrs. Walters. How are you doing?" Emmylou asked.

"Just fine, dear. Thank you."

Lindy stepped out of the kitchen to stand behind the counter. "Hi, Mrs. Walters. What can I get for you?"

"The usual." Widow Walters came in every Saturday and ordered the same thing. "How's that fiancé of yours?"

Lindy got all gushy and smiley. Emmy looked back to Scarlett.

"Been sucking lemons?" Emmylou immediately smoothed the wrinkles in her face. "You know some day that will be you."

"Nope. That'll never happen. I'm not getting married."

"Hmm." Scarlett covered any further reply with her cup.

This was not going the way that she wanted. Emmy knew she should've talked to Lacy instead of Scarlett. At least Lacy would do her best to spin it so Emmy heard what she wanted to hear.

"So I hear your date with our new doctor went well."

Emmylou shifted in her seat and stared at Mrs. Walters. "I didn't go on a date with the new doctor."

"Are you sure? Because I have it on good authority that you were over to Glenwood at the theater with him last night."

Emmylou narrowed her eyes wondering how in the world word got out so fast. The theater had been empty. Then, she raised her head and looked Mrs. Walters in the eye. "Did you happen to have your car serviced this morning?"

"Why, yes I did." That familiar, wily light in Widow Walters' eyes had Emmylou nodding her head.

"Well, thank you, Mrs. Walters. I certainly appreciate you stopping in and visiting with us."

The silent exchange between Mrs. Walters and Emmylou made it understood they were on the same page. When Mrs. Walters left the shop, Emmy turned back to her friend.

"Tim." They echoed, sharing the same expression.

"What did I ever see in that man?"

"Muscles and a sexy smile."

Emmylou let out a self-deprecating chuckle.

"Oh, you can bet that Mrs. Walters will squash any gossip she hears about it and everyone else is too busy shoveling snow to care what is going on in this town."

"At least the first part of that is true." Emmylou faltered and shot upright in her chair with who she saw in her window. "Oh, my God!"

"That's always the look I wear when someone *I* hate shows up."

"Oh, shut up." Emmylou scowled and tried to duck down while Scarlett continued to smirk at her. The bells jingled. Emmy could feel the heat flooding into her cheeks. She directed her gaze at Scarlett's shoulder.

"Hello, Dr. Newbury." Scarlett smiled at him over her coffee cup.

"Oh, hello there."

Emmylou could hear the smile in his voice, and his presence was sending a warm vibration through her. She knew he was standing there, waiting. She took a deep breath in her battle to ignore him.

"Hi, Emmylou."

She pressed her lips together before shifting in her chair. "Hi, Doctor." Her hands shook when her gaze settled on his face.

"Oh, I think you can call me Shane." His wrinkled nose and the delighted twinkle in his infuriatingly deep brown eyes annoyed her.

"No, I don't think I can." She met his gaze, fighting not to give anything away. The moment dragged on.

"How's the coffee today?"

His question flagged the memory of the last time he'd insulted her coffee, and the moment broke. Emmylou remembered just exactly what she despised about him. He was an ass. "I'm afraid it hasn't changed since the last time."

"Really? I would've thought you would change the pot even if you hadn't sold it all."

Emmy perched her eyebrows up and stared at him. "Were you born without a filter or are you just socially impaired? Because I was taught if you couldn't say anything nice, you shouldn't say anything at all."

*****

Shane wasn't really sure why he was here, especially with the five mile drive to town. He was fully capable of making his own coffee, but something inside of him had had him grabbing his keys and driving to Emmylou's bakery. He had to see her. He felt that they had left some things unresolved last night. He couldn't pinpoint what those things were exactly, but the twinge inside of him said they were there.

"I was just trying to make a joke. I'm sorry if it offended you. I didn't mean it that way." He kept his hands balled into fists inside his coat pockets even though they itched to touch her hand. It looked so soft. He glanced in Scarlett's direction, hoping she didn't think he was a jerk, too. The attentive glow in her expression told him she was enjoying this little scene immensely.

"I thought it was funny."

Shane silently thanked Scarlett for the lifeline even while Emmylou shot her friend a quelling look.

"I think I'll risk it, anyway." He watched Emmylou for a moment, unable to leave her company. He'd had the same problem last night. That mass of blonde hair pulled into a knot on top of her head was enchanting. He wondered what it would look like spread across his pillow and what it would feel like running through his fingers. He had to clench his jaw and look to the letters on the window behind her in order to squash that thought.

"Lindy's back there. She'll take your order."

"Thank you." He smiled in spite of his disappointment and walked to the counter. This time when he looked at the loopy, girly chalk writings, he appreciated the creativity of naming each drink and pastry with a catchy name. He imagined her long fingered hand gliding over the chalkboard, creating the titles. It made his heart race. Then his stomach clenched, and his chest tightened.

He shouldn't be feeling this way. Emmylou wasn't his biggest fan. Okay, who was he kidding? She hated him, and even if she didn't hate him, attraction and love had only brought pain and devastation to him and everyone he was close to.

The girl behind the counter was smiling politely, waiting for him to work through his emotional turmoil and place an order. Her dark pixie hair brought out her large blue eyes. He could tell they were kind eyes. He believed the soul dwelled in the eyes. He ordered the first things he saw on the menu just to get through the awkward moment and retreat to his house. He didn't turn, even though he could feel Emmylou's and Scarlett's eyes on him.

He paid and nodded to the women as he left the store. What had he been thinking? He couldn't behave like this anymore. Just because she brought out feelings he hadn't experienced in seven years was no reason to follow her around. Following her home from the theater last night should have been the end of it.

*****

Emmylou sat in front of her double monitors waiting for everyone to log on. She had been doing a series of webinars on the complexities of marketing. Today they would be discussing shipping of perishable items. Last week had been social media and how to use it.

As the names popped up, she recognized several as devoted followers. *Edibites402* logged in, and a message beeped several seconds later.

It was nice to see you and your store the other day.

Emmylou took a sip of her water and scooted her chair closer to the keyboard.

Thank you. It's always nice to put a face to the name.

She answered several other instant messages from her students and turned on her webcam. She typed the announcement that the class would now begin and hit the broadcast button. She had tried other formats, but being able to be both seen and heard saved her so much time in answering questions. Her students typed their question, and she was able to answer it in real time without taking the time to type it all out. She could also run a PowerPoint presentation and show them the proper tools and techniques right then, instead of trying to describe it and show pictures.

Twenty minutes into the presentation, another message from Edibites402 popped up.

Your hair looks beautiful today.

Trying to be nice, she smiled and thanked him in the middle of talking about the cost of refrigerated trucks. She went on to talk about the pros and cons of contracting out and the different avenues available to rural businesses.

Would you like to get together after this class is over?

She did a double take at the conversation box and paused in mid-sentence. She wasn't sure how to answer that, so she ignored it and continued on with her presentation. A few minutes before the class was over, she always opened it up for questions. She hoped that Edibites wouldn't make any more advances. It wasn't until the end that his name appeared again. This time it was on her private message board.

Sorry about my earlier question. I didn't mean to put you off or scare you. You don't know me from Adam, and it was inappropriate for me to put you on the spot. I was hoping that we could get together to talk about some recipe ideas that I have and maybe brainstorm about the bakery I'm opening. I understand if you don't want to.

She wrapped up the questions from her other students before messaging him back. She looked at the tiny picture next to his user name, remembering when he had paid a visit to her bakery. He was a little on the worse-for-wear side, but he had an easy smile. Still, something in her gut told her not to break her rules for anyone.

Thank you for apologizing. I don't usually like to personalize my work, but I would be happy to visit with you through Skype or email.

That was the offer she made with all of her students. After all, they were paying one hundred fifty dollars for the four week course. She liked to give them their money's worth. A smiley face showed up on the screen first, and she laughed at the toothy grin on the yellow circle.

I understand completely, and that would be wonderful. I would appreciate any help that you can give me. I'm still at square one with this business plan and unsure where I want to go next. The ideas of a woman who has been such a success in her own right would be a blessing to this clod with a dream.

Emmylou smiled at the screen. She had once been Evan Matthews, hungry for any bit of information on the bakery business. Her hands poised over the keyboard, and with every intention of setting up a time to Skype, she typed.

I guess since you are already in town, and you flattered my humongous ego, I can make some time for us to meet. Evenings are about my only free time, so if you would like to get together after five o'clock, I can do that any night except for Thursdays.

She was surprised that she had given in but wasn't sorry. It couldn't hurt to give some business advice in person. She preferred the protection that meeting through the computer gave her, or at least it made her feel protected to have that barrier, but he seemed like a decent enough guy.

Evenings are good for me, too. Uncle Steve has me helping out on the ranch, but we are usually done by 6. Would you like to talk over dinner? My treat. I could use a night out of the house.

Emmylou agreed to meet him at The Dove House at seven o'clock on Tuesday night. That was the night Mrs. Walters made chicken fried steak and Scarlett always had something tasty from her greenhouses. They both agreed and bid each other goodbye.

Emmy turned out the lights and locked the office door where she kept her recipes and the safe. She knew that living in a small town decreased the possibilities of being robbed, but her grandmother had always told her, "Trust in Allah, but tie up your camel". Her grandma had never steered her wrong, so she lived by that advice, always.

She was greeted with a blast of icy afternoon air when she opened the back door. It felt like a storm was coming in. Now she was dreading having to go to her production building and meet with Lorie, her manager.

"Daddy!" Emmylou wasn't expecting her father to be by the back door when she walked outside. She hadn't been sure he knew her place had a back door. Or a front door. George Bennett had hardly came to the bakery. He had never approved of her career choice.

"Hi, darlin.'" He had a distracted look about him when he leaned in and kissed her on the cheek, and she got a sick feeling in her stomach.

"What brings you by?"

"Oh, nothing." He clasped his leather gloved hands in front of his still trim middle.

"It isn't mother, is it?"

"No, no. She's perfectly fine. Meeting with the Community Foundation this afternoon." His greying mustache twitched beneath his nose.

It wasn't her birthday, and since that was the only day in the whole year he ever dropped by to see her, her qualms were doubling by the second. Emmylou chafed her arms and waited. She knew better than to interrupt her father.

"Can we go inside?" He gestured toward the door.

"Uh, sure," she stammered, taken back. She unlocked it and ushered her father inside, flipping on the light.

It was probably the first time since she opened five years ago that he had been back there. He looked around with his back to her, touching a large stainless steel bowl hanging from a rack over her work station, making it clink. Finally, he turned around. The panic in Emmy's chest had spread to her hands. They shook and tingled despite her best efforts to get them under control.

His blue-green eyes were sorrowful when he focused on hers. "Honey, you know that loan you secured eighteen months ago when you expanded into mass production?"

"Yes." She swallowed hard. She remembered all too well the two-hundred thousand dollars she had borrowed from her father's bank and the price she had to pay for it. He had had to pull strings to his great chagrin, and she had to live with his demands and skepticism.

"Well, do you also remember that the bank sold that loan along with a dozen others to a larger bank in Kansas City?"

"Yes, Dad. I still have the letter, and that's where I send the payment every month." She really hated when he addressed her as if she were a fifteen-year-old in a high school business class. He had been discussing business with her around the dinner table since she'd moved out of her high chair.

He pressed his lips together, nodded and looked away. At least he understood he had been talking down to her. "I hate to tell you this, honey, but that bank went under last week, and the government is now collecting all the loans."

Emmylou crossed her arms over her chest. "I'm guessing that's bad news since you came here in person."

He took the five steps to close the distance between them and placed his hands on her shoulders. "Emmy, that means you have sixty days to pay the loan in full, or they foreclose."

Chapter 10

Emmylou sat in solid darkness, her feet propped on her coffee table, sipping a glass of cold wine. She and her dad had talked over all of her options which, as it turned out, weren't many. She could take on a partner with money, she could sell to someone else, or she could default on the loan and go into bankruptcy. None of those sounded very good to her. And she knew that her father would only go so far to help her. His parting comment was, "Oh, honey, it's not all that bad. These things have a way of working out."

Normal supportive parents meant that as encouragement, but George Bennett was telling her she could now go to law school like he had always intended her to do with the silly bakery out of the way.

She had known the risks of taking on that loan and expanding, but she wanted to prove to everyone that she wasn't wrong, that she could be successful with her passions for baking and business. That blind ambition was coming back to bite a humongous chunk out of her butt.

She dropped her head against the cushion of her pillowy couch. Her production and distribution branch was doing well. Just not well enough to be able to pay off her two-hundred thousand dollar loan in sixty days. She would have been able to do it within the next five years, though. It was booming and taking on new clients every day.

Lorie had just informed her that they had now had online orders from all of the lower forty-eight states. In one year, she had gone from personally driving orders up to two-hundred miles away, to contracting with a nationwide trucking company to deliver all of the baked goods that her production staff created in mass every day.

Hot tears pooled in her eyes, but she refused to shed them. The faces of the thirty-one people she now employed flashed through her head. Maria was about to have a baby, Donnie was going to school at night to get his degree in accounting so he could manage the office, and Lorie… Two tears slipped out before she could stop them.

Lorie had worked harder for Emmylou than anyone had a reason to. When Emmylou had hired Lorie, she had just been abandoned by her husband and was checking groceries at McCarthy's Grocery Store trying to eke out a meager living. She had dropped out of high school when she got pregnant and married the baby's father. But Emmy knew Lorie had potential and was hungry to prove the town wrong about her. Emmylou had been looking for a bright, ambitious person who could accept a smaller paycheck to manage the production house, and Lorie fit the description.

Emmylou had had a good feeling when she brought Lorie on, and that feeling had proved more right than she had imagined possible. That place was a well-oiled machine. Lorie had everything mapped out, cataloged and scheduled into a computer system she had begged her brother to build. Not that she had to try hard, Wesley Marshall would have done anything for his big sister.

Emmy jumped when the phone rang. She slammed her shin into the table and let out a yelp before answering on the fourth ring.

"Hello?" Emmy tucked the phone between her chin and shoulder and reached over to flip on the light. She flinched and shut her eyes. How long had she been sitting in the dark?

"Emmylou, what's wrong?"

Emmy kept her eyes closed and dropped her shoulders. "Nothing, Mother."

"You aren't *entertaining* are you?"

A mental image of her mother's pursed up mouth and narrowed eyes flashed in her head. "Eww, mother. No, I don't have anyone here."

"Well, with your social life, I never know if it's safe to call on a Saturday night."

Emmylou rubbed her forehead. Just what she needed, more ridicule. "What did you need, Mom?"

"That's actually why I called. I was wondering if you were entertaining a certain young gentleman."

"I'm not entirely sure what you mean by that, but no, I assure you I'm all alone."

"Oh."

Was that more disappointment Emmylou heard?

"Well, I thought that perhaps you were with Dr. Newbury again."

"Again?"

"Yes. I heard that you two were at the movies in Glenwood last night."

"That was simply a coincidence, Mother. We happened to be there at the same time. It wasn't planned, and it most certainly wasn't a date."

"Why would you say it like that?"

Emmylou sat in her dining room chair, bracing for a battle. "Because I can't stand him. In fact, I'm pretty sure that I hate him."

"You don't need to be so dramatic, dear. I don't think you hate him. How could you? He's such a wonderful young man."

"Have you even met him?"

"Well, no. Not yet. But he's a doctor. And he's young. And available. I was just –"

"Well that makes him downright perfect then, doesn't it?" Emmylou shot out of her chair, gripping the phone. "Maybe I should go over to his house right now and propose. I think we would have just enough time to make it to Vegas and back by Monday. With any luck, I could be knocked up with your grandchild before we get off the plane."

Emmylou's heart was thundering in her chest. Silence buzzed on the end of the line.

"I didn't mean to upset you, Emmylou. I was simply hoping that you had finally made a good decision in regards to your personal life."

"Sorry to disappoint you again, but there is absolutely nothing between me and Shane Newbury but a shared animosity. Looks like your darling daughter has screwed up again."

"That's not what I said, but I know what a hard time you've had with the men you've chosen to date, and I wanted you to finally get one you could be happy with."

"No, Mother. You wanted one that *you* could be happy with."

"That's not true."

"I've got to go, Mom. I'll talk to you later." Emmylou hung up without saying goodbye. She dropped the phone back in its cradle and leaned against the doorway. She knew her mother only wanted the best for her. She could hear it in her voice. She didn't mean to be critical, but the way that she said it grated on Emmylou's pride. She jammed her hands through her hair, sliding them to the base of her neck.

Her life was a disaster. Everything that she touched turned to crap. Maybe she should buy a cabin in the middle of nowhere and live out the rest of her days alone. The knock at her door brought an ironic smile. She wanted to be by herself right now, but there were only two people in the world who knocked on her door instead of ringing the doorbell.

"Hey." Scarlett's dark head popped inside when she pushed the door open. She kicked the snow from her boots and stepped inside holding a paper sack. "What's the matter?" Without removing her boots like she normally did, she walked across the floor, dropped the sack in the chair and wrapped Emmy in a tight hug.

"Oh, nothing. I was just thinking about running away from home."

Scarlett pulled away and looked into Emmy's eyes. "Why? What happened?"

Emmylou closed her eyes and shook her head, still trying to wrap her mind around the trouble she was in. "I think I may have to close the bakery. Well, at least the production side anyway."

93

"It isn't doing well? I thought it was starting to take off."

Emmylou and Scarlett went over to the couch where she proceeded to tell her everything that had happened today.

"That was one heck of a day. I can't believe your mother actually said those things to you. Well, I can. But still. Didn't your father tell her about the trouble with the loan?"

Emmylou shrugged. "I don't know. Even if he did, that would only encourage her to push me toward marrying the good doctor. Maybe I should. Do you think he has any money?" She half-groaned, half-laughed and scrubbed her hands over her face, then walked to the cabinet to get another wine glass for Scarlett. While she poured, Scarlett took her coat and boots off and wrapped her legs beneath her.

"Thank you. So what are you going to do? Do you think you can get another loan?"

Emmylou propped her elbow on the back of the couch and rested her head in her hand. "I'm going to try. I won't go down without a fight. I can't let everybody down like that. Lorie has worked so hard to get that place running smoothly." She took a sip of her wine. "It seems so unfair to her and the whole crew."

Scarlett got a funny, far-away look while she sipped her wine. She nodded a couple of times. "Oh, I brought you something." Scarlett went to the sack she had brought and pulled a glass container from it. Emmy could only guess what was inside; the waxed paper was hiding the contents. Scarlett opened it and held it out. "Chocolate covered strawberries. All of it is organic."

The scrumptious scent of fruit and chocolate wafted up, making Emmylou's mouth water. She plucked one of the gigantic berries out. "These look like edible art, Scar."

"Oh, pshaw." Scarlett placed the container on the coffee table and settled back onto the couch. Her cheeks bloomed red. "I also brought you some more packets of the tea you like."

The strawberry burst in her mouth when she bit into it, and the chocolate melted to blend into an intoxicating combination. She licked the corner of her mouth and held the treat at an angle to keep it from dripping on her.

Scarlett grew her own strawberries. She was an amazing gardener and herbalist. She had two greenhouses just south of The Dove House, Lacy's bed and breakfast, where she mostly tinkered with her plants and sold to the locals. She also worked for Lacy in the kitchen most days and sometimes as a fill-in maid or front desk clerk. Scarlett was happy with her quiet and simple life. It hadn't always been so quiet or simple.

Emmy finished the strawberry, then helped herself to five more while they talked of other things. Scarlett still had that distant, thoughtful look when she left, but Emmylou knew better than to prod her about it. Scarlett was an old soul who preferred to keep things inside until she had fully processed them. The time would come for them to discuss what was on her mind.

*****

Three a.m. came too early for Emmylou. She hadn't slept well, but the muffins and pastries wouldn't bake themselves. The morning routine was just that; routine. She didn't mention anything to Lindy. They simply went about business as usual. Even though Emmy couldn't get her dilemma off her mind, she tried to act as normally as possible. And when Lindy brought up the making of her wedding cake, Emmy only paused for a moment to sweep away the thought that she would probably be baking and decorating it from her home kitchen after this place shut down.

"I've got a great sketch up in the office of what you told me you wanted. You can go in and grab the book if you want."

Emmylou finished packaging the items she was going to take out to The Dove House like she did every Sunday. She was closing the box when a breathless squeal announced Lindy's foray back into the kitchen holding the sketch book.

"This is going to be the best cake you've ever made!" Lindy's eyes were still focused on the page, so she didn't see Emmylou's sad smile. "It's exactly what I want. Four tiers. Flowers cascading. Oh, Emmy. Thank you." Lindy's eyes glistened with tears when she looked up. She pulled Emmylou into a hug and sniffed at her shoulder.

"I haven't made it yet." Emmy returned the embrace wholeheartedly. She worried she was holding on too long and putting too much of her worries into it, but if she was, Lindy didn't notice. When she pulled back, the grin splitting her face made Emmy sick to her stomach. What if she couldn't deliver on her promise? All of her promises? Emmylou couldn't stand the thought of Lindy losing her job just as she was starting a new life with her husband. She should have the security of her employment.

"I'm going to put this back and get out front. The morning rush will be here soon." Lindy hugged the book to her chest and gave Emmylou one last hopeful smile.

Emmylou loaded the back of her SUV and set off for her deliveries. She only had three stops, and The Dove House was her last one. She parked in front of the steps and bundled her scarf tighter around her neck before opening the hatch.

"Hey, you! I want you to know I've called the cops."

Emmylou grinned and kept sliding boxes forward, listening to the thudding of footsteps on the wooden stairs.

"We don't take kindly to trespassers around here."

She looked up, straightened and dropped her hands on her hips. "Well, then they'll be here just in time to haul you away." She paused a second to narrow her eyes in her best attempt at a threatening stare, then threw her arms out for a hug. "What was your name again?"

"I've had so many I can't remember."

Emmylou returned the bear hug she was receiving. "It's good to see you again, Kyle. Welcome home." He kissed her cheek and released her. "How long are you here for this time?"

Kyle grabbed two boxes in each hand. "For good, I hope."

"Be careful with that one on the bottom. I'm sure Lacy was glad to hear that."

"Lacy who? You know I only have eyes for you, beautiful."

Kyle's grin was contagious and larger than normal. Impending fatherhood agreed with him. She clapped his broad shoulder with her gloved hand and joined him in walking into the house. They went to the large dining room, and Emmylou retrieved the silver platters from the antique buffet.

"It's going to be a busy day today. Did you bring the cake?"

Emmylou shook her head. Kyle was never this enthusiastic about hosting events at the house. He didn't like crowds and was mildly suspicious of everyone. After what happened last fall to Lacy, who could blame him? It really shakes one's trust when your assistant takes the one you love hostage and tries to kill her. "That's why I told you to be careful with the bottom box."

"Oh." He slid the top box off and opened the one containing the cake. "This looks great. You're going to make every one of my son's birthday cakes, right?"

Emmylou paused in her stacking of the muffins to look at Kyle. "Son?" At the mention of the word, Kyle turned into a glowing Halloween pumpkin.

"Kyle McClintock!"

Both Emmy and Kyle jerked their heads to the doorway where Lacy was entering the room. Her stomach was finally starting to grow. Emmylou had never seen her look more content or more beautiful. "Son?" Emmy repeated to Lacy.

Lacy rolled her eyes and continued walking until she stood with her arm resting on Kyle's. "I let him watch the ultrasound, and he's certain we're having a boy."

"Well, honey, it's my child, so if it were a boy it would be obvious. And believe me, I've seen it. It's a boy."

Lacy looked at Emmylou and shook her head. Emmy was thoroughly enjoying the two of them squabble. It was adorable and refreshing. She had never seen a married couple completely enjoy each other's company like the two of them did. Her own parents acted as though every time they were together they were conducting a business meeting. It was no wonder she was an only child. Another one had never been on the agenda.

"Yes, my darling. I'm sure you're right."

"I'm glad we can agree on that." Kyle kissed his wife, making her blush. "I'm going to check on the kitchen."

The women watched him leave, drawing closer together.

"Now I understand about the birthday party." The two women leaned against each other. "He's practicing for the future."

Lacy picked up a muffin and began arranging them. "It's the craziest thing. Since he got back from selling his house in Garberville, he's been as giddy as a billy goat in green grass. I'm just glad he's excited about hosting a seven-year old's birthday party today. You know how he is with commotion around here."

Emmylou offered her friend an understanding grimace. She knew everyone was still recovering from last fall's incident. She didn't think Lacy would ever be the same. It had left scars. Deep ones. Emmylou knew *she* would never look at the world the same after having seen a lifeless body impaled on a garden sun dial when the woman fell from a second story window.

"You would think after working on a dozen movie sets, he wouldn't flinch when a door slammed or an unfamiliar car pulled into the driveway." Lacy frowned at the muffins.

"Real life is different. There's no director around to yell cut." Emmylou recoiled at her own comment.

Lacy tucked her arm around Emmylou's waist. "Kyle hates Marcus for what he did to you."

"I appreciate that, but he doesn't need to. I think deep down I knew it could never work out with him. I'm a small town girl who never wants to leave, and he's a top-drawer director. You couldn't find a more incompatible pair."

"That doesn't make it any easier."

"I know."

A family of four walked into the room, and Lacy smiled and greeted them, took their order and went back to the kitchen where Mrs. Walters was cooking. Emmylou offered them a muffin and made small talk about where they were from and what they were doing in town. She had to dodge some of the questions they asked about Kyle, though. Obviously they were fans who were unaware he had no plans to make another movie any time soon. Perhaps never again. She happily turned over hostess duties to Lacy when she got back.

Emmylou hadn't intended to stay all morning, but Lindy's text informing her that it wasn't too busy at the bakery was all the encouragement she needed. Emmy needed the comfort of being around her friends in one of her most favorite places.

She helped Lacy put up streamers and bundle balloons, then put together the cake and punch table. She was grateful for the distraction. For an hour she didn't think about losing everything and putting over thirty people out of work. They were hanging the birthday banner over the fireplace when Scarlett walked in with a steaming plate in her hand.

"Time for your breakfast Mrs. McClintock," she gibed and placed it on the nearest table.

"Oh, thanks, doll." Lacy dropped the banner and made a beeline to the food.

"Hey!" Emmylou had to gather the end before almost dropping it into the flame.

"I'll help." Scarlett was already underneath Emmy, ready for her end of the banner.

"Sorry," Lacy spoke over a mouthful of eggs.

"No problem. I can see that we don't want to stand between a pregnant lady and a meal."

Scarlett and Emmylou finished up while Lacy scarfed her breakfast down. Kyle returned just in time to see Lacy wiping her plate clean with the remaining scrap of toast.

"Glad to see you're feeding my son." He kissed the top of her head, then transferred his attention to the room. "Good job, ladies. It looks like a party supply store threw up in here. It's perfect."

Scarlett and Emmylou moved the chairs back and joined the couple at the table.

"How generous are you two feeling toward me right now?" Kyle glanced from Scarlett to Emmylou.

"After your comment about our decorating, I'd say you're pretty low on our priorities list. Why?"

"Betty and Badger need an outing, and I don't like Lacy to ride very much right now. I've been taking them in turns, but with the party today, Lacy needs the extra hands. Are you two up for it?"

Scarlett and Emmylou exchanged looks.

"Or you can stay here and help with the party. Sixteen seven-year-olds." Kyle nodded slowly and widened his eyes. "All hopped up on punch and cake." He waved his hand. "You know what? I think I will take them out."

"NO!" they answered in unison.

"We can do it," Emmy finished, and Scarlett nodded in agreement.

"You're saints." Kyle grinned and his killer-blue eyes sparkled.

"You're not." Emmy rolled her eyes.

Chapter 11

Damn that Kyle McClintock! No wonder he had won every award under the sun and the devotion of millions of fans. He grinned, twinkled and arched a brow and got usually sane women to agree to anything.

Emmylou was still grumbling when she stuck her foot in Betty's stirrup and settled into the saddle. They were shorter than she needed, but she knew they wouldn't be running or jumping fences with all the snow on the ground. A little exercise was all the horses needed today.

"Tell me again why we are doing this?" Emmy turned to Scarlett when she stopped Badger next to Betty.

"Because we're amazing friends." Scarlett adjusted her stocking cap and tugged her gloves up. "And because Kyle McClintock is a manipulative jerkface."

Emmylou returned Scarlett's annoyed grin. "It's just a good thing we love him so much."

Scarlett agreed and nudged Badger forward.

Once they were outside, it wasn't as bad as Emmylou had thought it would be. The ground was still stable, not too much ice, and the air was crisp, but the sun was warm. Both she and Scarlett were swimming in the coveralls they had borrowed from Kyle, but Lacy's would have been too small. Emmy's hands were wrapped in fleece-lined, leather gloves which made it difficult to know how tightly she was gripping the reins. Betty would let her know if she was getting out of hand.

They headed north on the road leading out from The Dove House and stuck to the gravel until meeting the convoy of pick-ups headed out for the birthday party. They decided to go through the fence and out into the pasture. Scarlett's greenhouses were tucked into the background fifty yards from a stand of cedar trees.

"How are your crops doing?" Emmy looked like a steam kettle when she spoke.

"They're doing really well. I've propagated a new variety of strawberry that is supposed to be good for jams. Super sweet so you don't have to add any extra sugar."

"Was that what you brought to me last night?"

"No, those were the *Fragaria Virginiana.* My new berries are a type of Alpine, *Fragaria vesca 'Alexandria'.*"

"I love when you talk garden nerd to me," Emmylou cooed.

"Really? Well then, let me tell you all about this batch of compost I'm making."

Their giggles echoed over the hills.

The next moment, an icy blade of fear sliced down Emmylou's spine and into her gut. She jerked harshly on Betty's reins, apologizing when the mare jolted to a stop. "Did you hear that?"

Badger stopped too. Scarlett was wide-eyed, her breathing quick and shallow. She twisted in her saddle, scanning the white tundra for the animal they were both certain they had heard. Emmylou looked in the other direction. Her gaze examined the patch of trees, the hay bales and the grooves of the hills searching for movement, for fur, for anything suspicious. The horses shifted nervously, flicking their tails. Betty's ears perked straight up, and she raised her head.

Emmylou finally let loose the air she had held, trying to calm her panicked nerves. "I think we're –"

The unmistakable scream of a cougar rent the air, and Emmy's insides turned to ice. Scarlett whimpered. Emmy was pretty sure she had made the same noise. She was having a hard time keeping Betty under control. The mare spun and shifted. A direct reaction to Emmylou's terror.

"Okay." Her voice shook. "Do you see where it is?"

"No," Scarlett's breathless answer worried Emmy. Her friend's face matched the snow, and her sea green eyes resembled silver dollars. Emmy knew she must look about the same.

"From the sound of it, I don't think it's closer than a couple hundred yards." Emmylou tried to steady her voice. She patted Betty's neck and cooed, trying to calm her. "I think it's to the south of us, so we're going to need to cut through Mrs. Walter's field and take the long way back."

"Okay. That sounds good to me."

Scarlett probably would have agreed to strip naked and streak through a packed football stadium if she had thought it would get her out of here safely. Emmylou would have, too.

Emmy's alertness was at a twelve on a scale of one to ten as she and Scarlett nudged their horses into a walk. She knew better than to tear out of there like their hair was on fire. The giant cat would surely give chase. They tried to act as normally as possible, even though Emmy's heart was about to pop out of her throat.

Every nerve in her body started to tingle, and her chest tightened. She turned in her saddle. And all hell broke loose. She cried out and the horse launched forward – or the horse launched and she cried. The cougar was right behind them! It's sleek, powerful body was gaining ground. Emmylou's body was going to break apart if she continued to flail in the saddle while Betty charged across the prairie. She wasn't sure if the pounding was her horse, Scarlett's horse or the cougar. With a herculean effort, she got herself under control, gripped the horse with her thighs, loosened the reins and hunched low over her neck. Finally, she could glance to her sides to find Scarlett. First right, then left. No Scarlett!

Emmylou craned her neck to see behind her. She scanned the area, but there was no sign of her friend. Betty kept her pace at a full run while Emmy did her best to search the area for any sign of Scarlett or Badger. Nothing.

"Whoa!" She yelled and pulled the reins, slowing Betty. The cougar would just have to take her on. Except there was no giant cat behind her readying itself to pounce. "What the hell?" she spoke to the wind.

Betty was heaving and adjusting the bit, skittering beneath her. "Sorry, girl." Her glove patted the lather at the mare's neck. She squinted and hooded her eyes from the sun, scanning the wide-open prairie. Her fear competed with her good sense, almost winning. Her face scrunched with building tears. Where was Scarlett?

Emmylou clapped her hand over her quivering mouth. "Oh, God. No." *The canyon,* she finished silently. Her anguish tripled. She directed Betty to the southwest and prayed she was wrong as the mare ran over the hard ground kicking up snow and dirt. Emmy wasn't just scared for Scarlett; she was scared Betty would hit ice and break her leg, but she had to hurry. She would risk it if she could save Scarlett.

She tried her best to pick the path that would keep them both safe on her way to the canyon. Betty was moving too fast for Emmylou to see the ground properly and check for tracks. She was going with her gut on this one. When they reached the ridge, she stopped Betty to scan the area for Badger and Scarlett. Scarlett was an accomplished rider having grown up on a ranch with her grandfather working her half to death every day. Emmylou knew she would still be mounted and riding... unless.

Before she could control it, a graphic image of Scarlett being attacked by the cougar flashed through her mind. She swallowed hard and closed her eyes against the vision. Her hands were shaking, but she gripped the reins and kicked Betty into action. She leaned back in the saddle trying to distribute her weight so Betty could handle the steep path down to the bottom of the canyon. They zigzagged down the fifty feet to the base. The ground was hard and uneven. It was a difficult task, but they finally made it.

Emmylou pointed Betty in the direction of the place she knew Scarlett would go if she had been forced to come down here. They had ridden here many times over the years. Lacy's mother had been obsessed with horses – rather, stablemen – but the job of keeping the horses in shape had fallen to the girls.

Emmylou stuck to the middle of the broad-based canyon in case the cat was lurking, waiting to pounce from above. She knew better than to start yelling for Scarlett. She tried to move quietly. Every nerve was razor sharp and standing on edge. She was scared the cougar would be able to hear her raging heart, but she kept on until she reached the area where she had been hoping to find Scarlett.

"*Scarlett.*" She used a hoarse whisper and advanced on the brush covered cliff. There was a cutout large enough for a couple of horses that they had used as kids to hide from Steve the horse trainer. Scared of what she would find, hopeful it would just be a scared Scarlett, she moved forward calling for her friend again. If she had been cold earlier, she was now a human furnace. Sweat trickled down her temples and neck. She pulled her scarf free.

Emmylou and Betty both jolted with the crunch of branches and pulled back. She forced the horse, and herself, to hold their ground. Her breath stalled and her body trembled, but she stayed.

"Scarlett." Relief poured out of her when her friend rode Badger out of hiding, unharmed, from the thicket. "Oh my God." Three red, swollen and bloody scratches striped Scarlett's cheek.

"It's fine. It's from the stupid tumbleweeds covering the cavern. I hauled ass inside just in case the cougar was still following me." She swiped at the blood with her glove. "Ouch. Is it bad?"

"Not really. It just scared me." Emmylou looked around, worried that the giant cat was close by. "Do you know where it went?"

Scarlett chewed on her bottom lip and looked in the opposite direction. "No. We'd better get out of here and back to the barn. We have to call Game and Parks to report it."

They decided to head further south in the canyon before climbing out and going back to The Dove House. Once on top they picked up their pace, but the scattering of ice pockets near the stream forced them to slow and change directions. They couldn't risk injuring the animals.

A chill ran through Emmylou when they started to pass a grove of trees. She wished they could stay in the open of the prairie, but the snow hadn't melted and formed ice in the grove, so it was the only path to take. The horses' ears perked with the sound of cracking branches. Emmy and Scarlett sat straighter and started a targeted inspection of the trees and tundra while moving forward. The nervousness of the horses was cause for alarm. The cracking was too close to be coincidence. Emmylou looked above and to the side, then let out a yell, spurring Betty into action moments before the cougar screamed and launched itself from the branch, landing feet behind the horses.

The hooves pounded the ground as Scarlett and Emmylou ran them, hell bent on breaking from the tree cover. The cougar would be too fast for them once they hit open ground, but Emmy didn't know what else to do. Betty was leading, Badger close behind, when they charged from the trees and sped toward home. She didn't dare look behind her; she just prayed for a miracle that the cat would lose interest or they would outrun it or anything to get them home and safe.

She could hear Scarlett yelling for the horses to go faster, and soon Badger was outpacing Betty. Emmylou felt the change in direction as Scarlett took the lead. Fear simmered in her brain, but she let Betty follow. A white barn appeared on the horizon, and Emmylou cried out in relief. God help them get to it in time.

The report from a rifle echoing across the prairie drew Emmylou and Scarlett's attention, slowing the horses. The two women frantically searched the area. Blood was charging through Emmylou's veins; she was still panicked the cougar would pounce with them stopped. Suddenly her attention landed on a man covered head to toe in winter gear and carrying a rifle, running toward them.

"Are you all right?" He was panting hard through the fleece face mask. He had to be in great shape to traverse the uneven ground as quickly as he was.

Emmylou looked down at him, her reflection in his sunglasses. She didn't like what she saw. "I think so." She swallowed back her own panting and looked to Scarlett who had a hand pressed to her chest. Her stunned gaze was fixed at the ground behind Emmylou. She turned and quailed. Fifteen feet from where the horses were fidgeting was the lifeless body of the cougar lying on its side in the snow, blood oozing from its neck. She stared in horror at what could have happened. Thirty more seconds and that animal would have brought her horse down.

"I heard the lion's scream earlier and went out looking for it."

Emmylou drug her attention back to the man. He had pulled the mask down and propped his sunglasses on his head. He was resting his rifle against his leg, still trying to catch his breath. He came closer, placed a firm hand on Betty's nose and murmured to her. She instantly obeyed his commands to settle down.

"Thank you. I don't know what..." She looked back at the animal at a loss as how to finish that sentence.

"You saved us," Scarlett said. "Thank you."

"It was nothing. I'm sure Emmylou could've handled a measly old mountain lion."

Emmy snapped her gaze back to the man's face, noticing the chin dimple. Recognition hit her, and she ducked her head and looked away. "Damn," she mumbled under her breath. In all the chaos, she hadn't realized who her champion was.

"I'm sure glad you're a good shot." Scarlett had taken her hat off and was tugging her hair out of her face. Her hands were shaking, and she was struggling with the routine task.

Emmylou discovered she was shaking from head to toe, too. The adrenaline from the terrifying chase was beginning to dissolve now that her heart rate was slowing. A hand landed on her knee. She snapped her head and found Shane Newbury looking up at her.

"Are you sure you're all right?"

An insult shot to the tip of her tongue, but logic and manners had her swallowing it. "Yes. I'm fine. Thank you."

She met his gaze. The instant they connected, her heart thumped hard. She melted into the bronze-flecked depths staring at her in earnest. His eyes spoke to her soul, and what they said was wreaking havoc on her resolve to hate him. Even with her layers of clothing his palm was radiating heat through her body. Her limbs were turning to jelly.

"What the hell were you doing out there? You should know better."

Emmylou bristled at his criticism. "We were exercising the horses. They needed it."

"Well, if you anything, you would know never to go out without protection. You could've gotten yourselves killed!" Shane backed away and ran his hand over his mouth and chin.

"We were handling it! I didn't know there was a mountain lion in the area! Don't you think we would have been more careful had we known?" Emmylou's cheeks were hot with anger and shame. She knew he was right, but it didn't make him less of an ass.

"With you? No, I don't think you would have been more careful. I think you thrive on being careless. I think you don't care about anyone else, and you don't pay attention to anything outside of your own mind." His dark eyes were like daggers, and his face was harsh with anger.

"How dare you talk to me that way! You don't know anything about me."

Shane looked taken aback with that statement. He shifted his attention to the ground before returning it to her. Her anger with him dropped a notch with the expression on his face. Betty shifted beneath her, bringing Emmy closer to Shane.

"You're right. I don't know you that well and I…" He swallowed hard and wrinkled his forehead. It looked like he had tears welling in his eyes. But it may have been a trick of the sun. "I was out of line. I'm sorry."

"It's okay. We're all upset and emotions were running high."

Shane nodded, jerkily, keeping his gaze averted. "I'd better get the cat loaded in my truck. You'll want to cool the horses down and check them for injury. You two were riding hell bent for election out there on some pretty dangerous ground."

Emmylou nodded. How could he be so rational at a time like this? With one last glance, she watched him walk the short distance to the dead cougar. When she looked back to Scarlett, she found her friend tilting her head and inspecting her with a thoughtful smile.

"What?" Emmylou cleared her throat when it squeaked.

"Nothing." Scarlett's tone said it was much more than nothing.

Emmy's cheeks burned and she urged Betty to move forward.

*****

Shane watched Emmylou and Scarlett trot across the frozen ground. His body started to tremble. He hadn't realized how upset he had gotten about the incident. He raised his hand to wipe the sweat from his upper lip and inhaled horse. He blinked and shook his head with the shock of emotion that fragrance caused. He hadn't had contact with a horse since two weeks after Katie's accident, when he sold his stallion.

Shane inspected the giant cat with mild regret for having had to bring it down. It was a full-grown female. He wrinkled his forehead and twisted his mouth, then looked up. He probed the landscape looking for cubs. That was the only answer for why the cat had given such an aggressive chase to Emmylou and Scarlett. These solitary creatures were fiercely protective of their cubs. The two women must have come too close to the animal's daybed and stirred up her protective instincts. And with it being winter, she was most likely teaching her cubs how to hunt. Food was scarce, and two horses would have been a welcome meal.

How could they have been so stupid? Out here alone and unarmed? Now that the ordeal was over, his rage was inflating by the second. They could have been seriously hurt. Or worse. He swallowed hard and squeezed his eyes shut trying to get a grip on his rioting emotions. If he had come across them even five minutes later, it would have been too late. *So stupid!*

The thought of losing another woman to a horrible accident made Shane physically ill. He couldn't live with that. No person should have to endure that kind of pain once, let alone twice. His eyes flew open, and he found himself hunched over with his hands on his knees.

What was he thinking? He didn't have Emmylou. She wasn't his… anything. He took several deep breaths to balance his erratic breathing. He told himself that it was just the memories of Katie's broken and bleeding body that were bringing about this response to the mountain lion chase. The two incidents were close in nature, and it was dragging up things he didn't want to ever live through again. Things he had shoved to the back of his mind and buried beneath an iron will to live on.

He cradled the heavy cat and trudged back to his truck with his rifle strapped across his back. He slid the cat into the bed and slammed the tailgate. Emmylou's screams were echoing on the edge of his mind, but he was practiced at controlling his thoughts. They stayed on the fringes, along with the images of his fiancé and out of control horses, while he drove the half-mile back to his home.

He hadn't told the truth when he had explained that he was out looking for the mountain lion. In truth, he had heard screams first and picked up two names on the wind; Scarlett and Emmylou. It was a lucky thing that he had been on his way to his truck to drive into town when he heard it. He always kept a rifle in his vehicle. A habit never lost from growing up on a farm. He never wanted to pass up an opportunity to shoot a coyote or rabbit.

He hadn't made it far into the pasture behind his house when he had caught sight of the racing horses and the women holding on for dear life. In the next instant, he had identified the mountain lion and was launching out of his truck with the rifle. Instinct had taken over at that point because he couldn't remember pulling the trigger or hitting the cat. But thank God that he had.

He parked in the drive, all thoughts of the meal he had been craving when he left the house gone. He was going to be spending the afternoon with the Game and Parks Commission now that he had illegally harvested an animal that had only recently been moving into the Plains of Nebraska.

With a sigh he searched for the correct number and dialed the phone. He explained the situation to two people before being connected with someone who could actually help.

"Yes, Mr. Andrews. That's right. I have it in the back of my truck." Shane held the phone in one hand and retrieved a beer from his refrigerator with the other. "Really? I wasn't sure about the laws –" Shane paused to listen to the officer explain. "I can assure you she was threatening the women."

They talked a few minutes longer about mothers and cubs and so forth before setting up a time for Mr. Andrews to come out and interview Shane and dispose of the animal properly. The beer was refreshing but not soothing his raw nerves like he had hoped. If he didn't have to go into the clinic first thing in the morning he would sit and drink himself into a coma, but he had never been one to handle his liquor well, and he was the only doctor in town.

Chapter 12

Valentine's Day was a mere five days away, and Emmylou was running around like a chicken with its head cut off. Bake My Day had set a new record for the number of monster heart cookies ordered, easily outstripping last year by triple. It was the second Valentine's Day for the production bakery, and internet sales were climbing every hour. That radio ad was really paying off. Thank goodness, since it had cost a small fortune to produce and air.

Lorie was calling her every twenty minutes with the reports. This was unbelievable – better than her wildest dreams. And it could all end. The enormity of that fact hadn't fully sunk in. She was still hopeful that it was going to work out. After this week she would sit down and start making contacts for money. Someone would find this a viable business. They wouldn't let it go under.

She weaved between the chairs with the tray balanced in her hand, delivering orders to her customers and making small talk. Inside she was screaming that she didn't have time; she needed to be in the back getting the ovens going so they could make all these confections that were being ordered. She should be checking with her trucking company about ETAs and making sure they had enough packaging supplies, because if not, they would have to be overnight shipped at an astronomical cost. But she made time for everyone in her bakery, smiled warmly and chatted about the snow pack in Wyoming being able to feed the river this year.

She delivered the last espresso and tucked the brown tray under her arm, heading back to the kitchen. All the things on her mind had presented themselves in a scowl.

"Hello, there."

The voice drew her up short.

"Whoa. You look like you're beatin' the Dutch." Evan

Matthews stood up, studying her thoughtfully. His intense green gaze was hypnotic.

Emmylou knew she must look awful. She hadn't slept at all last night after her ordeal with the cougar. And Shane Newbury. She caught her chaotic strands of hair and tucked them behind her ear. "It's a busy week, and I could use about ten more workers."

Evan's lopsided smile charmed her. "Ah, yes. Valentine's Day. A baker's worst nightmare. The only thing worse is the June wedding cake season."

Emmy laughed and shifted the tray in front of her. "Yeah. Listen, I know we had scheduled dinner for Tuesday, but I don't think I'm going to be able to swing it this week. I forgot all about how busy this week is for me, and with the way things are going, I'm probably going to end up in the production house slinging frosting every night this week."

He placed a large hand on her bicep. "I understand."

She usually didn't welcome physical contact by complete strangers, but there was something about him that seemed sincere and harmless. Of course, that was how most of her bad relationships had started out, a seemingly innocent man flashing a smile at her.

She backed away and he dropped his hand, unfazed by her action. "I'm glad you understand. I'll message you with another time." She took a step around him but was halted by his tall frame moving in front of her.

"Actually, if you need the help." He shrugged and ducked his head. Once again she was caught up in his mossy gaze. "I'm just barkin' at knots out at the ranch. I'd love the opportunity to observe the master in her element."

Maybe it was the old-fashioned way he talked, or maybe it was her desperation, but she didn't consider his offer for more than five seconds. "Really? I can't pay you more than eight-fifty an hour."

"You don't have to pay me anything. Call it an internship." He drew up her right hand and cradled it between his.

She felt the pink creep into her cheeks. His warm hand sent

vibrations up her arm. "I couldn't ask you to do that."

"It would be an honor to work under you."

She puckered up her mouth and regarded him from beneath lowered lashes. She made a disgruntled humming noise through her curving lips. "I'm still going to pay you something. I couldn't live with myself."

Evan chuckled. He kept her hand in his and shook it playfully in his excitement. "Great!"

"Go to the kitchen and get yourself an apron. Lindy will show you around."

"I won't let you down." He tugged her closer and planted a kiss on her cheek. "Thank you, Miss Bennett. You don't know what this means to me."

The feel of his lips on her skin shocked and pleased her. It had been a long time since a man had appreciated something she had done for him. She watched Evan strut back behind the counter and into the kitchen with a feeling of satisfaction. Why couldn't all men be that kind to her? Really, was it too much to ask?

She was interrupted from further introspection by the vibrating phone in her apron pocket. The text read *"911"*. It was from Lorie. Emmy cursed under her breath. Lorie never sent messages like that. The woman was always full of positivity. Emmylou was praying that Lorie was just stressed out. Lord knew *she* was on the edge of sanity.

She swung the door open, laying the tray down and jerking off her apron in one motion. "Evan, looks like you're getting tested on your first day. I've got to go to the production facility and see what's going on. You think you can handle it?"

"Of course boss lady. We got this." He barely looked up from the trays he was arranging. Emmy wondered where he had found the ball cap he was now wearing; not that it mattered. He was looking as good as one of the strawberry popovers he was handling. She jumped out of the way of Lindy pushing a cart. She rolled her eyes at Emmylou and Emmy snickered. "Sorry," she said out of the corner of her mouth.

"It's fine. He's actually pretty good in the kitchen. I still think he's weird, but I'll manage until you get back."

"I know you will, doll." Emmylou patted Lindy's shoulder and swept to the back door.

Steve had been out to Prairie Goodness early this morning to plow the new snow off the parking lot. She parked at the end and hustled inside, on the lookout for billowing smoke or an ambulance. So far it all looked normal.

Even though she had walked into this building hundreds of times, she never grew tired of the heavy fragrance of sugar, flour and vanilla. She had recently installed a new conveyor system to make it easier for the decorators to get the finished product to the packaging area. She had looked into revolution ovens to amp up production, too, but honestly she hadn't thought her little Midwestern business would take off quite this fast.

Emmylou hadn't made it fifteen feet into the building when Lorie rushed up to her.

"I got your text. What's wrong?"

Lorie grabbed her by the shoulders, her brown eyes frantic like a cornered animal. "Oven number four has broken down. It was working fine this morning, but Angie went to take out the batch of cookies, and they were just puddles of semi-cooked dough."

"Okay. I'll take a look at it. It's probably a breaker or something. We've been working them pretty hard."

"I've already had Wes here looking at it. I wouldn't have troubled you, but he says it's the heating element. It's toast."

"Shit." This was bad. This meant a whole new oven. The two women hurried back to where the cluster of ovens was located. Angie was standing back, biting her thumb nail.

"I'm so sorry, Emmylou. The timer went off and I opened the door, but when I reached for the sheet, they weren't done. I thought I had accidentally shut it off or something, but we've tried everything."

Emmylou rubbed Angie's arm. "It's not your fault. These things happen." She tried to silence her inner panic by projecting a calm and authoritative front. She hoped it was working because she was freaking out about being an oven down during her busiest time of the year. Emmy looked down at the parts scattered across the floor. Wes's large and very fit body was half inside the oven. "Thanks for coming to take a look, Wes."

He ducked out of the appliance and stood up with a wavy metal piece in his hand. He shook his dark hair away from his face and grimaced. "It's no big deal. I'm used to saving my big sister's butt." He grinned at Lorie, and she returned it with a less-than-impressed stare. "It looks like you're going to need a new oven. I'm not sure it's just the heating element that went bad. It may be the whole panel that went, frying the element."

Emmylou tugged at her bottom lip and nodded. "Okay, it's not even a year old. I'm sure it's still under warranty, but getting a new one or getting it fixed if we can is going to be a pain in the ass."

"Sorry to be the bearer of bad news." The manly dent in his chin was more pronounced with his dark stubble. Emmylou was sure he wasn't used to being out of the house at this hour, especially in the winter. He managed the implement dealership on the edge of town, and there wasn't as much call for tractors and combines in the winter.

"It's not your fault, either. I just appreciate you helping me out like this."

Wes placed the part with the others he had removed and wiped his hands on his jeans. "Let me know if you need anything else. The boys can hold down the dealership for a couple hours." He twisted his mouth and shrugged. "Any excuse to get out the poker table or build elaborate mouse traps out of scrap metal." He kissed Lorie on the cheek and told her he'd see her tonight for dinner. She answered back that Tucker had basketball practice after school, so he didn't need to pick him up until five-thirty.

Wes was the best brother in the entire world. He had picked up the slack when Lorie's husband had run off. Emmylou was pretty sure that had to be humbling to Lorie. She was the oldest in their family and Wes the youngest. That kind of role reversal upset the balance in sibling land. Not that Emmylou understood that much about siblings.

116

Emmy climbed the stairs to her office. This calamity was going to take the rest of the day.

Emmylou slammed the phone down on the desk. She had spent the majority of the last forty-five minutes on hold. In the four minutes when she had been able to talk to a human being and not an automated message, she had discovered that, while her oven was still under warranty, the repair man wouldn't be in the area for another four weeks. Nor would she be able to hire anyone locally since they were not "certified" and it would "void her warranty". She had been so angry that she screamed into the phone that the oven was already in several pieces on the floor, so she was pretty sure the warranty was already voided.

"Damn it," she hissed to the room and plunked her hands on her hips. She couldn't finish those orders without working the ovens – and her people – twenty-four hours a day. And she wouldn't ask them to do that. "Enter," she growled with the knock on her door.

Lorie stuck her head through the crack in the door. "What did you find out?"

Emmy dropped into her chair and rubbed her forehead. "We can't get anyone here for four weeks. "And with Cletus still recovering in Denver, there isn't another repairman available to get this thing going."

"Can't you get someone from Glenwood or even LaGrange?"

Emmy shook her head. "They don't have anyone available this week. Apparently there is a convention in Las Vegas, and they are all in attendance."

Lorie stepped into the room and shut the door. "I closed orders on the internet and called Lindy to tell her not to take any more at the bakery.

"Thank you. What a disaster."

"It's gonna be okay, Emmylou." Lorie sat in the folding chair by the door. "I'll stay late. Wes can take the kids. It's no big deal. We can get the orders out. I promise. I can get some of the others to pitch in and help too."

Emmylou drug her hands down her face and looked up at an

eager Lorie. Emmy was slumped in her chair, mentally exhausted. She picked at a small hole in her jeans. "It's worse than just the oven breaking down." She took a deep breath. She had to tell her manager about the bank situation. She forced herself to look Lorie in the eye. The woman had no idea, and Emmy's heart squeezed painfully. "Lorie... there's something I need to tell you."

The door to the office flew open, and Donnie Burton burst into the room. "We've got a problem!"

Emmylou stared at him for several seconds, not able to process. "What is it?"

"You'd better come and take a look."

Emmylou and Lorie followed Donnie down the steps and through the baking room to the refrigeration room. He pulled the handle on the galvanized steel door; the familiar whoosh of cool air hit her. Emmylou was about to ask what the problem was, but when she looked back up, a grey mouse scurried across the floor from a hundred pound sack of flour and disappeared between two sacks of sugar.

Both she and Lorie let out a scream. But hers wasn't in fear – it was in outrage.

"How did this happen?" she hissed.

"I'm not sure," Donnie replied, stepping inside the walk-in refrigerator.

Emmylou pulled air through her nose, keeping her mouth locked in case she was tempted to say something she would regret. She adjusted her shoulders in an attempt to relax them, but it was no use; she still felt strung tighter than a gallows rope after a hanging. She looked at the red numbers of the temperature gage on the wall. They looked okay. She followed Donnie inside as two more mice dodged between bags.

"Damn it!" Emmylou looked at the hundreds of bags of flour and sugar that she had just gotten in for this week. "We can't use any of these, can we?"

Donnie shook his head. A look of disbelief and defeat etched his face.

"Donnie, I want you to get on the phone to the supply company and rip them a new one. I want new supplies delivered today at no cost to us."

Donnie hesitated.

"What are you standing there for? We have got to get this replaced so we have a *chance* at getting our orders filled!"

"But Emmylou, we don't know if this is their fault or something that happened on our end."

Emmy ground her teeth and took two steps toward Donnie, about to grab him by the collar and shove him out the door, but she drew up short and slumped against the cold steel wall. "You're right." She dropped her head back and stared at the ceiling. "I need you to find out what happened, and I need you to do it now." She twisted her neck and sighed, forcing her brain to work. "What do we have left on the floor? And has it been tainted too?"

"No, everything out there is from last week's supplies. We have about three hundred pounds of sugar and maybe two hundred pounds of flour."

Emmy nodded. "Lorie, I need you to get on that fancy program of yours and find out what we can make to stretch that as far as we can and then tell the bakers."

Lorie took off to do as she was told.

"Donnie, do whatever it takes to get the answer to this." She wrinkled her face in disgust. "I'll be up in the office taking care of what I can. Let me know as soon as you figure it out."

Back in her office upstairs overlooking the production floor, Emmylou's first order of business was to make a fresh pot of coffee. While it brewed she stood at the window watching everyone working their stations. She had to regroup so she wouldn't be erratic when she started making phone calls. Finally, she pushed away from the sill and settled behind her metal desk. This office wasn't nearly as cluttered or as nice as her one at Bake My Day, but she wasn't here as often. Now, it looked like she would be spending the remainder of the week here.

She picked up the phone, paused, then dialed the familiar number.

*****

Shane told himself he was being stupid, that she didn't want to see him, and that she would most likely kick him right back out the door. But he entered the bakery anyway, and he even walked confidently to the counter. He had been worried about Emmylou and Scarlett after their run-in with the mountain lion yesterday. He had to check on her if he wanted to get any sleep tonight. He wouldn't admit that there was more to it than that. Not out loud anyway. He wasn't ready to deal with the torrent of emotions that Emmylou brought.

"Can I help you, sir?"

The sound of a man's voice snapped him out of his reverie. He did a double take to make sure he was in the right place. He finally focused on the tall man behind the counter. He had a red Huskers ball cap on, a freshly shaven face and interesting green eyes. Shane didn't like him. He looked shifty. "Where's Emmylou?"

The man sobered and straightened at Shane's tone. "Miss Bennett is unavailable. But I would be happy to get you anything you like."

Shane gave him another once-over. He really didn't like him. "I've never seen you in here before. How long have you worked here?" Since Shane was new to town, he didn't think he could ask the other questions swirling in his mind.

"About an hour, sir."

"Oh." Shane shifted. He didn't have a lot of time left before his next patient. "Can you tell me where I can find Emmylou? I'm a…" he choked, unable to find the right word, "friend of hers."

"I'm sorry, sir, I don't know when she will be back."

Shane narrowed his eyes at the smug man. "Well, that wasn't what I asked. Was it?"

Lindy, exiting the kitchen door with a tray of fresh cinnamon rolls, drew his attention. "Lindy. Where's Emmylou?"

She lowered the trays and slid them into the case. "Hey, Dr. Newbury. She had an emergency she needed to take care of."

"Oh my God." He was prepared to race all the way back to the clinic to help her.

"No." She shook her head and smiled ruefully. "Not that kind of emergency. She had to go out to the production facility to take care of something. She didn't say what."

"Oh, okay. Thanks for your help." Shane transferred his gaze back to the man at the cash register. "I didn't catch your name."

"I didn't give it to you."

Shane probably deserved that, but it didn't make him dislike the man any less. "I'm Shane Newbury." He held his hand out. The man looked at it, then accepted the handshake.

"I'm Evan Matthews."

"Nice to meet you, Evan." They released hands. "Would you mind getting me a large cup of coffee to go, please?"

"And Dr. Newbury likes half and half in it," Lindy added.

Shane grinned, but Lindy was bustling about, restocking shelves and moving empty trays.

"But no sugar." She pointed at Evan and disappeared to the back.

Evan moved to the coffee machine. "Just straight Columbian?"

"Yeah. I don't much care for that froufrou stuff the ladies like to serve." Shane dug in his pocket for his wallet. "So are you from Primrose, Mr. Matthews?"

"Mostly." Evan brought the paper cup and set a small white pitcher next to it. "I've got an aunt and uncle here. They raised me."

Shane understood about complex family matters; he saw them every day in Lincoln at the hospital, so he didn't press for any more information. He tossed two bills on the counter. "Thanks." He took an invigorating sip. He didn't know what Emmylou did to it, but the coffee here was magic, he'd swear to it.

When he got back to the clinic, he asked Abigail to pull Scarlett Pearson's file for him. After a surge of late morning patients, he found the file on his desk when he went to his office to have lunch. He flipped it open and found the phone number. At that moment his courage faded. He came up with every possible excuse not to dial it and ask the questions burning in his brain. He ate his entire turkey sandwich before allowing himself to think about calling again. Finally, after an intensive, name calling self-lecture, he punched in the numbers and waited.

"Hello?"

Her voice was sweet and cut to the tender scar of Katie's memory. It took him a moment to speak, and when he did, his voice was shaky. "Hi. Uh, Scarlett. Miss Pearson. This is Shane. Uh, Doctor Newbury that is."

Her soft laugh quickened his uneasiness. She reminded him so much of his darling fiancée. "Yes. And you can call me Scarlett, Doctor Newbury. I think after saving my life you are allowed to address me informally."

He let out a contorted, scoffing laugh and leaned over his desk. "Yeah. That's actually what I was calling about. I wondered if you were doing all right."

"I am. Thank you."

There was something in the way she said it. It was as if she knew he was avoiding asking about Emmylou and going to her instead. "That's good to hear. You know it may be a good idea to come into the clinic and have a check-up, just to see. Or to talk. I'd be happy to visit with you. That kind of stressful situation can have residual effects. Are you sleeping okay? Have you noticed a hypersensitivity to noise or uncomfortable situations?"

She laughed again. "I'm doing just fine Doctor. In fact, I met with the game warden this morning to discuss what happened."

"Glad to hear that, Scarlett. I've been worried. Well, not worried. Concerned. And I'm glad you met with him. He came and got the cat yesterday. So you and Emmylou met with him?"

"No. It was just me. Emmylou was busy, as usual." Again she was using that tone of knowledge. She must possess some kind of super power. Shane could just slap himself. This conversation was not going the way he had planned. He never played it as cool as he wanted.

"Did you know that mountain lion was a mother?"

He snapped his head up and stared hard at the wall across from him. Scarlett suddenly sounded so angry. "I knew she was a female, and Mr. Andrews and I thought perhaps she was protecting some cubs. We thought that might be why she came after the two of you so hard."

"Well, Mr. Andrews and I found them."

Shane narrowed his eyes in confusion. "Scarlett, if I hadn't killed her, she would have attacked you or Emmylou."

"Maybe. But did you have to murder her to do it? Couldn't you have shot at the ground in front of her? You could have scared her off instead of killing her."

This was not what he had expected. "Scarlett, she was just about to pounce. She wasn't more than ten feet from Emmylou's horse. She could have killed her. I had to do it."

"Three babies. She had three babies in a day bed in the canyon."

Shane didn't know what to say. He had done the right thing. But Scarlett was calling him a heartless murderer. "I'm sorry, but that's the way it is. She's an animal and you're people. People take precedence over wild animals."

"That's just the attitude the white men had about the buffalo. It doesn't matter. There are plenty of them. We can take what we want, do what we want without any concern to the animal or anyone else!"

Shane swallowed to keep himself from bursting out in defense. "Scarlett, I'm sorry that that was the way it happened. I assure you I'm not a heartless murderer. If there had been another way..." he faded off, not sure how to finish because he wasn't sure he would have done it differently. He had been taught the principles of hunting and shooting at an early age. It was second nature to him to take an animal that was a threat or that could be a meal.

He heard a sniffle and a sigh on the other end. "Scarlett?"

"I'm sorry, Doctor Newbury. I'm not trying to say you're a murderer. I know you did what you had to do, and believe me when I say that Emmylou and I are very grateful that you did, but Mr. Andrews and I went out to find the cubs." She hiccupped and sniffed again.

"Oh, I'm..." Shane was at a loss again. He had thought that perhaps the cubs hadn't made it. And he felt bad about it.

"No, no. They're fine. Actually, Mr. Andrews took them to a rehabilitation center for orphaned animals. He hopes they will grow and be released back into the wild." Scarlett's voice was still shaky but stronger.

"That's good to hear."

"You should tell my neighbor that."

Shane was surprised by the venom in her statement. "Why's that?"

"He said they should have destroyed the cubs. That they were a *parasite* and would only become a nuisance."

He would never tell Scarlett that he tended to agree with her neighbor, whoever that was. Mountain Lions were not native to Nebraska. They could get out of control easily and people were at risk. Instead, he answered, "Well, I'm sorry to hear that. I'm glad that you got them into the right hands and they will be taken care of."

"Thank you, Doctor Newbury."

"You're welcome. It's good to hear that you have recovered from your incident." He hesitated before he continued, but he couldn't stop himself from asking, "How is Emmylou faring?"

"Like she always does. She's a tough one to beat. She and Lacy have always been strong."

Shane smiled at the receiver. "There are all kinds of strength, Scarlett."

"Hmm."

She didn't believe him. Interesting. "Well, I'd better get back to work. It was nice talking to you."

"It was nice talking with you, too."

"Don't tell Emmylou I called and asked about her." Shane closed his eyes at his stupidity.

He could sense that she was perplexed by his comment. There was a loaded pause on her end of the phone. "Okay," she drawled.

"Bye." He hung up and swiveled his chair with his forehead resting in his palm. "That went well," he addressed his office.

Chapter 13

Scarlett and Lacy walking into her office was manna falling from heaven for Emmylou.

"The cavalry has arrived." Lacy, always meeting a problem like a general, marched to Emmy's desk with her arm in the air and her jaw set, her rounding stomach poking out between the buttons of her coat. The shirt that had been loose on her at Thanksgiving was stretched tight.

"Praise the Lord," Emmylou sighed in relief. "I've never asked you for a bigger favor."

"I don't think you've ever asked us for a favor." Lacy looked to Scarlett for confirmation.

"Not that I can recall. I'd say it's about time." Scarlett's pretty face was set in determination.

"You're the best friends in the world."

"And don't you forget it," Lacy teased.

The three women surveyed the staff on the floor and the data that Emmylou had in her hand. Lorie had switched up the baking schedule so the bakers could make the most of the supplies they had left. Right now that meant the only thing they were making were the personalized candies that sold by the dozen. It was also a tedious project for the decorators. But, really it was good that they were getting the hard stuff out of the way. Now if Emmylou could meet the rest of her orders, it would be nothing short of a miracle.

They weren't taking in any new orders, which was a shame. They were missing out on quite a chunk of revenue. Much needed revenue.

"How's this affecting your bottom line?" Lacy asked after talking with Maria about the process she used for cookie decorating.

Emmylou saw in her friend's eyes that she knew about the trouble Prairie Goodness was in. "It isn't good. I really don't know. We had more orders than I had expected. A bunch more, but if we can't fill them, the long term effects it might have on my reputation -" Emmy broke off, scowled and shrugged. "If we have to close, then it won't matter."

"Oh, you won't close. I'll see to it." Lacy was looking down the production line, so she missed the look on Emmylou's face. "Kyle and I will take care of it if you need us to."

"No!" Emmylou said it too loudly, drawing more than just Lacy's attention. She moved closer to a frowning Lacy and lowered her voice. "Lacy I don't want you bailing me out."

"It's not like that. What happened is a complete crock." Lacy's eyes were flashing, but not at Emmy.

"I know, but I couldn't take your money and go on being your friend. It would be something that hung over us all the time." Emmy touched Lacy's arm when she tried to object. "Believe me, no matter how we say it won't matter and that it won't change us, it will. It's not twenty dollars for dinner. We're talking ten thousand times that amount."

"Kyle has it." Lacy held Emmy's gaze for an extended moment. "Okay, but if it gets down to the wire, you promise me you'll let us help you any way we can. Promise me you won't let your dream die because you're too proud to borrow money from your friends. Besides, with as many times as you went to the theater to watch Kyle's movies, a sizeable chunk of his bank account belongs to you anyway."

They both laughed and did a sideways hug, squeezing each other's shoulders, and Emmy dipped her head to rest on the top of Lacy's. They straightened when Scarlett walked up with a clipboard in her hand.

"Donnie just told me that the staples will be delivered Wednesday, and they're discounting you thirty percent."

Anger flashed through Emmylou. "Thirty percent! They should be giving it to us, and they should be here tomorrow! They sold me tainted goods!"

Scarlett fidgeted and pursed her lips. "I don't think they did."

"Why do you say that?" Seeing her friend having such a difficult time meeting her eyes, Emmylou tempered her fury at the company.

"I talked to Donnie about it, and I looked for myself, Em. I don't think the mice were brought in by your wholesaler. I'm not sure how they got there. I don't know if we'll ever know."

"But we keep that area so clean and locked down, and the door is the correct height from the floor. I don't see how they could get in there. We put the health codes to shame. The inspector himself said it was the cleanest place he had ever been in, and he's been doing his job for almost twenty years."

Scarlett tucked her dark hair behind her ear. "I'm not saying it's your fault either. I'm just telling you what I found. It's like they dropped from the ceiling."

"Could that have happened? We have vents in there."

Scarlett shifted and shook her head. "I don't know. Maybe."

Emmylou looked from Scarlett to Lacy, an almost unbearable stabbing pain in her chest. "What the hell is going on? I'm not sure I can make it through this."

Scarlett and Lacy each took one of her hands in theirs.

"We're gonna get you through it. I will *find* where the mice came from. After managing three greenhouses in the middle of a field, I'm an expert at tracking the little boogers." Scarlett squeezed Emmylou's hand.

Emmylou, Lacy and Scarlett were working shoulder to shoulder piping frosting onto cookies, the sun having ducked below the horizon hours ago. Emmylou had sent the rest of the staff home with a request to be back at three-thirty a.m., but Lorie, God bless her, had refused to leave. She was placing the finished cookies into boxes, distributing the protectors evenly and securing the lids, getting them ready for the shipping line to package and label them.

Lacy's phone peeped like a bird, bringing them all out of their concentrated assembly. "It's Kyle. He's at the door." She couldn't hide the pleasure in her glowing face.

"Better go and let him in." Emmylou placed her hands on her lower back and arched, trying to stretch the kinks from it. She picked up her water bottle, and the other two women did the same, obviously grateful for the break. She hadn't noticed how long they had all been working. "Sorry, ladies. We should all call it a night. I'm sure it's well past dinner time."

"You're right about that." Kyle's voice boomed as he strutted across the room, carrying pizza boxes.

Emmylou's stomach growled at the sight of them. She hadn't eaten all day. A pleasant relief washed over her. "Kyle, you're too sweet."

He stopped in front of her and presented his cheek. She chuckled and obliged him with a peck to his bristled skin. "I know. It's a curse, really." His eyes gleamed with humor, and he placed the four boxes on the stainless steel counter. He turned his attention back the way he had just come, and Emmylou mimicked his movement. When her eyes locked onto what Kyle had been searching for, her stomach plummeted. Suddenly she wasn't hungry anymore.

"Hope you guys don't mind, but I brought along a friend."

Emmylou clenched her teeth as Lacy escorted Shane Newbury into the group. His dark-eyed gaze darted from Scarlett and Lorie to Emmylou. He blinked quickly, then looked away. He was uncomfortable with the attention, or perhaps it was the company. Kyle clapped him on the shoulder.

"Of course we don't mind." Lacy grinned at Shane and rubbed the arm she had been linked to just seconds ago. Shane placed the cooler down that he had been carrying and jammed his hands in his back pockets.

"I don't want to intrude, but Kyle here insisted I come along." Again Shane made eye contact with Emmylou. She swallowed at the flurry of electricity stinging her nerves. She wanted to hate his presence in her factory, but she could tell he had been bamboozled into coming here.

"And you all know how persuasive I can be," Kyle announced unapologetically. "The good doctor was going to take his pizza home and dine alone. I simply couldn't have that. This man will be bringing my son into this world. Right, Doc?" Kyle tilted his head at Shane, and Shane met his inquisitive gaze with bemusement.

"That's right." Shane crossed his arms over his chest. Lacy let out a disgusted grunt of outrage. "Your *child* is in good hands. And you," he pointed at Lacy, "better be taking it easy." The emphasis of the word child made Kyle narrow his eyes and study Shane. Shane wasn't giving anything away.

Emmylou couldn't help but laugh. She knew Lacy and Kyle were butting heads about whether or not they would discover the sex of the baby ahead of time, and the good doctor was staying true to Lacy's wish not to know.

"Thought I had ya." Kyle clucked his tongue and flipped open the first pizza box. "Eww, this one must be yours, Doc."

Shane looked at the steaming pizza covered in black and green olives, beef, pepperoni, onions and cheese. "That's mine." He hadn't taken offence to Kyle's disgust at all. Kyle handed him the box, and Shane stepped toward Emmylou.

She caught a whiff of the concoction. "Bleh, what *is* that?"

"Pizza."

She rolled her eyes at him. "Not where I come from."

"You must not get out very much." He leaned against the work station counter, pizza box balanced in one hand, while retrieving a heavy slice with the other.

Emmy witnessed his first bite into the monstrosity with disgust. "I'll remind you that I am a professionally trained chef."

He swallowed and leveled his gaze on her. She wished he wouldn't look at her like that. His damnable heavenly eyes were like tractor beams she found impossible to drag her gaze from. "Professionally trained *pastry* chef. Forgive me if I don't think you're an expert on pizza." He licked his lips, drawing her attention to their pink smoothness. Her hand flexed with the urge to reach out and rub her thumb over his bottom lip. Why was she always attracted to assholes?

"I'm an expert on everything."

His eyes sparkled while he chewed his next bite. "That's because you're a woman. They generally think they are."

"Amen, brother," Kyle agreed and was rewarded with a jab to the ribs from his wife.

"You were the one who said his pizza was disgusting." Emmylou gaped at Kyle who was serving pizza and breadsticks to the others.

"We weren't talking about pizza. We were talking about women."

"Yes, we –" she shook her head. "Never mind." She took the paper plate Kyle handed to her, still miffed about what Shane had said about women.

Shane continued watching her and chomping on his pizza with a bemused expression.

"What?" Emmy was feeling self-conscious now.

"You want a slice?" He held the box of stink-pizza toward her.

"Noooo." She dragged the word out in her disgust.

He arched his dark eyebrow and shrugged. "Then how will you know?"

"Oh, trust me. I don't need to eat garbage to know what it tastes like." She looked at her own pizza, not wanting to eat it with him watching her.

"Things aren't always as they appear, Princess." He helped himself to another piece.

"Don't call me Princess." Emmylou resented that pet name. Her father used to call her that, and she had spent most of her life proving she was anything but a princess. She could sense her friends watching and listening to the entire exchange between them. Normally she wasn't shy of being in the spotlight, but in this case, she wished they would all start talking amongst themselves or that Shane would focus his attention away from her.

Emmylou turned sideways and picked up her slice of pizza. The others were either too hungry or too uncomfortable to make conversation until, finally, Kyle started asking Lorie about raising boys. She had two, so she was a veritable cornucopia of specifics.

Emmylou couldn't shake the challenge she had heard in

Shane's voice. *"Things aren't always as they seem, Princess."* The pressure was building inside her, that uncontrollable need to win, to never be thought of as lacking.

She glanced at him and his pizza from the corner of her eye, then snapped her gaze back to the stairs leading up to her office. She tapped her foot, peeked over again and clenched her jaw. *The arrogance of that man!* He was still smirking at her with an irritating gleam in those brown eyes. He wiggled the pizza box while chewing, with overstated enjoyment, the slice he held in front of his mouth.

Damn! She turned and stamped over to him, meeting his mocking gaze with a challenge of her own. She reached out and lifted a piece of heavily topped crust. With a narrowing of her eyes, she sunk her teeth in and tore off a bite, never breaking eye contact. She chewed, knowing she would hate it and want to spit it out. She wanted to be able to swallow, pull a disgusted face and throw the unfinished slice back in his stupid box. Except… something was happening inside her mouth. It was an explosion of flavor. The salty sour of the green olives matched well with the meat combination of beef and pepperoni.

She couldn't hold his gaze any longer. She continued to work on the piece in her mouth while trying her best to come up with something nasty to say about it.

"See? What did I tell you?" Shane gibed. "I know how to pick pizza, honey. I've been a bachelor longer than you've been a chef."

It was a throwaway term of endearment, but it had made Emmylou's heart flutter. Even with that feeling, she wasn't about to admit to him she liked the pizza. "It's okay."

He laughed outright and it rankled her. "Is that why you made that cute little grunt of appreciation?"

Her mouth dropped open. "I did *not* grunt."

"Tell yourself anything you want, Madam Chef, but you grunted when you ate that. I could tell it was a culinary fiesta on your taste buds. You may as well have closed your eyes and sighed in ecstasy with all the pleasure you were getting out of it."

Emmylou faltered at all of his double meanings. "Do you always act this superior to people, or is it just a complex caused by your profession, *Doctor*?"

Shane bunched up his mouth in thought. "I never took a psych rotation, so I can't discuss the deeper nuances of my personality." He shrugged. "I can't help it if I'm right nearly all the time or that you seem to take great issue with being proven wrong."

Emmylou was gathering all her force to launch a full-blown reality check on the high-and-mighty doctor when a chorus of raucous laughter distracted her. She turned furiously toward the noise to find her two best friends, shoulder to shoulder, laughing up a storm. Emmy continued to stare them down with a mixture of disbelief and anger at their disloyalty.

"I have never seen that before," Lacy stammered between breaths and giggles.

"I know," Scarlett agreed. "It's like watching a couple of bulls in a tight pen."

"Excuse me?" Emmylou drawled and narrowed her eyes.

"I'm sorry, hon, but I have never seen a man draw swords and do verbal battle with you. This is the greatest thing I've ever witnessed." Lacy was leaning against Scarlett as though the scene had sapped her strength.

Emmylou glanced from Lacy to Scarlett several times. They both seemed to be enjoying her humiliation at the hands of Shane Newbury. "I didn't realize I was such a tyrant and had been submitting you all to torture with my thoughts and opinions."

"You haven't, Em." Scarlett's face was still flushed from her laughing. "We love your wild tirades and tangents. You're the one who always knows what you think and what you want, and you aren't afraid of vocalizing it." She took a breath and sobered a little. "We've just never seen you do it to a man before."

That statement took her back. What was she usually like around men? She didn't think she was any different, but her friends obviously thought otherwise. She listened as Lacy and Scarlett complimented Shane on a job well done, wondering why it was so satisfying to them to see her put in her place. Nothing had been right since Shane had come to town. His slights and comments had burrowed under her skin from the first day he had insulted her bakery. He had continued to blindside her at every turn, but she may have been able to overlook some of those things if his personality wasn't so awful.

"Well, I'm glad I could make your day." She addressed the group in an effort to mask her inner havoc.

"Oh, Emmy, please don't think we're being mean," Lacy implored. "We're just glad you finally found someone to spar with. It's refreshing to know there is someone out there who is your equal."

Emmylou couldn't believe that Lacy was serious, but the sincere face she exhibited said just that.

"If everyone is finished, I think we should get back to work." Kyle's voice boomed, covering the awkward mood that had settled among them.

"That's a good idea." Emmylou hadn't planned on the dinner break and knew she would be here well after midnight if she had a hope of making a dent in the orders. And that was if the supplies held out. Donnie had bought them some extra time by purchasing every scrap of flour and bag of sugar within a fifty mile radius. The grocery shelves were bare, and even a few neighbors had sacrificed their stores to help her out.

The group was reorganizing, but Emmylou noticed Kyle and Shane weren't leaving like she had thought they would. They were walking in the opposite direction of the door. "Don't you boys even think about pilfering one of those cookies," she called after them.

"Wouldn't dream of it." Kyle raised his hands in defense. "We're going to take a look at that oven."

She wanted to laugh but managed to keep it from escaping. "I don't have time to entertain the fire department tonight, Kyle."

"Hey, I'm offended by your lack of faith in my handyman abilities."

"Kyle, my dear, tell me what a rodeo king slash movie star knows about fixing appliances other than calling the repair man and he shows up?"

"What? You mean to tell me you haven't heard about my skills in the small appliance department?" Kyle clasped his chest in mock horror.

"Sorry."

He straightened and sobered his expression. "That's because I don't have any. But." He raised a finger, then stretched out his arm to pull Shane beside him. "The good doctor assures me he is an expert in oven repair."

Emmy transferred her attention to Shane and eyed him warily. "He's an expert all right," she mumbled under her breath and crossed her arms over her chest. Once again, the challenge he was presenting flashing in the cocky set of his jaw forced her to push him. "Fine, you break it, you buy it." Emmylou gestured for him to lead the way to the oven.

He nodded, "I can accept those terms."

Chapter 14

Shane wasn't sure he could keep his concentration while being this close to Emmylou. As they bent over the open door of the oven, he inhaled a delightful scent of vanilla and citrus encircling her. She was covered in food coloring, chocolate and frosting, and her long blonde hair was twisted into a sloppy bun. He had often wondered what it would feel like running between his fingers. It was thick and shiny and reminded him of the wheat fields at harvest. He had spent every summer in those very fields with his family.

"So, Mr. Fix-It, what do you think?"

Shane had only been looking at the oven for thirty-seconds. "It looks like someone has already removed most of the important parts."

"Yes. That's very astute, considering most of them are sitting right there on top of it."

Damn she was sassy. His mouth involuntarily curved, and his gaze drifted to her plush mouth. As soon as he did that, Emmylou's face contorted into an irritated scowl. He cleared his throat and turned back to focus on the oven. He went through a series of familiar diagnostic tasks while she was bent over with her hands on her knees, watching him. Her attention was making his hand shake.

"Wes has already worked on it, and he said it was the heating element that went caput."

The sound of another man's name on her lips stung. It shouldn't. He didn't like her; he was physically attracted to her. It had been a long time for him, and Emmy was simply the first woman to draw his interest. She was too obnoxious to trouble with. He only liked getting her riled up; she wasn't the girl for him.

Forget the hours he spent thinking about her or the fact that he had been so emotionally overwrought by the attack of the mountain lion, he had lost sleep.

"Well, did this Wes know what he was doing?" His guess was no.

"Of course he did."

"Hmm," was all he could answer. She seemed awfully protective of the man. He wondered if he was her boyfriend. "It would really help if you had a volt meter. Do you have one?" Her blue eyes drew him in as they always did. They were such a deep shade, he thought they could almost be purple.

"I don't know. What is a volt meter?"

Some of her hair had come loose, and he had the urge to tuck it behind her ear, but he restrained himself. "It's a little tool to check for electrical current." It took superhuman effort to turn his attention to looking around for the tool. He scoured the floor, but only found a few parts lying on a dish towel.

He blew out a sigh of frustration, picking through his brain for ideas. And then one hit him. "Have you checked the breaker? Your guy went through all the trouble of tearing the thing apart, but did he check the power source first?"

Her mouth dropped open as it seemed to do after he spoke.

"Of course he did." But he saw she wasn't sure of that. "And what do you mean 'my guy'? Wes is Lorie's brother, and he helps us out – a lot – free of charge."

"So he's not a repair man or an electrician?" Shane asked, but he had the answer he really wanted. Wes wasn't her boyfriend.

"No. He runs the implement store west of town. And he would have been smart enough to check the breaker. Besides, one breaker runs two ovens, and the other one is working just fine."

Shane shook his head. "That isn't to code then. They each need to have their own circuit. Where's your panel?"

Emmylou pointed in the direction of the breaker box, and Shane got to his feet. She trailed him as he strode to the wall. "Where is the key?"

"In my office. I'll go get it."

He watched her walk away, enjoying the view. When she disappeared, he turned his attention to the group back at the conveyer table. They were talking and working, smiling the entire time. The sight made him homesick. His family had been the same way, always pitching in to get the job done no matter how long or difficult. His chest constricted. It had been too long since he had talked to them.

"Here you go."

It took Shane a moment to remember what he was supposed to be doing. Emmylou held the key out to him. She was truly beautiful, even now when he could see the stress lines in her forehead and around her mouth. Kyle had only told him that Emmylou was having trouble with her oven and was worried she wouldn't be able to get all the orders out.

"Thanks." He took the key and turned to open the box. "You know, I had no idea you did all of this." His eyes roved over the building. "I thought you were just the coffee shop owner who made amazing muffins."

She smiled and looked around the huge building. "Yeah, this has been my dream since I was in high school and took a home ec class. I liked the structure of recipes, how a specific mixture of all those ingredients could turn into this completely different creation. It reminded me of myself and all the complexities I have inside."

She became shy after she had spoken, and he smiled when he realized she had never told anyone that before.

"So a love of mixing ingredients became a full-fledged baking empire?"

"What can I say? I also liked all my business classes."

He chuckled at her impish grin and sparkling eyes. "Well, it's amazing."

She blushed with his praise, and a pull of attraction tugged at his gut. He wanted to pull her close, to touch every inch of her ivory-pink skin, kiss her full lips. Hell, he had to clench his fist to keep from reaching for her hand. The moment dragged on; Shane finally forced himself to unlock the cabinet. He blinked hard, drawing his focus onto the task at hand. He drew back in surprise.

"It's unlocked." He furrowed his forehead; the padlock was there, but it wasn't connected. "Did you give the keys to Wes so he could check the box?"

It took Emmylou several seconds before she looked from him to the box. "No." She shook her head. "Not that I remember, but maybe Lorie got them for him."

The lock didn't look tampered with, and even though Shane had a strange feeling about it, he accepted that Emmylou trusted her employees explicitly. Still, he found himself scolding her anyway. "You really should be more careful about those things."

"What difference does it make? It's the electrical box. My staff has to have access to it. I'm not here all the time."

"I don't think it's smart to allow *everyone* to have access to it."

Emmylou straightened and crossed her arms. "Well, this isn't your business, it's mine, and I will run it however I want. Even if *you* think it's stupid."

Shane sighed. Why did he always say the wrong thing around her? "I'm just trying to help."

"Yeah. Fix the oven, not give me lectures on my lack of intelligence."

"That's not what I meant." Shane wanted to say more, but he knew it would only get him in deeper.

He turned to the box and read the panel, moving his index finger through the breakers. When he reached the switch for oven number four, he found that even though the switch was on, the red wire running to it looked like it was stripped and had shorted out.

"That's strange." He explained to Emmylou what he had found and what he thought.

"You mean I'm going to have to change every wire in that whole box?"

"It looks that way." He looked over the wiring again; what he saw confused him. "I don't know, but it looks like these are old wires. It's either that or they have been tampered with somehow."

"Great." Emmylou slumped against the wall, a crease etched between her brows and a faraway look in her blue eyes.

"I can fix this." Shane wanted to reassure her with more than his words. She rolled her head against the wall to look at him. He thought she might be on the verge of tears, and he took her cold hand in his. "It's going to be all right, Emmylou."

The hilarity that escaped her wasn't humor. It was more like a deep panic and despair exploding from its cage. "I don't think it is."

She looked away from him, and he clasped her hand tighter. She didn't pull away, but neither did she return the gesture. He waited, his instincts telling him she wanted to say more. He held his breath in anticipation, but instead she squeezed her eyes shut, took a ragged breath, then straightened. "How are you going to fix it?"

He rubbed his upper lip with his free hand. "I'm not some city bred doctor come to the country."

"No? Really? What are you?" Her eyes were red rimmed, but she didn't shed the tears. "Doctor by day, electrician by night?" She tugged her hand free of his. "Oh, and lest we forget, you sideline as a knight in shining armor here to save stupid girls from wild animals and sticky situations."

Shane crossed his arms but held his ground. "That's right, I am. And it seems I've got my work cut out with you."

She threw herself away from the wall and rounded on him. "I didn't ask for your help. I don't need your help. I don't know who you think you are, but you aren't my savior."

"Look, sweetheart. I understand the whole strong business woman in charge of her own destiny routine, but let me ask you a question." He paused to see if she would have another outburst. She narrowed her eyes but held her tongue. "Do you see anyone else around here willing to help you out? Or maybe you know how electric boxes work."

She was struggling with holding back from telling him to go to hell. He gave her credit for at least having a fraction of good sense. "That's what I thought," he said with a nod and turned back to the box. This was the first time he hadn't stuck his foot in his mouth when talking to her. He clamped down on the smile that threatened to curve his lips.

*****

Emmylou watched his long fingers prod and shift the wires coming from her electrical box. They were steady, confident in their actions. She leaned against the wall. Studying him was better than worrying about whether or not her entire production bakery was going to short out or burst into flames. She studied his profile, noticing a scar at the edge of his eyebrow. She checked the impulse to run her finger over the groove.

"How did you get that scar?" The husky words escaped before she could stop them.

He glanced at her, and a wry smile curved his firm mouth. With his attention back on the breakers, he answered, "You would have to ask my brother for the full story. The details are still pretty foggy for me, but it involved a green broke stallion, a piglet on the loose and a fence."

The picture those hints conjured made her chuckle. It wasn't at all how she had imagined his life. "So you have a brother?"

"Three of them." He pulled a handyman tool from his pocket, unfolded it into pliers and went back to work.

"Wow. You really came prepared."

"I never go anywhere without these. You'd be surprised what these babies have done."

"Open-heart surgery?"

He chuckled; she was beginning to really like the low natural pitch. It gave her a warm, tingly feeling in her stomach. "Close."

A comfortable silence settled between them for several moments.

"What was it like living in a whole houseful of boys?" She didn't know when her loathing of him had lessened. Maybe it had never really been. Maybe her friends were right about having someone to challenge her. Lord knew he was good at that.

"Probably worse than what you're imagining." He twisted the pliers and removed something.

"I feel sorry for your mother."

"You should feel sorry for my sisters." He rolled the black object in his hands. "When are you going to be finished with your ovens?"

"Sisters? You have sisters, *too*?" She was enthralled with this new side of him and the imaginings of a big family.

Shane nodded and toyed with the object. "Yep. I have three of them. So the ovens?"

Emmylou still couldn't picture this stoic doctor coming from a family with seven children. "I'm really feeling sorry for your mother."

"Why? She came from a family of eleven. Seven was a walk in the park. You still haven't answered my question about your ovens?"

She sighed, hating to end the conversation. "Probably tomorrow when I have to close up shop because I can't fill the orders."

His chocolate eyes gleamed for a moment while he watched her, waiting for her serious answer. Why did it feel like he knew her better than she knew herself?

"When do you need me to be done with my ovens?" she gave in.

He grinned in appreciation, and she felt herself blush. She thought she had lost her ability to blush. With her experience, there wasn't anything she hadn't seen. Until Shane smiled at her.

"Would five minutes be too soon?"

The apologetic puppy-dog face he was giving her was enticing. She smiled at him, feeling herself slipping. *Back into old habits.* She jerked with the realization, moving away from the wall and straightening. She wet her lips and cast her gaze around, composing herself.

"I have two questions Doctor Newbury." She spoke, using his title to distance herself and put the brakes on this careening vehicle of disaster. Shane dropped his hands and tilted his head, waiting. "First, how do I know that by letting you shut down the electricity, this entire place won't be put out of commission for the week? And second, you're not an electrician; how do I know that you won't send this place up in flames taking everything with it?"

Finally, her business brain was replacing the mushy-in-love-brain from moments before. It felt good to be back to normal. She watched him struggle with her switch back to their earlier formalities, but he managed to do it, and when he answered, she was happy to see that he had understood what she was doing.

"Well, Miss Bennett, you don't."

That was not the answer she was expecting. She stared, befuddled at him, and crossed her arms over her waist again. "Excuse me?"

"You don't know that those things won't happen," he answered frankly and toyed with the tool in his hands. "You don't know that I'm not the one that sabotaged this thing or if I'm the one trying to put you out of business."

That sent her reeling. "What?" Her voice was a mere whisper.

He didn't look in the mood to sugar-coat his reply. He pointed with the pliers at the box. "This wasn't an accident or bad wiring. I'm guessing that you had this place wired for a commercial kitchen when you set it up?"

His intelligent, sharp brown eyes fixed on hers. She reached for the nearest support to keep her from doubling over. She expected him to extend his support like most men would have. He stood resolute.

"Okay, I take that as a yes. Well, unless you hired some fly-by-night operation to do the work or someone who doesn't know a thing about electricity, like Wes, then this box has been tampered with."

Emmy shook her head over and over, staring at the floor. Her mind was jumping in a thousand different directions. "How can you be so certain? Maybe *you* are someone who doesn't know anything about electricity." She raised her eyes to his.

Shane made a face of agreement. "That's a good point."

She narrowed her gaze and gaped at him. "Would you stop agreeing with me? It doesn't make me feel better."

"I'm not agreeing with *you*, just your thought process."

God, he knew how to raise her hackles faster than anyone she knew, and that included her mother! Before she could offer up a series of criticisms about his intelligence, his communication skills and his legitimacy, he shifted his weight to one leg and continued.

"You don't know me," he stated. "You couldn't know that I spent three winters as an apprentice to a journeyman." He flinched when he imparted this information, but Emmy didn't think he was lying. "I was also a farm kid who worked on more pieces of equipment than you can name, and we lived too far from town to rely on someone being available to come and fix any household problems in a timely fashion. What I learned was hands on and by men who had grown up the same way I did, working beside their daddies. What I know would make your head spin, Princess, and would fill more books than the inventory of the Primrose Library."

Shane realized he had advanced on Emmylou and took a step back, but she didn't mind. She was intrigued with what he was telling her. None of this had been in his resume when he had applied for the doctor's position.

Their gazes were locked. Shane was breathing heavily, and Emmy knew the color was flooding her cheeks again. If she had thought him attractive before, she was now finding him irresistible. Such passion about his heritage. Emmylou didn't have that with her own family. She had come from a long line of only children and distant relations she never saw. Even her best friends were only children.

"Now, would you like me to help you out and fix this, or would you like to wait around for the fire department to come? Because, by the looks of it, that would have happened sometime tomorrow at the latest."

Shane's intensity stabbed at the core of Emmylou's anxieties. The feeling of violation this news evoked was stronger than her determination to overcome any obstacle. "What does that mean?"

Shane softened under her croaking plea. "I'm not sure what it means. All I can tell you is these wires are damaged, the box has been tampered with, and you were lucky that the oven shorted out when and how it did." He sighed and gave her an apologetic grimace, then reached out and stroked her shoulder.

Emmylou shook her head trying to absorb and process Shane's words. Her brain was rejecting the information like a computer virus.

"Do you know anyone who would want to do this? Some competitor or, I don't know, unsatisfied customer?"

Emmylou let out a tense laugh. At least it relieved a tiny bit of the pressure inside her. "This is Primrose, Nebraska." It was the only answer she could come up with, and the meaning wasn't lost on Shane.

He rubbed his chin and stared into the distance. He understood what she had meant right away. This was a small town and, here, everyone was family. No one was out to damage her bakery or injure her staff. Except someone was. The proof was right there in front of her. Emmylou began shaking with the shock of knowing someone would carelessly endanger innocent people.

"Why would someone do this?"

She was asking herself more than she was Shane, but he answered anyway. "There's always a reason." He patted her arm. His expression was soft, and his eyes warm. A drugging feeling of warmth spread through her. "While you think about it, I'm going to get to work. Would you tell everyone that we need to shut the power off, please?"

She nodded and took several steps before his arm hooked her elbow, pulling her back. "Emmylou?"

A stampede of elephants was charging through her stomach, and a firestorm was spreading through every pore, leaving her throat parched and making it impossible to speak. She did manage a jerky nod, though. The urge to close her eyes and savor his touch swept over her. She battled it and won.

"Don't mention this to anyone, okay? We don't know enough, and I don't want you scaring off the culprit."

His hand was still holding her arm. She used her free arm to push her heavy hair from her damp forehead. "But it's just my friends over there. They didn't have anything to do with this, and the fact that you would insinuate it disgusts me."

"I'm not accusing your friends, but it's better to be safe. You

144

can tell them later when the threat of fire isn't immediate. I don't want to deal with a lot of hysteria and questions while I'm working over here. And you still have one employee in the mix."

Emmylou followed his gaze to Lorie and was instantly angry. She pulled her arm free. "Lorie's my best employee. She and I go way back. I trust her implicitly."

Shane turned to face her fully. "But it was *her* brother who came in to fix the stove." He tipped his head, and she finished his thought.

Even though it galled her, she had to admit that he had a point about the hysterics – the rest of it was crap. Lorie and Wes were included in her list of old friends. Shane was still an outsider who didn't know that they had all grown up with each other. Rather than roll her eyes at him, she bobbed her head in agreement.

"Okay," she hissed when he looked skeptical. "I'll ask them all to go home."

Chapter 15

It took a desperate call to Dennis Moore, the owner of the lumber yard, at home to get the supplies that Shane needed to fix the breaker box. They were sitting on the counter finishing off the pizza. It was nearly two a.m., but Emmylou still had as much energy as an eighteen-year-old at an all-night bonfire. Or her body was in shock from the disastrous day.

"So, it's safe to say you have this whole town wired?" Shane asked before popping the last bite of crust into his mouth.

She grinned through her chewing. "Pretty much." If that were true, she would be able to find out who was responsible for the damage to her bakery. She still wasn't convinced it wasn't just arbitrary. She had been sifting through all the possibilities, even down to her own employees, but no one stood out to her. So until something else happened, she was going to go with the theory that it was a series of coincidences that had made the wires deteriorate. It could be that the place wasn't vented properly or that it was too hot due to all of the ovens running.

"I installed a new lock, but I would suggest installing some security cameras." Shane jumped down off the counter and dusted his hands of crumbs.

"Thanks, but I'm not going to do that to my employees. I don't want them thinking they are being monitored every minute of the day. That would destroy the trust we have, and they wouldn't work as hard for me."

Shane turned to look at her. A dozen worms on hooks started wriggling in her stomach. The way his eyes had the ability to take every bit of her in and not look away was alluring. She had never had a man look at her like she was fascinating and intelligent. "Your psychology is sound, but I fear it may do more damage now that you've had this breach."

She marveled at him.

"What?" he asked, and the small dent in his chin drew her attention.

"I've never had anyone to talk business to."

"What about Kyle? He's seems pretty savvy."

She flung her head to get her hair out of the way and avoid his contemplation of her.

"Kyle and I don't have that kind of relationship, and honestly, he's only been around for the past six months."

He wisely kept his opinions about her two best friends to himself. Even though neither of them were accomplished business women, Emmylou loved how they helped in other ways. She couldn't ask for better. And with Kyle's help, Lacy was learning quickly.

"What about your parents?" He rested his hands on his trim hips. "I'll take that as a no."

"Why do you say that?"

"Because of the way you reacted to the question. It's okay. I get it. Parent-child relationships are complicated."

Emmylou bristled. "Thank you for that psycho analysis. I must have missed that rotation in Psychology on your resume."

"I don't need one to see that you are adamantly opposed to talking to your parents."

"I was simply getting more comfortable."

"And exercising your face?"

She puckered her mouth to stop from smiling. "I heard they are the first muscles to weaken."

"Read a lot of health magazines, do you?"

"Mmm-hmm." She flicked her gaze to his half-grin. His potent magnetism was drawing her closer.

With a deep breath, he placed both hands on the counter beside her, and hunched over. "I'm going to be worthless tomorrow if I don't head home."

Disappointment darted between Emmylou's ribs. "It is tomorrow."

He looked up at her with a sparkle of appreciation. "Good point."

Had he been any other man, Emmy would have taken the look as an invitation, but with Shane, she wasn't so sure. There were flickers of interest, but what kind of interest eluded her. "I'd better get to the bakery and get started." With great reluctance, she jumped down from the counter.

"You're not going to go home and sleep?" Shane straightened.

"Nope. I've got to get the day's stock ready."

"Don't you have employees for that?" Shane stretched his muscles, and stepped within eight inches of her.

"I have Lindy, but I can't stand her up like that." A charge of electricity frolicked over her skin with his nearness.

"What about that other guy? The two of them can't handle it together?"

"Wha–" Emmylou clamped her mouth shut when she remembered that Evan Matthews was now in her employ. With everything that had happened in the last eighteen hours, she had neglected to check in with Lindy. "Well, he's new, and I'm not sure how much Lindy likes him. Anyway, I've seen how you work all day after emergency calls that last all night, so don't talk to me about overdoing it."

He held up his hands in surrender. "Okay, I won't tell you your business, but as your doctor, I will tell you that it isn't good for your immune system to get run down. So don't come crying to me when you come down with the flu."

"You're not my doctor." She tilted her head and raised her eyebrows.

"Fine, then as your friend, please take my advice."

"Are we friends?" Her voice was soft.

"Well, if we aren't you owe me several thousand dollars for the electrical work. Pizza isn't going to cut it." The playful challenge in his voice was delightful, making it even more obvious that their banter was a welcome liberation.

"I guess that makes us friends." Emmylou reached out and playfully slapped him on the shoulder, unsteadying him. "Buddy."

"I thought so."

They cleaned up the pizza mess and gathered their winter items, maintaining the good-humored camaraderie until they reached the door. Emmylou turned out the lights and held the door for Shane. The keys jangled in her hand as she searched for the right one. He walked past her, then halted and turned back.

"I had a really good time tonight. I'm glad I came with Kyle."

The clouds from their breath meeting the cold air drifted above them. Her throat constricted when their gazes connected. "I did too. Thank you for helping me. I can't tell you how grateful I am." She managed to draw the words past the lump.

He leaned closer, resting his hand on the door knob, pulling the door and her toward him. "Don't mention it." His mouth was an inch from hers, his breath tickling her skin. His features were hard and intent; a light glow of moonlight played on his cheekbones making his eyes as dark as sin. "We're friends, remember?"

A nod was all Emmy was capable of. She had been robbed of speech, of breath, of thought. Her body tensed in anticipation. Shane swooped in to capture her mouth, while simultaneously pressing her body to his. Emmylou dew a quick breath, and the keys clattered to the floor just before she clamped her hands behind his head, drawing him tighter to her. He pushed forward against the door, and it gave way, swinging open. Emmylou was lost in the satin of his lips moving on hers, tasting her as though she were whipped cream on top of a dessert. Gentle, insistent, sensual.

The door slammed shut with a kick of his foot, cutting off the bite of cold air. He used the closed door as a stanchion for the onslaught of passion he lavished on her. Her brain was swirling in a fog of desire, her fingers working of their own accord. His soft locks slid between her fingers, heightening her excitement. The heat of his invading tongue formed waves of tremors bent on destroying any sense she had left.

She slid up the door to get closer, to make the kiss deeper. Shane wedged himself between her legs to assist her pursuit. His hands cupped her face, traveled down her neck and splayed at her rib cage. Her breasts ached and swelled. His lips worked her pliable, sensitive mouth, instructing her in exactly the right way to please him. She thrashed against him unable to get close enough, to touch his hot skin enough.

Her body screamed for more, but none of her extremities were communicating with her brain. Her powerful need for this man was more than she had ever experienced. Overwhelmed and confused, she reacted on instinct to his roaming hands, probing lips. Blood thundered in her ears; she whimpered when his mouth broke from hers. Her arms clamped around him in an effort to bring him back, but a fresh tremor rocked her when his moist lips tugged at a sensitive place on her throat and slid down her skin. Her hand convulsed against his head, and her eyes rolled up.

Her hoarse voice pleaded with him as her body thrust against him. He murmured against her ear, and she shivered. His hands gripped her hips, and he wedged her harder against the door, then reclaimed her mouth for one more scalding kiss. She was on fire. She pulled at his coat, wishing she was shed of her own.

Suddenly, she became aware of his waning intensity. He turned his head and raised one arm to lean against the cold metal door. He was panting as though he had just sprinted the length of a football field. The puffs of air scattered her hair. She nuzzled his neck once and got no reaction. A stab of rejection pierced her.

"What is it?" She was as out of breath as he was.

"Nothing." His answer was flat, and he didn't look at her.

Emmylou wiggled to free herself of Shane, smarting with shame.

"No." He snapped his head around and settled his hand at the curve of her neck and collar bone. "I didn't mean for this to happen."

Emmylou wanted to get away from him, but his weight was still pinning her. "I'm sorry." She pushed at his shoulders with her hands and made to get past him.

"No." He urged her back, his face only a few inches from her, staring into her eyes. "I'm sorry. I always say the wrong thing. Every time you're within five feet of me, I stick my boot in my mouth." His self-deprecating half grin relaxed her a fraction.

"I just thought it was a social disorder." She bit back a smile.

He laughed and its warmth flowed from the tip of her nose to the tip of her toes. "I assure you I only get it with you. Normally, I'm not such a jackass." He smoothed his hair back but kept her immobilized with his hard body.

"Or maybe you just *think* you're not." It was becoming hard for her to breathe again but not from his weight. The way he looked at her, the fact that his hand settled comfortably at her hip was just about to undo her.

He appeared to be considering this. "Nah." He shook his head. "I'm a pretty great guy."

She smiled and it made his eyes gleam with pleasure. "I'll be the judge of that."

He glanced at her mouth. "I'm sure you will."

The moment stretched on, becoming increasingly charged. His wrist watch beeped.

With a deep breath of regret, he pushed away from Emmylou, and the cool air was a shock to her system. "Reality calls."

"What time is it?" Emmylou blinked and straightened her jelly legs.

"Three-thirty." She could hear the disappointment in his voice, and it made her feel good. With the way she had behaved during their kiss, she was glad to find that she wasn't the only one who had enjoyed it more than expected.

"Then I'm late. I'd better get going." She rearranged her clothing, stopped and turned her head. "Why does your watch beep at three-thirty in the morning?"

"It doesn't usually, but I have an important date I can't miss." He was adjusting his clothing with some discomfort. His head was down as he aligned the zipper on his coat, so he couldn't see her expression, which Emmylou was grateful for.

"Oh, I see." She twisted the door handle, and the sting of cold air helped her return to reality, along with his admission. She was a fool. Always a damn fool when it came to men.

Shane's boots echoed on the floor while she held the door open for him. Her back ramrod straight as he passed, she used the heavy door as an anchor. Really, what she wanted to do was bang her forehead against the metal.

He stopped and turned his shoulders toward her, hands in his coat pockets. "I'd like to see you again."

Emmylou tried but couldn't look at him. She settled her attention on a point over his shoulder. "I don't think that's a good idea." Her throat tightened, and she had to swallow. She hated the weakness that revealed.

Shane leaned in closer. "Emmylou." It was a whisper, a question, a plea, and she weakened inside but held as firm as she could on the outside. He was a kitten whisker from her cheek, his breath played on her skin. She still stared past him, even when he moistened his lips and the wet heat kissed her. She blinked and clenched her teeth.

"I n-need to go," she stammered. Every instinct instructed her to lean into him, to wrap herself around him and hold on forever. She didn't do it. The promise she had made herself after Marcus broke her heart poked her sub-conscious.

He ducked his head back and studied her. She could feel his confusion and a hint of annoyance beneath his dark perusal. "Emmylou?" There was a smile in his voice. "That date."

"It doesn't matter. You don't need to explain anything to me. Really." She forced her gaze to meet his.

"That's nice to know, but you didn't let me finish. That date I have is with my sister. It's her birthday today, and she lives in Georgia. I have to call her at 4 a.m. to catch her before she goes to work. Different time zones."

She did a poor job of hiding her shock and relief at his confession. She had said it didn't matter, but it did, and that was dangerous. "Your sister's birthday. That's nice. That you call her I mean."

"I try." He was enjoying this way too much.

She huffed a sigh and shoved at his shoulder. "Get out. I need to go and so do you. You've got a date."

He laughed and turned on his heel. She locked the door. When she turned around to go to her car, her hand went to her heart, and her steps faltered. Shane was scraping the ice from her windshield.

*****

The day had been grueling, and it was only lunch. She had fielded more phone calls and emails about orders than Amazon on Christmas Eve. The dollars flying out the door turned her stomach. Lorie had been by earlier to update her on the situation. Emmylou had to fill her in on the electrical. That was an awkward conversation. Shane had warned her not to discuss anything that had happened in case someone from the factory was responsible. But Shane didn't understand that Lorie couldn't operate on half-knowledge.

The crew was turning out as much product as they could, but Emmylou knew the supplies were going to run out any minute now if they hadn't already. Her cell phone buzzed in her apron pocket just as she sat down at her desk in the back of the bakery. She closed her eyes, sighed and braced herself for the news.

"Hey, Donnie," she answered the call and listened to his short reply. The supplies were gone; he was sending the crew home. "I understand. Thank you. Really, Donnie, thank you."

"I'll stick around for a while and clean up. Maybe wait and see if the truck shows up, but they got another storm out East. I don't think it's gonna happen. I talked to the driver yesterday and told him it was an emergency. He said he would do his best." The defeat in Donnie's voice broke Emmy's strength more.

"I appreciate it. Let me know if there's any change."

They hung up and Emmylou buried her head in her hands. "Emmylou?"

"Yeah." Her voice was muffled; she was beginning to hate her own name. Nothing good followed it. She turned a fraction toward Evan standing in her office doorway but didn't look up.

"What's wrong?" He slid into the room and placed a heavy hand on her shoulder. The support she felt from that simple gesture was nice. "Can I do something for you?"

She looked up knowing her make-up was gone, her eyes were

red-rimmed and her hair was an absolute disaster, but Evan's concern was there in his green eyes.

"No, you're doing what I need you to do here helping Lindy. From what I hear you're a natural, and coming from Lindy, that's high praise. She isn't one to hand out compliments."

His smile was charming. She wondered how old he was. He had the look of someone who had lived a lot of years in a short time. A hardened and weathered exterior stretched over a young man full of stifled dreams. "She's been very helpful." He sat in the chair next to her chaotic desk.

"By that you mean she's ridden you pretty hard." Emmylou couldn't help but smile at his tactfulness and intelligent eyes dancing with amusement.

"She demands perfection and I'm okay with that. You have a good employee in her."

Emmylou twisted in her chair, picked up a pen from her desk and toyed with it. "I know. I hope she never leaves me."

"Does she act like she would?"

Emmy darted a look to Evan, puzzled with his anxiousness. "No. But she's getting married next month, and you never know."

"No, I guess you never know." Evan looked off for a moment before shaking whatever thought he had had and returned to his lighter self. "Well, I have a few things to finish up and then I guess I'm off until tomorrow." He slapped his leg and stood.

"Okay. Tomorrow is another day." She answered the question in his voice. He nodded and stepped to the door. "Evan." Emmy turned and looked up at him. He raised his brows, waiting with his hand resting on the door frame. "How do you feel about staying on here for a while longer?"

He grinned. "I'd love it."

"Great. It's nice to have someone here that can work with Lindy and do such a good job."

"Thanks." He gave her one last smile and returned to the kitchen.

Even though she wasn't sure she could pay him or keep the doors open, he was a great addition to her team, and she needed the help right now.

The back door opened bringing Scarlett and Lacy. They stomped their boots on the rug and removed their outerwear while Emmylou approached.

"Hey." She hugged Lacy. "I already thanked Scarlett this morning, so now I'm gonna thank you." She gave Lacy another hug. She and Scarlett exchanged a greeting. She had seen Scarlett first thing this morning when she brought in two boxes of chocolate covered strawberries for the case.

"You're welcome. Are we going again today? I've got Kyle on the B and B, so I'm all yours." Lacy had purple smudges under her eyes but was smiling and glowing despite her obvious exhaustion.

Emmy ushered them to the office and closed the door. She hadn't really told Lindy or Evan what was going on at the production site and didn't want them to overhear.

"I don't think we'll be working at the factory today. The supplies just ran out, so there isn't anything to do except pray and wait. Donnie and Lorie have done everything they can, but it's at a standstill."

Lacy had settled herself into the chair Evan had occupied minutes earlier. The smug face she was making and transferring from Emmy to Scarlett made Emmylou suspicious.

"What?" Emmy glanced to Scarlett who shrugged and looked to Lacy.

"I kind of made a few calls. Well, Kyle did."

"Lacy," Emmylou scolded.

"Hey, what good is it being married to a powerful man if you can't use it from time to time?"

"What did you do?" Emmylou crossed her arms and lowered her chin to pin Lacy with a heated stare.

"I told you, I didn't do anything." She raised her hands in defense and continued when Emmylou made a threatening gesture. "Kyle called someone who called someone who called someone in the restaurant industry, and you should be getting a call any minute."

"A call for *what*?" Lacy was digging in her purse for

something, pointedly ignoring Emmylou's annoyance.

Lacy pulled out a giant candy cane, peeled back the noisy wrapper and broke off a chunk, filling her mouth. "Sorry," she mumbled through the crumbled pieces. "Low blood sugar." She crunched away, roaming her brown eyes from Emmylou to Scarlett, stalling for time.

"Damn it Lacy, I haven't had any sleep, and my patience is about as long as a tick's hair."

Lacy made a production out of swallowing, Emmylou's phone buzzed, and the look of reprieve and relief on Lacy's face was comical.

"Hello?" Emmylou adjusted the cell phone against her ear to hear better. "Yes, this is Emmylou Bennett." She pressed into the crackling distant noise. "You what?" The voice repeated his information and Emmylou straightened. "Okay. I'll be right there." She turned and stared hard at Lacy who had the look of a fox poised at the mouth of a rabbit hole. "I don't know whether to hug you or throttle you."

Lacy giggled and rubbed her hands together. "Shall we go?"

Emmylou's heart swelled during the drive to Prairie Goodness. Not necessarily from excitement, but more from stress. A delivery was being made to the production house. That was all the caller had said. Knowing her friend and her obnoxiously generous husband, it was probably an entirely new baking system. Whatever it was, it was big enough to fit in an enormous moving truck. They pulled into the parking lot to see a large *U-Haul* truck backed up to her overhead door.

They had their choice of parking since the staff had been sent home. Lacy bounded along like a little puppy, squeaking and fidgeting with delight. She wouldn't tell Emmy what was going on, and Scarlett was her usual intractable self. If she knew, she wasn't talking either.

"You Emmylou Bennett?" the man standing behind the truck asked.

"Yes." She couldn't help staring at his hat. It had a camouflaged bill and fuzzy, fake grey hair sprouting from the top.

He held out a clipboard.

"Sign at the bottom please." He gnawed on a toothpick, and his aviator sunglasses reflected her dumbfounded look. Emmylou took the paperwork and pen. The man pulled a pair of leather gloves from his back pocket and released the latch on the door of the truck. He threw it open. It made the clicking-thudding noise and a bang when it reached the top.

She was too distracted to care that the man took the clipboard from her hands, set it on the floor of the truck and climbed inside. Emmylou was overwhelmed with gratitude and disbelief. Lacy grasped Emmy by the shoulders and squeezed her with an excited noise. Emmy patted her friend's hand, still standing in amazement.

"Thank you, Lacy," she whispered, staring at pallets stacked with sacks of flour and sugar. "I'm paying you back for all of this."

She could feel Lacy's grin. "You didn't read what you signed."

Emmylou tipped her chin toward Lacy who was still clinging to her. "What did I sign?"

"The invoice," she chirped.

Emmylou lifted the clipboard. At the very top, the yellow and green logo for Lansky Foods jumped out at her. She had tried last year to get them as a supplier, and they had turned her down. She was outside their distribution area. "I didn't know you knew Harold Lansky."

Lacy shrugged. "I don't. I just got the stuff here. Well, *he* got it here."

Lacy nodded her head in the direction of the parking lot. Emmylou turned to see two men walking to them.

"Y'all want to help me get this unloaded?" The driver's gritty voice didn't defer her attention from the men approaching.

"We got it," Shane instructed the driver. He looked like the proverbial cat who swallowed the canary with the look he flashed Emmylou before climbing inside the truck to help.

Emmy dragged her attention from Shane to Kyle, who had joined the group as well. "Thank you, Kyle. I can't tell you what this means to me."

"I didn't have anything else to do today. I don't mind throwing around some heavy bags. It means I won't have to work out 'till tomorrow." He moved to the back of the truck, waiting for the first load.

"No, I mean the supplies. Thank you for getting them here. Whatever strings you had to pull – I really appreciate it."

Kyle shrugged. "No biggie. They weren't my strings."

"I'm sorry?" Emmylou narrowed her eyes and shook her head.

"They weren't my strings," he repeated.

Emmylou was still confused. Two stacks of heavy bags thudded in front of Kyle.

"They were his." He nodded at Shane, and Emmylou shifted her openmouthed attention upward. Shane dusted his hands, turned and walked back to get more bags.

Chapter 16

The ultimate look of dumbfoundedness was worth the phone call Shane had made begging Harold Lansky for the flour and sugar.

"You gonna stand there gaping, or are you gonna open that door?" He had to turn to conceal his laughter.

"Yeah," her startled reply followed him to the stacks of supplies. He heard the jangle of keys, the release of the lock and the rumbling of the overhead door being rolled up.

Kyle lifted a stack of heavy bags and entered the building beneath the watchful, contemplative eyes of Emmylou. Shane was enjoying this far too much. He hadn't thought Emmylou would be *this* stumped by his surprise. She didn't know what to do or what to say.

"Oh, no." She fluttered to life and shuffled behind Kyle. "I have a cart for unloading heavy stuff."

"Don't bother," he answered. "I told you I need the workout. Where do you want these?"

The two of them disappeared into the building, and Shane and the driver kept stacking.

"Hey! Superman!"

Shane turned to see Scarlett resting her hand on the floor of the truck and scowling up at him. He straightened and placed his hands on his hips, waiting for her to speak her piece. She had obviously been waiting for this moment.

"This was pretty nice of you." She narrowed her eyes. "But don't think for one moment this will soften her up for you."

He raised his hands, palms up. "What makes you think that was my plan? Maybe I was just trying to help out."

She shifted her mouth in thought. "No. I don't buy that. I see how you look at her. I saw you two battle last night. You like her."

Shane sobered and swallowed. Hearing someone else say it out loud brought his feelings into a whole different light, and it made his stomach squirm. "Doesn't everyone?" His attempt at flippancy sounded hollow.

"Well *we* do." Scarlett indicated Lacy. "And so does Kyle. You would do well to log that up there in that brilliant mind of yours before you go getting any ideas about Emmy." She nailed him with a look, and those soulful sea green eyes pierced through him. It was as if Scarlett knew every impure thought he had had since puberty.

"I got it." And he meant it.

"Good. Because if she gets hurt one more time, Lacy and I swore to each other that we would take care of the man who did it."

The fire kindling behind her pretty eyes enforced her message. Shane knew she meant business. He didn't have to imagine what kind of punishment she would mete out for her best friend. Growing up on the farm with three sisters and a mother, he knew country girls well and knew what they would do. None of it was pleasant.

"Scarlett, I understand. I really am just trying to help out."

His sincerity must have rung true. Scarlett relaxed, nodded and moved so Kyle could get more flour sacks.

Shane's heart stopped when Emmylou emerged outside. He couldn't tear his gaze from her. A different feeling moved through him this time. A stronger one. Her blonde hair beneath the knit hat lifted in the breeze; her cheeks were rosy from the cold making Shane want to touch her skin, to feel it warm beneath his palm. Blood rushed when memories of the heated moments in the dark of her bakery flooded his mind. She had been so responsive; he had been almost too anxious. He had come within a millimeter of losing control.

He wondered if she wanted to do it again, if she wanted to spend more time with him. They had left things unsettled with an awkward good-bye. He had showered and gone to the clinic after speaking with his sister; she had gone to work although she didn't look like she had gone without sleep. She looked the picture of health.

"You know I could get you a forklift to help with this kind of work?" He wiped his sweaty forehead with his leather glove.

"I think you have done more than enough. Thank you." He could see it was hard for her to say it. She wasn't used to accepting help. Shane would give Emmylou the world if he thought it would win her heart. As soon as that realization quaked through him, a panic gripped his chest. He didn't want to want someone like this. The women he chose didn't thrive with his affections; they crumbled. They died.

The pain spread to his stomach and arms, causing his grip to falter. Two fifty pound bags of sugar dropped to the floor.

"Looks like we might need that forklift after all," Kyle joked.

Shane let out a muffled laugh and stacked the bags on the edge of the truck floor. *Damn. Why had he let himself get so deep into this?* It had all gone too far. Emmylou would get hurt, and he had just promised Scarlett that he wouldn't let that happen.

"Well, that's all of them," the driver piped up.

Shane nodded and jumped out of the delivery truck. The driver followed and slammed the door shut, latching it. He released the invoice from the clipboard and separated the copies.

"The address for payment is right there on the top. It's due in thirty days."

"Thank you," Emmylou answered and took the white copy.

Shane had moved away, not far enough to draw attention, but enough to make a statement of distance. The group stood in the parking lot and watched the truck leave. He was still shook up from the realization that Emmylou was becoming a part of him. She had slipped in under his armor, and he couldn't handle it.

"I'm going to need a ride back to the clinic," Shane addressed Kyle.

"Sure, just let me kiss my wife, and we'll get out of here."

Shane's heart sunk with Kyle's comment. He had to look away. His mistake was looking in Emmylou's direction. Her beautiful blue eyes were filled with gratitude. He suppressed a regretful sigh. Despite her earlier curtness, she was happy it was him who had helped her. He was familiar with the emotion written on her face. He really had let this go too far.

"Thank you, again, Shane." Her voice had an element of kindness he hadn't heard before, and it slivered his heart. He had wanted this, had created it with his charm and cajolery and now he had to put a stop to it.

"It's no problem. I know the owner. It was just a phone call." He shrugged a shoulder and kept his attention away from her. He scuffed the packed snow with the toe of his boot, hoping Kyle was finished mauling his pregnant wife. He winced. The uncomfortable silence dragged on.

"I better get to work," Emmylou finally said, and her two friends followed her to the door of Prairie Goodness. She was disappointed and confused.

Shane stared at Emmylou's back, hoping that she had taken his cue and wasn't hurt by it. It had been one moment of weakness. One incredible, unforgettable moment. At least he would have that to hang on to. And his patients. His practice was going quite well, even with a few older skeptics. Word had gotten around fast in this little town about his care of Mr. Perkins.

Kyle dropped Shane at the front of the clinic. It was nice to have a friend in town. At first he had thought it a great relationship to cultivate. He liked Kyle and befriending him put him in proximity of Emmylou. Now he wasn't sure he should maintain this close contact with the McClintocks. Lacy was a patient, and they were both very close to Emmy. This would undoubtedly get messy. Too bad.

Kyle had been the one to start up the friendship with his easy conversation at the pizza parlor. Shane had been quick to see that Kyle was a great guy and obviously looking for a friend, too. He was famous, a legend in this town, and everyone here idolized him. Not a great scenario to garner close friendships.

"Hey, Shelby. What have we got going this afternoon?" His red-headed nurse set down the file she had been looking over, and with both hands, grabbed the stethoscope hanging on her neck. "We're gonna be busier than a whore house on nickel night. The phone hasn't stopped ringing all day."

Shane noticed that their office lady, Abigail, was at this very moment cradling the phone between her ear and shoulder and typing on the computer. "Okay. Let's get to it."

Shelby nodded, picked up her energy drink can and finished it off. She tossed it in the trash as they walked to the examination rooms. He had just been provided a day full of excuses to keep him from Emmylou. Now, if he could keep it going for eternity, he would be out of danger's path.

He knocked and entered the exam room after the occupant's acknowledgement. He wished he had eaten more lunch than the package of crumbled crackers he had found in Kyle's glove compartment, but the delivery truck had come, and he had to rush out to help. At least he had thought he needed to help. He probably should have allowed Emmylou to handle it on her own. He should have remained anonymous, but the need to see her had been too great.

Shane forced a smile when he reached the patient seated in the green vinyl chair next to the computer desk. "Hello. I'm Doctor Newbury."

He would put the woman in her mid to late fifties, and if he had to guess, he would say she was someone of some importance in this town. Her hair was still blonde, but not without the help of a stylist, and she had perfectly applied make-up. She was slender and stately in a grey pantsuit with practical black flats. Her eyes were devouring him, and her lips were curved in a bemused, tight-lipped smile that often adorned the face of high society women. It set his teeth on edge, and he prepared himself to be told how to do his job.

"It's very nice to meet you, Doctor." Her voice was pleasant. It didn't fit the straight lined suit and perfectly styled hair.

"How can I help you today?" He clasped his hands in front of him.

"Well, funny you should ask. I came here to ask you to dinner."

Had she told him to strip naked, he wouldn't have been more surprised. "I'm sorry?" he stammered and ran a hand down the front of his white coat.

She smiled. There was something about it that was familiar. "I would like to take you to dinner."

He had been flirted with as a doctor by many types of women, but the deliberate forwardness of this woman was a first. Shane cleared his throat, "That's a very kind offer, but –"

"My husband will be in attendance as well." Her light brown eyebrows were raised in expectancy.

He opened his mouth several times but found no response. "Um, ma'am. I'm not sure I'm understanding you." He used the files in his hand as a barrier, keeping them pressed to his waist.

She uncrossed her legs and scooted forward in her chair with another smile. "I'm sorry. I didn't introduce myself. My name is Susan Bennett." She placed a graceful hand on the collar of her suit jacket.

"Oh." He nodded.

"My husband is George Bennett."

He nodded again, still confused, until something slid into place. "Oh, George Bennett. His picture hangs in the reception area. I understand your family donated a sizeable amount to build this new clinic."

"Yes, that's right. And I used to be on the Board of Directors here. I have since passed that duty on to my daughter."

Finally he remembered his manners and held out his hand to Susan Bennett. "It's a pleasure to meet you. I'm sorry if I seemed confused just now. I'm new here and haven't had a chance to meet everyone."

Susan took his hand in a delicate handshake. "It's quite all right, Doctor. I understand you have been very busy during your first week with us." Once again she gave him that familiar smile, throwing him off balance trying to place it. "So how about we treat you to dinner? It would be wonderful to get to know you better."

Shane didn't like this part of the job. Politics should never be hand in hand with health care, but these people were advocates and financial supporters of the place where he now worked, so he couldn't turn down the offer. "That sounds terrific."

"Wonderful." She clapped her hands together and stood. "Friday night, then? Shall we say seven o'clock at The Dove House?"

"Sure, that sounds lovely. Is there anything else I can help you with today? A checkup perhaps or a flu shot?"

"We'll get to that in a moment. I wanted to secure your company at dinner first." Her eyes lost their luster and her smile faltered, but she took a quick breath and rallied. "My daughter will be pleased to hear you accepted."

"Your daughter will be joining us as well?" *Why were these things never simple?*

"Yes, I believe you know her. Emmylou Bennett."

His hand clamped the files, and he blinked in disbelief. His chest tightened, and his stomach dropped at the mention of Emmy's name. He hadn't put that all together. "Ye- yes, I do," was all he could manage to utter.

Susan lifted the corners of her mouth, and he could have sworn her eyes glimmered with some secret delight. And he knew what that delight was. Mothers often knew everything their children didn't want them to. "Great. So there won't be any awkwardness at dinner."

"None at all." Shane knew his face was giving his lie away. He nodded, and made his way to sit on his stool. "What else can I help you with today?"

"I'm sure when you open that file, Doctor, you'll know."

*****

Forty-five minutes later, he shook Mrs. Bennett's hand with sickness twisting his insides.

"Have a nice day Doctor Newbury."

"Thank you; you as well."

Susan left and shut the door. Shane went straight for his office, dropped into the chair and closed his eyes. Not only had he agreed to dine with the woman he had vowed to stay away from, he was dining with a patient who was also a major benefactor to his place of employment. How do things always get so complicated?

He glanced up at the wall calendar and rolled his eyes to the ceiling. This Friday was Valentine's Day. "Great," he sighed to himself.

Chapter 17

Shane had been as jumpy as spit on a hot skillet to get back to the clinic, so Emmylou hadn't been able to talk to him about what he had done for her. And she'd had more eyes and ears around them than she had wanted. When the two of them had left the production house that morning after their incident, they had left most things unspoken. Just bid each other an awkward good-bye.

The kindness he had shown in scraping the ice from her windshield and opening her door for her made her nervous. She had never had someone be so thoughtful toward her. Except for her two best friends, and Kyle on occasion. If it weren't for Kyle, she wouldn't have known that nice men existed. He had shown her what a real man was and what she wanted her relationships to be like.

Marcus hadn't fit the bill. He was far too self-absorbed to be concerned with other people's feelings. But Shane did. He was a nice man, a real man, a man that she wanted to be with. And the chemistry between them was like sodium and water; volcanic explosions. She had promised herself that she wasn't going to be with another man for a while, but that was when she was dating jerks. Shane wasn't a jerk.

"Earth to Emmylou." Lacy waved a hand in front of Emmylou's eyes, bringing her back to attention.

"Sorry, just thinking."

"About war in the Middle East?" Lacy smirked.

"Of course," Emmy joked.

Emmylou felt it before she saw it and turned to Scarlett, studying her. She lifted the corners of her mouth into a small smile to answer the question in her friend's eyes. She hated when Scarlett contemplated things. Her conclusions were always right.

"So, do you need our help after all?" Lacy chimed in.

"You know what? I'm giving you both the afternoon off. I'll call the crew in, and we'll knock out these orders. Thank you though."

Lacy grumbled and made a face. "Aww, man, I was looking forward to making more cookies. I had a great idea for one. What do you think about making sarcastic cookies?"

Emmylou giggled and braced herself for what came next.

"Something like, 'It's not me, it's you.' And maybe, 'Alien lips', 'Fine ass'." Lacy grinned while Scarlett and Emmylou hooted with laughter. Her next suggestions brought about a fit of hilarity, and Emmylou thought Lacy might be onto something. She may have to add a line of sarcastic valentines to her order list next year.

Donnie called the production staff in and got them to work. They were still an oven down, but maybe now that they had these supplies and more coming tomorrow, they could make their quota.

Emmylou spent an hour talking with Lorie about what had been going on. She trusted Lorie and needed to have her on board looking for anything out of place or anyone acting suspicious. Lorie had actually had some good insights as to who might have tried to sabotage things since she worked here every day and had close contact with everyone on staff.

Emmy turned down Lorie's offer to have Wes come in and put the stove back together. She wasn't sure he was the man for the job. Maybe she would call up Shane and ask him to help her with it. He had done such a great job of rewiring the breaker box and knowing what needed to be fixed. And it would give her an excuse to spend more alone time with him.

They still hadn't figured out where the mice had come from, so Emmylou was keeping the new shipment of dry goods in the refrigerator with the eggs and milk. It was packed to the gills, but at least there weren't any mice in there. She paged Donnie to her office so they could talk more about the situation and get an update on production.

After their brief meeting, Emmy made a note to call Scarlett and have her do some investigative work about the mice, but first she had to make another call. She looked at the clock and leaned back in her chair with disappointment. Shane was still at the clinic, and she didn't want to call him while he was helping people. Anyway, if she called she would be talking to Abigail. She would have to leave a message, and that didn't sit well with her. She didn't want anyone to know that she was chasing after the good doctor. Of course, she could say it was board business. No, that had trouble written all over it. She would just wait until later.

Her cell phone buzzed on her desk. "Hello?"

"Miss Bennett?"

"Yes. Evan is that you?"

"Yeah. Lindy gave me your number. She said to tell you that she has the orders for all of the drop offs ready to go and will be out delivering them. Then she was going to go home unless you needed her for anything else."

"Okay. Thank you. Go ahead and tell her that she is free to go home. I know that she's trying to get some work done on her wedding. I appreciate you calling and checking in, Evan."

"That's no problem. I hope everything is going well out at the production house."

"It is." *Now*, she thought. But with her track record, it could change at any moment.

"Are you sure? You sound... a little frazzled."

"You must be a mind reader." She smiled at how comfortable she was talking to Evan.

"No, but I know how stressful this season is for bakers. Is there anything else you need me to help you with, Miss Bennett?"

"Please call me Emmylou; everyone does." She leaned back in her chair and swiveled it.

"I will. Thank you. My offer to help is purely selfish you know. I don't have anything else to do, and I really like learning from you. In the past two days, I've had more experiences than in the whole time I was at school. This hands on learning is so much more valuable, and anything I can learn from you now will help me in the future."

"That's so nice of you to say. I had to learn so many things the hard way, I'm glad I could help you." His eagerness was so sweet. "I could use an extra pair of hands out here to get the orders ready."

"Say no more; I'm on my way."

They hung up and Emmylou went down to the floor to find a place for Evan.

When he arrived, enthusiasm was bursting from his every pore. "I'm glad you found it." She couldn't help but return his excitement. She remembered when she had walked into her bakery for the first time.

"Small town. It's not hard to find anything here."

She agreed and led him to what she called baking row. "I thought that since you want to know the ins and outs of a bakery, I'd start you here." She trailed her arm through the air, encompassing the baking floor. "Where it all begins."

Evan glanced around with a huge grin. "That sounds great!"

Emmy motioned Donnie over. "Donnie, this is Evan Matthews, and he's here to help us out. Just tell him what you need done."

"Sure." Donnie's annoyance at training new staff was evident in his tone.

"He's been working at the bakery the past two days."

"Two whole days? Wow, are you sure he needs me to show him the ropes?"

"He'll do fine," Emmy answered with a cautionary look and a pat to his shoulder. Donnie was gruff with everybody. It was actually one of his best traits, helped him keep the staff motivated and working.

"Got it. I'll take care of him."

"I knew you would." She winked at Donnie, and he gave her a grudging pursed lip, gleaming eye face. "Thank you, Donnie." She turned to Evan who was surveying Donnie with narrowed eyes. "You're in good hands."

"Okay." Evan nodded and smiled at her. She liked his smile. She knew nothing about him but felt a keen camaraderie with him and was glad that he had joined her team.

She excused herself to continue the rounds and check in with Lorie. She was sure that things had rounded a corner and would turn out for the better – as soon as she could figure out some new funding. She nearly skipped her way through the production house back to shipping where she knew Lorie would be supervising the packaging and printing labels.

Her cell phone vibrated as she reached the sorting tables. She groaned at the caller ID and stuffed it back in her apron pocket. She talked to the crew and checked packages. They were still behind schedule but were willing to put in a couple of extra hours to get caught up. Emmy was disappointed that she had had to shut down internet orders, and she knew that it was too late to open them back up now. She hated that Lorie had had to put "out of stock" on everything. But Lorie had made a good point; she thought it made them look in demand and popular, so it might help down the road.

Hopefully, they still had a "down the road". Emmy's phone beeped indicating voice mail. Her mother always left her scalding messages. She hated voice mail. Probably because Susan Bennett thought of herself as too important for someone not to take her call. And she never thought of Emmylou as a busy person. Her little hobby, as her mother referred to her business, was a distraction until she found a real job or a man, and not in that particular order.

It wasn't five minutes later when her phone buzzed again. Emmylou set down a stack of boxes she had been carrying to the back cargo door for pick up and dug her phone out. Her mother again. It must be important.

"Mom, I can't talk right now. I'm in the middle of shipping out seven hundred boxes of baked goods." Emmylou had to plug her opposite ear to hear her mother, and even then, she didn't catch it all. "Sorry, what did you say?" Emmylou shook her head at Lorie when she held a clipboard up for Emmy's inspection. "You did *what*?" She ducked behind a pallet of supplies.

"It's this Friday, dear." Her mother's no-nonsense voice informed her.

"Mother, I can't make that! That's Valentine's Day! Do you know how many deliveries I have to make on Friday?"

"I'm sure you'll manage just fine."

"Maybe I have a date for that night."

The soft guffaw on the other line frustrated Emmylou. She narrowed her eyes and gripped the phone tighter. "Do you have a date for Friday?"

Emmylou tried to lie and say she did, but instead the opposite came out. "Well, no. But I could. And the fact that you just *assumed* that I didn't upsets me."

"Which part upsets you, Emmylou?"

An indistinct sound of disgust escaped Emmy's throat. She couldn't answer that; either way would result in another round of tug-o-wits. Emmylou wanted to bang her head against the cement block wall. "No, Mother. I won't be there. There's no way I can do it."

"The reservations are for seven at The Dove House. I'm sure you know where that is."

Emmy closed her eyes and pursed her lips at her mother's criticism. She had never approved of Emmy's friends, and the only reason her mother had made the reservation there was because it was the only place to eat in town besides the diner, and her mother would rather endure an hour of Lacy than endure the shame of eating at a short-order restaurant. "Yes, mother. I know where it is."

"Good! Then we will see you there."

Emmylou tried to protest, but her mother cut her off. "And Emmylou, it is important to your father that you are there. I won't tolerate anything less than your smiling presence at the table. Oh, and please wear your hair down. It covers your ears."

"What's wrong with my ears?" Emmylou's question met with silence. Her mother had already bid her good-bye and hung up.

Emmylou stared at the phone with astonishment. *Every time!* Emmylou shook her head. When would she learn? Her mother did the same thing to her every time. Susan Bennett was the master of railroading.

Her only bright spot in this situation was that Valentine's Day was two more days away and anything could happen in that time to prevent her from going. And she would have two days to come up with a really good excuse.

She tucked the phone away and went back to counting. For all the stress of the holiday, she was holding up pretty well. She didn't see any reason why she couldn't turn a profit and present her case to the bank after all the receipts came through. She had an appointment with her accountant about her taxes at the end of the month; maybe she would have some ideas for other possibilities. There were two hours left to go in the shift, and Lorie thought they would be almost caught up by the end of it. After another hard day tomorrow they would be on track or maybe even ahead of schedule.

Emmylou sat on a stack of pallets and tugged her hair free of the pony tail, massaging her scalp. It had been a very long couple of days. Being in the clear was almost euphoric. She had just leaned against the wall when a blaring alarm sounded. She shot up, looking around. The red alarm on the wall was flashing, and the warning was blaring.

Only a flicker of panic wiggled through her. It could be anything. A batch of cupcakes or cookies forgotten in an oven; a towel or oven mitt accidentally dropped on a heating element.

Emmylou wasn't prepared for what she saw when she rounded the corner into the production room. Heavy, black smoke filled the room, and orange flames were crackling and lapping toward the ceiling. They spanned the length of baking row.

She was glued to the floor, her mind blank, trying to take it in and formulate a thought, some kind of reaction. Nothing. The thunder of the big overhead door rolling up, bringing a blast of sunshine and frigid air snapped her to attention. The smoke swirled and the flames grew as the light struggled to pierce them.

Emmylou screamed for everyone to get out. Her legs finally started working, and she trudged forward, pushing shoulders and yelling. She knew she should be counting heads, but couldn't. Safety was all that mattered. Her staff's lives were in danger, and she was scared for them. She saw Evan at the door swinging his arm, urging everyone to safety. Emmylou was filled with gratitude. Her burden lightened knowing he was helping.

Suddenly, he ran back inside. He was too far from her to hear her pleas to stop; to get out. He disappeared into the choking blackness. Emmylou had to stay and make sure everyone was exiting the building. She couldn't run after him. Her throat ached from her hacking coughs and full-volume yells. She covered her mouth with her arm and squeezed her scratchy eyes shut to moisten them. When she opened them again, an explosion of white foam shocked her. It was swiftly coating baking row.

First left, then right, down, then up. Evan was brandishing the red extinguisher and firing it over the flames. Emmylou was jolted into action. She ran to the wall opposite her, smashed the glass with her elbow and released another fire extinguisher from its case. It was unexpectedly heavy, and it banged against the floor before she got control of it.

She hitched it against her hip, pulled the pin and hurried toward the heart of the flames. She squeezed the handle, and a burst of foam shot out. She aimed for the outside and worked in, counting in her head. When she got to twenty, she moved the stream to another area. The adrenaline charged through her veins, and she shook with the effort to stay focused. She had every urge to chuck the extinguisher into the flames and run outside.

Sweat streamed from her pores, her arms were scalding from the heat and singed hair mingled with the thick acidity of smoke in her nostrils, but she continued counting and shooting.

A hand on her shoulder made her jump and swing the red cylinder. The foam coated the perpetrator's black and yellow suit. Another pair of hands relieved her of her burden and yelled something she didn't understand. The gloved hand waved in the direction of the door. Before she could move, another person was manhandling her and forcing her toward the large opening.

She went, not because she wanted to save herself or breathe fresh air, but because the hands were so insistent. The moment she emerged, she flinched from the brightness and hunched against the fireman's abrasive bunker suit. Flashing lights flourished the parking lot, while faces covered in soot and tears passed before her. Emmylou's heart broke at the sight. Her employees, her friends, people she loved were huddled together staring in devastation at Prairie Goodness. She wanted to gather them all into her arms, but once again, she was passed to another set of hands.

This time she was forced onto a gurney as a man and a woman started checking her over. She heard chatter about establishing a line and felt a cold, wet swiping at her arm, then a pinch. She didn't care what they did to her.

"Shelby." Emmylou didn't recognize the rasp coming from her mouth. Maybe she had only imagined speaking. She clawed at the woman's arm, grasping it firmly. "Shelby," she repeated, stronger this time.

Shelby's pale eyes focused on her and her red hair glowed in the sun. "Just relax, Emmy. I'll take care of you." She secured the plastic mask over Emmylou's face before she could scream that she didn't care about herself. She wanted to know if everyone had gotten out. Where was Evan? Was he okay? Did the firemen get to him, too?

"Just breathe." Shelby stroked Emmylou's matted and filthy hair.

They clipped something on her index finger and slid her into the ambulance. Emmylou's voice dissolved into a coughing fit, or she would have argued and fought harder to get answers. The blaring siren pounded against Emmylou's ears, along with the two EMTs talking and passing things back and forth over Emmy's prone body. A monitor to her right was blipping, and James, the other EMT, was watching it and giving reports to Shelby.

Finally, she was able to lock eyes with Shelby, who smiled at her. "I know this wasn't what you had planned for the day, but we're taking you to Glenwood Community Hospital."

Emmylou shook her head and glared at Shelby. She tried to talk through the oxygen spewing through the plastic mask but ended up coughing again and being urged to lie still and be quiet. She wanted to scream that she was fine, that they needed to take her back immediately.

"I'm sure that Scarlett is there by now with that police scanner she keeps in her dining room, and Lacy won't be far behind. Let them take care of things there, and you take care of you.

"This is stupid." Emmylou mumbled through the heavy, restricting mask.

"Yes, I know, dear. All these things that save lives are simply ridiculous," Shelby answered without looking at Emmylou.

Emmylou closed her eyes. It was too much work to explain to Shelby what she had actually meant. It was thirty minutes to Glenwood under normal driving restrictions. In a speeding ambulance, it takes twelve. And during all twelve of those minutes, Emmylou thought she might die. Not from smoke inhalation or carbon-monoxide poisoning, but from worry. She was living under a dark cloud, a cursed sun, or perhaps she was God's personal whipping boy because this was getting insane. This many bad things couldn't happen to one person.

The ambulance slowed and swayed. They must have arrived at the Emergency Room door. Soon the back doors opened, and James jumped out. Emmylou was resigned to sticking with the program. She knew Shelby wouldn't hesitate to get out the restraints and clasp them on Emmy's arms and feet if she put up a fuss.

The roller legs hit the concrete. "What's her pulse-ox?"

Emmylou's eyes were in danger of popping from her head. "*Shane!*" She felt a rush of relief when his brown eyes flared with concern.

Shane faltered in his attempt to retrieve his stethoscope from his neck, staring at Emmylou. "Um—" he swallowed then held out his arm in direction. "Get her inside."

Chapter 18

Shane hadn't been that frazzled since his first day in rotation treating the victims of a tragic car accident. Seeing Emmylou covered in soot and lying on that stretcher had done things to him he didn't think possible. Those feelings had died inside him long ago. He had worked to master his control and treat patients objectively. Emmylou had blown that all to Hell.

His hands had shook, and the nurses must have thought he was possessed by the way he snapped at them, but he wasn't taking any chances with Emmylou. He wasn't going to lose another one. Things had crystalized in the seconds he had spent staring at her when she came out of the ambulance. In two seconds he had understood how important she was to him and how much he had grown attached to her.

It wasn't just her pretty face; in fact he hadn't thought she was that beautiful in the beginning. She wasn't his usual type. But her wit and her guts and her unfailing focus was what had won him over. Treating her in the emergency room and having her question and criticize his every move had told him more than the physical examination. She was going to be fine.

She had spent the entire time peppering the staff about her employees and asking for someone to get her a phone. She had started off making polite requests, but as the examination went on, she had become more and more demanding. He was sure one of the nurses re-attached her face mask just to get her to be quiet. But, Shane was finally satisfied with his findings and had had Emmylou moved from Emergency to a regular hospital room, which only irritated Emmylou further. She was frustrated and wasn't keeping it a secret.

"I'm keeping you here overnight as a precaution."

"The hell you are! I need to get back and check on my staff and my bakery."

He hid a smile behind the pretense of making notes on her chart. "Sorry. You need to take care of yourself first."

She blew out a burst of breath and smacked her hand against the bed. "I knew you were an idiot. I didn't realize you were such an autocrat."

The fire in her eyes was impressive, but he didn't cave. The challenge was too much of a temptation for him. "Well, that's what I went to school for. I live for telling people what to do, and a medical degree entitles me to do it every day."

She narrowed her eyes and jutted her jaw. "Aren't you clever?" She grabbed the covers and made to throw them off, but he restrained her with a firm grip of her wrists. "Get your hands off me!" Her mouth opened and she shot him a look that promised bodily harm. "I told you, I have to get back. I'm fine and I need to take care of things." A fit of coughing hit her, and she doubled over, hacking and sucking air.

"Thank you for making my point. You're staying here." He wanted to stroke her back, to pull her hair from her face and hold her close, but he didn't dare.

With a moan her coughs faded. "Isn't there some kind of form I can sign to get me out of here? Or maybe you could get me a *real* doctor? Someone who actually knows what they're doing?"

Shane bit his tongue to keep from laughing. "Hmmm. Yes, that would be nice, but sorry. I'm all you've got."

"What? What kind of cut-rate hospital is this? You're it? You're my only option? Where's the nurse? She'll let me go. She'll get me whatever I have to sign. Nurse! I need you!" Emmylou kicked her feet over the side of the bed and hastily adjusted her hospital gown. "And then I'll see to getting you replaced. This is what happens when the board gets desperate. They'll take any warm body. I told them you weren't the doctor for us. And what did –" her words froze and she angled her head, looking hard at him.

"What did you say?" Shane's grip on her wrist slackened. "You

178

were on the board that hired me?"

She swallowed and shifted, looking at her hands. "Yes," she murmured.

"And you were against me?" he stared hard at the side of her face.

"Uh, well. Not really."

"That's not a difficult question, Emmylou. Either you were or you weren't. It's a simple yes or no answer."

"It's not simple." She pulled back when she caught the look he was giving her. After regrouping, she straightened and answered quietly, "Yes. I was against you."

Light was breaking through the dark sky as all the pieces clicked into place. "I have been wracking my brain trying to fix whatever I broke when we first met. I thought you hated me because I made the mistake of criticizing your bakery and spilling your coffee tray. I thought if I could just make amends that – " he cut himself off before revealing anything else. "But you were never gonna like me. You were dead set against me. This whole time." He looked at her with new eyes, rubbing his hand over his mouth. The room had shrunk, and his lungs became tight. She looked vulnerable sitting on the hospital bed, beseeching him with her eyes, but this time it didn't touch his heart.

That delicate organ he had encased in lead and ice after Katie and that had been thawing over the past week, immediately hardened. Thicker this time. He couldn't stand to look at her. He shook his head and stared at the fiberglass chair against the wall.

"Did you need something?" the nurse rounded through the doorway.

Shane moved his head in her direction and talked over his shoulder. "Yes, Miss Bennett will be staying with us overnight. Can you take care of that, please?"

"Certainly."

Shane followed the nurse out of Emmylou's hospital room without glancing at her. She said nothing as he left. No apology, no calling for him to stop, to listen to her. Nothing. That hurt more than any of the other things. His stupidity about Emmylou Bennett cut to the quick. There would be no one who could fill Katie's place. He had been naive to think for one second that Emmylou might be special to him.

She was stubborn and selfish, completely single-minded and heartless. His cell phone buzzed in his coat pocket. "Dr. Newbury," he answered automatically. "Yes, hello Mr. Lansky." Shane dug his thumb and forefinger into the corners of his eyes and clamped them shut. "Sorry. Harold," he corrected with a grimace. "Yes, she did. Thank you so much for doing that for me. I can't tell you how much I appreciate your helping like that."

Shane chuckled at Harold Lansky's reply. "I'm glad that you think of me as a friend."

They made small talk about Shane adjusting back to country life and about Harold's wife, Emily. Emily would always occupy one of the only warm places left in Shane's heart. She had given him unconditional love when he didn't deserve it. They promised to talk again soon and hung up.

The call didn't sit well with Shane. He had called in a favor from Harold Lansky on behalf of Emmylou when he thought had he was helping out a friend, a friend with potential for something more. Now, he was sorry about it. It had cost him a chunk of pride to make that call in the first place, and now it had all been for nothing.

*****

Emmylou backed away from the doorway of her hospital room and leaned against the wall. She felt disgusting, and it wasn't the heavy coating of soot, fire and sweat on her skin. Her soul was swimming in sewage.

She had followed Shane to the door to stop him. She wanted to explain but stopped in her path when she heard the name Harold Lansky. Shane had answered his phone and was talking to the man who had delivered much needed dry goods to her that morning at Shane's request. She had planned to wait until he was finished and then speak with him. She prayed he would at least hear her out. She hadn't meant what she'd said.

But when Shane had asked about someone named Emily, it had startled her. The softness in his voice, the way she could sense his smile, even if she couldn't see it. Emily was someone special to him. It ripped her heart to hear him speaking sweetly about another woman.

Damn it! She had fallen for him!

Her breathing was shallow and still painful and she had to force herself not to give in to the fit of coughing that was bursting in her chest. She refused to let him know she had been at the doorway, that she had been following him. He was obviously involved with another woman. Emily Lansky had ownership of his heart. It was no wonder the supplies were shipped overnight to her. Emily's father, Harold, would do anything for his daughter's beau.

And from the sound of it, Shane and Harold had a friendly relationship, so it was nothing to him to ask a favor of his sweetheart's father. Maybe they were engaged. The memory of their moment of passion in the bakery now came into focus. It was just that, a moment of passion. A weakness. It was nothing to him, and deep down she knew it. He had shown her kindness but nothing more after their kisses.

"Where can I find Emmylou Bennett?"

Dread rushed through Emmy at the ring of her mother's superior voice. It wasn't panicked, or hysterical like any normal parent's would be when their daughter is hauled off in an ambulance. At best Susan Bennett spoke with mild concern. She didn't want to deal with her mother right now. This would give her more ammunition to get Emmylou back in business school. And then really start pressing for a law degree. Emmylou becoming a lawyer was about as likely as fruit punch raining from the sky.

Emmylou hurried to her bed, jammed the monitor clip onto her index finger, pulled the covers over herself and pretended to be sleeping. With any luck her mother would see her and leave her in peace. She heard her mother's shoes on the tile and felt her presence enter the room. She concentrated on keeping her breathing even and her eyes still while listening to her mother getting settled in the chair against the wall.

Emmy strained her ears with the sound filling the room. She wasn't sure, but it sounded like crying. Her mother was trying hard not to be loud, but those were most definitely the sounds of a crying woman. Maybe it wasn't her mother who was sitting there. Maybe she had imagined her voice earlier. There were only two other people who would be upset about her circumstances, and Emmy would gladly wake from her "slumber" to see them.

She opened her eyes, fully expecting to see Lacy or Scarlett sobbing into a tissue next to her bed. She blinked several times, not believing what she saw.

"Mom?" Emmy's voice still wasn't normal, and it seemed to bring her mother pain to hear it.

"Oh, Emmylou!" Her mother reached out and braced Emmylou's arm in a firm grasp. "I just…" she buried her face in a tissue again, and her shoulders rocked with sobs.

"Mom, it's okay. The doctor said I'm going to recover and be fine." Emmylou was confused and touched by what she was witnessing. She knew her mom loved her, but her mom wasn't one for hysterics. Or emotion.

"It's not okay." Susan hiccupped. Her eyes were puffy, and her makeup was smudged. "The last conversation we had was an argument. And if I thought that —" her breath hitched and she shook again. "I love you more than life itself and hope that you know that."

Emmylou was shocked by the fierce look in her mother's tear-reddened eyes. "I do," she nearly whispered. Emmy reached over with her free hand and covered her mother's shaking hand clamped on her arm. Her mom leaned over and kissed Emmylou's hand and rested her head there while continuing to cry.

Emmylou was lost for words. She had never seen this side of her mother before. They stayed like that for many minutes. Emmylou even began to lightly stroke her mother's hair. She couldn't think of a time they had spent in tenderness and quiet. Maybe they never had.

Finally, the mood lifted. Emmylou heard her mother's breathing even out, and she raised her head. They looked deeply into each other's eyes. Her mom's slight smile and adoring gaze meant more than a hundred bakeries and ten thousand cookie orders.

"You're all I have, Emmylou."

That statement spoken with such conviction hurt. "You have Dad."

Susan looked away and sat straighter. "Yes, of course. I have your father."

Emmylou's world tipped, and she had a strange sinking feeling in her stomach. "Mom, what does that mean?"

"Nothing, honey." Susan's voice was too high for normal. "When do you get out of here? I'd like to drive you home and then you can stay at the house."

Emmy's eyes narrowed. Her mother had changed back, making Emmylou wonder if their moment had even happened. "I have to stay tonight. But Mom, I'll go back to my house. I'm fine. I don't need a babysitter."

"I know that. But it would make me feel better if you would stay with us. Just for a few days to make sure."

Emmylou wasn't up for an argument. She was tired and her throat and lungs burned with the exertion she had already spent. She wanted to know more about what was behind that statement her mother had made, but her strength was sapped. "I'm going to rest now Mom, okay? We'll talk later."

"Okay, honey. You rest. I'll be here when you wake up."

Emmylou wanted to tell her to go home, but her eyes were already closed and darkness was filling her head.

*****

Emmylou woke with a start. Her eyes were difficult to open. Her face was covered by a heavy plastic mask, and her arm was being held by cold hands and a scratchy cuff.

"Sorry," the nurse whispered. "I have to take your blood pressure."

The cuff became tight with the air pressure. Emmylou blinked hard several times, trying to acclimate herself. She looked to her right, and the chair was empty. Her mother had left. She wasn't sure if she felt relief or disappointment. Her feelings were so discombobulated she didn't know what to think. She reached up to remove the annoying mask emitting air into her face but was stopped.

"No, no. You need to leave that on until the doctor has checked you. We had to put the mask back on several hours ago."

Emmy contorted her face and tried to speak.

"Yes, you have been asleep for quite some time."

Emmylou didn't recognize this nurse. Not that she spent a lot of time at the hospital. Actually, it had been many years since she'd had to be here. If it had been someone she had known, she would have told her where she could stick the mask, thrown the covers back and marched out of the room and back to her house.

The nurse continued to check Emmylou to her complete an utter irritation. She couldn't speak through the heavy oxygen and constricting mask, so she tried her very best to relate her feelings through the changing looks on her face. She didn't like knowing Shane had been in here while she'd been sleeping. He wasn't happy with her, and she hadn't been able to explain, not that she was sure she could talk to him after what she had overheard in the hallway.

She didn't know how to handle the fact that he had someone in his life. She had wanted to be his someone. Her feelings for him were there and very raw, especially after the emotional rollercoaster of yesterday. Maybe it was better she had been out of it when he was there after all. Maybe she would feign sleep when he came back.

The nurse nodded, asked if Emmylou needed anything else and smiled and left after Emmylou shook her head. She had to get out of here! Where were her friends when she needed them? They would break her out of here. She hadn't had any news about the bakery, and as far as she knew, there weren't any others being treated at the hospital, but not knowing the details was going to drive her mad.

"Oh. You're awake." Her mother came through the door

holding a bottle of water and a granola bar. "Would you like to have this?"

Had her stomach not been trying to leap from her body and devour the snack for her, she would have said no, but the sounds of an angry cat echoing from her belly were hard to ignore. Emmylou slid the mask away. "Sure." She took it from her mom and finished it in under thirty seconds.

"Would you like me to go ask about a tray for you? You slept through dinner."

She was still chewing but managed to answer, "I'd take a couple more of those if you have them. Jell-O and instant potatoes don't appeal to me right now." Her voice was closer to normal. "What time is it?"

"Two in the morning."

Emmylou was impressed. Her mother looked good for the middle of the night. "Why are you still here? I thought you would go home, get some rest and be back tomorrow."

Susan Bennett fidgeted with her water bottle and lowered herself into the blue chair. "I said I was staying with you."

"Yeah, but I've been out for quite a while. It would have been fine, Mom. You haven't been this protective of me since I was a teenager." Emmylou was trying to use her tone to get her mother to open up, but she may as well have been trying to open an oyster shell with a toothpick.

"You're my daughter and you're hurt. Where else would I be?" Her voice was hollow.

"I don't know Mom. You tell me. We've been dancing around this for a while now, so how about you just tell me what's going on?" The oxygen was tickling her neck, and she was still a bit light headed, but she tooled every effort into concentrating on her mother.

"I told you. I'm concerned about you."

"And I appreciate that Mother, but I'm sure you've talked to the doctor at least ten times since I've been here, and I'm sure he's done everything he can to alleviate your worries. He said I'm fine, and I can go home tomorrow. So what is it? Is it Dad? Has he done something?" Her throat was closing up, so Emmylou reached for her cup of water and took a long draw from the plastic straw.

"I haven't spoken to your doctor. He's been on another emergency and unavailable."

"But what about my oxygen mask? I thought that he had ordered it to be placed back on."

"No, dear. The nurse thought that your breathing was a bit rough when you were sleeping and your levels were lower than what they should be, so she put it back on and said we should wait until the doctor came in." She raised her brows and held her gaze steadily on Emmylou. That usually had the effect of quelling Emmy, but either her emotions had gone on strike, or she was tired of all the games.

"Okay. Well, whatever." Emmylou pushed her hair from her face; she would think about Shane Newbury another time. "What's up with you and Dad?"

"Nothing. We're fine. Why is it so hard for you to understand that I want to be with you? I want to protect you and make sure that you're fine. I want to be here in case you need anything. I am your mother."

Emmylou watched her mother carefully. "You are my mother, and I'm not questioning whether or not you care for me; I'm questioning why you're hanging around here. It's out of character for you."

"Maybe you don't know me as well as you think you do, Emmylou. I know that you don't think I was a good mother to you and that I'm always critical of your choices, but I'm not here under any other circumstances other than I'm scared for you, and I want to be with you."

"So there isn't anything wrong with you and Dad?"

Her mother sighed and pursed her lips. "We're fine." She rested her exacting gaze on Emmylou. "Your friends came by earlier while you were sleeping. They said they would be back in the morning."

Emmylou was left with a bad feeling, but obviously her mother was done talking about it. "Okay." She wished they would have awakened her, but she wasn't about to argue with her mother about it. Scarlett and Lacy would have had information about the bakery, the damage and the staff that Emmylou was dying to know, but her mother would only shut that down if Emmy asked her, and that was assuming her mother had talked to her friends.

Emmylou let out a sigh. She could go crazy being cooped up here. She wasn't meant to be stationary.

Chapter 19

The nurse took Emmylou to the shower first thing in the morning, and while getting clean was certainly a welcome pleasure, the wide open, impersonal and cold atmosphere left something to be desired. Emmylou had finally convinced her mother to leave the hospital. It was only to go to a restaurant and get Emmy something to eat that wasn't hospital food, but at least she wasn't sitting shotgun to the hospital bed anymore.

She settled back into her clean bed under protest. She had been patient – relatively speaking – about staying here, but enough was enough, and she was ready to leave. She had things to tend to.

"The doctor will be in shortly to check on you."

"That's what you said an hour ago. Where is the good doctor? Taking a leisurely stroll through the gardens?" The nurse nudged her into the bed, and Emmylou had a strong urge to fight her like a child.

"He is tending to other patients."

"Don't you mean he's ignoring me?" She couldn't believe she had vocalized her thoughts.

"Emmylou, I can't discuss other patients with you. He is doing his best, but right now he is handling the workload of three doctors and trying to maintain the clinic in Primrose."

Emmy felt churlish. It was her pride talking. It had taken quite a hit yesterday with her outburst and discovery. Her stomach was heavy with dread at the impending meeting, as much as her heart was fluttering with the anticipation of being near him. She didn't know what to expect, and she didn't function well under uncertainty.

"Good morning, Miss Bennett. The nurses all tell me you are anxious to leave."

Emmy's heart leapt with the timbre of Shane's voice, but her hope shriveled and died with his autocratic manner and impersonal nature. The word's jammed in her throat, and she found herself making incoherent noises.

"Let's check you over and see if you are fit for release today."

Emmylou felt weak and defeated. She rested against the pillows, heartsick. There was no sparkle in his eyes, no half-grin on his lips, no teasing or light-hearted reprimanding. She had lost him. He had been pulled back to his Emily. She gritted her teeth against the tears and allowed him to examine her while trying to answer his questions about her condition with short replies.

He was so detached from her, and her throat ached so much from stuffing the sobs inside that she kept her attention on the latch hook wall hanging of an orange flower. He smelled so good, and her fingers twitched to stroke his cheek, to draw him to her and gaze deeply into his eyes. The question of whether she had pushed him away with her hurtful comment or if a relationship was no longer possible bothered her more than his reserved treatment of her.

"Looks like we can send you home." Shane wrapped the stethoscope around his neck again and picked up her chart to scribble something on it.

"That's great." Her voice was even, emotionless, just like her heart. He hadn't *looked* at her since he walked in the room, and there wasn't anything she could say to change it. She knew it just as she knew when a soufflé was finished baking.

"I'm sending you home with a prescription, and I want you to rest at home today."

She scoffed and took the slip of paper.

"I mean it, Emmylou. I know you don't think so, but you aren't invincible, and you need your recovery time."

She latched onto his gaze like a deer tick. Hope flowered and she bit her bottom lip, praying he had softened. "Thank you," she poured every emotion, every apology rampaging through her into those two words. And for one fleeting moment, she thought it had worked, but just as quickly as it had come, the light extinguished and he dropped his gaze.

"Yes, well." He shrugged and cleared his throat. "That's my job. And you will want to do a follow up with one of the doctors here in about a week. Dr. Ramsey will be back by then." He fidgeted and his jaw flexed. "I'll – take care of yourself."

Whatever he had started to say died, and he turned from her. "Shane." It burst from her before she could pull it back. "I'm sorry," she spoke to his back, desperate for him to turn. All she saw was the side of his face before the slightest of nods and then he lowered his head and walked from the room.

She placed a fist to her forehead in agony. That was it. Another man walking away from her. The only man who had been kind to her. She hadn't known she had wanted him until he was gone. He had been a total surprise, and she had blown it. She should have realized it sooner, and maybe she could have won him away from this Emily. She had been stupid and wasted her chance.

"Hi, sweetheart."

She looked up at her father standing in her doorway in his usual suit and overcoat, his black leather gloves clamped in his left hand. "Hi, Dad."

"Your mother says we can take you home as soon as the doctor has a look at you."

She licked her lips, trying hard to bury her misery. "He was just here. He said I can go."

"That's great, pumpkin."

She nodded and looked down at the white sheet folded over her, wanting to burst into tears, knowing she couldn't show that kind of weakness.

*****

Emmylou wasn't about to take the doctor's advice. She had to see her production house. Her parents had brought her home after a stop at the pharmacy. Thank goodness she had been able to talk her father into being sensible and allow her to go to her own home instead of being forced to camp at their place. It was her childhood home, but it didn't hold the same sentimentality as normal children's. It wasn't a warm, welcoming place for her.

She had allowed her mother to set her up on the couch with trashy novels and magazines, snack foods, a blanket and her inhaler before bidding them goodbye and falsely promising to stay there all day.

The front door closed, and she waited a few more minutes before picking up the landline and dialing it. She had lost her cell phone in all the chaos.

"Scarlett?"

"Emmylou?"

"Yes, it's me. Listen –"

"Why are you calling me when you should be resting? How are you?"

"I'm fine." She paused when she heard Scarlett's sound of skepticism. "Have you been to Prairie Goodness?" She could tell from the long pause the answer was yes.

"I don't think you need to be worrying about that until tomorrow."

"That's a yes. Come get me; I need to see it. I've got to know."

Scarlett let out a long, grumbling sigh.

"I would drive myself, but my car is still there, and my parents wouldn't stop and pick it up on our way home."

"They've finally caught on."

"What's that mean?" But Emmy knew exactly what that meant, and Scarlett wasn't wrong.

"Really, I need to explain that?"

"No. Just come over. Quit trying to distract me; you know it's not going to work. Don't make me call Lacy. I don't want to have to disturb her. She needs her rest, too."

After one more annoyed sound, Scarlett caved like Emmy knew she would. "Fine. I'll be there in ten minutes. But we aren't staying long."

"Of course. Just a peek."

"Mm-hmm."

Scarlett knew Emmylou was lying, but she wouldn't let her friend down. She would be there and stay at PG as long as Emmy needed her to.

Ten minutes later they were loaded in Scarlett's white Jeep and on the road to the production house. Emmylou was sick to her stomach. She could only picture her beloved Prairie Goodness charred beyond recognition, the roof collapsed and debris covering the mangled appliances.

The sun was midway through the sky casting shadows over the parking lot, when they pulled in. Emmylou's eyes were glued to the blackened overhead door that was closed over the scene of the accident. The roof didn't seem to be missing or even shot with holes. The place looked surprisingly normal except for the door.

The women got out and walked to the metal door, neither talking, both inspecting the exterior for signs of devastation. The only sound was their boots crunching against the ice and snow. Emmylou removed her keys from her pocket.

"I'm glad everyone got out safely."

"Almost everyone," Scarlett corrected. "It doesn't look like I thought it would. When I heard the call over the police scanner, I thought the worst. I called Lacy and we rushed over, but with all the commotion, I didn't think to check the building. We were so frantic to find you."

Emmylou smiled and twisted the key to unlock the door. "Thank you."

"What are you thanking me for? We didn't even get to the hospital in time to see you before you were asleep."

"Knowing you were there is enough."

Both women slowly crossed the threshold and stepped inside. Light was streaming through the high window, and the air was heavy with floating particles. Emmy held her breath and flicked the light switch, not expecting the lights to come on. But they did. Her eyes roved over every space, every surface. There in the middle of the production floor was the aftermath. Their boot steps echoed as they cautiously moved forward.

"I was expecting worse. I was expecting the whole place to be destroyed, but it looks like it's just the oven area." Emmylou looked from blackened and broken ovens to puddles of black water pooled on the floor.

"I was expecting that, too. The way Lorie talked when we met her outside made me think the fire was too big to control. And with firemen and people scrambling around, I didn't think to ask anyone else. And then Wes came running up to take care of Lorie, and Lacy and I were bombarded by most of the staff all asking questions about you. They weren't too happy to learn that we were more unaware about it than they were."

She couldn't respond to that. Emmy was touched beyond words. Her employees were the most important thing in the world to her. "And how do I repay them? By burning up their place of employment." The unbearable weight was more than she could handle. She was powerless and overcome with anxiety. Scarlett caught her in her arms, and Emmy hung on with the strength she had left.

"It's gonna be okay," Scarlett whispered into her hair, and the dam of tears broke loose. "It's not as bad as it seems. We'll have this cleaned up in a couple of days, and you'll be back to baking in no time."

Pain filled her lungs as she sobbed and sucked in air. "It doesn't matter," Emmy blurted between stuttering breaths. "I can't fill orders, and we can't afford to be out of commission for any length of time."

Scarlett stroked Emmy's hair as she held her in a tight embrace. "*You* can do it. As long as I've known you, Ems, you have been able to accomplish anything you wanted. This isn't hopeless, and it isn't impossible."

Emmylou jerked free of her friend. "Oh look around, Scarlett! This –" she swept her arm through the air, "– is impossible. It's over. Done. Prairie Goodness is out of business. I can't pay the loan if we don't have a stream of income. I can't win this one."

Scarlett watched Emmylou in the way that she often did when she was thinking how to approach a topic. Emmy didn't want to hear logic or reason. She wanted to wallow, to throw a big fat temper tantrum and break things. She wanted to take a board and beat the daylights out of every ruined oven in this place. "Go

ahead. Tell me I'm wrong. Tell me there is a way to fix *this*!"
Emmy pointed at the destruction. "Please, Scarlett, if you have an
idea I'm all ears." She paused and stared at Scarlett, waiting for
her brilliant idea or another pep talk.

Scarlett merely watched Emmylou. She wet her lips and folded
her arms over her stomach.

"That's what I thought. And you know what? I'm okay with it.
I don't have to fight anymore. I won't have the stress of running
such a large and demanding business. I can have my small bakery
and have a simple existence, maybe keep up my webinars. So
what if I'm a failure? So what if I'm a complete and total fraud
who can't live up to what I teach?"

Scarlett reached out and rubbed Emmylou's shoulder. "You're
not any of those things, and you aren't meant for a simple
existence. This is just a setback. A little bump in the road."

Emmylou snorted and let out a disgusted laugh.

"Okay, so maybe it's a mountain in the road. But, Ems,"
Scarlett paused and shook Emmylou to get her attention, "you
know what this means?"

Emmylou shook her head and looked into Scarlett's beautiful
eyes.

"Get your hiking boots on and get going."

Emmylou closed her eyes briefly before looking back. She felt
her lips twitch with the steady, confident gaze Scarlett was giving
her. "Why do you have so much faith in me?"

Scarlett grinned. "Because you are Emmylou Marie Bennett.
You are the girl who convinced all of our parents that we were
going on a college visit over Spring Break. In Tampa. And you are
the one who defied all expectations and followed your passion.
And you, Emmylou Bennett, will come out on the other side of
this victorious."

Scarlett pulled her close and rested her head against Emmy's
while they looked at the damage. "And how do you suggest I do
that?" Emmylou asked.

"I told you. Go get your boots. This place isn't going to clean
itself."

*****

Shane sat in the darkness nursing a beer for the second night in a row. He was numb and his whole body felt heavy. He may as well be a part of the chair with as useless as he felt. He had covered two shifts at the hospital, kept up with the clinic and treated Emmylou without a break. The last duty was by far the hardest. Too many emotions were attached to that woman, and he had experienced every single one of them in a twenty-four hour period. Now he was empty. He had been surviving on hate and betrayal, but even those had petered out. He should be able to sleep, but her stupid-beautiful face was embedded in his brain, and it wouldn't get out. The feel of her smooth skin was branded on his hand, and the silk of her hair lived in his skin.

And he hated her.

She had invaded a place that had been dead; she had lit him up and brought feelings that he couldn't control. Truth be told, he hadn't wanted to. But she was a heartless witch. He was done with her. His vulnerable heart couldn't handle her. She was comfortable with playing puppet master, but he wasn't comfortable being the marionette.

She didn't consider anyone other than herself, so he was done. He needed a compassionate woman, one who would value him and treat his heart with care. Emmylou wasn't that woman. He didn't know how she had wiggled beneath his defenses, but he would be sure that it wouldn't happen again.

Lesson learned.

The terrifying fear and anguish of Katie's death had lessened over the years of treating patients in varying states of injury and even death. Treating those victims had helped him compartmentalize and work through his guilt and sorrow. Somehow he had allowed his emotions to play too big a role where Emmylou was concerned. She hadn't been just a patient he was trying to save; she had been something more.

Passing her on to the doctor on staff at the Glenwood Hospital was the only answer. It placed her care in more objective hands and separated Shane from temptation. Tomorrow was his dinner with her parents. He planned to call and cancel with a vague promise to reschedule. He didn't usually cower from awkward situations, especially when they included the largest donor to the new clinic where he was employed, but this was an extreme set of circumstances.

He didn't think he could be gracious or even very good company tomorrow night.

The silence in his house was disturbing. He didn't have any cable or internet to distract his thoughts yet. He had been desperate enough to watch YouTube videos on his smart phone, but even those had only worked for a while before he had grown tired of watching the same things. None of it had been able to yank Emmylou from his brain. She wasn't in his heart any longer, but she still occupied his thoughts.

Why did it have to be this way? Why was he fascinated with such a selfish woman? Katie had been selfless, kind and wonderful, and he had loved her completely. Emmylou was nothing like his wonderful Katie.

His phone vibrated on the TV tray beside his chair, and the urge to smash it into tiny pieces nearly got the best of him. The name on caller ID made his whole body sag with exhaustion.

"Hey, Shelby. What is it now?"

Her knowing chuckle tickled his ear. "Relax, Doc. You're off the hook. This isn't an emergency call. Go to your front door."

Shane let out a heavy sigh. "Why?"

"Because I'm standing on your doorstep in my underwear."

"*What?!*" Shane slammed the foot rest down and sat up straight looking around.

"I'm just kidding. I only wanted to get your attention. Just go to your door. You won't be sorry."

Shane stood and shuffled to the door. He opened it and looked down. A grin split his face. "Thanks, Shelby."

"No problem. Enjoy it."

"I will."

"See you tomorrow." Shelby hung up before Shane could thank

her again.

Chapter 20

Emmylou dropped onto her couch and curled her feet beneath her. It had been an awful and a great afternoon. She and Scarlett had cleared out some of the smaller debris, taking stock of the damage and what could be saved. Thirty minutes into it, several of her employees had stopped by, mentioning seeing Scarlett's car and had come in to help. Shortly after that, more of them had come; then Lacy and Kyle had arrived with food for everyone.

As it happened, the stock they had already packaged was still viable. The fire had been contained to the kitchen area. Evan's quick work with the fire extinguisher had seen to that until the fire department had come. Emmy needed to call and thank him for his heroic efforts. Without his help getting people out and shrinking the fire, the place would have been a smoking pile of rubble.

Lorie had been in the shipping room checking orders while the others cleaned up the mess and had found that they would only be able to fill two-thirds of the orders that had been placed. For some reason, Emmylou was glad. It was a small victory in an otherwise crushing defeat. The clock was ticking on her bank loan trouble. She had done nothing to figure out a plan for keeping her production line open. She had pinned her hopes on having a stellar Valentine's season, and that was turning out to be anything but successful.

Even with all of that on her mind, Emmy was oddly relaxed. Her lungs were still a little heavy feeling and sore when she coughed, which was sporadic, but overall she felt good. She had hope that it was going to work out. The support of the people around her lifted her spirits.

She was pondering a nice hot shower to shed the sweat and soot when the doorbell chimed indicating that it wasn't one of her friends or a family member. With some effort, she heaved herself from the couch and ambled to the door.

"Evan!" Emmy leaned against the door with her hand resting on the handle. "I'm glad to see you."

His grin was wide and brightened his face. "I didn't know if I should come over, but I heard you were out of the hospital, and I wanted to check on you." He was relieved and bashful.

"That was nice of you." Emmy smiled and held the door open further. "Would you like to come in?"

"Is it all right? I don't want to wear you out with my visit. I know you need your rest."

"Of course it's all right. You saved my business from burning to the ground! I think you can come in and sit down for a while."

Evan bowed his head as he stepped into her home. She wondered what kind of life he had led that he was uncomfortable entering a friend's house. She ushered him to the couch, but he chose the wing chair instead, so she settled onto the corner cushion and leaned against the armrest across from him.

Evan was glancing around her small house. "I'm happy you're here," she repeated, hoping it would put him at ease.

"I hope it isn't any trouble."

"Of course not." She smiled and looked expectantly at him. "So what brings you over?" She wasn't used to awkward conversations or quiet people.

"I was worried about you and..." he trailed off, rolling his shoulders further forward.

"Your job?" she helped. He skidded a glance across her, and she smiled and nodded. "It's okay, Evan. I completely understand, and for now we are still in business. I'll have to talk with the insurance company tomorrow and see what the next step is, but Scarlett and I were there today doing some clean up."

Evan perked up and tilted his head toward her. His blue eyes sharpened. "How's it looking?"

"Not great but we can salvage most of the shipment. I think the ovens will all have to be replaced, and Lord knows when we can get running again. I think we can do some of the production using the ovens at Bake My Day, but not much, and they would be running around the clock."

"I could take another shift. I'd be willing to work at night, too. Anything you need, Emmylou."

Emmylou couldn't believe his willingness to pitch in. He was a worker. Or maybe he just needed a job that badly. He had seemed such a desperate soul the first time they'd met. "Thank you. I may be taking you up on that, but I also have thirty other employees that are currently out of job. So they will need the work as well."

Evan moistened his lips and leaned back in his chair a little. "I understand your concerns. Please don't think I'm trying to gait ya. I'm not plannin' to pull up stakes any time soon. I'm here and I will help any way you want. I already feel at home at Prairie Goodness."

"I'm glad you feel that way." Evan's accent was so interesting. It was such a combination of worlds. Emmy wondered if he was a country boy unable to shed his roots or a city boy trying to fit in with the country folk. Maybe a bit of both. She didn't know that much about him other than he spent time here with his aunt and uncle on their ranch near Primrose. "I want everyone who works for me to feel that way. I wasn't trying to put words into your mouth or insinuate that you were pushing for work."

"You weren't…" He was going to finish, but laughed lightly instead. He looked into her eyes, merriment playing in his, and sighed. "It seems we're both trying to be overly polite and not step on each other's toes here." He leaned against the armrest of his chair, and Emmylou found herself drawn forward. "So let's just put it this way. You call me when you need my help, and I will come. I'll still plan on working at Bake My Day like I was before?" He raised his brows, waiting for her response.

She nodded. "That sounds like a reasonable plan."

"Good. And if it changes at any time, you let me know, and I will adjust."

Emmylou grinned. "Thank you."

He nodded and closed his eyes, then settled against the wingback.

"I'm usually better at this," Emmy confessed.

"You've been through an ordeal. It's to be expected."

She watched his hands, his elegant fingers folded in his lap, knowing it wasn't the fire or the hospital stay that had her off her game. It was Shane Newbury. After her outburst in the hospital room, she didn't trust herself to speak without causing harm or offense.

"Have you eaten yet?"

"No, I haven't." She was surprised by the invitation in his voice.

"Pizza?"

"*No.*"

She must have said that with too much disgust. Evan pulled a face. "Okay." He glanced in the direction of the kitchen. "Got anything in there?"

She followed his gaze, then looked back with a sideways smile. "I don't know."

He pushed himself out of the chair and held out his hand. "There's only one way to find out."

She contemplated his outstretched hand for a moment before placing hers in its warmth. He lifted her up.

*****

How pathetic did a person have to be to have a date with a middle-aged couple on Valentine's Day? He was accustomed to being alone or working a shift at the hospital on this stupid holiday. Not in a restaurant surrounded by dating couples and talking business with donors.

Shane was dreading dinner with the Bennetts. He would rather cut off his right arm than have to make small talk with Emmylou's parents. He wasn't happy with her, and he knew he wasn't going to be able to stomach the praise for her they would most likely be heaping upon him. What wasn't there to be proud of really? As a parent he would probably be proud of Emmylou's accomplishments, but her people skills and selfishness were unimpressive to say the least.

The beer and bullets that Shelby had brought over last night were the best things he had received in a long time. Somehow, that lady always knew the right thing to do. She may be direct and a bit harsh, but she had a heart the size of the Grand Canyon. Her note attached to the package still had him chuckling. *"If you can't drink it away, blow it up. Cheers."*

He had tried both and had felt better for a while, but now that he was facing two hours of misery in dim lighting and austere surroundings, he wished he hadn't used it all. He could really do with some target practice on a silhouette target – with Emmylou's face in the middle.

Last night had served as a great release of anger and frustration, but he wasn't quite finished. Maybe if he didn't feel like such an idiot, he could get over it. If he didn't feel like she had tricked him, lied and flirted her way into making him retire his defenses, he could forgive her.

She had been stressed and in shock when she'd crushed his heart. Her cough made him cringe even thinking about it now. He was certain she didn't understand how lucky she was. She could have been seriously injured in that fire, all because of that damn hard head of hers. And hadn't he warned her about the electrical issues in that building?

His hands slowly stilled at the half tied Windsor knot at his throat. He stared hard at the tan colored wall. He had been working on the electrical panel one day before the blaze. Tremors racked his body, and he sat on the mattress trying to process it all. Was he responsible for the fire at Prairie Goodness? Had he been careless and left a wire uncapped or a circuit overloaded?

Emmylou had been such a distraction that night. Her fragrance, her hair and that smile; mischievous and charming. Had he missed something? Had he caused another accident that could have harmed the woman he loved?

Sickness filled his stomach and tightened his throat. What had he done? He dropped his head into his hands and jammed his fingers into his hair, pressing on the sides of his head. He was a cursed man. Any woman he loved was in danger. Emmylou had

had a close call. Katie hadn't been so lucky. If he hadn't learned his lesson before, he had now. He wasn't meant to have a woman in his life. He would be okay with that. His work kept him busy enough; he didn't need the distractions.

Shane slid into his suit jacket and pulled on his boots, but he couldn't shake the thought that he was responsible for Emmylou's fire. He settled his Stetson atop his neatly combed hair and grabbed his keys. And if he was responsible, how was he going to make it right? He just thanked God no one had been seriously hurt.

The Dove House was only a few miles from his place, but the drive felt like hours. The night he'd fixed the electric box at the production house played over and over in his mind. He picked apart every step that he could remember, but every one of his memories was clouded with Emmylou's presence. When he parked his truck, he was more convinced than before that he had been the cause of the fire.

If he could just go back and take a look at the box. He needed to inspect his work, that was if the fire marshal hadn't been in there already checking for arson. He walked across the snow covered grounds, up the stairs and through the glass door with the chalkboard sign proclaiming it was open.

"Well, hello there!"

It took Shane a moment to realize that the chipper voice belonged to Lacy. He narrowed his eyes, making it seem like he was glaring at her. He saw her draw back and fold her hands.

"Table for one?"

"No." He placed his hand on her shoulder. "I'm sorry, Lacy. I was distracted when I came in here. Please excuse my rudeness."

She brightened with his smile and nodded in acceptance of his apology. "So if you aren't here to sample Mrs. Walter's prime rib, then what brings you in? I'm feeling fine."

"And you're looking fine. Pregnancy agrees with you, ma'am." He tapped his finger against his hat.

"I'm certainly no ma'am, Doctor."

He believed her. She was too much of a spitfire to ever be mistaken as a dried up, old married woman. "I'm meeting Mr. and

Mrs. Bennett here tonight."

Her eyebrow lifted and a clever gleam entered her eyes. "Really?"

The way she said it made him uncomfortable and squeamish. "They invited the new doctor to dinner," he said, attempting to play it off as a pity invite.

She nodded with a knowing smile. "In that case, they're right this way, sir." She waved at him to follow.

Shane removed his hat and placed it on top of the hat rack just inside the doorway to the dining area. It was decorated in western antiques and artifacts. This was what it must have looked like a hundred years ago when it was an upscale brothel. Being a Nebraska native, Shane had heard of this place but had never been here before moving to Primrose. The last time he was here, it was for an emergency, so he hadn't looked around. And, of course, Emmylou had been on his case with her insults, making a tour an even smaller priority.

The heavy green curtains were pulled back showing the ivory lace and dark night beneath. He was following and gawking, so he nearly ran into Lacy when she stopped. "Sorry."

"No problem." She patted him on the shoulder. "Your server will be right with you."

He wanted to laugh at the professional side of Lacy; it seemed so out of place. Something more along the lines of *"Grub'll be out in two shakes of a lamb's tale,"* seemed more appropriate. Lacy nodded at the table and walked away.

Shane turned his attention to the chairs, ready to shake hands. "I hope I'm not late." He started to smile, taking in the setting. He mentally counted, One, two... *three!* He had expected to be dining with two Bennetts. Not three. And the third was shooting him with red hot daggers from her eyes. Emmylou remained seated even though her parents had risen to greet him.

"Doctor Newbury, this is my husband, George Bennett," Susan introduced.

"A pleasure, sir." Shane shook the man's hand.

"The pleasure is all mine after what you've done for our

daughter and…" he bit the rest of his sentence off and cleared his throat. Shane understood and let it slide without so much as a twitch. "It's an honor to meet you. Our little hamlet is lucky to have you on staff here."

Shane felt his stomach drop with George Bennett's compliment. If only the man knew *all* he had done for his daughter. He could very well be the person to put her out of business. They could sue him for tampering with the electrical system and causing a fire. It was very likely that the next time they met, it would be over a conference table discussing liability and settlement.

"Really, it was nothing, sir. Just doing my job." He could feel the heat from Emmylou's glare on his cheek. He wanted to look at her but knew he couldn't. She would see the guilt in his eyes; he wouldn't be able to hide it from her. This was the most unnerving situation he had ever been in, and that included the time he had had to tell the mother of his fiancée she had died in his care. At least then he had received a modicum of sympathy. He wouldn't be getting the same here.

"Have a seat, please. Of course, you know our Emmylou." George was smiling like the ward boss on rent collecting day as he sat down.

"Yes, of course I do." Did his voice just quiver? "Emmylou." He flicked a tentative look in her direction but felt the heat under his collar rise up his throat. "How are you feeling?"

"Perfectly fine, thank you." From the corner of his eye, he saw her lift her wine glass.

"You won't want to mix that with your medications." The moment the words were out, he wished he could reel them back in.

She rolled her head in his direction. "I'm not on any medications."

He finally turned to look at her fully. She tipped her nose in the air and took a drink of wine, never taking her eyes off him. "I'm sorry. Force of habit. You understand?"

She swallowed and set the glass back down. "Yes, I do. I'm a *very* understanding person."

Shane chewed on the inside of his lip instead of shooting a snappy comeback. "Mm-hmm," he answered instead and slid into his awaiting seat. This dinner was going to be ranked number two on his list of worst nights ever.

Chapter 21

Emmylou was a boiling ball of emotion. When Shane Newbury had walked up to the table, it became crystal clear to her what her mother was doing, and she wasn't going to stand for it. She was already angry at her for forcing her to keep their Valentine's Day plans instead of allowing her to stay at home and rest. His flashy smile had cemented the truth of the situation. This was a setup.

"We're so glad you could pry yourself away from your duties to have dinner with us tonight," Susan Bennett spoke to Shane with a calm smile.

"A night out and away from the demands was a welcome change."

All heads turned in Emmylou's direction when Emmylou snorted. She tried to cover it with her wine glass, and the three of them were tactful enough to return to the ridiculous dinner small talk. She slumped against the cushion-backed chair and crossed her legs. Her mother had requested that she wear her navy blue, dolman style dress tonight and, to avoid another argument, Emmylou had obliged. Now she was wishing she had come in her grey sweats and a pony tail.

Shane Newbury wasn't worth the effort she had put into her appearance. She should have taken Evan up on his offer of another quiet dinner. Last night he had prepared a simple pasta in butter sauce and green salad. It had been an easy night of conversation with no pressure on her performance. She could be herself around him because she knew he wasn't interested in her for anything other than friendship. He had talked about having gotten out of a six-year relationship and not being ready for anyone new. It was why he had come to Primrose. She was keeping the apartment they had shared in Denver, and he didn't want to move in with any of his friends, so he had come home for recuperation.

Laughter broke out around her, snapping her reverie. She glanced around with narrowed eyes, not really caring what the big joke was. She wished she were at home figuring out what to do next. She needed to talk with Lorie. What she didn't need was her mother's baited questions, her father's jovial back patting or Shane's charm.

The restaurant was a buzzing hive of schmoozing couples. It turned Emmylou's stomach. How many years had she been half of one of those couples? She tried to remember if she had had a repeat boyfriend over those years but couldn't come up with anything.

Scarlett bustled over to stand at Emmylou's shoulder and spoke without taking in who she was addressing. "Happy Valentine's Day. Would you like to hear... the specials?" she finished lamely with wide eyes.

Emmylou saw her friend quickly surmise what was happening and come to her own conclusion. She licked her lips and raised her brows, waiting for someone to answer her. God love her, at least she was trying to play it cool no matter what she was thinking.

"I would love to hear what you have on special tonight, darlin'."

Emmy stuffed the snort that nearly escaped. Her father used that country boy drawl when he was trying to be charming. Had he stayed on the family farm instead of becoming a banker, it would have rung true. As it was, he sounded like a middle aged man in the midst of a mid-life crisis trying to pick up college girls.

Scarlett regaled them with the menu choices in her ultimate hostess voice but winked at Emmy in the middle of the side dish description. That made Emmy feel justified in her feelings.

Everyone placed their orders. Emmylou expected the good doctor to reprimand her when she ordered the large serving of prime rib, but he now seemed to be ignoring her and opting for studying the room decorations. Well that was just fine with her.

"That one there was the original owner of The Dove House, Emma Schuster, Lacy's great-great grandmother," George Bennett was so kind to point out when he noticed Shane's attention had settled on her portrait.

"She was a famous madam." Emmylou felt her cheeks bloom pink with her outburst. She hadn't meant for it to sound so bad. Actually, Lacy's ancestors had been amazing business women.

"Yes, I know," Shane answered with barely a glance at her.

Emmy had an overwhelming urge to stick her tongue out and mimic his condescending comment. He was turning her into an eight-year-old she realized with a sigh. She opted to remain silent while her parents kept the conversation going. She was repeatedly maneuvered to join in but managed to reply with minimal responses. Pretty soon she could feel her mother's blazing gaze boring into her. Emmylou didn't care.

"So Doctor Newbury –,"George began.

"Please call me Shane."

Emmylou rolled her eyes and snatched a piece of bread from the basket on the table, tearing off a chunk.

"Shane." George grinned, something Emmy usually liked about her dad and would tonight if he wasn't such a traitor. "Tell me, do you have someone special back in the big city?"

Emmy's heart dove into her shoes. She involuntarily turned her attention to Shane, completely proclaiming her interest in him. Her stomach ached because she already knew the answer, but this time she would hear it from his lips. Her chest burned from holding her breath, and she tried to release it in a slow, inconspicuous way. Shane smiled and looked down at his plate with a strange smile ticking at his lips.

"No, sir. I don't."

"Liar!" Emmylou hissed.

The brown eyes that turned to her were flagged with sorrow and confusion. "Excuse me?"

"You heard me. I called you a liar." Her voice wavered and she was poised to flee the scene but battled the urge to storm from the table.

Shane opened his mouth, then closed it thoughtfully.

"Emmylou Marie Bennett! You apologize to Doctor Newbury

right this minute. I will not tolerate you speaking to our guest in this way!"

"Oh please, Mother. I can't stand this any longer. And don't tell me that this isn't a *date* that you set up between the two of us."

Susan Bennett's lips flattened, and her left eye twitched as she pierced Emmy with her stare.

"I would like to speak with Emmylou for a moment in private if that's all right with both of you?" Shane looked from Susan to George, getting their nodded agreement. "Thank you." He pushed his chair back and stood holding his hand out in front of Emmylou.

She jutted her jaw and gaped in outrage at his hand and his audacity. He stared hard into her eyes, and a muscle ticked in his jaw, but his stance exuded nothing but calm. "May we speak privately?" His lips pursed forcing his nostrils to flair.

Emmy didn't even consider declining his request. She simply slid her chair back and stood without taking his hand. He straightened with a sharp intake of breath at the slight and ushered her with a hand to lead the way. She tossed her napkin into the chair, flipped the skirt of her dress and shoved her shoulders back as she marched a path through the chairs.

She hung a right down the hallway and back to the study. The Dove House had been a second home to her; she knew it as well as her own. She flicked the overhead lighting on and staved off a chill. Ever since Lacy's incident with Lauren last year, this room gave her the creeps. Knowing a woman had crashed through the window in here and died was something she couldn't quite get over.

Emmylou could feel Shane only two feet behind her. Or maybe it was his anger she sensed. When she made it to the desk, she turned and leaned against the cool surface, folding her arms over her chest. Shane planted himself in front of her, but just out of striking distance. His gaze was unnerving, and Emmy found she couldn't hold it. *Coward!* Her brain screamed, but she ignored it. She set her attention at his collar instead.

The seconds stretched and she struggled under their weight. He had asked for this meeting, and she would be damned if she spoke first.

"This is ridiculous!" Emmy broke her own promise.

"I agree with you."

She glared straight into his brown eyes, understanding his meaning and not liking it. "Then why are we in here? You wanted to speak in private, so here we are. Speak." She gestured with her hand.

"I'm not sure where to start. I'm not one who angers easily, but I find you spark that fire faster than lightning on a hayfield in October."

She narrowed her eyes. "You know, when you talk like that it almost makes me think you're human."

"Almost, but not quite," he surmised and she assented.

"So is that why we're in here? So you can tell me I anger you?"

His jaw clenched and he crossed his arms. "Not exactly. We're in here so I can tell you that you're acting like a spoiled child and embarrassing your parents. Two things I find detestable."

"A lesson in manners? That's why *you* embarrassed *me*?"

"Well somebody needed to stop you. Your parents were being too polite to tell you that ladies don't guzzle wine and sling insults at dinner guests."

"I'll sling more than insults at you!" She slapped her hands on the edge of the desk and leaned forward. "You have more guts than a turkey buzzard!"

"And you have about as much grace as an elephant in a tutu!"

"How dare you call me fat!" Emmylou charged forward.

"What are you talking about?"

"You called me an elephant!" She advanced but Shane held his ground.

"There you go not listening again. I didn't call you fat, I called you uncouth."

Her mouth gaped open, and her eyes flared with fury. "*Uncouth? Uncouth?* Who do you think you're calling uncouth?!"

He moistened his lips and tightened his folded arms. "No matter how many times you say it, it doesn't change the fact that you have been acting like a gangly little filly with her tail in a snit and prancing around like an entitled princess at her debut ball."

"I am not a princess," she hissed through clenched teeth. "And you are an overgrown, self-righteous, narcissistic, pain-in-the-ass man with a God complex. If you spent half as much time trying to get to know someone as you did diagnosing their personality defects, you might actually get along in this town, but I can tell you, *Doctor* Newbury, that you won't last long here at the rate you're going."

The half-cocked grin he gave her spurred her rage more than the insults he'd been hurling at her. She was standing toe-to-toe with him trying to make herself as threatening as possible, and he was enjoying this!

"You seem to be the only one who doesn't like me. Everyone else has been very welcoming." He rubbed his chin thoughtfully with one hand. "Actually, you were pretty welcoming the other night."

Her eyes narrowed to slits. She opened her mouth, but no words came out. Her brain was assaulted by the memory of his delicious kisses, his caressing hands and her overheated body. It had been a moment of weakness; a wonderful, awful moment. She swallowed and his face softened. His gaze wondered over her face and settled on her lips making heat burn in her cheeks.

"Yeah, that's what I thought about it too."

She whipped her head up to stare hard at him. She wanted to feel outrage and anger at his presumption, but the way he caught his lower lip with his teeth squashed it. "It didn't mean anything," her voice wavered.

"I know." His lips flickered into a smile, and he lifted his hand to tuck her hair behind her ear. "But maybe this one will." He tilted his head and lowered his lashes.

Emmy found herself helpless at his touch. He leaned forward and she tipped her chin up. "I'm still mad at you," she whispered and closed her eyes.

"And I'm still mad at you." His breath brushed against her mouth a second before he caught her lips in a soft kiss.

212

*****

Being seated next to Emmylou made it hard for Shane to stare leisurely at her. The short time they had spent in Lacy's study still had his temperature spiked. The anger they had been feeling had erupted into something more. The feelings he had wished gone had come charging back like flood waters. The two of them were like magnets; the pull was too great when they got close.

The lights were dim, and Emmylou's blue eyes sparkled in the candlelight. He had walked in here with a chip on his shoulder, but within fifteen minutes, she had humbled him. He could still feel her pliant skin beneath his hands. Like the twist of a fishing reel, his attention was drawn to her. The rosy glow perched on each cheek bone was enchanting. He couldn't fight the urge to touch her, to be near her. He had staked his claim on her the night he had kissed her in her bakery.

A bolt of electricity charged up his leg and zinged into his abdomen. Her foot wiggled against his boot, pulling his pants tight around his ankle. With all the will he could muster, he propped his elbow on the table, rested his chin in his palm and stared at Emmy's father. His other hand stayed in his lap ready to defend against Emmylou's ever rising foot.

"Um-hmm," he agreed with George through tight lips. He swallowed and flicked a killing glance at Emmy. She returned it with a bland smile. *How could she be so calm?* Blood was racing through him to places that shouldn't be getting extra stimulation. Especially with her parents at the table!

"Don't you agree, dear?" Susan addressed her daughter after picking up her wine glass.

Emmylou turned casually toward her mother, presenting Shane a view of her delicate profile. "Oh yes, Mother. I also think we have a state-of-the-art clinic, and isn't it just lucky that we have positioned Doctor Newbury there?"

Shane was going crazy. Did Emmylou actually say *positioned* with significance? Why would she say that?

"Quite right, darling." George Bennett raised his glass in a toast. Everyone at the table followed suit. Shane needed something stronger than white wine. As it was, he took an extra long gulp to fortify his frazzled nerves.

"So, Emmylou, have you found anything out about the fire at Prairie Goodness?" He hadn't intended to chill the mood at the entire table; he had only wanted to distract Emmylou from her toe choreography. Maybe if he'd had more blood flowing to his brain, he would have thought the question out better.

"I don't think we need to discuss business tonight." George's smile clearly deemed the subject closed.

"Isn't that what you have us here for, Dad? To talk about the clinic and your generous support of it?"

Shane stared in amazement at Emmylou.

George directed his smile solely at Emmylou. "No. Tonight is about getting to know each other better."

"Oh, I see," Emmy's sardonic drawl tightened the mood further.

"Let's not do this tonight please," Susan looked from her husband to her daughter.

"I'm sorry. I didn't mean to bring up such a sensitive subject. I can understand that –"

"It's not a sensitive subject," Emmylou interrupted turning her attention from her mother to Shane. "To answer your question, no, we don't know anything, and the Fire Marshal won't be here until Monday to assess the damage and determine the cause. Thank you for your concern." She made pointed looks to her parents with that statement.

Shane nodded and took another drink. When was the food going to be ready? Asking about the fire had twisted his stomach into knots. He had been distracted about his possible involvement until that moment, and now that it was out there, it had become the hole in the boat. It was all downhill from here on out. This evening would soon be like wreckage on the bottom of the sea.

"A bouquet for your sweetheart?" Mrs. Walters appeared at George's shoulder with a large clutch of multi-colored roses. She seemed oblivious to the prickly climate at the table, though Shane didn't know how that was possible.

"Kathleen! How are you this evening?" George flipped like Judas Iscariot and beamed a smile at the woman. He reached for his wallet. "I would love one yellow and three reds." He pulled out some money while Mrs. Walters picked out the roses.

"Here you are George."

Mrs. Bennett made a strange noise in her throat and tried to pass if off as a cough.

"Thank you." He presented his wife with two red roses and Emmylou with the yellow. "Hang on a second, Kathleen." He waited until Mrs. Walters turned back and he held out the third red rose to her. She smiled and shook her head.

"Happy Valentine's Day," he said.

"You're too sweet, George." She accepted the flower. "Y'all enjoy your evening."

"What do you think of your –" George brought himself up short when his gaze connected with that of his red-faced wife. "What?"

Susan tossed her roses down on the table. "Don't pretend that you don't know why I'm angry. We've been married for over thirty years, George Bennett. I think you know me well enough to understand."

Shane wondered if he could duck under the table and crawl away without being missed. The dinner had gone from cordial to family feud, and he had been the instigator. Susan Bennett wouldn't be as upset if Shane hadn't started talking about the fire.

"All I did was give an old family friend a flower for Valentine's Day, Susan. She's also a valued bank customer, and at one time, she was your friend."

Shane looked to Emmylou hoping that she would get them both out of there, but she was intent on listening to the argument. In fact, she seemed to have a stake in it. She appeared curious instead of embarrassed. He didn't know what to do. This was a private moment taking place in a very public setting. Several of the couples at nearby tables had broken off their conversations to stare at the Bennetts.

"Oh yes, some friend she was, too."

George leaned forward, taking the challenge. "You've had a burr under your saddle for the past twenty-five years about that woman. I thought we could all finally get along. I thought we were all grown-ups here. I didn't realize marrying you would destroy your friendship. If I had I would've –" George was searching for an answer.

"Would've what, George? Not married me? Married her instead?"

"I think I will excuse myself. We can finish our dinner another time." Shane rose from his chair and placed the napkin on the dinner plate.

"Here we are!" Scarlett announced while placing the serving stand down next to the table. "Sorry it took so long. We're backed up in the kitchen with Kyle's Valentine's surprise for Lacy. He's been working in there all evening on some sort of special meal."

Scarlett took in the scene with a sweeping glance, then focused her attention to Emmylou. She raised her eyebrows a fraction. Shane looked to Emmylou and lifted the corner of his mouth as she faintly shook her head at her friend in response. Scarlett paused, then went to work placing the meals on the table. Shane was fascinated with the silent communication the two of them had.

"Mr. Bennett, here are your steak, baked potato and fresh green beans prepared special by Mrs. Walters."

Susan Bennett shoved her chair back, slapped her napkin down on the table, and with a snap of her head, strode from the dining room, back straight, chin high, and with all eyes tracking her progress.

George knocked his chair to the ground when he followed her.

"What did I say?" Scarlett asked with a plate still in her hand.

"Nothing, Scar. You didn't say anything," Lacy answered while standing. "I'll…" she swept her hand over the table.

"Yep. It's fine." Scarlett nodded.

"Thanks." Emmylou rushed after her parents. Her stiff nods and lack of eye contact with the other diners made Shane go after her.

"Small towns," he mumbled to himself.

Chapter 22

"Thanks for the ride." Emmylou pulled her coat around her neck and scooted toward the door of Shane's truck. The awful scene at the restaurant had cocooned the truck cab in silence, and it still hung heavy in the air. Her earlier boldness was replaced with pensiveness.

"It's no problem, really."

They had followed her parents outside to see their car pulling away and her father yelling for her mother to come back.

"It was nice of you to take my dad home, too."

"I hope the two of them can work it out."

"I'm sure they'll be fine," Emmy lied.

The dashboard glow cast Shane's features in a sharp outline. His cowboy hat didn't help Emmylou in being able to read what he was thinking. It didn't matter; she already knew. Her family was appalling and the meal had been a disaster. All three of the Bennetts had behaved like common trailer park domestics. Bad manners, tantrums and public arguments had dominated the evening, and it was embarrassing. Her normally very reserved, proper family had split at the seams, and the fetid core had bubbled out.

"I want to apologize again for the way the evening went. I behaved horribly and my parents…" She didn't know how to finish because she didn't want to share the dysfunction of her family. It wasn't her fault that Mrs. Walters had been her father's high school sweetheart, and her mother couldn't get past it.

"Hey, don't worry about it. We all have a little crazy in our gene pools." Shane pounded the steering wheel with his hand and looked away shaking his head. "Sorry. That didn't come out right."

She laughed. Most of their relationship could be summed up in that sentence. "No. You're right. How could you think anything different after what happened? It was like having dinner with the Kennedys."

Emmylou wanted to die. When was it going to end? She had hopped from disaster to disaster, and somehow Shane had been witness to nearly all of them. It was a humbling experience to have a stranger know all the worst things about you. At least her friends knew that *part* of her life was normal.

"Thanks, again. I'm sure I'll see you around." Emmylou pushed the truck door open.

"Wait!" Shane's hand touched her shoulder, and she turned to see him slide from his truck. He hurried around the hood and held open her door. She accepted his offered hand, and his warm grasp sent a shiver through her. She wobbled when her heels met the snow-packed sidewalk, and he held her closer to stabilize her.

"Thanks." She seemed to be thanking him at every turn tonight, and she didn't like it.

"You're welcome." His voice was silky and created fog clouds in the cold air. He wrapped his arm around her and escorted her to the door. Her heart pounded so hard in her chest that she thought it might jump right through her ribs. They made it onto the porch, and she reached, with shaking hands, for the door handle. He was standing inches from her, the heat from his body, his wonderful smell all mixed together to send her nerves into a meltdown.

"I've got it." He laid his agile hand over hers, then moved it away.

All feeling left her body; she stood trembling in anticipation as he held her hand and angled toward her. Her breath stalled in her throat when he tipped his hat higher on his head, and his hand slid from hers to cup her face and lift her chin. Shane gave a half smile before pressing his moist lips gently against hers.

He braced a muscular arm along her lower back, and Emmylou went limp against him. Her hands grasped at the front of his coat to draw him closer. The kiss in the study was nothing compared to this one. It had been charged and passionate. This time his lips made slow caressing movements. They molded and tugged her mouth, stealing her breath and quickening her pulse. Her head was spinning. He flicked his tongue inside making her moan and clasp tighter to him. He deepened the kiss and she nearly shattered. Shane was in complete control.

He shifted to use the house as support, his leg pressed between her legs, his broad frame blocking her from the cold wind. His mouth traveled from her lips, down her throat and to her collar bone. It was heaven. His silken hair slid between her fingers, and the stubble on his jaw scraped against her delicate skin. She gripped the back of his head as he traveled along the sensitive bone and back up to her cheek.

He whispered sweet things in her ear, driving her closer to the edge of euphoria. He kissed her lips again with more control and hunger than she had ever experienced before. His hard body moved along hers, and her breasts ached with need.

"Let's go inside," she rasped, unable to control her hands from holding him tight to her.

Her eyes flickered open when he stilled. His dark eyes shone with desire, and his breath came in pants. He stroked her hair and brushed his thumb over her swollen lips. "I'd love to."

"Great." She let out a sigh and groped for the handle. He stopped her hand and turned her back to him.

"But I can't."

It was like a hard slap across her cheek. "*What?*" She shook her head to realign her senses. "Did you just tell me no?" She couldn't believe it. She had never been turned down. He caught her again when she tried to rush through the door. "Get off me!"

"Not until you listen." His hands were strong, but his words kind. "Please, Emmylou."

Her name was a plea, and the sound of it on his lips painfully beautiful. She kept her face averted, but stopped struggling to get away. His ragged breathing tore at her heart, signifying the intensity of a moment before.

"I don't want it to be like this for us. No! You don't understand." His words grew in urgency when her body tightened and shifted with the insult. "I've... damn it!"

He had both of her shoulders pinned beneath his hands, pushing her into the boards of the house. When she looked at him, what she saw sent a riot charging through her. He was wild with panic and confusion. She relaxed beneath his urgency and stared hard at him. "You what? You have someone else? You're married or have a fiancée somewhere?"

"No! I told you that I don't. There is no one else in my life." Shane's face was harsh, but his eyes pleaded with her. She forced herself to settle against the house and wait for him to continue. "But." He swallowed and her heart throbbed. "I did once."

A huff of disbelief escaped her. Tears burned her eyes. Whatever she was feeling wasn't relief, and it wasn't anger. It was... sickness. A sick, twisting disappointment. The scorch of betrayal roared through her.

"I was engaged once. We were young and she..." he choked.

Emmylou slowly managed to turn toward him. She crumpled at the sight of him. His head was bent against his arm, his eyes squeezed shut and a tortured mask had claimed his handsome face. This woman had broken his heart. Hers ached with compassion. She lifted her hand to his face and cradled it in her palm. He leaned into it.

"I'm sorry," she whispered and kissed the side of his mouth.

He breathed deeply. He was sagging beneath the weight of burden. She wanted to wrap him in her arms and chase away the pain. This feeling of fierce protectiveness was reserved only for her friends; she had never felt it so strongly for a man.

"So am I. But you need to know something. We were twenty-two and were visiting her parents to tell them about the engagement." He swallowed hard. Her body trembled with the need to smooth the anguish in his face; vanquish it from his soul.

"It's okay. You can tell me." She laid her hand on his chest and felt the thunder of his heart against her palm.

"Emmylou? Are you all right?"

Shane and Emmylou jolted at the interruption. She suddenly felt the whip of cold air. They had been shielded from the outside by intimacy, and it had been whisked away. Shane straightened and dropped his arm that had been keeping her sheltered against the house, and Emmy was weakened with emptiness. Approaching footsteps crunched on her sidewalk.

"Emmylou? Are you all right?" the voice repeated finally breaking what was left of their moment.

She cleared her throat, and Shane sidestepped with one last desolate look.

"*Evan?*" Emmy raised her hand to her coat lapel. "What are you doing here?" Her mind couldn't catch up with her shock.

"I was coming over to see if you wanted some ice cream." Evan lifted a paper sack. "With hot fudge. I remembered you saying last night at dinner you didn't have anything going on tonight so -" he shrugged and took a couple of steps forward but hesitated when his attention shifted to Shane. "I can see you're busy."

"She's not busy. I was just leaving." Shane walked to the top of the steps.

"Wait!" He turned and she was at a loss for words. His face was harsh and blank, his posture rigid. She pleaded silently with her expression and outstretched hand. "I -" her mind strained for the right words. She wanted him to stay, to finish what he was telling her.

"It's fine. I can see you have a busy schedule to juggle. My time is up." Shane descended the stairs, and she called after him. He stopped next to Evan but didn't turn back. "Y'all have a nice evening."

"But -" Evan came up the stairs and grinned at her. "Hang on a sec, okay, Evan?" Emmy charged down the stairs and hurried over the snow covered sidewalk. Shane was getting into his truck when she finally caught up with him. She grabbed the door, refusing to let him close it. "Stop!" She panted and clutched her dress from the gust of wind that sent ice shavings over her skin. "You can't do that to me."

"Do what to you Emmylou? We were having a conversation, and it was interrupted by your date. Maybe you should have a chat

222

with your boyfriend."

"Don't do that. Don't take your pain out on me." She let out a heavy sigh. "I think we were doing more than just having a conversation on my porch. You were about to tell me something very important. What was it? I need you to tell me."

He tilted his head so his hat covered most of his face. "I told you what I wanted to tell you. More than -" he bit off the next words before looking at her. "I have to go and so do you. Your boyfriend's waiting for you." He tugged the door free of her and slammed it. The truck fired to life. Shane flicked a glance at her from the corner of his eye and she stepped back as he drove away.

*****

March rolled around in a haze for Shane. He drank too much, thought too much. When he thought, he drank. He spent most of the time expecting the police to show up and arrest him for arson, or at least serve him with a lawsuit from burning down Emmylou's production house.

Those thoughts inevitably brought about more memories of Emmylou, which generated more drinking. It was a horrible cycle he was trapped in. Every day passed without any word, and the knot of anxiety hardened into a crater in the pit of his stomach.

He hadn't had any hospital work, but the daily operations of a small town clinic came with plenty of distraction. He had currently researched more severe conditions than he had in all of med school. It seemed to him that the area was plagued with an onslaught of rare and serious ailments. He hadn't diagnosed anything graver than a case of pneumonia, but it was just a matter of time.

He sat eating his lunch at his desk while looking over an interesting case of a seven-year-old boy's chronic neck pain. His boots were resting on the corner of his desk, and he had just stumbled upon some fascinating information about the boy's symptoms.

"Doctor Newbury?" Shelby's sturdy frame materialized in the doorway.

Shane slammed his laptop shut. "What is it?"

Her light eyes narrowed on him, and her lips thinned. She marched into his office and dropped a stack of files on his desk. He looked from them to her annoyed face. She braced her hands on the edge and leaned forward.

"What in the hell is this?" Her eyes flashed down to the files and back up.

Shane reclined in his chair and laced his fingers together over his stomach. "I'm not sure I understand what you mean." Heat was rising under his western shirt.

"Oh come off it, Newbury! These are nothing more than colds and flus and one broken wrist. You referred Doris to an internalist?" She straightened and plopped her hands on her hips.

"Yes, I think she may be suffering from diverticulitis."

"That's ridiculous! Doris Murphy has a hankering for Scarlett's rhubarb-blueberry jam and chooses to forget that her old stomach can't take the bite of rhubarb anymore. All she needs is some antacid and a kick in the backside. I told you that three days ago when she came in here."

He twisted his chair back and forth and watched her tap her foot on the floor. "I think you're wrong."

"Bullshit! I don't know what you've got going on, but you've been a moody, overanalyzing sergeant-major for the last three weeks, and I'm sick of it. If you don't get your head out of your butt soon, I'm going to get a suppository and help you out!" Shelby slammed her hand down on the files fixing him with a fiery glare. "You are going to cancel all the incorrect recommendations in these and put them in the cabinet yourself."

Shane leaned forward and steepled his fingers to match her glare. "Who's the doctor here?"

Shelby narrowed her eyes. "That is a really good question."

She pushed her weight off the desk and spun on her heel. "Fix it!" she instructed as she stomped from his office. "And stop using WebMD!"

Shane stared at the empty doorway. How in the world did she know he was searching online websites? He pitied the man who was married to that fireball. Looking at the stack of files, he wondered if she was right. He knew he had been short with the staff lately, but he hadn't realized it was as bad as all that. Shelby was a great nurse, and her personality was a dynamic match for his own. She was smart enough and had enough experience to be a doctor herself. He threw himself against the chair and looked at the wall that held his degree and license.

That damn blonde would not get out of his head. He could still feel her soft skin, smell her vanilla filled hair. Every time he turned around, something reminded him of Emmylou. He'd nearly had a panic attack when he saw Lacy's name on the schedule. The last time she was in, Emmylou was with her. He didn't want to see Emmylou or talk to her. He was furious with her for lying to him again. He was angry at himself for telling her about Katie.

The crunch of his pop can crushing in his hand filled the room. She wasn't letting any grass grow under her feet. She had thrown him aside and moved on to the man who worked in her bakery. A man who wasn't worthy of her. Or maybe he was. Maybe she wasn't as special as he had imagined. Maybe she was fickle and narcissistic. He was a fool to want her.

Shane stayed late reevaluating the cases that Shelby had brought in. He had been distracting himself by making his work more than it was. Now he was going to have to make phone calls and apologize to his patients, as well as cancel lab work and appointments with specialists at the hospital in Glenwood.

It was pitch black when he left the clinic. Shane had lost track of the time. He checked his watch and saw that it had reached ten-thirty already. His stomach growled and clenched to remind him he hadn't eaten since lunch. He started his truck wishing for the first time that he were back in the city. There he could get any kind of food at any hour. Here he was going to have to go home and slap something together or nuke it in the microwave.

Out of habit he drove down Main Street past Emmylou's bakery. He knew it was cowardly, but he had to. He had avoided her at all costs in the daylight hours, but somehow knowing that she had been there drew him in. He was traveling at one notch above turtle, trying only to look from the corner of his eye. A movement caught his attention. He slammed on the breaks and snapped his head to the side.

"What the hell?" He rolled his window down. "Hey, Evan! What's up?" That was nicer than what he was thinking. He really hated that guy.

"Hey, Doc!" Evan jammed his hands into his coat pockets and walked away from the bakery door to the edge of the sidewalk. "Just out for a walk. I was going past, so I thought I'd check to see if we had locked up. It was a busy day, lots going on."

Shane narrowed his eyes, taking in the whole scene. "Man, you must really like to walk at night. In winter." He sincerely hoped he caught the reference to Valentine's night.

"I do," he let out a nervous laugh. "Clears my head."

"Uh-huh." Shane knew a lie when he heard one. He dealt with them on a daily basis. Nobody was truthful about their health. And Evan Matthews was no different than any of his patients.

"What are you up to this fine evening?"

The way he was shivering meant anything except fine evening. "Oh, just catching up with some paperwork at the clinic."

"Yeah, I can imagine you're busy this time of year."

"Uh-huh." Shane was hoping he would garner more information if he didn't add too much to the conversation. Evan nodded and looked up the street. "So where ya' headed now?"

"I'm not sure. A bit more walking and then home I guess."

"Yeah? Did you grow up in Antarctica or something? It's like two degrees outside." Shane's arms tensed and his heart thumped. He was giving it his all to remain casual.

"Nah, I just like the cold."

Damn! Evan wasn't offering up any kind of information. Shane tapped the side of his truck with his hand. "Well, I guess I'll let you get after it then."

"Okay. You have a nice night, Doc."

"You, too." Shane rolled his window back up. That was a load of crap. He didn't know what Evan Matthews was up to, but it wasn't a leisurely stroll in two degree weather late at night. He was a baker and bakers were early morning people.

He watched Evan in his rearview mirror. He was walking in the opposite direction with his shoulders hunched against the cold. Shane would eat his boot if Evan actually liked being out walking in winter. Evan turned the corner, disappearing from Shane's view. With hesitation, Shane turned and drove home. He didn't know why he cared; Emmylou had chosen Evan. If he was a sleazebag, then it was on her head. He rubbed his chest when his heart ached but chose to focus on the road instead of turning around and investigating.

Chapter 23

"Dad?" He was the last person Emmylou expected to be in her office.

He stood in the doorway, shifting the brim of his hat around in his hand. "Hi, darlin'." His mouth twisted into an apologetic smile.

Emmylou turned fully in her chair. "Come on in. What are you doing here?" She hated unannounced visits from her father. The last one had brought the worst news possible; this one didn't look like it was going to be any better.

He shuffled in and Emmylou pulled a stack of papers from the metal chair and set them on top of the files next to it. "Sorry." Emmylou didn't have this office set up for visitors. This was where she did her bookwork and kept her recipes and sketches. The room on the other side of the kitchen was where she met with her clients.

"It's no problem. You weren't expecting me."

"No. I wasn't." Emmy hoped that was enough of an opening for him. Instead of speaking he fidgeted in the small chair and rubbed his hands together. He looked like he had aged five years in the past three weeks, and the stress lines that he often got on his forehead were deeper. "Dad? What's wrong?"

If it was another problem with her business, she was going to go drown herself in Sunset Pond. She couldn't take any more bad news.

"How are things going here?"

He wouldn't meet her gaze, opting to glance around pretending to be interested.

"They're going well. Why?"

He propped his arms on his knees and leaned forward. "Just

curious."

"Really? The bank hasn't decided to foreclose? They haven't found that I actually owe more money than they thought, and I'm going to have to figure out how to come up with that too?"

"Not that I know of." He pressed his lips together and then his palms.

"I got the insurance check," she offered, hoping that would spark his interest and he would start talking.

"That's great, honey. Did it cover everything? They didn't try to screw you, did they?"

Her dad livened up and a spark of relief hit her. "They tried. But I'm George Bennett's daughter. They didn't get very far."

He grinned. "That's right you are. What did the Marshal's report say? What was the cause?"

"Faulty wiring behind one of the ovens. The insurance company tried to say we didn't have sufficient capabilities on our panel, but the Marshal said that was crap and had Johnny from Dietz' Electrical come out and look. They found it was all regulation." She stopped herself from telling her dad that Shane had been the one to fix the problem or she could have been found at fault for the fire. Then she would have had to go after the business that installed it. It would have dragged the whole thing out. It could have been a year or more before it was settled.

That was the only good news she had had in months.

"That's good. I'm glad it all worked out. Are you up and running yet?"

"Not yet. It'll probably be another couple of weeks before everything is repaired and the equipment installed so the staff can return to work. I have most of them at Prairie Goodness helping as much as they can. The rest are putting in some hours over here. But it's a struggle for everyone. I'm trying to use the insurance money to supplement lost wages."

"That's awful nice of you, Emmy. You're a good boss."

Emmylou thought her heart had stopped. Her father hadn't paid her a compliment since her college acceptance letter had arrived in the mail with a full academic scholarship. "Thanks, Dad," she fumbled.

"I don't say it enough, and I'm sorry. You really have made quite the business here."

Her chest tightened and sickness washed over her. "Are you dying? Is that why you're here?" Panic filled her voice and her heart.

"No," he chuckled lightly. "That's not it."

"Then, is Mom? Seriously, Dad, you have me worried." Numbness spread through her, preparing her for the worst.

"No."

Emmy could feel her cheeks pale. Her breathing had become erratic. She held her father's blue-eyed gaze, building up her internal armor.

"I've been wanting to talk to you since the night of our little dinner."

Emmy clamped her hands together and tried to remain quiet.

"I don't know what you thought that night, but I wanted to explain." Emmy nodded and waited while her dad took a deep breath. "I guess it's a harder thing to explain than I thought."

"It's all right. I'm listening. Explain it however you want."

"Well, I guess we'd have to go back to when your mother and I were first married. You see we had gone to high school together, but we never dated. Actually, I had gone steady with Kathleen. Mrs. Walters," he added when Emmy wrinkled her face.

"I knew that."

Her father nodded. "Okay. But did you know that Kathy and I were engaged and that she broke it off when I went off to college?"

"No." A riot of emotions charged through her. Her father had wanted to marry someone else?

"She was a year behind me and didn't want to have a long distance relationship. I think that she just changed her mind about me."

"So what does that have to do with mother?"

He held out a quieting hand. "Well, Kathleen and your mother were best friends in school. The three of us had spent time together, but I never really thought about your mom that way. She always seemed so refined and graceful. What would a girl like that see in a dusty old farm boy like me?"

Emmylou couldn't quite grasp the picture of her parents in their youth. She had never thought of them as idealistic young kids. They never talked about how they met or anything much about their childhoods. She knew her dad was the second youngest son in a family of three boys and two girls, and that her two uncles took over the family farm while he went off to school and then became a banker and that her mother was an only child, raised in a prominent Primrose family. All of Emmylou's grandparents had passed away before she had turned twenty, so she didn't know anything much about her dad's family.

"I'm confused. How did you two get together?"

Her dad's eyes sparkled. "That happened when were in college. It was the seventies." He lifted his shoulders and fought off a smile. "Let's just say she looked good in those white go-go boots and short skirts, and I saw her in a whole new way."

"Oh, Dad! Gross!" Emmy threw herself back in her chair and covered her ears.

He scowled playfully and patted her leg. "Emmylou, your mother was perfectly respectable. I was trying to say that I now saw her as a woman and not Kathleen's prissy friend. Things sort of fell into place after that. We came back to Primrose and got married, and the rest is history."

Emmy was seeing her parents as people for the first time. People who had a love story, a history, perhaps dreams. She would have liked to have known them when they got married. By the look on her father's face, they had had a good time together. She had always wondered about that. Her mother was so uptight and proper, and her dad was the businessman everyone liked, but it seemed Emmy didn't know either of them and what she had presumed may have been very wrong.

"Dad." She waited until he focused on her. Emmy moistened her lips trying to frame her question. "What part of that history is Mrs. Walters? By the way mom behaved at our Valentine's dinner, I don't think she just went away, married Mr. Walters and led a separate life from the two of you. Mom isn't the jealous type to stay mad at an old high school girlfriend of yours."

He tilted his head and studied her with a strange look. It made her stomach ache. "Isn't she? She's a woman you know. She's a lot like you, actually. Maybe not the side she shows the world, but I know her better than you."

Emmy felt tears sting her eyes. She wasn't anything like her mother. Emmylou showed people that she loved them; she didn't put unrealistic demands on them and then express to the world her disappointment in their behavior with frowns and reproving glares.

"So you're saying Mom hates Mrs. Walters because thirty-five years ago you were engaged for ten minutes?"

"No. I'm saying you don't know your mother quite as well as you seem to think, and what I didn't realize until now is that you are a spoiled brat who has no real feelings for your mother other than a mild tolerance. I knew there was friction between the two of you, but I thought that was because of your similarities. I thought this rebellious side of you was due to your independent nature. Now I see that you go your own way because you want to show the world – or prove to yourself – that you're nothing like her."

Emmy's body was lit with humiliation. She didn't like the tone her father was using. He had never been so directly criticizing. And right. That was exactly what she did.

"Do you have any idea what your mother went through for you?"

Her eyes burned with tears. She knew if she spoke she would break, so she shook her head.

"Do you know how hard it was for her to get pregnant, let alone carry you to term?"

She shook her head again, and a tear slipped down her cheek.

"We went through eleven miscarriages and eight years of doctors who either blamed your mother, or told us it would happen if we just relaxed and let nature take its course. Eight years, Emmylou."

Her dad took his handkerchief out and offered it to her. She could barely look at him. She was so ashamed.

"She was depressed and I was scared for her – for us. So I went to Kathleen. I thought that if your mom had someone to talk to, someone who might be able to comfort her and bring her back that we could at least save our marriage. But what I didn't realize was that Susan would think Kathy and I were having an affair."

Emmy thought her chest might collapse with the straining pressure against her heart. Her poor parents; she had no idea. She wiped her eyes with the soft white hanky.

"I'm sure you can image what happened when Kathy came over to talk to your mother one afternoon." His face was drawn, and his laced fingers were white from squeezing them together. "She practically threw Kathy in the street and hurled every name imaginable at her." He swallowed and looked down. "Your mother and I worked through it, and we were blessed to have you. She didn't care that she had to stay in bed for nearly six months to keep you. She would have done it for two years if it meant we could have a baby."

Emmylou let the dam break and sobbed into her hands. "I'm sorry, Daddy," she choked out between hiccups and tears. "I – had – no – idea." She sucked in a breath. "I knew I was trouble." She rushed through the words before emotion took her voice.

"You weren't trouble." He laid his hand on her knee and looked at her with a meek smile. "You were work."

Emmy tried to laugh, but a shuddering breath racked her. She blew her nose.

"So you can imagine what giving that flower to Kathy meant to your mother. It was my mistake. I thought it was all water under the bridge, but, as we men often find, women are extremely complex, emotional beings that we will never figure out."

She was able to laugh at that revelation. "I didn't expect that I would have ended my day like this."

"I'm sorry, honey. I didn't come here to upset you, but when you didn't call your mom after the scene in the restaurant, it tore her to pieces. I knew you needed to be hear the story. You needed to understand her better."

Emmy rubbed her forehead in misery thinking about the wasted years, of all the times she had praised Mrs. Walters in front of her mother, and of how her mom would stoically listen and nod. All the while, she had been harboring those horrid feelings for the other woman. Suddenly, she snapped her head up and stared hard at her father. "Dad?"

"No, darlin', I didn't have an affair with Kathy. Your mom is the only one for me. I would never fool around on her."

"Too scared of her?" Emmy quipped and swiped a smear of mascara from under her eye.

"Too much in love with her."

His smile wavered as he held her gaze. She saw the play of emotion twitch across his handsome face, and a volcano of tears erupted in her again.

*****

"That's amazing."

It was Thursday night dinner with friends, and Lacy had been enraptured the entire time Emmylou was conveying the story her father had told her.

Scarlett's forkful of peach cobbler had been forgotten halfway to her mouth. "So that's why you spent your childhood in doctors' offices. Your mom was so worried she might lose you."

"I guess so." Emmylou reclined against the sofa at The Dove House. They had moved into the living room after a succulent dinner of beef stew and kale salad. "I wonder why they never told me any of that before."

"That is a lot of important stuff, but I'm sure they had their reasons." Scarlett leaned forward to set her plate down and missed the eye roll from Emmylou. Scarlett idealized parents too much. Emmylou imagined that growing up without any parents would cause a person to do that, but she wasn't ready to forgive and forget yet. She had a lifetime of lies to get over.

"Who knew old Widow Walters and your dad were an item?" Lacy shook her head, staring into the fire. "I just thought she was the kooky lady with too much money who liked to help people out. I never really thought of her as anything other than John Walter's widowed wife. I assumed living alone for more than twenty years was a choice, but what if…" Lacy sat up, an excited glint in her eye. Scarlett and Emmylou gathered closer while Lacy rearranged herself against the pile of pillows on the floor. "Do you suppose it's possible she has been pining away for your dad all these years?"

"Ewww!" Emmylou wailed and smacked Lacy's arm in disgust at her beguiling exposé. "No! My dad said there was nothing to my mom's suspicions. He was just trying to get my mom some help."

"Maybe he wasn't interested, but that doesn't mean that *she* wasn't." Lacy folded her legs beneath her, having to rock back and forth to get it done. She cradled the bottom of her stomach as though it were the most natural thing in the world.

"Come off it, Sherlock. Mrs. Walters is happy with her life just as it is." Scarlett gathered the plates and stood up, effectually ending the little intrigue.

At this point, Emmy wasn't ruling out any possibility. She had heard it all and wasn't going to scoff at the impossible. Nothing was impossible to her anymore. Maybe Mrs. Walters did have a thing for her dad, but neither one of them were doing anything about it, so, for Emmylou, it was all over.

"You stay," Scarlett commanded Lacy. "You get the cobbler and help me in the kitchen," she jerked her head at Emmylou, and Emmy obeyed.

"I'll pick out a movie," Lacy said and wiggled toward the remote on the coffee table.

Once they entered the kitchen, Scarlett rounded on Emmylou. "Are you really okay? That's a lot to take in."

"I really am." And she meant it. "I finally understand my mother – and my parent's marriage. If only I had known this earlier, I would've probably treated my mom differently."

Seeing the pained grimace when she remembered how indifferent and judgmental she had been most of the time, Scarlett rubbed Emmy's shoulder. "Yes, you probably would have, but you can't dwell on that, honey. You didn't know, and you were simply reacting to your circumstances. Most of us would've behaved the same way."

"You wouldn't have." Emmylou frowned.

"It doesn't matter. She's not my mother, and I didn't grow up in your house. Well —"she drawled and they both laughed because they knew different. Scarlett had spent as much time at the Bennett's house as she was allowed to; anything to get away from her grandfather.

Scarlett loaded dishes into the dishwasher, and Emmy put the leftover food into containers. "I hope you're growing me another crop of strawberries, Scar. I can't keep them in the shop for more than twenty minutes."

"I am." Scarlett was wearing a strange smile.

"What? What are you thinking?"

"Nothing, yet. But I was going to talk to you about it. Do you think we could get together next week?"

"Sure." Emmy studied her impassive friend, wondering what mystery she had behind those pretty eyes.

Scarlett and Emmylou talked about the cleanup and repairs at Prairie Goodness and the progress being made before Lacy came into the kitchen and asked for their vote on the possible three movies to watch.

Emmylou wrapped an arm around each of her friends as they returned to the sofa. She didn't know a luckier person in the world.

Lacy started the movie as they all settled under a blanket. They all turned when heavy boot steps echoed on the wood floor. Kyle's quick, sure strides spoke of something serious.

"I hate to interrupt ladies, but the Sherriff just called looking for you, Emmylou."

Her stomach dropped and she sat upright. "What is it?"

"It's your mom."

Chapter 24

"Just calm down, Emmylou." Shane met Emmylou and her friends as soon as they entered the emergency room.

"Don't you dare tell me to calm down! Where's my mother."

"I will tell you whatever I want." Seeing her after his three week hiatus was like taking a shot after an all-night bender. He wanted to hold her and shake her at the same time.

"Look here you arrogant S-O-B, I will call the president of the board and have you shot out of here faster than a rocket full of monkeys."

"Of course you will. You didn't want me here in the first place. You've just been waiting for an opportunity to get me out of here. Well go ahead, make the call. I'll wait." He crossed his arms and met her blazing stare with one of his own.

She was wavering and he was glad. It was about time she backed down first.

She let out a grunt of pure frustration and flung her arms out. "Fine! Just take me to my mother."

Shane held up a hand, stopping her before she charged forward. "First, let me say what I was going to say." Her lips clamped into a tight circle of anger, and flames were practically shooting from her, but she kept silent. "Your mom is fine. She hit a patch of ice and her car skidded off the road. She has a bump on her head and bruise from the seat belt, but other than that she seems to be doing okay."

"How about my dad? How is he?" She had lowered her voice and slackened her tense shoulders.

"Your dad?" he echoed, confused. "I assumed he would be with you."

"No. Why would he be with me? He's with my mother. Why

else would you call me?"

Shane could see her conviction melting away with every word. He stepped closer and she hugged her arms around her middle, her face twisted. "We couldn't get ahold of him. We tried but he didn't answer."

"Did you call his cell phone? That's the one that you can - oh for heaven's sake." Emmylou whipped her phone out of her pocket and pushed on the screen. "I'll call him. You obviously didn't try his cell phone."

Shane's insides were shredded. He was angrier than he had ever been at another human being, but seeing Emmylou so upset was killing him. He reached for her, wanting to comfort her, wanting to hold her close and stroke her hair, to tell her to slow down. But she was a freight train barreling down the track with no engineer. She spun and paced two steps away from him with the phone up to her ear.

Kyle clapped a hand on his shoulder. "I called the two numbers Susan gave me. She said one was the home number, and one was George's cell," Shane spoke over his shoulder and Kyle squeezed it once before removing his hand.

"I know. Emmy's just upset. Let her do this."

Shane nodded and watched Emmylou pace with her thumbnail between her teeth.

"I'd like to tell you she isn't always a ball of commotion, but I can't. She's been this way as long as I've known her. It's why she's so successful. She's like a rat in a maze; won't give up until she finds the cracker no matter how many dead ends she hits."

She rounded on Shane. "Voicemail! I never get his voicemail!"

"Did you leave him a message?"

"And say what? Mom's in the hospital, possibly dying, the doctor is standing out here like an idiot instead of taking care of her, but no big deal. Get here when you can. Take your time."

Her pretty face was flushed with anger. He had to clamp his teeth together to keep from smiling at her. "Your mother isn't dying; she's resting. And I thought you preferred that I stay away from patients. You know, with my incompetence and everything."

His anger began bubbling again. "By the way, did you contact the board to get me thrown out on my ear? I'm sure you can't wait to get rid of me."

She raised an eyebrow and pursed her lips. "As a matter of fact we're meeting next week."

That hurt more than he had thought. He didn't realize she had absolutely no feelings for him at all. He had hoped that their moments together meant more to her, but again, he was being a fool when it came to Emmylou. "I'm sorry you couldn't get it arranged for an earlier date. I didn't figure you had that much trouble arranging dates."

Damn that felt good!

He struck a nerve with his cheap shot, and he didn't care. Emmy's chest puffed up and her jaw jutted out. "If only you knew anything about dating me," she hissed.

"I know enough to never make that mistake." His blood was whooshing though every vein and his hands shook with the adrenaline. He had never behaved this way to anyone outside of his sisters and brothers.

"Okay," Lacy drawled and stepped between them. "As much fun as your little pissing match is, I think we've gotten away from the situation at hand." She looked from Shane to Emmy and back to Shane. "Can Emmylou see her mother now?"

The floor dropped out from under him. Lacy's grim smile indicated she knew what he was thinking. He had been outrageously unprofessional. "I'm so sorry." He pressed his hand to his chest to still his heart and faced Emmy. "She's right this way." He held out his hand in escort. The sheepishly proud look on her face was all he needed. She felt the same way he did and was sorry.

Emmy brushed past him, head held high, and out of habit, he breathed in her scent. It was heaven and shot straight to his knees. If Kyle hadn't chosen that moment to rest his hand on Shane's shoulder, Shane would have dropped to the floor and snatched at the hem of Emmylou's coat.

Kyle sighed heavily. "You know, I fought it too. But in the end

I had to admit defeat. You'd do us all a favor if you just admitted it now and started the process of humbly accepting the collar and leash."

They walked down the white hall behind the ladies, "You know, Kyle, you could do me a favor and butt the hell out."

Kyle's resounding laugh made Shane want to punch him in the face.

"Mom!" Emmylou rushed to her mother's side and gently covered the woman's hand with her own. "Are you okay?"

Susan smiled weakly. "I'm just fine. Dr. Newbury has taken very good care of me." She transferred her tender gaze to Shane, and a pleasant warmth sifted through him. He stepped forward to stand on the opposite side of her bed. He looked at the monitor and moved the oxygen line to a more convenient place.

"You're a model patient."

He smiled when she patted his hand. "Oh!" she touched her cheek and ran a hand over her hair. "I didn't know you would be bringing everyone with you, dear."

Emmylou was huddled close to the bed. Shane saw the shimmer in her eyes but no tears escaped. Shane tensed with the pain etched in her face. She opened her mouth to answer, but nothing came out. She was on the edge of breaking. Shane's hand ached with the need to comfort her. Damn her for making him feel this way! He hated her! She was heartless and dangerous.

"We were so worried about you, Mrs. Bennett," Scarlett answered for Emmylou and moved forward through the group.

"Thank you, sweetheart. I'm sorry I caused such a ruckus. It was stupid really. The car hit a patch of ice just outside of town, and I went sliding into the ditch like some inexperienced teenager."

Everyone smiled at her description. Everyone except Emmylou. She was staring hard at her mother.

"What were you doing outside of town?"

"Oh, nothing." Susan diverted her attention away from Emmy's scrutinizing gaze.

"But you live on Walnut Street. That's on the west end of town.

Nowhere near the edge of town. Were you going to visit someone?"

"Not really, dear. I was just out for a drive." Susan's words were halted and unsure.

Emmy wasn't about to let it drop. She tried to press her mother for more information.

"I think Susan has had enough excitement for one night," Shane interrupted. "How about we all clear out of here and give her a chance to rest?"

Emmylou's friends all agreed, wished Susan Bennett goodnight and shuffled out the door. "You, too." Shane gave Emmy his best authoritative look.

"Why me? I'm her daughter. I can stay as long as she wants me here."

Her pleading blue eyes were almost too much for him to handle. There was a catch in his voice when he spoke again. "I'm the doctor and I say she needs her rest. You can come back tomorrow." He cleared his throat and straightened his shoulders.

She narrowed her eyes trying to intimidate him but he didn't falter… much. She rose gracefully, her gaze never leaving him. "Fine." With one last twitch of her eyes she looked to her mother. "I'll come back first thing tomorrow." She spoke with such loving concern. What a great little actress she was.

She left the room with a dignified stride. Shane had to give her credit. She certainly was tenacious.

"Thank you, Dr. Newbury. I didn't have the heart to tell her the truth."

He looked down into the woman's sad eyes and sighed with a grim smile. "You really need to. It isn't fair to her."

"I know." Susan swallowed and looked away.

Shane squeezed her hand and brushed the tear from her soft cheek. A few moments later, he left her room feeling dejected and sick to his stomach. Keeping information from family was one of the hardest requirements of his job.

*****

Emmylou sent everyone else home and paced the waiting room. Her father had to show up. Any minute he would come rushing through the glass doors, frantic about her mother. Where in the world could he be?

This time when the phone went to voicemail, she left a message. A very clipped and hurtful message. If he didn't get here in the next twenty minutes, she would go search the streets for him, and when she found him, he would be sorry. How could he ignore all the calls?

She turned to make another trip across the linoleum floor when the white coat caught her attention. She jammed her cell phone into her coat pocket and marched forward. He stopped and rested against the counter to talk to the nurse.

"What the hell is the matter with you?" She propped her elbow on the high counter and stared at the side of his face with only a slight flutter in her stomach.

"I thought I sent you home." His voice was tired and his head bent. When he finally turned, she had to check the impulse to reach for his hand and stoke his face. Somehow she had always been able to read his eyes. They spoke to her, and right now an overbearing weight pressed against her chest with what they said to her.

"I can't go home." She shrugged and let the rest of her thought hang in the air. As angry as she was with him for everything he had put her through, storming out, speeding away, and ignoring her for the past three weeks not to mention the scene in her mother's hospital room, she still cared for him. More than she had any other man on earth. She hated it. She hated being vulnerable to him.

He had shifted to face her, still resting against the nurse's station. "Did you reach your dad?"

She shook her head.

"I did call him you know."

She felt awful. He should be yelling at her right now. Instead, he was speaking gently. It nearly broke her. She could handle confrontation, but tenderness was invasive. She didn't know how to battle it. "I know," she sighed. Her skin tingled in anticipation when he started to reach for her, and every hope collapsed when he checked it and withdrew his hand to tuck into his lab coat.

Her jaw clenched but she didn't fold. She stacked it with the millions of other hurts she had been awarded and used it as shoring. Although, this one carried more weight.

"Look, Emmylou, you should go home and get some rest. Your mother is okay. I want to keep her here for observation, and she will most likely be going home in the morning. There isn't anything you can do by camping in the waiting room."

"I could stay in Mom's room," she chimed in.

He blinked and his gaze faltered. "That's not a good idea. Let her rest."

"Okay. I get it. You're trying to blow me off in that nice doctor way."

His half-grin was so enticing. "That would be an accurate summation."

She chuckled but the weight in her chest was still there. She had missed him desperately. Even when he was sarcastic and angry, she wanted to be near him. His smile was contagious and she had never felt safer in her life than during the times she spent with him. His gaze traveled over her bringing a quick heat spreading all the way to her toes.

"You'll call me if anything changes?"

"Of course." His voice was low. Her breath hitched when he locked his attention on her mouth. "I'm sure one of the nurses has your contact information."

She jerked back. Then hit him on the shoulder with her palm when she saw the look on his face. "Not funny."

He lifted one shoulder. "You never gave me your number."

She opened her mouth to argue then stopped. "You're right. I never did." She straightened and settled both her hands in her coat pockets. "Well, I'm sure you'll be able to find it somewhere around here." With a challenging lift of her eyebrows she turned on her heels. "Thanks, Doc. I'll see you tomorrow," she called over her shoulder.

Just because she had never officially given him her number she knew he had it. He had simply refused to use it the past three weeks. Well, if he wanted to get ahold of her badly enough, he would.

*****

Emmylou came stumbling out of her room with a baseball bat slung over her shoulder. She banged into the door on her way out of her bedroom flipping her hair out of her face. Another set of banging on her door rent the air.

"Emmylou! Open the door!" In her befuddled state she wasn't sure if she recognized the voice.

She made it to the door and pressed her cheek against it to look though the peephole. She turned the lock and whipped the door open. "Where the hell have you been?"

"I'm sorry, honey." Her dad rubbed his hands together and rocked on his heels. His breath made a steady puff of white smoke.

"Get inside." She moved away and jerked the bat marshaling him through the door.

"Thanks. It's damn frigid out there tonight." He walked past her and she shut the door.

"It's March in Nebraska, Daddy, not Hawaii." She shuffled behind him as he walked into the living room.

"It's nice to know you come to the door prepared."

She looked at the bat and back at him, then rested it on her shoulder. "I find it works better than a gun."

"You would."

"Dad," she scolded, bringing him back to the subject.

"I just left the hospital and couldn't wait to see you."

"Glad to hear you could find time in your busy phone–call–ignoring–day to drop by and see Mom after her car accident." Emmylou hoped he caught every bit of sarcasm in her accusation.

"I wasn't ignoring your phone calls; I was in a meeting."

She stood like a soldier ready to do business. "And after my number popped up on the *tenth* time, didn't you wonder if,

244

perhaps, something was wrong?"

"I'd left my phone in my truck, honey. I'm sorry."

She looked at him, holding her words, waiting for him to explain.

"Look, Emmy, you can be pissed at me later. There's something I need to tell you, and after I do, you have my permission to whack me with the bat."

She stared at him for a moment. "Fine. Is this something that's going to take coffee?"

"Probably something stronger."

Her heart thumped against her chest watching him get settled on the couch and pat the cushion next to him. She padded over to him, leaning the bat against the coffee table.

He waited until she was facing him before he spoke. "Your mom didn't have a car accident tonight. At least not from hitting a patch of ice."

She felt like a drawer ripped from a desk and dumped on the floor. "What are you talking about?"

The sadness in his face split her heart open. He reached for her hand and turned to face her fully. "Emmylou, your mother has a condition."

*****

Shane shot upright with the sudden pounding on his door.

"Open up you sorry sonofabitch!"

More pounding, yelling and name calling followed. He ambled to the door, still half asleep. He didn't need to look through the peephole. He knew who was standing on his doorstep, and he knew there were only two reasons she would come out here in the middle of the night. He jerked the door open and saw Emmylou pull back in shock a moment before she planned to unleash more anger.

"Come on in." He leaned against the door and ushered her inside with a wave of his heavy arm.

Emmylou marched inside, and he closed the door. She rounded on him after only a few steps. Shane pulled back, realizing she was wielding a baseball ball in her right hand. She really was furious at him.

"Now Emmylou, I don't think violence is the answer." He held his hands up and spoke with his soothing doctor's voice.

"I'm not so sure about that." Her eyes were dark and set on him like a lion's on a zebra. "Who the hell do you think you are?"

He took a breath, keeping a steady eye on her. "I'm not sure how you want me to answer that. How about you tell me why you're here."

"Don't pull that sanctimonious doctor crap on me! I'm sure you think it keeps you out of a lot of trouble, but I'm here to tell you that trouble has found you!"

The sight of her in her pajamas and snow boots, gripping a bat and standing like a beat cop, didn't add up to him. "Would you like to sit down?"

"No. I would *not* like to sit down."

"Would you like to bash something to pieces? I can offer you whatever's in the cupboard but I'll ask you to stay away from the television. It's all I have."

She glared at him, but his ploy was working; she had loosened up a shade. "Emmylou, tell me what's wrong."

She swallowed hard and her lashes fluttered when he spoke her name. "You know what's wrong."

"Well, there are so many things wrong between us, I'd hate to guess and be wrong. You might take a whack at me, knocking what's left of my good sense out."

Emmylou looked at the bat, then lowered it to the floor. "My mom. Why didn't you tell me about my mom?" Her chin quivered and her eyes filled. "She could die and you didn't tell me." Her words were broken by her sorrow. She buried her face in her free hand and her sob shattered the ice in his chest.

"I couldn't. She begged me not to, and I can't discuss my patient's help with anyone." He stepped closer and placed his hand on the bat, removing it from her loose grip. Her hand joined the other at her face, and she was racked with sobs. He wrapped her in his arms, holding her tight to his chest. It felt so good to have her there.

Shane stroked her hair and rocked her back and forth, whispering encouragement while his heart ripped from his chest with her anguish.

"What did she tell you?"

Emmy's arms slide up his back and clutched his shoulders. She pressed her head into his neck with a sniff. "She didn't. My dad came over and told me she needs to have surgery on her heart. That was why she crashed her car. It wasn't the ice. She passed out at the wheel and went off the road because her heart isn't pumping enough blood."

He held her tighter. It was heaven. "She's going to be fine. It's a simple procedure. She would've done it sooner if Dr. Miller hadn't passed away."

More tears flooded her eyes and dampened his chest. "Why?"

He closed his eyes against her plea and rested his head against hers. "I don't know." He had to swallow back his own tears. Her warm body fit his perfectly. She clung to him and he stroked her back until her crying turned to sniffles and she loosened her grip on him.

"I'm sorry." She took a step back, and he reluctantly let go.

"That's what I'm here for." His body already missed hers; he could have held her the rest of the night and been a happy man. It hurt so much to know that she didn't want him.

She wiped her eyes with her hand and tossed her hair away from her face, sucking in a heavy breath. "I don't know why I'm here. I just got in the car and started driving. I was so angry —"

"And the bat?"

She laughed and looked at it leaning against his entryway table. "I keep that for protection. It's a long story." She shrugged and he marveled at her beauty and strength. "I better go. I'm..." she was searching for what to say.

"How about some tea?" he offered. "I won't be able to go back to sleep after that." His nerves were wired, waiting for her to mull his invitation over.

He was genuinely surprised when she answered, "Okay."

Emmylou

Chapter 25

It was like some pyrotechnic was systematically dismantling her life. Every day a new explosion took out another piece, blowing it sky high and sending it crashing down. The rubble that was left seemed so overwhelming Emmy wanted to bury herself beneath it and die. Life wasn't meant to be this hard all the time. Was it?

Sitting on Shane's sofa, a hot cup of tea in her hand, made it seem a little less devastating. When she had gotten in her car and taken off after her father's visit, it was with the intention of having it out with the man who had been the secret-keeper. In her mind Shane was the blockade to all of her problems. They started when he came to town, and at every turn he was there, blocking her path to happiness.

Her undeniable attraction to him was just another sick twist in the macabre state of affairs. Shane sat on the opposite end of the sofa and rested his arm across the back. He was relaxed, facing her then propping his feet on the coffee table. He was in pajama bottoms and a blue T-shirt still soaked in her tears. He was the most marvelous being she had ever seen. Her stomach clenched with nerves. She shouldn't be here.

"Feeling better?" he asked.

She nodded and looked into the amber liquid. "A little."

"Good. I can't discuss your mom with you, but I might be able to answer some of your questions."

She shook her head, still unable to meet his gaze. "That's okay. I think my brain is full."

He made a noise in his throat and repositioned himself on the cushion. "I'm sure it is. How's the bakery?"

She scoffed and raised a hand to rub her forehead. "It's been better." She held the cup with both her hands, but that little warmth did nothing to heat her insides.

"You can talk to me, Emmylou. I meant it when I told you I was here to help."

She shivered and raised her head. She searched his features. He was so handsome and welcoming, she had the urge to crawl over to him and wrap herself in his strong arms to block out the world. Something about him always made her feel like he would protect her from anything. Even when she hated him, he was a safety net, a place of refuge. She had rushed out here in her darkest moment without a second thought.

Something that had been niggling at her for weeks poked through. "Tell me what you were going to say that night on my porch." The moment her thought was vocalized she wanted to pull it back in.

He tipped his head back and rested it on the sofa cushion. Pain marked every muscle, every feature, and she regretted asking. "Never mind. I'm sorry. That was presumptuous of me." She ran her thumb over the rim of her cup with an aching heart. Being in his home suddenly seemed inappropriate. She placed the cup on his table and made to stand.

"I've never told anyone what I told you. The only people who knew were our families and the people of my hometown. It wasn't like we were national news. These things happen every day to a lot of people."

His words stopped her, and she looked at him. He shrugged and Emmy felt the distance he had traveled. He was staring into the distance, obviously remembering something very painful. His Adam's apple slid down and up his throat, as if he were swallowing back a memory.

"I told you I was engaged once a long time ago. Almost eight years, now." His brows narrowed and he rubbed his chin. "Her name was Katie. Katheryn Ann Lansky, and she was my whole world."

Emmy's heart collapsed with that. He was in anguish, remembering the love of his life. Emmylou would never be anything to him. His heart wasn't just occupied by another, it was owned by her. Emmy's nose burned. She wanted to run from here, but she was frozen with devastation.

"We were young and she was so beautiful; the kind of beautiful that drew every drop of attention in a room. She was like a saint and a movie star rolled into one. A clear sky after a month long monsoon. Her smile could reach the darkest corners and, for some inexplicable reason, she picked me to love."

Emmylou didn't think it was all that mysterious. He was easy to love. She couldn't tear her eyes off him no matter how much she wanted to. It tore her to shreds knowing this amazing man would never be hers. His watery smile was her undoing. Her throat closed and a tear slid down her cheek.

He cleared his throat. "We were at her family's place, out riding horses, when it happened." His voice was soft, and he chewed on his lip before continuing. "I can still see her. Sun shining in her hair, wearing the shirt my sister gave her for her birthday. It was green – like her eyes. She challenged me to a race. She teased me about the weight I'd put on at college and laughed. It lifted into the leaves, making the birds fly. I always loved her laugh."

Shane looked down at his hands, and Emmy wanted to reach for them. She was so cold inside, wanting to hurry from this house and never look back, but drawn to stay by his enchantment with his love.

"So we took off, charging our horses over the prairie grass. 'To the trees,' I heard her yell, and we angled for the stand of cottonwoods. 'First one there picks the wedding date,' she hollered behind me." He blinked hard, opening his mouth but nothing came out. "I knew she wanted a Christmas wedding. So I…" he sniffed and rubbed away the tears that had leaked from his eyes. "I held back on the reins so she could pass me and win. I didn't care when we got married. I would've married her that day, the next year, whenever she wanted."

Emmylou's entire body was numb. Watching this man talk so lovingly about another woman was ripping her heart out. He was

251

in so much pain, and Emmylou would have done anything to take it away. Still, after knowing that he was forever linked to another, she would give him her heart if it would heal the agony he was suffering. Her hand slid over the cushion but stopped before touching him.

"She turned to look back at me as we reached the trees, and I yelled – I stretched out my hand – but…" he fell forward with his head in his hands. Sobs shook his shoulders for a brief moment before he snapped his head up and sucked in a deep breath. "She didn't see it, and I couldn't get to her fast enough. She ran into a low branch. Her horse was almost at full speed." He shook his head as if he wanted to get the memory out. "She was knocked to the ground. I jumped from my horse and ran to her. There was so much blood." He faltered on the last word, covering his mouth with his hand. "It was everywhere. I couldn't stop it. I tried so hard, but she had landed on a rock." He bowed his head and raked his hands through his hair. "She was gone." When he raised his head, he turned to Emmy, and the look of complete desolation broke what was left of her heart.

"Oh, Shane, I…" she reached out but stopped.

"I rode with her cradled in my arms back to her house. It took a long time." He stared at the wall again for what seemed like forever. Emmylou had played the whole scene in her head as he spoke. She was devastated for him, for Katie, for what they had together. That kind of living nightmare would destroy a man. She finally understood why he was unattainable; why he turned away from her.

"We buried her on a Tuesday. With red roses on her casket. She was twenty-two years old."

The air was so heavy and her body strung so tightly, that the chime of his mantle clock shook her in her seat. She wiped her tear-soaked face and tried to get control of her breath. The only movement Shane was making was the slight rise and fall of his chest. Frozen in indecision, Emmylou sat and watched him for a long time.

A tear escaping his beautiful brown eyes drew her over to him.

She moved to his side and tentatively curved her arm around his shoulders. Her heart was burning with the need to have him close, to soothe the hurt and tragedy from his soul. He leaned into her, and she held him tighter. Soon Shane was clinging to her. Emmy held him so close she could feel his heartbeat through her shirt, its rhythm in tandem with her own. He occupied every space of her. She was connected to him, and it destroyed her to know that he would always belong to someone else. She had finally met the man for her, but they would never be anything more than they were.

His hair was smooth against her cheek and his skin warmed her palms. They sat in the weighted silence of his home, bound together by heartbreak. She had come to him with her own worries and found that his were bigger. She still had her mother. There was a good chance that her mother would recover and live a long life. Shane didn't have that possibility. His Katie was gone forever in a senseless accident. One moment in time had changed the lives of so many. Even eight years later.

*****

The sun was streaking through the window when Shane dared open one eye, then slammed it shut with the glare. He had slept like a hibernating bear. Something was different about this morning. He moved his head and soft hair tickled his cheek. His eyes flew open, and his heart bumped to life. Careful not to move too quickly, he took in the moment.

Emmylou was lying cradled in his arms, her head on his chest, and her legs intertwined with his own. Memories of last night flooded his brain, and sickness filled his gut. He had told her everything. He hadn't meant to be that detailed, but once he started, it was impossible to filter out the facts of that awful day. The day he had lost his beloved Katie. Usually the mere thought of Katie stirred sorrow and longing in his chest, but this time it was only a sadness that squeezed his heart. He wasn't consumed with grief for the first time in eight years.

The only thing different this time was the woman in his arms.

She had wept with him for his lost love, and he felt more than gratitude. He felt – light. His burden had lessened. Telling Emmylou his tragic story had revoked the authority that event held over his life. His hands tightened on her back, pressing her into him. He tipped his chin to look at her. Her pink skin shimmered in the sunshine. She was so peaceful, her breathing deep and steady. He relished this moment of joyful quiet even though his desire was to wake her.

Last night had been incredible. The shackles of death and responsibility had fallen away with every word he had spoken. She was his savior, and he loved her. He had loved her all along, but had needed permission to accept it. Emmylou had given it to him by listening and staying. He squeezed his arms tighter. He needed her as close as he could get her, and still it wasn't close enough. He drank in the scent of her, feeling it all the way to his toes. He could stay in this place forever.

She jerked awake, pushing away from his chest.

"Good morning," he said with a smile.

"Morning?"

He swept her long hair from her face, resting his hand on the curve of her jaw. "I'm sorry I woke you."

She shook off the grogginess of sleep, squinting against the sunlight. "It's morning." She threw herself up. "No, no, no, no." She whipped her hair over her shoulders and bent over, reaching for her boots. "What time is it?" she yelled and shot him a furious look. "Why did you let me fall asleep?" She shoved her foot into a boot and dropped it on the floor.

"It was late. We were both exhausted." Shane lifted himself into a sitting position.

"I shouldn't have stayed." She got the other boot on and stood up.

"Why not? Nothing happened."

She gaped at him like he had suddenly turned purple and sprouted horns. "Okay, but now I'm late for work." She rubbed her wrist in frustration.

Shane glanced at the wall. "It's six-twenty."

"Damn it." She snatched up her coat and tucked it under her arm. "I've gotta go. This is unbelievable." She rushed to the door and Shane hurried after her.

"Wait. I'm sorry but…" he swallowed unsure of what to say.

"Look, I've got to get to the bakery. I'm sure Lindy will have a search party out soon. I never miss opening." She looked at him one last time before leaving him standing there like an idiot.

He heard her car start and pull out of there like a stock car at the starting line. That hadn't gone like he had hoped. He was thinking breakfast, maybe a little conversation, but she had run out of his house with her hair on fire. Something in his gut told him it wasn't just that she was late for work. She was running away from him. Again. This time he wasn't about to let her go.

*****

Emmylou was still in her pajamas when she slid into the parking lot behind Bake My Day. It was six forty-five. She was almost three hours late for work. She rammed her hair into a pony tail, securing it with a long strand of hair. She ran to the back door and threw it open.

"Sorry, I'm late. I…" she didn't have an excuse. Not one she was about to share with her staff, anyway. "I overslept. What do we need to finish?"

"It's quite all right, Emmylou." Evan strolled from the ovens with a pan of éclairs and a grin. "Lindy and I got started and several of the others came about an hour later. We got it handled and even had time to make these." He spun the éclairs in his hand.

"I'm impressed." She nodded her head at him and smiled.

"I'll go put them in the case."

"Perfect. Thanks, Evan."

He sighed playfully. "It's not easy being this perfect."

They both laughed and he left the kitchen. Two of her other workers were talking by the mixers while they whipped up what looked like fresh cream for the éclairs. "Morning," she called to them.

"Good morning, Emmylou!" they both chimed.

She felt so strange. It was like a month had gone by in one night. The events of last night were still fresh in her mind. She was exhausted and disoriented. Too many things had happened, and her brain had shut down. She couldn't process it all.

Emmylou ducked into her office and attempted to shut the door. It made it about halfway with the stacks of boxes and papers all over the floor of the tiny room. She sat at her desk trying to process everything and get to a place where she could think clearly. She picked up a pen and rolled it between her fingers. She couldn't shake the delightful tingle of Shane's hands on her body. She couldn't remember falling asleep; she only knew it was the most amazing feeling in the world, lying there in his arms.

Shoving that aside, she focused on what her father had told her last night. Her mom would be getting out of the hospital today, and she should be there to help. Of course, that would probably bring her in close proximity of Shane, and she wasn't sure she was prepared to be around him knowing that she couldn't be with him the way that she wanted. He would never get over Katie. Losing the love of his life had scarred him deeply, and he hadn't recovered from it. From the looks and sounds of it, he never would.

She closed her eyes against the onslaught of agony slicing through her. She wanted him more than anything in the world. She covered her face with her hands and scrubbed, trying to scrub away the thought of him, the memory of his wry grin and dark eyes. Her shoulders slumped, and a whimper escaped her throat.

Gathering every bit of resolve she possessed, she straightened and slid closer to her desk. She grabbed the stack in her inbox and laid it in front of her, then opened the drawer and removed her checkbook. Nothing like paying bills to bring her back to reality. After a few minutes she picked up a white invoice. The yellow and green Lansky Foods logo stood out.

That had been such a strange couple of days; the loan, the mice, the oven. Shane had come to the rescue by getting her the supplies. He had helped unload them and then fixed her wiring problems. The next day he was saving her life, and she was yelling at him. Why had she behaved so stupidly? She had been frantic and scared. She didn't like hospitals or doctors. She had had her blood drawn more times than a person could stand. She held her pen over the check to make out the amount when something rang in her mind.

She sat up, thinking back. Lansky Foods. Harold Lansky had been on the phone to Shane the day of the fire. She had heard part of the conversation when she followed him to apologize. Lansky. Why was that name standing out to her?

"Oh my God." She dropped the pen and shoved away from the desk. "Katie Lansky." She covered her mouth and shook her head, remembering what Shane had said last night. He had said the name Katheryn Ann Lansky. That's why he could get the supplies she had needed. That's why he had been so friendly over the phone. Shane had been engaged to Harold Lansky's daughter. Then who was Emily? Harold's wife? Katie's sister? It didn't matter. Emmylou had jumped to the wrong conclusion. Emily wasn't Shane's girlfriend. She had punished him for three weeks over a misunderstanding.

Emmy eye's filled with tears. She wished that knowledge made a difference, but it didn't. She had been there last night when he poured out his soul to her. She had seen what Katie meant to him. Obviously the entire Lansky family was important to him. He would always be linked to them. And that wasn't what bothered her. She could deal with him being close to a family he shared so much history with. What she couldn't handle was knowing that Shane's heart would always be Katie Lansky's. She was his everything, even after eight years.

There was no chance that Shane would be free of that loss. He held tightly to it, and she understood. She hated it, but she understood. She wrote the check and placed it in an envelope. It seemed to be the first step in disconnecting from Shane–something she had to do. She would eventually find her way back. She had suffered heartbreak before and bounced back.

The next paper in the stack was the official notice from the government stating she had ten days left to submit payment or statement of refinancing. She burst into tears. She couldn't do it. She hadn't found a way. None of the banks wanted to take on the risk, especially after the fire. Her income had evaporated. She had become too high risk for them. A couple of them had asked for a co-signer before they would even look at her application.

It was hopeless. Prairie Goodness would close. Thirty people would be out of work, and she would be a failure. She folded her arms over her desk and dropped her forehead on top of them. For the first time in years, she allowed herself to succumb to pity.

The sound of the door hitting cardboard boxes wrenched her from her misery. She shot upright in her chair, quickly wiping away her tears and clearing her throat. She pretended to be busy at her desk.

"Emmylou? Sorry to bother you but we were making your raspberry-peach strudel, and we can't agree on the spices that you use in it. Can we get your recipe, please?"

"That's all right, Evan. You won't need the recipe. Put in three cups of honey per one hundred with the fruit, then mix the cinnamon with the cream cheese before layering. Are you folding the phyllo or braiding?"

"Braiding."

"Then dab a little butter between the braids so it doesn't flake too much."

"Okay. Thank you." Emmy started to turn back to her work, but Evan hesitated in the doorway. "I, um, I do better with written instructions. If I could see the recipe, then I would be sure to get it right."

"Have someone write it down for you, Evan. I'm busy with paperwork," she clipped.

"If you just show me where they are, I could get them for you."

Emmylou popped out of her chair. "It's just three cups of honey, cinnamon with the cream cheese and butter between the braids. It shouldn't be too difficult. Now, if you'll excuse me." She advanced as she spoke, backing him out of her doorway, then pushed the door shut in his face.

What the hell was he bothering her about some recipe for?

Wasn't he a world class baker, taught by the finest teachers on the planet? He should be able to figure out how to make a simple strudel. Emmy returned to her paperwork but didn't get much further. She couldn't help being a clock watcher. When it hit nine o'clock, she left her office.

"Lindy, I have to go take care of something. Can you hold down the fort?"

Lindy looked up from changing out empty trays for full ones. "Sure. It's no problem."

Emmy shoved her arms into her coat before turning back. "Lindy." She waited until Lindy made eye contact. "I'm sorry for being so absent lately. I've been leaving you to take charge a lot, and I really appreciate you stepping up and running things for me here. I haven't worried at all, knowing you're here. You're amazing and I want you to know how grateful I am."

A rare smile graced Lindy's face making her look older. "I know you are. I haven't minded at all. Robbie and I both agree that it's been good for me to have more responsibility. You've had a lot on your plate with everything going on at Prairie Goodness. I'm glad you haven't had this place to worry about, too."

The mention of her fiancé reminded Emmy of Lindy's impending wedding. Two weeks from today, the two of them would be married. "I don't want you and Robbie to worry about your wedding cake. Even with the mess we've had, I will get it done, and it'll be the most beautiful cake I've ever made." Emmylou would see to it. There was no way she could let Lindy down.

"Thank you, Emmylou. That means a lot to me. I wasn't worried. I figured it would all come together one way or another."

Emmy tried to reassure Lindy with a smile, but the weight on her heart wouldn't quite let the smile happen. Lindy didn't know how deep the trouble Emmy was in reached. She hadn't told her anything about the loan or that the bakery was probably going to have to close.

"And it will." Emmy tried to convince herself at the same time. "I'll see you later. Thanks again."

Driving to the hospital in Glenwood gave Emmylou twenty minutes of thinking time. She tried to go over all her options, but something about the landscape kept distracting her. First, she had to drive past Shane's place, which brought back the emotional rollercoaster of last night and this morning. Then, she had to drive past The Dove House, which made her think of her friends. They were beyond wonderful. She couldn't understand why they had stood by her all these years. She was one disaster after another with a crazy family. But they were there for her no matter what.

It hit her that things were starting to show signs of the coming spring. More birds were on the telephone lines and fences than she had seen in months. A coating of short green grass was beginning to blanket the western slopes of the hills and all along the ditches. The land was awakening from its winter slumber, but she wasn't. Winter had been long and desolate for her. Emmylou usually felt a refreshing revival when the days got longer and warmer. This spring wasn't bringing her any kind of renewal. She still felt dead inside.

Chapter 26

Emmylou reached the hospital after Shane had been and gone. He had released her mother, but it took three more hours before they were able to take her home. She wasn't sorry she had missed Shane. It would have been an unbearable discomfort to be in the same room with him. She had run out of his house with a heavy heart and wasn't prepared to be in close proximity to him knowing all that she did now.

"We're going to leave for Lincoln first thing in the morning," her dad informed her after they left her mother in her bedroom to rest.

"Okay. I'll pack some things and be over here." Emmylou went into the kitchen, and her dad followed.

"I don't think that's a good idea."

Emmy grabbed a cup from the cupboard. "Why not? You don't want me with you when Mom has her surgery?"

"It's not that, darlin'. I just thought that you might need to be around for the bakeries."

She filled the glass with water from the tap. "I don't think me being here will make any difference, Dad." She leaned her back against the sink and took a drink to gather her courage. "It's over. I can't get the funding." She couldn't meet her father's eyes, so she stared into the clear glass in her hands. His arm slid over her shoulders as he joined her. He tipped her head down to rest on his shoulder.

"I'm so sorry, Emmy."

Tears burned her throat and filled her eyes. "I couldn't do it, Daddy," she said on a sob as the tears streaked down her cheeks.

"Shhh. It's all right."

She shook her head against his shoulder. "No, it's not. All those people." She sniffed and dug her thumb along the rim of her glass. "They depend on me. They believed in me." She swallowed hard, pushing back more sobs. "And I let them all down."

After a long moment her father finally spoke. "I believe in you."

A scoff rushed out before she could check it. "No you don't. I'm one big disappointment to you and Mom."

Her dad grabbed her shoulders and spun her to face him. "You are *not* a disappointment! We love you."

"I didn't say you don't love me. I said I disappoint you. They aren't the same thing."

He moistened his lips. "Emmylou, this may not have been the career we wanted for you. Don't roll your eyes at me. Just listen."

Emmy clamped her lips together and stared at him. She hadn't seen him this insistent since she had dropped out of college.

"You have done an amazing thing. You went after your passion, and your mother and I can't fault you for that. We didn't like it, but you proved to us that you were capable of even more than we thought. You are amazing and we are proud of all that you have accomplished."

He was serious. A strange wiggling took over her body. She wasn't accustomed to praise from her parents, and it made her feel weird. She had developed embattlements against them over the years to protect herself from their disappointment in her. Her father was tearing them down, making her vulnerable. She hated that feeling. Weakness wasn't acceptable.

"You're just saying that to make me feel better that I failed. You got what you wanted. I went against you and mom in everything, and now you're being proven right."

He pulled away from her, still studying her with his unwavering blue eyes. "Is that what you think, Emmylou? You seriously think that your mother and I have been waiting for you to fail so we can swoop in and point our fingers at you?"

Heat flooded her cheeks, and her chin trembled. He had vocalized her feelings exactly and now that they were out there, she heard how ridiculous they sounded. She bobbed her head in the merest nod.

"I see. Again, we're having a giant miscommunication. I didn't realize we had done such a terrible job of raising you to feel loved."

"It wasn't the love, Dad. It was the respect. You never respected my decisions. You always made me feel like I was letting you down. That the *real* me was an embarrassment to you. Every mistake I made was discussed at length. It was hashed over and replayed so we could find out where I went wrong, what I could've done better." Saliva was building in her mouth affecting her speech, but she continued through the onslaught of emotion constricting her throat. "You never just hugged me and told me it was okay, that I had done my best, and it simply hadn't worked out."

Finally, she had said it. It had hurt to speak the truth, and she was sure that it wouldn't change a thing, but it was out there instead of taking up all the room inside of her. Her dad dropped back against the counter, his forehead wrinkled and his eyes thoughtful. Emmy swept the tears from her face and folded her arms over her stomach.

"I'm sorry, Emmylou. I didn't realize..." he shook his head and rubbed his chin. "We never meant to make you feel like you weren't good enough. Actually, sweetheart, we thought you liked to tear it apart. You always came back stronger and better after we did. We thought that was what you wanted. You were so driven all the damn time. We thought you needed that critique from us to help you."

A sorrowful smile played at her mouth. "I did. I respected your insights, but it would have been nice to have the hug, too."

A change swept over her dad, and he reached for her, pulling her into a tight embrace. They stood like that until all the bitterness and misunderstanding washed away.

Her dad took a deep breath and looked at her with new eyes; she looked at him the same way. "Now, about the bakeries, don't you have work to do?"

She let out a laugh of disbelief. "I guess I do."

"That's my girl. I'll take care of your mother. I've been doing it for more than thirty years." The wry twist of her expression made him smile. "Okay, so she's taken care of me. It's my turn. We'll be fine."

Emmylou hated missing her mother's surgery. She really felt that she should be there, but she also knew it was a battle with her dad she wouldn't win. "Okay. I'll stay if you want me to, but I'll be checking in. I want minute-to-minute updates."

"Deal." He finally let go of her and got a drink of his own. "Emmy?"

"Yeah?" She asked while placing her cup inside the dishwasher.

"Have you been looking for an investor?"

She turned herself fully to him and studied him. He had crossed his ankle over his knee and was semi-reclining in the chair like he didn't have a care in the world. "Sort of, but nothing serious. Why?"

"Just curious. You know I –"

"You're not going to give me your retirement money to infuse my business," she cut him off.

"We could manage."

"No. Besides you don't know what's going to happen with mom. You may need that money."

"Well, the offer's always there if you change your mind."

The grey in his hair and the wrinkles around his eyes and mouth seemed to be more prominent in that moment. There was no way she would jeopardize her parent's retirement. "Thank you, but I'm sure there's another way. And if not, then Prairie Goodness closes. I'll be fine."

"You don't always have to be so strong, darlin'."

"Yes. I do."

*****

The contractor called to have her come out to Prairie Goodness and do the final walk-through. He was in the parking lot when she arrived. They chatted while making their way to the baking room.

He began explaining everything when Scarlett came out of the refrigeration area holding a metal cage.

"Scarlett! What are you doing? Why would you bring one of your creatures to the production house? It didn't get loose did it? Is that why you were in the refrigerator? Oh my God! It didn't get in there with the flour and sugar did it?" Emmylou was hurrying forward, appalled at her friend's poor judgment.

"Why would you ask me something like that? If you'd just settle down for a second, I'll explain."

"Sorry." And she was. Emmy knew Scarlett wouldn't do anything like that to her. The past couple of months had her so twisted around that she now *expected* something to go wrong.

"Hi, Scarlett," the contractor said with a bashful smile.

"Hi, Tim." Scarlett's reply was far more frank. She had no clue that men adored her. "Last winter I had a tiny hole in greenhouse two." She was talking only to Emmylou. As far as Tim was concerned, he could have been running around naked and Scarlett wouldn't have noticed. "It was behind the hydroponic tank, clear down in the corner. When I was in there working, I would notice that the fabric from the cooling panel in the back was shredded and scattered on the floor. It took me weeks to finally figure it out. But, I did."

"Scarlett, I love you, but does your story have a point?" Emmylou was exhausted and out of patience.

"Yes. What I was going to say was, I had a mouse problem. Several of the little boogers got in there and made a nice little house in my cooler wall."

Emmylou wasn't following the story. To her it still had no point. "Okay. And?"

With an exasperated sigh, Scarlett continued, "And, I had an idea about your cooler." She straightened and lifted the cage.

"Eww! Scarlett!" Emmylou reared back in disgust from the three furry mice darting around in the cage.

"Oh, grow up," Scarlett chided and turned the cage to look at her quarry.

"Do you know how many diseases those disgusting things

265

carry?"

Scarlett shot her a dead pan stare.

"Sorry, of course you know, Queen of all Living Creatures." Emmylou performed a mock worshiping bow and Scarlett chuckled.

"That's right, which is why I know that these aren't field mice." She shook the silver cage sending the mice scurrying.

"I don't know what that means." Emmylou's head was spinning.

"It means that these are domestic mice. Raised by a breeder. Probably came from a pet store or something."

"Okay?" Emmylou drawled, really trying to put all the pieces together but coming up blank.

"Emmy, I love you, but you really have to pay more attention when I talk. You might learn something."

"Fair enough," Emmylou conceded. "I'm listening now."

"Good. Domestic mice don't come from the wild. So…"

"So, someone had to have released these little guys."

Emmylou and Scarlett both turned and gaped at Tim, who had finished Scarlett's sentence and taken the cage from her hand.

"What?" He shrugged and looked into the cage. "I was a little boy once. I know all about snakes and mice, and Scarlett's right. These guys –well guy and two girls– didn't come from the wild. Their fur is too nice, and their color is all wrong for them to be wild. And I would say someone was hoping they would breed and make more little balls of trouble for you."

Emmylou's head hurt. What did it all mean? Domestic mice in with her dry goods? "Maybe we're jumping to conclusions. Is there any way they could've gotten in her on their own?"

"I suppose so, but I'd say you have a better chance of winning the MegaMillion lottery than these critters did of wondering in here without help."

"Tim's right, Emmy. The coolers don't have any exterior walls and I did a complete inspection around them. I didn't find anything. "

Emmylou saw the look of fascination on Scarlett's face when

she looked at Tim. Maybe one would get through that thick heart of hers yet. "Okay. I get it. But who would have done that? Do you think one of the employees would've brought in domestic mice, released them in the cooler and stood back and waited? For what? Why?"

Scarlett took a deep breath, contemplating her questions. "I don't know. Has anyone been acting strange? Have you had any problems with one of them?"

Emmylou thought about that. She wracked her brain for anything that stood out as strange or out of place. "Not that I can remember. I don't think any one of them would have done something like this. It sabotages their own job. Everyone here seems so happy."

"You'd be surprised, Emmylou. People act for all kinds of reasons or no reason at all." Tim placed a hand on her shoulder and shook his head. "Last month one of my guys took a skid-steer out for a joy ride. Caused three thousand dollars worth of damage. His reason? He just wanted to see how powerful it was." He shook his head. "Do you see what I mean?"

The three of them spent several moments looking at each other and processing this new information. Emmylou was cataloging all of her employees in her mind, wondering if one of them was capable of an act like this. Did one of them secretly hate her? Did they just want to see what would happen? The answer was still no.

"Do you have security cameras?"

She shook her head. Shane Newbury had suggested she get some when he fixed her electrical system. Even though she wouldn't have seen who had put the mice in the cooler because that happened before his work on the wiring, it may have been useful in observing who was acting strangely. Now the damage had been done and it really didn't matter. This place would be closing. Repossessed by the government and either sold to someone else or left to ruin.

Emmylou couldn't catch a break. She should've kept the insurance check and taken a vacation instead of rebuilding and having faith it would all work out.

*****

The final walk-through only depressed her more. She went home, consumed an entire bag of potato chips, and took a long, hot bath. She had tried everything she could to get out of the mess that she was in, but every time she made progress, another hole opened up, and she was sent spiraling down it.

She shuffled through her house with wet hair, in cushy slippers and flannel pajamas. Tomorrow was her only day off, but she wasn't looking forward to it. That meant another day of stewing. When she wasn't busy, she would dwell on her problems, and no matter how many times she went over it, she didn't have any answers.

She took a book to bed, hoping it would distract her, but no luck. It was Saturday night, and she was alone and depressed. She had graduated into the sad-single ladies club. All she needed was a couple of cats and an obsession with public television.

Her cell phone rang, and she ignored it. She wasn't in the mood to talk to anyone, even her friends. They would either be sympathetic or want to fix the problem. She couldn't handle a conversation yet. She had to come to grips with reality, and neither Lacy nor Scarlett could help her with that. Her cell dinged indicating voice mail. Out of curiosity she checked caller ID. She didn't recognize the number.

She dialed her voice mail and listened. It was Shane! Heat and nerves darted through her at the sound of his voice.

"Hey, Emmylou. It's Shane." He sounded so uncertain and jittery. "Um, give me a call when you get this. I, uh, just wanted to check on you."

She wondered how he had gotten her cell number. She had never given it to him. She had no intention of returning his call. Not tonight, not ever. She couldn't cope with loving a tortured soul on top of everything else.

Staring at his number on the phone keypad stirred unwelcome feelings. Shane was always coming to her rescue. First the electrical system, then the food supplies. He helped her after the fire when she was hospitalized, he rescued her and Scarlett from that mountain lion, and he was even at the movies when she had a run-in with her ex. Even keeping her mother's illness from her was protection. He was an amazing and compassionate man.

He was different than any man she had dated, but she had a terrible record for choosing men. She was perpetually drawn to the wrong man, and Shane could very well be the worst of the bunch. He had wormed his way into her life by playing the hero, and she had fallen for him. She hated that she liked him helping her. She hated admitting that she wasn't as strong as she thought she was.

All of those revelations tumbled over each other in her mind, falling into a clear picture. She sat up as the truth snapped into view. She was head over heels, jumping off a building, soaring with the eagles in love with Shane Newbury!

"No," she said to the room. "Oh, no." Shane was still in love with his dead fiancée. He was untouchable. And he was the one she wanted more than anything in the world. Even more than her bakery and production house. She'd give it all up to spend the rest of her life earning his love.

There was no way he felt anything more than compassion and responsibility for her. She was constantly at him; she insulted him, yelled at him, and embarrassed him. She was difficult on their best days together.

And he was the one for her.

Chapter 27

Shane hung up the phone with a pit in his stomach. He had called Emmylou three times. Each time had been harder to dial than the first. Why wouldn't she answer? He thought they had connected. He thought that after telling her the story of Katie's death, she would understand why he had been distant. He had hoped that that would help in bringing her closer to him.

He dropped into his recliner and chewed on the tip of his thumb. It was a nervous habit he had picked up in med school. He replayed every moment of Friday night. She had come charging over here like a bull in the arena looking for blood. He hadn't been sure why she had come until she started yelling about her mother's health.

He had known that was going to be an obstacle in their relationship. He'd had to keep it a secret from her at her mother's request. Susan had her reasons for not telling Emmylou, and he had to respect them. Then again, maybe it really was Katie that was keeping Emmylou away. Maybe he had shared too much, but she had asked, and if had felt so good to finally have it out there.

He had been hoping to catch her at the bakery on Saturday, but he'd met that jerk Evan Mathews there instead. He loitered around for a bit waiting for Emmy to come out from the kitchen but ended up ordering something so he wouldn't look foolish. Evan didn't need to know what he was doing there. And it was possible Evan was still Shane's competition.

Damn it! That was probably it. He had poured his heart out hoping it would bring Emmylou closer to him, but she was probably just being nice and listening to his sappy outpouring of emotion before she went back to Evan.

Shane hated Evan more than he had hated anyone in his life.

Where had he even come from? He said he was "sort-of" from Primrose, but was he really? Did anyone know his history? Probably not. Emmylou didn't seem the type to do a background check on the people she hired. She was a trusting woman. And rightfully so. When you grow up in a small town, you tend to think people are honest. You have no reason not to.

But this Evan character was standing in Shane's way, and he had a feeling that Evan wasn't who he said he was. His story was just a little too shaky to believe. It was Sunday, so the only investigating Shane could do was on the internet, but he was going to get to the bottom of this. Evan Matthews would be sorry he'd ever stepped foot in this town. He would pay for coming within ten feet of Emmylou. Shane would see to it.

He felt better now that he had the answer to his problem. Emmylou didn't know that Evan was bad news, and if her ex-boyfriend at the movies was any indication of the type of man she dated, then he had the rest of his explanation.

Shane opened his laptop to do a search when a thought jammed his research. What if Evan wasn't the problem at all? Emmylou had been driving to Prairie Goodness yesterday. After leaving the bakery, he had followed her part of the way until she turned off. There had been several vehicles there even though he knew it wasn't reopened yet. He concentrated on remembering what the vehicles were. A white Jeep with a black top and a red Ford truck with a sticker on the side of it. He didn't know what it said, but he would bet his life savings it wasn't *Prairie Goodness Delivery*.

Who was she meeting out there?

He slammed his laptop closed. "Oh my God! What if she knows?"

*****

Emmylou spent the next two weeks on tenterhooks. She knew at any moment Shane was going to stroll through her door, and she wouldn't be able to pull off the acting job she needed to. He would see right through her, so she wouldn't be able to hide her feelings from him.

He had stopped calling her, and she still didn't have any answers to who was responsible for the fire. Emmylou despised uncertainty most of all. She was trussed up like a turkey wondering which crisis she would be dealing with first.

The production house was up and running, but the fire had taken its toll on business. Being shut down that long had turned customers away. She had done her best to keep her retail outlets by purchasing products from another bakery and sending them on, but she had received complaints about the quality. Now she was playing catch up and having to smooth things out, but it seemed to be working. She still had a few more days before the loan was due, and her dad thought that more than likely they wouldn't move on her case for another couple of weeks. She hadn't been the only one on their list.

Emmylou sat perched in front of Lindy's cake applying the fondant lilies she had painstakingly air brushed. Lindy had taken the week off to get ready for the wedding so Emmylou could work freely on the wedding cake. Each layer had been designed, carved and decorated by Emmylou. No one else was allowed to help. It was her gift to the employee who had been so wonderful to her. It was a symbol of their friendship, and hopefully, the perfect statement for the perfect couple.

She got a little teary every time she thought about Robbie and Lindy getting married. She had poured her heart into that cake. It wasn't the most difficult cake she had ever built, but it certainly was the most beautiful. She took her ball tool and curved the petals of the flower to perfection. Emmylou had been so engrossed in studying her work that a knock at her back door startled her. She looked at the clock and pushed away from the table.

"Scarlett! Hey! Come on in!" Emmylou had been avoiding her friends for the past two weeks knowing she couldn't keep her suspicions to herself.

Scarlett hugged her. "You've been hiding out, so I thought I would track you down."

It was so good to see her friend that she nearly screamed. "I know. I've been so busy with opening PG and preparing for

Lindy's wedding. I couldn't get away."

"That's why I'm here."

"Lindy's wedding?" Emmylou wiped her hands on a dish towel and motioned for Scarlett to sit on the stool next to hers.

"No. I'm here to talk to you about Prairie Goodness." Scarlett slid onto the stool and set down a file folder.

"What's that?"

Scarlett placed both hands on top of the file. Emmylou recognized the look on Scarlett's face. It was the same one she had worn when the principle informed her she was the valedictorian and would have to give a speech on graduation.

"You can tell me. What's wrong, honey?" Emmy reached out and rubbed Scarlett's hand.

Scarlett blew out a breath and opened the file then drew out a small piece of paper and placed it gently in front of Emmylou.

It was a check.

A very large check.

A check made out in the amount of two hundred thousand dollars payable to Emmylou Bennett and signed by Scarlett D. Pearson. Emmylou was blown away. She stared at the check in confusion and wonder before placing it in front of Scarlett.

"Thank you, Scar, but I can't accept your money." She gazed at her friend with such gratitude she was sure she was grinning like a fool.

"It isn't a gift. I want in."

"In what?"

Scarlett chuckled and shook her dark head. "I want to be your partner."

"My partner?" Had Scarlett said she wanted to be a motivational speaker, Emmylou wouldn't have been more surprised.

"Yes. I've got it all worked out." She pushed the folder toward Emmy.

Emmylou opened it and read the first page. *The Future of Prairie Goodness: Scarlett Pearson's proposal of Partnership.*

"Wow, Scarlett. You're serious."

"As a heart attack. Sorry," Scarlett retracted the instant she said it. "I didn't mean to say it like that."

"That's okay. Mom is doing fine. She's fully recovered from surgery and back on the warpath." Emmylou smiled knowing her mother's prognosis was good and that their relationship was better than ever. "So, what's your proposal?"

Scarlett straightened in her seat as though she were a girl who had just been asked to tell someone about her favorite stuffed animal. "Well, I was thinking we could combine both of our skills. Your baking and my ability to grow fresh produce."

"Yes," Emmylou answered and closed the file to her friend's astonishment.

"Yes?" Scarlett shook her head to clear it. "But I have more. It's all in there." She indicated the folder.

"I know it is and I'll read it. The answer is still yes. I agree. Let's be partners!"

"Are you sure? You don't want to hear my pitch?"

"Scarlett." Emmylou looked deep into Scarlett's sea green eyes. "I don't need to hear it. I already know it'll work. Your chocolate covered strawberries fly out of my case. I've tasted your hand-blended teas and herbs. I've even eaten your flowers. I know what you can do. Together we'll be the dream team. It's perfect. I don't know why I didn't think of it myself."

"Okay." Scarlett took a breath and held out her hand. "Partners?"

Emmylou took her hand to shake. "Partners," she said with a firm nod.

They both laughed, then traded the handshake for a hug.

"I'm so excited!" Scarlett said as she pulled away from Emmylou. "I can't wait to get started. I've had this idea for a while, but I wanted to have all my ducks in a row before I talked to you about it. I figured that way you would know I was serious and – I had to get the money together."

"I would've taken you seriously," Emmy assured her.

"I know, but without the money, I think you would have felt like you were carrying me."

"Not a chance." Emmylou smiled. "Now you're carrying me."

"No way! Fifty-fifty. As long as that works for you."

Emmylou nodded appreciatively. "That sounds perfect to me. By the way, where did you get the money?"

Scarlett sobered, clamped her lower lip between her teeth and looked away. "I sold Grandpa's place."

A weight dropped into Emmy's stomach. "Why?" That was the only thing that Scarlett's grandpa had given her that was of any value. He was a mean old bastard who had probably died from all the bitterness and hate he kept wrapped up inside of himself.

"It's the only thing I had. And, honestly Emmy, I was happy to sign those papers. It felt good."

Emmylou watched Scarlett for a moment and decided that what she said was the truth. Scarlett was settled with her decision. Maybe it was good for her to rid herself of her childhood home. It hadn't been a happy place. "Then I'm glad you did it."

The faraway look on Scarlett's face meant she was in another place. Emmylou remained quiet until Scarlett shook off her memories of the past.

"Is this the cake?" Scarlett pointed at Lindy's wedding cake. Emmy nodded and moved closer to her confectionary masterpiece. "Oh, Emmylou, it amazing," Scarlett spoke with awe as she moved to inspect it closer. "The details." Scarlett's eyes roamed over the five tiers, taking in every subtle detail, and Emmylou grinned at the delight in Scarlett's expression.

"I thought it would be perfect for Lindy."

"She's going to love it! Boy am I glad we're in business together. You're going to make me a fortune on your cakes alone."

"What?" Emmylou didn't understand.

"It's all in the plan." Scarlett pursed her lips and arched her brows in a look of such absolute superiority that Emmylou snickered. "And you agreed without reading it."

"Oh no. Maybe I'd better get my lawyer to go over that document to see what I got myself into."

They both laughed and hugged. This day couldn't get any better. Prairie Goodness was saved, and Emmylou was in business with one of her best friends. Soon she would be watching two dear people joined together for eternity. It was all coming together. Now if she could catch her saboteur and carve Shane Newbury out of her heart, the world would be perfect.

*****

Shane had been waiting for the flashing lights and sirens to come blasting into his yard. Any day he would be arrested and hauled to jail. And for what? Just for trying to help someone out. See what happens? No good deed goes unpunished. How could he have been so stupid – so careless?

Emmylou Bennett had had him all tied up in knots since the day they'd met. He had been distracted, surly and irrational. She had wiggled her way into his life – his heart – and now he was paying the price.

Shane had kept his distance, steered clear of any place he thought she might be. He didn't want the pain that would come from an encounter with her. She still occupied his every waking thought. Everywhere he turned he saw her, and every time that happened, his heart leapt with elation and terror.

He was scared to see the disgust in her beautiful eyes for what he had done. She would feel betrayed, and who could blame her? He had screwed up and destroyed everything that was important to her.

Word around town was that Prairie Goodness was going to close. He felt responsible for it. And the more he played it over in his mind, the sicker he felt. The fire had closed her down for too long. Not very many businesses could recover from something like that, and definitely not within a month.

He felt awful and he didn't know what to do about it. Maybe he should go and turn himself in. Just take the punishment. Ten years in prison would be better than the fear that gripped him every minute of the day. He was walking around the clinic like the floor and walls were covered in nails and slowly closing in on him. Soon he would be pierced through with thousands of punctures, and he had nowhere to turn.

Habitually, he knocked on the exam room door after removing

the file from the door and entered after his patient invited him in.

"Lacy!" *Crap.* He wasn't prepared for this visit.

"Hi, Dr. Shane!"

"How are you feeling today?" He couldn't meet her gaze, opting to look at the file even though he wasn't reading a word of it. He waited for her to light into him. He knew how close she and Emmylou were.

"Pretty good. I'm the picture of pregnancy health." She held her arms out finally drawing his attention to her. Her smile was warm, and her eyes sparkled with delight. He narrowed his eyes, wondering if she knew the truth about him or if Emmylou had kept it to herself so she could catch him by surprise.

"That's good to hear. No more spotting? Any light-headedness? Rapid heartbeat?" He had relaxed a little with the assumption that she must not know anything that was going on. He wasn't sure if that was a good thing or a bad thing.

She shook her head as he rattled off questions. "Nope. I guess that early episode was a one-time thing. I haven't had any other strange symptoms. I feel great, and the little guy is just kicking the stuffing out of me." She ran her hands over her belly. Something he had seen other women do a hundred times, but for some reason, this time it made his chest ache. "So you think it's a boy, too?" He made notes in Lacy's file and listened to her laugh.

"No. That's just Kyle talking. He must be rubbing off on me. I think it's a girl."

"Would you like to know? We can find out today."

Lacy thought about it for one second before answering, "Nope. I'm holding strong. We'll wait until it's born to find out."

"Okay. Well if you ever change your mind, you can come in, and we'll check it out. No guarantees, but we should be able to give you the baby's sex."

"Thanks for the offer, but I really like torturing my husband with this. It has shown me sides of him I didn't know existed. He wants a boy so bad I'm pretty sure he would divorce me if it turns out to be a girl."

"No he wouldn't," Shane countered. Kyle adored Lacy. If she

gave birth to a raccoon, he wouldn't care.

"He might," she joked.

"Let's get you examined so you can go home and torture him some more." Shane stood and Lacy relaxed onto the examining table.

He thought it would be weird examining a friend, but it wasn't. Actually, it was nice knowing that he could be helpful to them during this life-changing event. Ten minutes later they were back to joking about Kyle.

"He can't wait for this wedding tomorrow," Lacy said as she wiggled into a sitting position on the rustling paper.

"Why's that?"

"He says it's so he can see if I can fit into the dress I bought two months ago, but I know it's really because he's sentimental. Don't tell him I told you, though."

Shane motioned a zipper on his lips and raised his hand.

"Thanks. He plays all those tough cowboys in movies, so he thinks it'll ruin his reputation if word got out he's really just a ball of goo. Are you going to Lindy's wedding tomorrow?"

"I was invited but I guess I hadn't decided yet."

"You should. Everyone's going to be there. Outside of the county fair, weddings are our only entertainment. It's a town requirement that we have at least six weddings a year whether we have willing couples or not."

Shane laughed. He loved Lacy's sense of humor.

"Emmylou's making the cake."

He drew up short with the mention of her name. "Really?" his voice broke and he cleared his throat.

"Uh-huh."

Damn, she knew he was in love with Emmylou. "Well, I'm sure it'll be delicious."

Lacy heaved a big sigh. "All right. I thought maybe you would spill it, but you're a tough cookie to crack, so I'm just going to say it. Ask her out already. I know you like her. Kyle knows you like her. I'm pretty sure even Jack Thomas's dog knows you like her, and he's blind – and deaf."

He shot her a sharp look. "What's that supposed to mean?"

"Look, Shane," she softened her tone, "Emmylou is my best friend, and she needs somebody like you. She hasn't had it easy in the love department. The guys she chooses – well, let's just say they aren't even in her league. She seems to think she has to settle, but with you she wouldn't be. I've seen the two of you together. You can't get more sparks off an arc welder."

Shane listened with growing agony. Lacy didn't know the truth. She didn't know what he had done to Emmylou, or she wouldn't be encouraging a relationship between them. It was torture to know that she was in favor of it because he knew that it was now an impossibility.

"Maybe you should ask her to go to the wedding with you."

"I'll think about it."

Lacy wasn't pleased with his answer, but she accepted it. Thank goodness.

They said goodbye and he went through the rest of the day resolved to stay far away from that wedding. He loved Emmylou too much to ruin it for her. Seeing him would only bring her misery, and he couldn't live with that.

Chapter 28

It was another Friday night that Emmylou was spending on her couch with a Hallmark movie and a bottle of wine. Prairie Goodness was saved, and she couldn't be more pleased about her best friend being her business partner. It was perfect.

So why was she still so miserable? Her dream was alive, and it was everything she'd ever wanted.

Not everything, she thought glumly.

The wedding was tomorrow. The fact that her far younger employee getting married wasn't bothering her like it used to. Now it was knowing that Lindy was marrying a man who adored her. She was marrying the love of her life. And Emmylou was more alone than ever. Lacy and Kyle were having a baby. They were going to be their own little family. Things would change. Heck, things already had changed.

And Scarlett. Well, Scarlett had never wanted a husband. She didn't care if she ever found someone to share her life with. She had her animals and her plants. She was happy.

Emmylou wasn't happy. And she hated it. She didn't want to be ungrateful for all that her life held, but it wasn't enough. She wanted more and she knew that was testing the universe, but it was the truth.

She wanted Shane Newbury. Everywhere she turned she saw something that reminded her of him. Her own bakery reminded her of Shane. But she knew that he wasn't hers to have. He was still grieving for Katie; he may never get over it. And how could she blame him? She wouldn't be inclined to find someone new when the perfect someone was lost in such tragedy.

She would get over Shane. She had to get over him. There were no other options.

She turned to look at her door when the bell chimed. She checked her watch. Who would be visiting at this hour? She toyed with the thought of ignoring it and hunkering down on the couch in case they looked in the window, but a fist pounding on the door changed her mind.

She wrapped her robe around her and tightened the belt as she walked to the door. Her jaw nearly unhinged when she saw who was standing there with his arm propped on the trim and his cowboy hat askew with rumpled brown hair across his forehead.

"Shane." She swallowed and reached for the fuzzy collar of her robe.

"Can I come in?"

She studied him for a few seconds before nodding and backing up. She shivered as he brushed past her. He was a man on a mission, and it didn't look like a pleasant one. He turned and kept his focus on a spot over her shoulder. She wanted to cry. He wasn't here to declare his love for her.

"What can I do for you?" she managed to ask.

He shuffled his feet, put his hands on his hips and then dropped them. His mouth was working on forming words, but none came out.

She crossed her arms over her stomach, raised her left hand to press her knuckles against her lips and waited for the worst.

"There's something I need to tell you. I just can't seem to find the words." His voice was hoarse, and it looked as though he hadn't slept in a week.

"It's all right, Shane. You don't have to. I understand." She crinkled her forehead to keep the tears inside.

He finally looked at her, but it wasn't a friendly look. He was upset. "You don't understand anything." He pressed his lips together and took a deep breath. "It was me."

Now she was lost. "*What* was you?"

"The fire!" He flung his arms in the air and turned away to walk into her living room. "It was me." He kept his back to her and talked to the blue vase of flowers on the table. "I'm responsible for the fire, for putting you out of business. For everything."

She followed him into the room. "Why would you think that?"

He huffed and slumped his shoulders while shaking his head. "Because it's true and you know it. I worked on the electrical box twelve hours before your place went up in flames. It's my fault."

Emmy didn't need any more proof that he was the man she would love until her dying day. "Shane." She reached out wanting to comfort him, but checked herself. It would only break her heart when he pushed her away.

"No, Emmylou. There is no excuse for what happened." He spun to face her and grabbed her hands. It was such a shock that she gasped. "Sorry." He dropped them and she hated herself. He focused on her, and the look of torture in his brown eyes was too much. She took his hands and stepped closer. He didn't pull away. And when his grip became tighter, she smiled with relief.

"Can you ever forgive me? What do I need to do to make it right?" He brought her hands up to his chest.

"Nothing," she drawled.

"You can't say that. I'll turn myself in. I'll give you my life's savings and take out a loan to pay you back. What do you want?"

She pressed against his chest with her trapped hands. "I want you to be quiet and listen."

He immediately straightened and clamped his mouth shut. She let out a sighing laugh.

"You didn't cause the fire." She shook her head at his disbelief. "In fact, the fire marshal said that what you did probably delayed the fire. It would have happened when no one was there to catch it. Instead, we were there to get it put out."

"And get you hurt," Shane interjected.

"I got myself hurt. That was no one's fault but my own. A captain always goes down with the ship. And, as I recall, you were there taking care of me."

"More like badgering you."

She tipped her head. "Would anything less work on my stubbornness?"

For the first time since his arrival, he smiled and slackened his tight shoulders. "Probably not."

"Look, Shane, you have done nothing but rescue me since you got here."

"Well, you get into a lot of trouble."

She blustered at his audacity. "Hey!"

His gaze softened and he moved her closer. "Are you sure that I had nothing to do with it, or are you just trying to be cunning and catch me off guard?"

"Now that I know what you think of me, I might just turn you in and let you go down for it."

Their locked gazes held until she could bear it no longer. She broke away and walked to the lamp in the corner of the room. "You have nothing to worry about." She spoke over her shoulder to hide her misery. It was too painful to look at him.

"Emmylou? What's wrong?"

"Nothing," she lied with a shrug. She felt his nearness before his hand landed on her shoulder. She turned with his gentle urging. She lifted her chin when he nudged it with his finger.

"Then why are you crying?"

"I'm not."

He wrapped an arm around her and pulled her against his tall frame. Her heart screamed out in joy, but her mind ached with sorrow. "Whatever it is, you can tell me. I can't fix it if I don't know."

Her eyes flashed when she glared at him. "I don't want you to fix it."

He didn't let her loose when she tried to get away. "Okay, then tell me what it is, and I'll just listen. I won't offer advice or assistance of any kind. Just think of me as your teddy bear."

She fought the laugh and swatted at him. "Oh, shut up!"

"You know you had a teddy bear you confided everything to." He grinned and held her tight as she struggled. "A bunny? Puppy? Dinosaur?"

She stopped and stared at him with an incredulous smile. "What?"

"You look like the kind of girl that would've had something like that. A stuffed dinosaur to share all your childhood grievances with."

"Why do you always do that?" She softened beneath his reflective gaze.

"Do what?"

"Make me smile and distract me with your –"

"My charm? Wit?"

"Shane," she groaned.

"Say it again." His words weren't joking. She lifted her head to stare into his eyes.

"Shane."

He stole her breath when he caught her lips in a sweet, demanding kiss. She melted into it, returning it with all the passion burning in her heart. She wished this could last forever. Her hands rested on his firm shoulders while she drank in the musky scent of him. This was heaven.

She took his face in her hands, moving her lips with his, wanting every kiss to tell him she loved him. A tear slipped down her cheek, and a moment later, Shane had drawn back. She kept her eyes shut tight, savoring the fleeting moment. She didn't want to see the goodbye she was sure to see in his eyes.

Finally, it felt foolish to be standing there like this. She slowly opened her eyes, but what she saw was tenderness and confusion. Shane kept his hands at her hips until he reached up and brushed away the tear. His throat convulsed with a ragged swallow.

"What is it? Don't you love me?"

The question was nearly torn from him. She threw her arms around him and hugged him close. "Of course I do!" One pained sigh escaped her. "I thought–" she moved her hands back to cradle his face and looked at him. "What about Katie?"

A slash of pain contorted his expression for a second, but he recovered. "Katie was special to me and a part of me will always miss her and love her. But, Emmylou–" he covered her hands with his own, "You're the one for me. I love you. I know you may not have always seen it, but I've loved you for a long time. Maybe even when we met in the bakery. You're different and special, and I want to spend my life with you. I just never knew what to expect from you."

"I didn't know what to expect from myself either. You're not anything I was expecting. I didn't know I would find my soul mate when we asked you to take the doctor's position."

"No, you didn't even want me here."

She smiled into his eyes. "And what an idiot I was. You're perfect for me. I love arguing with you, I love that you challenge me at every turn and I even love that you protect me. I love you, Shane Newbury." No one before him had had the honor of hearing those words. She had finally found someone who deserved to hear them. He was amazing.

He leaned in for a long, lingering kiss that sent her soaring over the tree tops.

*****

Wearing a light blue, one shoulder, ruched dress and silver heels, Emmylou stood in front of the cake table making the final adjustments to her masterpiece. The events of last night hovered on the edges of her mind. Her soul was feather-light, and every pore glowed with love. She couldn't wait to see Shane today. They planned to meet at the church for the ceremony.

Evan stood beside her, complimenting every aspect of the cake. She thanked him but was beginning to find him annoying. He was too over the top with his praise and his thanks. He had plum worn her goodwill out. The minutes seemed like hours. Shane was the only thing she could see. She focused hard on the cake, trying to maintain her professionalism, all the while wanting to squeal like a school girl.

"Evan, can you go out to the van and get me the container of yellow dust and my tool box? I need to fix that flower there."

"Sure thing. But I think it's perfect just the way it is. You're really amazing."

"Thank you." *Again,* she thought with an eye roll. Relief ran through her as he walked away.

She would fix the calla lily and then be able to get to the ceremony just in time. She looked around at the casual-elegance of the decorations. Everything about the reception hall was understated and beautiful. Lindy's colors were a soft yellow, white and black. It was just the kind of wedding Emmylou wanted for herself. Nothing over the top. It should be about the couple's love for each other, not a circus sideshow of entertainment. And in two hours, she would be here with her love.

Finally, Evan arrived with the supplies, and she quickly made the adjustment. "Perfect."

"Yes it is," Evan crooned. He reached his hand out and ran a finger down her face, tucking her hair behind her ear.

Emmylou jerked up and out of his reach. "Evan? What are you doing?" She brushed her hand over the place where he had touched her and stared hard at him.

He stepped closer. "Oh, come on, Emmylou. We've been dancing around this for weeks."

The smile on his face was disturbing. She hadn't seen this coming. Why hadn't she seen this coming? "Around what, Evan?"

"Around this." He curved his hand behind her head, pulling her close. He kissed her.

She was too shocked to instantly react. Finally, all her faculties returned. She jammed her arms between them and pushed him off. "Evan! Stop it!" She took several more steps away from him. "I'm sorry if I gave you the wrong impression, but I'm not interested in having a relationship with you. I've enjoyed our friendship, but there can be nothing more between us than that."

His eyes darkened and his features became harsh. "Whatever. You've been flirting with me since that night I came over to check on you and ended up staying half the night."

She shook her head. "I was touched by your thoughtfulness, and we had fun together, but, Evan, that's all. We had a fun night getting to know each other."

His nostrils flared as he sucked in air and straightened his shoulders. "Fine. Tell yourself whatever you need to."

With that he turned on his heel and marched away. Emmy

glanced around, her hand pressing into her stomach to calm it. No one else was there. Tremors of fear quaked through her. That could have been much worse. She was thankful he had gone. He was so angry. She had never see him like that before. He had always been so cheerful and helpful.

She hadn't been on the giving side of a set down in many years. It didn't feel very good, that's for sure. She gathered her things and left quickly.

The church was within walking distance of the reception hall. She left her purse and the cake tools inside her van, locked it, and hurried to join the gathering at the stairs. She scanned the crowd for Shane, Lacy and Kyle, or Scarlett. She spotted her friends first and rushed over, bumping into several people in her haste.

"There you are," Scarlett said and took hold of Emmylou's arm. "You're shaking. What's wrong?"

Lacy and Kyle instantly became interested in her appearance. All three of them had their attention tooled on her, and she felt like crying. Her gaze skidded away. She felt foolish. "Nothing. I just – " she took a breath wondering how to explain what had happened so it didn't sound as traumatic as it felt. "I had a little run-in with Evan. He misunderstood our relationship."

"What did he do to you?" Kyle's question promised bodily damage if necessary.

"Nothing. Really, I swear. He just caught me off guard, and there wasn't anyone else around. I'm sure I'm overreacting." She chaffed her arms to chase off the chill. She was sure her words were right. Having them out there made her feel a little better, but what she really wanted was Shane. Where was he? "Let's go in and get our seats."

Kyle wasn't satisfied with her answer, but she began moving with the crowd up the stairs and into the vestibule. Soon he was beside her with his arm around her shoulders. It was nice to have someone care about her enough to protect her. She just wished it was Shane. She scoured every row looking for his brown hair and strong shoulders.

She came up with nothing. He wasn't here yet. She twisted the delicate silver watch at her wrist. He still had time.

"We need to save a seat for Shane."

Kyle's smile grew wider, and his eyes danced. "Do we?"

"Oh, shut up, Kyle." She had said that more harshly than she meant. The incident with Evan still had her shook up. "Sorry."

"That's quite all right. I won't tease you – till later."

She managed a forced laugh.

The usher led them to the third row of the church, joking with Kyle about having the best looking trio of dates. He brought up Kyle's movie star appeal, and asked if he could borrow a girl.

"That's it!" Emmylou stopped in her tracks, bringing her friends to a halt. "Listen you little twerp." She pointed a finger into the usher's chest. "Do you think we're some kind of *thing* that you can trade around like baseball cards? That we don't have feelings? Are we all just interchangeable?" She slammed her hands on her hips and swayed her shoulders back and forth while she postured," Oh, tonight I think I'll have a blonde one; that'll go with my shirt color. Tomorrow, maybe a redhead." She angled closer to him. "You may be Lindy's little brother, Adam, and about eighteen-years-old, but I have half a mind to take you out back and give you the whipping you deserve. Don't you ever talk about women like that! Learn now while you still have a shot at being a decent man."

She felt Kyle's hand on her arm. "Emmy, I think we should take our seats now."

She glared at Adam to really drive home her point, then composed herself and walked past him with a snap of her head. Kyle gave him the "you asked for it" look and finished the ushering job himself.

Emmy settled into her seat with as much grace as she could manage. She was still fuming, but she knew that she had caused a scene too, so she opened her program to read it. A tap at her shoulder drew her attention.

"Nice job, honey. He deserved that. He made an obnoxious comment about my hat."

Emmylou turned in her seat and tried to hide her shock at the monstrosity on top of Mrs. Anderson's head. "Thank you, Mable. He's a repulsive young man. I can't imagine what he found wrong with it."

Dear God, she hoped she'd pulled that off. The thing had two birds in the middle of some purple tulle.

Chapter 29

Shane went out and did some target shooting Saturday afternoon with the ammo Shelby had given to him. He had offered to take her on-call shift this weekend. Any emergency that came up, he would cover, and unlike any other time in his life as a doctor, he had been hoping it was a busy weekend of emergencies. But that was before his conscience had gotten the better of him, and he had marched over to Emmylou's house to confess his sins.

It had turned out to be the best thing he had ever done. Now he was meeting her at Lindy's wedding and couldn't be more excited. He had come out to the field to clear his head. After declaring his love to Emmylou, he had had some residual guilt about Katie. Fresh air and guns were good therapy.

He took aim and blasted the bottle sitting on the post into dust. Damn that felt good. Just as he was adjusting the scope for a distance target, his phone buzzed.

"This is Dr. Newbury."

"When are you going to be here? We've got an emergency."

He shook his head. "Kyle?"

"Well it isn't Elvis."

"That's too bad, because I probably could've saved him."

Kyle laughed. "Seriously, we're in need of your services at the church."

"Oh!" Shane said with a jolt. "What's wrong?" He slid the safety on his rifle and started walking back to the house.

"Just bring your bag – and a lot of thread."

"That sounds bad. Maybe I should meet you at the hospital." Shane picked up speed across the rowed field like he was thirteen and hurrying home for supper again.

"No. He's not going to want to leave. And do you have a spare white dress shirt? This one's kinda' stained."

"Kyle, what in the hell happened?"

"You'll see when you get here. Hurry."

"Kyle! Is this man bleeding? How much blood are we talking about?" Full on doctor mode took over.

"Dude, just get here. Shelby's got a tablecloth around it, but it needs to be taken care of before the service."

"For heaven's sake! I'll be there in a minute."

Shane leaned his gun against the dresser and washed his hands in the bathroom sink, then grabbed a white shirt from the closet, his doctor's bag and truck keys. He had lost track of time pondering the future and the past, and now he was going to meet Emmylou in jeans and a T-shirt.

It was times like this he wished he had flashing lights attached to his truck. He had to swerve around three cars, a tractor and two trucks pulling horse trailers on his way to town, and it was only an eight mile drive. He double parked beside the horse-drawn carriage with his hazards on and rushed up the steps, bag in hand.

He reached the door and was immediately snatched by Kyle in the vestibule.

"Hey!" Shane yelled as Kyle shushed him and pushed him towards a door.

"Just keep it down, and get in there."

"Kyle if you made up some story to get me here, I'm gonna kick your ass."

The skepticism written all over Kyle's face was only overshadowed by the size of his biceps when he crossed his arms over his chest.

"Okay, I'm just going to be pissed off," Shane corrected.

Kyle pointed over Shane's shoulder. "There's your patient, Killer."

"You know that nickname isn't funny to a doctor?"

"Just get over there and work your magic." Kyle turned Shane and gave him a shove.

As he was projected forward, he saw three things: a pale faced man in a tuxedo reclining in a metal chair with his arm up, an annoyed Shelby with a blood soaked tablecloth, and Emmylou. The only thing that threatened to buckle his knees was Emmylou. His hands shook and his throat became a desert. No one had ever looked that good in a dress before.

"Did you want to help out here? Or are you going to stand there like an antagonistic ass?"

Shane blinked and turned to Shelby. The look on her face made his feet move forward. As he got closer, Emmylou raised an eyebrow and tracked her eyes over him with her arms crossed. He did the same, only with a look of pleasure. The exposed shoulder and creamy skin made his mouth water. He felt terrible about his attire.

It took great mental control to focus on what was in front of him, but his trusty self-discipline surfaced.

"I'm Doctor Newbury," he introduced himself to the injured man. "What happened, exactly?"

"I'm Robbie Hartman and I cut my arm – on some glass. It's no big deal."

The lack of color in his face would disagree with that. "Robbie Hartman? The groom?" He flashed a look at Shelby who returned it with one of her own. "I see." He turned his head. "The shirt is still in my truck," he said to Kyle over his shoulder.

"Got it."

His hair stood on end as Emmylou stepped closer. She smelled like a summer day, and the memories of last night flooded his brain. With a deep breath and a force of will, he dug in his bag for everything he would need. "Damn it!" He hit the side of his bag.

"What?" Shelby asked.

"No lidocaine."

"I can get some; where is it?" Emmylou's delectable voice and presence were going to be a constant distraction.

"Thank you, sweetheart, but I don't think we'll have time for that." He deflected Shelby's look of interest with a shake of his head. He knew the term of endearment was too much, but it felt right in the moment, and it made Emmylou blush.

"Oh. Well, Robbie, we're gonna see how much of a man you

are today. And if that little dance you were doing when you punched the window and sent your arm through it is worth it." Shelby's voice held no compassion, and Shane tried not to laugh when he looked at Robbie for permission to begin.

"Whatever. Just do it. My girl's waiting for me, and I don't want her getting any second thoughts about marrying a moron."

"We're all morons when it comes to the women we love." The words just fell out of his mouth and hung in the air. Shane knew all eyes were pointed at him, but he chose to ignore them and get started on the wound. No one had known about Emmylou and him, but he supposed that was all over now. This would make it official.

His eyes may not have been on her, but he knew Emmylou had barely moved beside him. He was so in tune to her he could almost tell how many times her heart beat in the moments he spent stitching Robbie's arm up.

Surprisingly, the young man hardly flinched and didn't even grunt with the repetitive piercing to his flesh. "There you are. Twenty-seven stitches."

Shelby was already wrapping the wound with gauze and giving him instructions on how to care for it.

"Yes, ma'am. I know," came Robbie's annoyed reply.

Shane laughed. It seemed everyone knew to toe the line with Shelby. "I have to say, Robbie, you handled that really well. Married life won't give you any trouble."

A snort came from behind him. He didn't have to guess who had made it. He patted Robbie on the shoulder with his best attempt at a smile. Then slid over and let Kyle take over as wardrobe technician. The room seemed crowded even though it was large enough for twenty people to stretch fingertip to fingertip.

He wanted to get out of there. He wanted to be alone with Emmylou. How was he going to get through the evening with her looking so beautiful? Every moment he would want to drag her into the coat closet and ravish her.

"Hi," he said as he joined her standing by the wall. She met his gaze with her sea blue eyes. He could stare into them for the rest of his life and never grow tired of it.

"Hi," she answered and bit her lip. Her hand touched his chest, and he wished to God he had dressed up for her.

"Sorry." He looked down at his clothes. He placed his hands on her waist and pulled her closer.

She made a face and raised a shoulder. "It's not a formal affair."

Her smile didn't reach her eyes, and it ripped the heart from his chest. He didn't know how to explain to her that he'd had to think things through, and 'I lost track of time,' seemed lame. "I'll do better. From here on out it's only the best for my girl." He rested his forehead against her and filled his lungs with the comforting smell that was uniquely Emmylou.

"That's good to hear." She gripped him closer, then drew back. "You can start making it up to me on the dance floor."

He grinned. "That I can do."

He watched Kyle help Robbie into his fresh shirt, a goofy smile on his face that spoke of realized dreams and complete contentment. Kyle, an idolized movie star with more money than God, was married to the love of his life, a hometown girl, and couldn't be happier, and Shane hoped his future held the same thing.

"Hey, Doc, thanks for stitchin' me up. And for the shirt. I owe ya."

Shane nodded with his arm holding Emmy close. "No problem. I may just owe you."

Emmylou was the only one who understood that statement.

*****

Sitting at the table with Shane by her side was Emmy's version of perfect. She had been worried when he wasn't there to meet her before the service, but he had explained why and she understood. This was a leap for him. He had loved Katie – still did. When a person sees his life so clearly as one way, stretching before him for eternity, and it turns out to be something completely different, it's hard to come to terms with the disillusionment.

She had been there with her career, and now the new path that she was on was better than she could've ever imagined or planned for herself. Things had a way of working out. Shane slid his hand on her knee and leaned in.

"Now, I may want a repeat of the last time we were dining at the same table," Shane said into her ear over the sounds of the DJ.

She stared at him in confusion. He lifted an eyebrow while she tried to remember. And then the memory of the Valentine's dinner snapped into place. She had been bold and slipped her foot up his pant leg. She had been angry and crazy that night. They had also shared one heck of a passionate kiss in the study of The Dove House.

"You want a public argument?"

He chuckled. "We could skip that part."

"My parents are right over there." She indicated the spot with a shift of her chin. "I'm sure we could wrestle up some sort of repressed emotion."

"I thought your parents had worked all of that out."

"They have. In fact, I've never seen them happier. Mom's successful surgery has brought them closer. It's weird." She twitched with the thought of her smiling, attentive parents acting like kids. "And I have you to thank for that." She leaned in closer, staring deep into his eyes. "Without you none of this would be possible. You truly rescued me. In everything."

He kissed her lightly, and she savored it. Hummingbirds were fluttering in her stomach. "And *you* rescued me."

Her phone beeping like a siren sent her shooting back in her chair. She frantically dug in her tiny black purse. "Oh, no." Her heart was in her shoes. The alarm at the bakery had been triggered. She slid her chair back, still staring at her phone. "I've got to go."

Without hesitation, Shane rose and walked with her. "What's wrong?"

"We've got to get to the shop. Something's happening."

They rushed out of the reception hall without retrieving their coats. The cold night didn't affect her in the slightest as they rushed down the sidewalk. "My van's in back."

Shane took her arm and redirected her. "My truck's over there. Get in."

They loaded into the truck, and Shane sped away to the bakery. "What do you think it is?"

"The alarm system doesn't tell me that. It only tells me that the door has been tampered with. I didn't opt for the mobile package, so I can't see what the cameras are catching."

His head whipped in her direction with a disgusted look illuminated by the dash lights.

"Yes, I got cameras installed."

"I could've done that for you."

"Well, I was avoiding you at that time, so Wes did it."

"*Wes!*"

"Oh, get over it. He's my friend."

Shane heaved a sigh that filled his entire chest. "How do you know he's not the one tampering with things?"

"You don't have to be so snotty. And why would the alarm go off if he's the one who installed it? Wouldn't he know how to disarm it?"

"Oh." Shane relaxed and turned the last corner. Four more blocks and they would know what was happening. "Maybe he's an idiot."

She didn't bother answering that.

He shut the headlights off and skidded to a stop.

"Why are you parking here?"

He killed the engine. "Because I'm not an idiot. We want to catch whoever it is by surprise."

"Oh."

"You don't have to sound so shocked." He got out and she followed, slamming the door with an echoing *Bam!*

He threw his hands in the air and gave her the what-the-heck-are-you-doing look over the hood of his truck. Which she returned with a toss of her hands and a silent apology.

Shane scowled and pointed for her to get against the building, followed by a "get behind me" wave. He traveled closer to the bakery, and she mimicked his movements. He dared a glance around the corner of her building for a second, then returned for a longer look.

"What do you see?" she whispered, too nervous to wait. Emmy tried to go around him so she could see what was going on. His arm shot out, pressing her against the wood siding. "Hey."

He spun and put his face an inch from hers. "Emmylou, if you don't hush up and let me look, so help me I'll barricade you in my pick-up until your fortieth birthday."

He kissed her nose, but there was no sympathy in his eyes. It pissed her off, but she understood that she was acting crazy.

"Did you leave a light on in the kitchen?" Shane whispered, staring through the glass as inconspicuously as possible.

"I don't know," she whispered back, wracking her brain for her last minutes at the shop. "Maybe. It was a crazy day having to get the cake to the reception hall."

He nodded. "Do you have your key?" Shane held his hand out, opening and closing it.

"My key?"

"Christ, woman." He turned to face her. "We're coming here to check on your place, and you didn't think to bring a key?"

She straightened and glared at him. "Well, I'm sorry. You hauled me out of there so fast I didn't have time to think."

"Aren't they in your purse or something?"

"My purse?"

He looked to the sky taking in a breath. "Damn it, woman."

"Stop calling me 'woman' like it's a cuss word! I can't believe you –" he covered her mouth with his hand and shushed her.

Pans clattering to the floor widened her eyes.

"Okay, I'm going to break the window."

She dragged his hand away. "I'm sure that won't scare them off at all."

"Well, what do you suggest we do? Stand out here while whoever's in there smashes your kitchen to pieces?"

Emmylou stood for a moment with his hand in both of hers, trying to think. "Wait! Why don't we just try the door?"

He angled his head as though to explain something to a small child. "Emmylou."

She rolled her eyes, walked around him, and gave the door a very small pull. It gave and she glared at Shane. "Give me your license or a credit card?" Now it was her turn to hold out her hand.

"Already? I thought that wouldn't start until after we were married," he quipped and dug in his pants pocket, so he missed the broad grin on her face. "Here."

She took it with a silly smile. "Thank you." Emmy squatted down with the credit card ready in the gap.

"What are you doing?"

She pulled the door enough to get the card through, slipped it in front of the sensor and pushed the door open. "Spoofing the bell."

He walked through while she held the card in place. "Very impressive, Miss Bennett."

She entered, shut the door carefully and handed him back his card. "I'm not totally inept."

"I never thought you were."

Another barrage of clanging came from the kitchen, drawing them out of their moment.

"Get behind me," Shane whispered, but Emmylou wasn't about to cower. Someone was vandalizing her kitchen!

"Sorry, Doc." She bolted past him behind the counter with him calling to her in a stage whisper. She slammed the swinging door open and barged through, hoping to catch the culprit off guard. She jolted to a stop when she saw Evan tossing a chair out of her office. Then anger annihilated her surprise.

"What the hell are you doing?"

He spun like a caged animal that had had water sprayed on it, and a touch of fear trickled down Emmy's spine. "I'm... uh." He ran a hand through his wild hair. "Looking for... uh." His eyes tripled in size and he stared at Shane who had come through the door.

Shane charged Evan like a bull, toppling him to the floor hard. More pots and utensils clattered and clanged while the two men rolled around exchanging punches and curses.

Emmylou fumbled forward, picked up Shane's cowboy hat and placed it on the work counter. She winced when Evan caught Shane across the chin, which was returned with a brutal crack to the nose. The fight was over in less than two minutes. Shane had pinned Evan with his knees, subdued him with one final hook and dragged him from the floor, securing his arms behind his back with a punishing sleeper hold.

"Call the police," Shane told Emmylou. He wasn't even out of breath.

Chapter 30

It only took Tyler Sheck, the sheriff's deputy, four and one half minutes to get to the bakery. In that time, Shane had encouraged Evan to spill his guts. Emmylou suspected it was the possibility of a broken arm that had Evan telling all his secrets.

"Emmylou!"

It took her friends five minutes to arrive and fifteen seconds to burst through the swinging door.

"Oh my God! Are you okay?" Lacy threw her arms around Emmylou and hugged her tight.

"I'm fine." She hugged Lacy back, released and was immediately snatched into an embrace by Scarlett.

"We came as soon as we heard."

Emmylou scoffed. Nothing stayed quiet in a small town. "Thank you."

Kyle gave her a quick one-armed hug, smiled into her eyes and made his way to where Evan was now handcuffed, sitting on Emmylou's stool and answering questions. The three women turned and observed.

"This place is trashed," Lacy said in disgust. "What happened?"

Emmylou related everything that Shane had forced out of Evan. He had been a student in her online classes and had decided that he wanted what she had. He had become obsessed with her and her business.

He came to Primrose with a story and a plan. He had intended to steal her recipes and start his own competing business, but then he had discovered her loan on Prairie Goodness had been called in and decided he would help the process along.

He broke in and released the mice in her freezer. Then, he

tampered with the wiring and set the fire.

"He called me a resourceful bitch," Emmylou told her friends with a half-smile. "I guess I am. When he learned that Prairie Goodness had an investor and wouldn't be going under after all, he must've gotten desperate. That's when he tried his little seduction scene, and when that didn't work, he broke in here looking for the recipes, again."

Scarlett rubbed Emmy's shoulder. "I'm so sorry, honey. I wish I had seen this coming."

"I *did* see this coming," Shane put in as he joined the conversation.

Emmy rolled her eyes. The group watched as Tyler took Evan to the back door. "Thank you, Tyler."

"No problem, Emmy. I'm going to need you down at the station later for your statement." Evan pulled against Tyler forcing him to get aggressive, shoving him against the door. "Tomorrow is fine. We'll let him sit for a while and think about what it's going to be like when his prison mates find out he's a pastry chef." Tyler turned and said the last words to Evan's face.

They all thanked Tyler again and watched him load Evan into the back of the patrol car.

Shane put his arm around Emmylou, and she cuddled closer, seeking his comfort and strength. He grunted when her head bumped his chin. She tipped her chin and kissed him lightly. "Sorry, sweetie. I didn't know you had such a glass jaw."

He looked down at her. "Glass jaw nothing. For a pastry chef, that guy has a hell'uva right hook."

Laughter filled the trashed kitchen.

"We should get back to the reception. I'm supposed to cut and serve the cake for Lindy," Emmy said with a sigh and a head shake at the destruction.

"You don't want to clean this place up? And did Evan find your recipes? You may want to check on that," Shane said as he released her.

"I don't need to. He could never have found them by destroying my office or even this kitchen." Emmylou had the interest of everyone in the room now.

"Why not?" Kyle asked.

"Because." Emmylou backed up, kicking a stainless steel bowl and slipping in a pile of flour. "I don't keep them in either of those places." She opened the door to the walk-in refrigerator and stepped inside. She quickly located the plastic-covered binder from behind the shelf where she kept it concealed in a box marked "Live Fish". She'd always thought that was clever. Emmy walked out with the binder in hand. "I keep them right here."

Everyone shared a smile and a laugh. "Mrs. Walter's always said the best ideas should be kept on ice until the world was ready for them. So –" Emmy shrugged and grinned at her recipe book.

"I'm in love with an evil genius."

All heads turned in Shane's direction, but he only had eyes for Emmylou.

"Yes!" Lacy cheered and held Kyle closer. "Told you."

"Did not. I told you," Kyle countered.

"Well, I knew it before all of you," Scarlett said and walked to the door.

"That doesn't surprise me," Kyle said, following her with his arm around Lacy.

The three of them teased each other as they weaved through the tables.

Standing in the kitchen in her fancy dress, looking at Shane who was covered in flour and frosting and sporting a shadow of a bruise on his chin, listening to her friends gibing each other, Emmylou realized she was a very blessed woman. To finally have everything she ever had wanted in life all at once was an indescribable feeling.

The bells jingled when her three friends opened it. She couldn't stop smiling at Shane. His eyes twinkled as he gazed back at her.

"Well, princess. Shall we go back to the reception?" He stepped closer and wrapped his arms around her waist.

"I thought I told you I hate being called princess." She arched her brow and ran her finger along his soiled collar. He swallowed at her touch.

"But there's no better name for you. Whenever I look at you, I want to be your knight in shining armor."

Emmylou curled her hands around his neck. "And that's a good thing because you seem to be riding to my rescue all the time."

"And you're the typical, ungrateful princess who thwarts me at every turn," Shane said with a playful grin.

Emmy moistened her lips and moved closer. "I see. However can I thank you?" She tipped her chin, inviting his kiss.

"Reward money would be nice."

His breath caressed her lips, and sparks danced across her skin. "Fresh out," she whispered. She nudged with her hands, and he coyly resisted, challenge in his eyes. Was it always going to be like this? Lord, she hoped so. She leaned the rest of the way and took his lips in a kiss meant to tease. She utilized every skill she possessed to make him give in and take control.

Finally, she won. He squeezed his arms around her, slanted his mouth and kissed her hard. She treasured every second of that kiss in her kitchen, with the man she loved who spurred and stimulated her.

With a sigh and a groan, Shane lifted his lips and settled his forehead against hers. "Thank you," he said.

"For what?"

"For being the one to love me. I'm so happy it's you."

"And I'm happy it's you who loves me."

"You know I do." He looked at her for a moment, and she laid her hand on his cheek. "Now, let's go to the party." He pulled away and took her hands in his.

Leaving to be around a bunch of people was the last thing Emmy wanted. "Why don't we go to my place?"

He shook his head. "Later. First, I owe you a dance."

And they danced hand in hand, and heart to heart.

<u>About the Author</u>

Nebraska native, Krista Kedrick, is the author or *Under a Prairie Moon*, *Family Ties* and *The Doves of Primrose* series. All her novels are set in Nebraska, a picturesque and diverse landscape perfect for her western romances. She is an avid outdoorswoman and is more often found digging in the dirt than wearing high heels. She resides in her hometown with her husband, two daughters and basset hound.

For more information on Krista visit:

www.kristakedrick.com

Thank you so much for reading Emmylou! If you would like to take a moment and leave a review, tell a friend or drop me an email I would greatly appreciate it.